About the author

J. **Kenner** loves wine, dark chocolate, and books. She lives in Texas with her husband and daughters. Visit her online at **www.jkenner.com** to learn more about her and her other pen names, to get a peek at what she's working on, and to connect through social media.

CLAIM ME

J. Kenner

headline

ETERNAL

Published by arrangement with Bantam Books,
an imprint of The Random House Publishing Group,
a division of Random House, Inc.

First published in Great Britain in 2013
by HEADLINE PUBLISHING GROUP

2

Cataloguing in Publication Data is available from the British Library

ISBN 978 1 4722 0607 7

Offset in Sabon by Avon DataSet Ltd, Bidford-on-Avon, Warwickshire

Printed and bound by CPI Group (UK) Ltd, Croydon, CR0 4YY

Headline's policy is to use papers that are natural, renewable and
recyclable products and made from wood grown in sustainable forests.
The logging and manufacturing processes are expected to conform to the
environmental regulations of the country of origin.

HEADLINE PUBLISHING GROUP
An Hachette UK Company
338 Euston Road
London NW1 3BH

www.headline.co.uk
www.hachette.co.uk

Acknowledgments

I almost hesitate to include this page because I am certain that I will forget someone, but I'm going to soldier on, wrangle my memory, and hope that whomever I accidentally slight will let me make it up to them with a martini (Damien Stark's Glen Garioch bourbon is a little out of my league).

Right up front I have to say that I am cheating a bit with this acknowledgment, because it is as much about *Release Me* as it is about this book, and I have to start off by thanking everyone who helped get *Release Me* and the Stark Trilogy as a whole out to readers.

Most especially, I want to thank my fabulous agent, Kimberly Whalen, my amazing editor, Shauna Summers, and everyone else on the team at Bantam, who have made diving into the world of Damien and Nikki such an absolute pleasure: Gina Wachtel, Jennifer Hershey, Maggie Oberrender, Susan Grimshaw, Alison Masciovecchio, Sarah Murphy, Matt Schwartz, Rachel Kind, Donna Duverglas, everyone I've missed (sorry!); the rest of the folks at Trident; Janet Stark and Sofia Willingham who brought Nikki's voice to life; and the wonderful publishers in foreign territories, especially the folks at Headline such as Kate Byrne and Veronique Norton, who have made Twittering across "the pond" such fun.

Special thanks to my "betas"—K.J., Heather, Stefani, and Liz. Thanks so much for the feedback!

And, of course, I have to thank my husband and my kids for putting up with "Mommy needs to write", and supporting me in so many ways.

Most of all, though, I want to thank the readers, especially those who have reached out to let me know how much Damien and Nikki have come to life for them. Every email, every tweet, every comment on my website and Facebook page is appreciated. Thank you! And a special shout-out to Kathy Womack, who coined the term "Damienized," which I have boldly appropriated, and to Redhotpolkadots on Twitter, whose #StarkOnSpeedDial hashtag made me grin—here you go, girl!

CLAIM ME

1

"Almost done?" I ask. "The sun's been down for at least five minutes."

Several yards away, Blaine tilts sideways, partially emerging from behind the canvas. I don't move, but in my peripheral vision, I can see his shoulders, bald head, and shocking red goatee. "In my mind, you're still bathed in light. Now stand still and be quiet."

"No problem," I say, and hear his growl of irritation at my blatant flaunting of his rules.

Despite the fact that I am standing naked in a doorway, our exchange seems perfectly normal. I am used to this now. Used to the way the chilled ocean breeze causes my nipples to peak. The way the sunset stirs something so deep and passionate in me that I long to close my eyes and abandon myself to the violent tapestry of light and color.

I've become blasé about the way Blaine's eye sweeps critically over me, and I no longer flinch when he leans in so close that he almost brushes my breast or my hip as he adjusts my stance to the proper angle. Even his murmurings of "Perfect. Shit, Nikki, you look perfect" no longer make my stomach tighten, and I've stopped imagining my hands closing into tight fists in protest, my nails digging into the soft skin of my palms. I am not perfect—not by a long shot. But it no longer makes me crazy to hear those simple words.

Never in my wildest dreams had I imagined that I could feel so at ease despite being so fully on display. True, I'd spent most of my life parading around on a stage, but during my pageant days I was always clothed, and even during the bathing suit competitions, my girl parts were modestly covered. I can imagine my mother's mortification if she saw me now, chin lifted, back arched, a red silk cord binding my wrists behind me and then trailing between my legs to twine gently around one thigh.

I have not seen Blaine's canvas for days, but I know his style and I can imagine how I look captured in pigment and brushstrokes. Ephemeral. Sensual. Submissive.

A goddess bound.

No doubt about it—my mother would have a cow. I, however, am enjoying it. Hell, maybe that's why I'm enjoying it. I've shaken off Proper Princess Nikki for Rebel Nikki, and it feels pretty damn good.

I hear footsteps on the stairs, and I force myself to remain in my pose even though I want nothing more than to turn and look at him. *Damien.*

Damien Stark is the one thing about which I've not become complacent.

"The offer stands." Damien's words drift up the marble stairs to the third floor. He hasn't raised his voice, and yet it is supported by such strength and confidence that it fills the room. "Tell them to take a good long look at their P and Ls. There isn't going to be any profit, and by the end of the year, there won't even be a company. They're in free fall, and when they crash and burn, every one of their employees will be out of work, the company dead, the patents tied up in litigation for years as creditors fight about the assets. They take this deal, and I'll breathe life back in. You know it. I know it. They know it."

The footsteps stop, and I realize he is now standing at the top of the stairs. The room is open, designed for entertaining, and normally someone climbing the stairs would be treated to a view of the Pacific Ocean spread wide across the far side of the room.

Right now, what Damien sees is me.

"Make it happen, Charles," he says, his voice now tight. "I have to go."

I have come to know this man so well. His body. His gait. His voice. And I don't need to see him to know that the tension in his tone isn't tied to the thrill of chasing a business deal. It's about me, and that simple fact is as intoxicating as champagne on an empty stomach. *An entire empire needing his attention, and yet in that moment, I am his whole world.* I am flattered. I am giddy. And, yeah, I am turned on.

I'm also smiling, which draws a sharp censure from Blaine. "Dammit, Nik. Get rid of the grin."

"My face doesn't even show in the painting."

"*I* can tell," Blaine says. "So stop it."

He's teasing me now. "Yes, *sir*," I say, and then almost laugh when Damien coughs, obviously hiding a chuckle of his own. The "sir" is our secret, our game that we play. A game that will officially end tonight, now that Blaine is putting the final touches on the painting that Damien has commissioned. The thought is a melancholy one.

True, I'll be happy not to have to stand stock-still anymore. Even the thrill of flipping the imaginary bird to my mother's overbearing sense of propriety pales in comparison to the way my legs cramp at the end of these sessions. But I will miss the rest of it, especially the feel of Damien's eyes on me. His slow, heated inspections that make me damp between my thighs and force me to concentrate so hard on remaining still that it becomes sweetly painful.

And, yes, I will miss our game. But I want more than a game with Damien, and I can't help the eagerness with which I face tomorrow and the knowledge that it will simply be Damien and Nikki with nothing between us. And as for any lingering secrets . . . well, with time, those will be brushed away, too.

Hard now to believe that I'd originally been shocked by Damien's offer: one million dollars in exchange for my body. For my image, permanently on display on a larger-than-life canvas; and for the rest of me at his command, whenever and however he wanted.

My shock had been replaced by blatant pragmatism laced with equal parts of ardor and outrage. I'd wanted Damien as much as he'd wanted me, but at the same time I'd wanted to punish him. Because I was certain that he saw only the beauty queen, and that when he got a peek at the damaged woman beneath the polished veneer he'd reel from the affront to his expectations as much as from the lightening of his wallet.

I've never been so happy to be wrong.

Our deal had been for a week, but that week turned into two as Blaine buzzed around his canvas, the wooden tip of his brush tapping against his chin as he squinted and frowned and mumbled to himself about wanting just a little more time. About wanting to get everything—that word again—perfect.

Damien had agreed easily—after all, he'd hired Blaine because of his growing reputation as a local artist, and his skill in handling erotically charged nudes was undeniable. If Blaine wanted more time, Damien was happy to accommodate him.

I didn't complain for less pragmatic reasons. I simply wanted these days and nights with Damien to last. Like my image on the painting, I was coming alive.

I'd moved to Los Angeles only a few weeks ago, intent on conquering the business world at the ripe old age of twenty-four. The thought that a man like Damien Stark would want me, much less my portrait, was the furthest thing from my mind. But there'd been no denying the heat that had burned between us from the moment I saw him at one of Blaine's art shows. He'd pursued me relentlessly, and I'd tried my damnedest to resist, because I knew that what he wanted was something that I wasn't willing to give.

I wasn't a virgin, but neither was I widely experienced. Sex is not something that someone with my history—with my scars—rushes into. I'd been burned by a boy I'd trusted, and my emotions were still as ragged as the scars that marred my flesh.

Damien, however, doesn't see those scars. Or, more accurately, he sees them for what they are—a part of me. Battle scars from what I have overcome and what I continue to fight. Where I thought my scars reflected a weakness, he sees an indication of strength. And it is that ability—to see me so fully and clearly—that has drawn me so irrevocably and completely to this man.

"You're smiling again," Blaine says. "I don't even need three guesses to know what you're thinking about. Or who. Do I need to kick our personal Medici out of the room?"

"You're just going to have to live with her smile," Damien says before I can answer, and once again, I must force myself not to turn and look at him. "Because nothing's making me leave this room unless Nikki is beside me."

I revel in the velvet smoothness of his voice, and I know he means what he says. We'd spent this entire afternoon window-shopping on Rodeo Drive, celebrating the new job I will start in the morning. We'd walked lazily down the pristine streets, holding hands, sipping calorie-laden frozen mochas, and pretending no one else in the world existed. Even the paparazzi, those vultures with cameras that have become uncomfortably interested in every little thing Damien and I do, paid us little heed.

Sylvia, Damien's assistant, had tried to put several calls

through, but Damien had flat-out refused to take them. "This is our time," he'd said to me, answering my unspoken question.

"Should I alert the financial papers?" I'd teased. "Doesn't it affect the market when Damien Stark takes a day off work?"

"I'm willing to risk global economic collapse if it means a few hours with you." He drew my hand up and kissed the tip of each finger. "Of course, the more shopping we do, the more we support the economy." His voice was low and sultry and full of enticing promises. "Or maybe we should go back to the apartment. I can think of several interesting ways to spend the afternoon that have no fiscal impact whatsoever."

"Tempting," I'd retorted. "But I don't think that I could stand the guilt knowing that I traded an orgasm for fiscal ruin."

"Trust me, baby. It would be more than one orgasm."

I'd laughed, and in the end we'd managed to avert global economic disaster (the shoes he bought me are truly awesome) and let me have my orgasm as well. Three, actually. Damien is nothing if not generous.

As for the phone, he'd been true to his word. Despite the constant vibrations, he'd ignored it until we'd pulled up in front of the Malibu house and I'd insisted he take pity on whoever was being so persistent. I'd hurried inside to meet Blaine, and Damien had lingered behind, reassuring his attorney that the world hadn't collapsed despite Damien's temporary absence from the cellular airwaves.

I am so lost in my thoughts that I don't realize that Blaine has approached me. He taps my lower lip with the end of his paintbrush and I jump.

"Damn, Nikki, you were in the zone."

"Are you done?" I do not mind posing, and Blaine has become a good friend. But right then, I just want him gone. Right then, all I want is Damien.

"Almost." He holds his hands up, looking at me through his

makeshift frame. "Right here," he says, using the brush to indicate. "The light on your shoulder, the way your skin glows, the mix of colors . . ." He trails off as he walks back to the portrait. "Damn," he finally says. "I am a fucking genius. This is you, kid. If I didn't know better, I'd swear you could walk right off the canvas."

"So you're done? I can come look?" I turn without thinking, realizing too late that he probably wanted me to stay still. But suddenly I don't care. All thoughts vanish. Blaine, the painting, the world around me. Because it's not the painting that I see. It's Damien.

He is right where I'd imagined him, standing on the top step, leaning casually against the wrought-iron banister and looking even yummier in real life than he did in my mind. I might have spent the entire afternoon with him, but it doesn't matter. Every glimpse of him is like ambrosia, and I will never get my fill.

I soak him in, my eyes lingering on every perfect feature. His defined jaw highlighted by the shadow of stubble. The wind-tossed black hair, thick and smooth and so familiar to my fingers. And his eyes. Those amazing dual-colored eyes that are focused so intently right now that I can feel the weight of his gaze upon my skin.

He is dressed in jeans and a white T-shirt. But even in such informal attire, there is nothing casual about Damien Stark. He is power personified, energy harnessed. And my only fear is the knowledge that one can neither capture nor hold on to a lightning bolt, and I do not want to lose this man.

His eyes meet mine, and I shiver from the shock of the connection. The athlete, the celebrity, the entrepreneur, the billionaire persona all fall away, leaving only the man and an expression that makes my blood heat and my insides curl with longing. An expression that is so raw and primal that were I not already naked, I'm certain that every stitch of clothing would have turned to ash, burned away by the heat in his eyes.

My skin prickles, and I have to force myself not to move. "Damien," I whisper, unable to resist the feel of his name upon my lips. The word seems to hang in the room, trapped in the air that is thick between us.

By the easel, Blaine clears his throat. Damien shifts enough to look at him, and I think it is surprise that I see on his face, as if he'd forgotten that we aren't alone. He crosses the distance to Blaine and stands at the artist's side in front of the huge portrait. From my position, I can see the wooden frame across which the canvas is stretched and, to the side, the two men studying an image that is hidden from my view.

My heart pounds against my rib cage and my gaze does not waver from Damien's face. There is something rapturous in his eyes, as if he is looking up at an object of worship, and his silent benediction makes my knees go weak. I want to reach out a hand and steady myself on the frame of the bed beside which I'm posing, but my wrists are still bound behind my back.

My immobility reminds me of the situation, and I fight another smile—I am not free. I am Damien's.

In Blaine and Damien's original concept for the portrait, I'd simply stood in this spot, the gossamer drapes set to flutter about me, my face turned away from the artist. The image was sensual, but aloof, as if someone was yearning for that woman but would never touch her. The portrait was stunning, but something was missing. Damien suggested that we contrast the free-flowing drapes that graze lightly over my skin with the constriction of a bloodred rope, and that we bind my hands behind me.

I didn't hesitate to agree. I wanted the man. Wanted to be bound to him. To belong to him. To be claimed by him.

No longer would my image be unattainable. Instead, the woman in the portrait was a prize. An ephemeral goddess tamed by a worthy man.

Damien.

I search his face, looking for clues to his assessment of the portrait, but there is nothing. This is his corporate expression, the unreadable mask he wears so as to not give away his secrets. Damien is extremely good at hiding his secrets.

"Well?" I ask, when I can stand it no longer. "What do you think?"

For a moment, Damien remains silent. Beside him, Blaine shifts nervously. And though only seconds pass, the air is thick with the weight of eternity. I can almost taste Blaine's frustration, and I understand the impulse when he finally blurts out, "Come on, man. It's perfect, right?"

Damien's shoulders rise and fall as he draws in a deep breath then faces Blaine with respect. "It's more than perfect," he says, turning to me. "It's her."

Blaine's smug grin is like sunshine. "I gotta say, I've never been shy about bragging on my own work, but this is . . . well, it's wow. Real. Sensual. Most of all, it's honest."

Damien's eyes never leave mine, and I draw a shaky breath. My pulse pounds so loudly it's a surprise I can hear anything else. I'm certain that the rising and falling of my chest must be visible, and I fear that Blaine can tell that I'm trying desperately to quell the wellspring of desire that bubbles violently within me. It takes all my effort not to beg Blaine to leave the room, to cry out for Damien to kiss me. To touch me.

A sharp *beep* shatters the heavy silence, and Damien yanks the phone out of his pocket, then spits out a curse when he reads the text. I see the shadows gather on his face as he slides the phone back, the message unanswered. I press my lips together as my skin begins to prickle with the first stirrings of worry.

Blaine, his head tilted as he inspects the canvas, is oblivious. "Nik, don't move. I just want to touch up the light right here, and—"

The shrill ring of Damien's phone interrupts Blaine's words. I

expect Damien to ignore the call as he had the text, but he surprises me by answering. But not before moving out of the room
with such swift, firm steps that I barely even hear the curt,
"What?"

He does not meet my eyes.

I force myself to stand still for Blaine, fighting a sudden wave
of fear. This is not a business call; Damien Stark does not get
upset over business. On the contrary, he thrives on the chase, on
the conquest.

No, this is something else, and I can't help but think about
the threats that have been made against him, and the secrets that
I know he still keeps. Damien has seen me stripped bare in every
way possible. And yet it seems as though I've only seen glimpses
of him, and those cast in shadows.

Get a grip, Nikki. Wanting privacy for a phone conversation
isn't the same as keeping a secret. And every phone call isn't
some grand conspiracy to hide either his past or some new
danger.

I know all of that. Even more, I believe it. But sane rationality
doesn't soothe the little pang in my heart or the knot of fear that
sits tight in my belly, and standing stock-still and naked and
bound is not a straight path to well-adjusted thoughts. Rather,
it's a twisting, winding road of angst, and I'm suddenly careening
down it without brakes, and hating myself for going there.

I want to hug myself, but my bound wrists make that impossible.

The truth is that I've been on pins and needles since my former boss made his threats against Damien. Carl's company had
pitched a project to Stark Applied Technology, and when Damien
declined, Carl blamed me. He fired me, too, but he didn't stop
there, and the last time I saw him he promised to fuck Damien
over. So far, nothing has happened. But Carl is determined and
resourceful, and in his mind, he has the moral high ground. As

far as he's concerned, Damien squelched one of Carl's most important business deals. The projected loss of capital must be in the millions, and Carl isn't the kind of man who would consider either the money or the slight to be water under the bridge.

That fact that nothing has happened in over a week bothers me. What could his silence mean? I've thought about it and thought about it, and the only conclusion I can reach is that something has happened—and Damien has chosen not to tell me.

I might be wrong—I hope I am. But worry and fear twist inside me, cruelly whispering that although Damien has shone a light onto all my secrets, his are still shrouded in gray.

"Well, hell, Nikki. Now you're frowning." Blaine's gripe is laced with a chuckle. "Sometimes I wish I could crawl into that mind of yours. I'd love to know what you're thinking."

I manage a smile. "Deep thoughts," I say. "But not bad ones."

"Good," he says, but there's a question mark in his eyes, and maybe even a hint of concern. I wonder what Evelyn, Blaine's lover who's known Damien since childhood, has told him about Damien's past. For that matter, I wonder if Blaine knows more than I do about the man who has consumed me so completely. The thought only makes me frown more.

Damien is gone only a few minutes, and when he returns I am overwhelmed by the urge to run to him. "What's the matter?" I ask.

"Nothing that looking at you won't make better."

I laugh, hoping he doesn't notice that the sound is hollow. Once again, he is wearing the face he shows the public. But I am not the public, and I know better. I look hard at him, waiting for his eyes to meet mine. When they do, it is like a switch has been thrown. The hard lines of his mouth curve into a genuine smile, and once again I am alight with the glow of Damien.

He walks toward me, and my pulse increases with the tempo of his steps. He stops only inches from me, and I am suddenly finding it very difficult to breathe. After everything we've done together—after every hurt he's soothed and every secret he's seen—how is it that every moment with Damien can feel like the first one?

"Do you have any idea how much you mean to me?"

"I—" I draw in a breath and try again. "Yes," I say. "As much as you mean to me."

I am trapped in the heat of his gaze and his proximity. He's not touching me, but he might as well be. There is nothing about me at that moment that isn't a reflection of Damien, of how I feel about him and what he's doing to me. I want to soothe him, want to stroke his cheek and run my fingers through his hair. I want to pull his head to my breast and whisper soft words, and I want to make love to him slowly and sweetly until the shadows of the night are gone and the morning light bathes us in color.

From his post at the canvas, Blaine coughs politely. Damien's lips curve up in a grin that matches my own. We've done nothing more than look into each other's eyes, and yet it feels as though Blaine has witnessed something deeply intimate.

"Yeah, right. So, I'm going to head on out. The cocktail party's not until seven on Saturday, right? So I'll come by that afternoon and see if she needs any last minute touch-ups. And I'll take care of hanging her when I set up the rest of the canvases on easels."

"Perfect," Damien says, not looking at him.

"I gotta say," Blaine adds, as he gathers his things, "I'm going to miss this."

For just an instant, I think I see something melancholy in Damien's eyes, but it passes almost immediately. "Yes," he says. "So am I."

I'm not sure when Blaine leaves, I only know that he's gone, and Damien is still there, and he's still not touching me, and that

I'm going to go a little crazy if I don't feel his hands upon me soon.

"Is it really done?" I ask. "I still haven't seen it."

"Come here."

He reaches out, and I shift to give him my back, expecting him to untie me. He doesn't, though. Instead he puts his hand on my shoulder and eases me toward the canvas. I have to move carefully because of the red silk cord wrapped around my left leg, but he doesn't make any effort to untangle me. And he certainly doesn't bother to pass me the robe that's laid out on the foot of the bed.

I grimace, lifting my brows in question. Damien doesn't even pretend to misunderstand. "Why, Ms. Fairchild, surely you don't expect me to sabotage such an amazing opportunity."

"Mmm." I try to sound harsh, but I'm pretty certain he can hear the laughter in my voice.

He doesn't respond, though, because we've reached the painting. I gasp—it's me, yes. The curve of my ass, the swell of my breast. But it's more than me. The image is alluring and submissive, strong and yet vulnerable. It's also anonymous, as Damien had promised. In the portrait, my face is turned away, and my golden curls are piled atop my head, a few tendrils spilling down to caress my neck and shoulders. In the real world, those curls no longer exist, my long tresses having recently been traded for a shoulder-length cut.

I frown, remembering the weight of the scissors in my hands, remembering the way I'd hacked at my hair when what I'd really wanted was to take that sharp edge to my flesh. I'd been lost then, certain that the only way back was to hold fast to the pain like a lifeline.

I shiver. It's not a memory I like.

Automatically, my gaze dips to the legs of the girl in the portrait. But her—*my*—thighs are close together and angled such that the worst of the scars aren't visible. The scar on my left hip is, though. But Blaine has managed to make that raised welt part of the beauty of the painting. The edges are blurred, almost as if it's in soft focus, and the red cord skims over the marred flesh, as if being bound too tight caused the wounds.

When you get right down to it, I suppose that's true.

I look away, unnerved by the inescapable reality that the girl on the canvas is beautiful, even despite the scars.

"Nikki?"

I glance out of the corner of my eye and see that Damien is looking at me, not the painting, and there is concern on his face.

"He's talented," I say, my lips flickering into a conjured smile. "It's a wonderful portrait."

"It is," he agrees. "Everything about it is exactly what I want." There's a familiar heat in his voice, and I understand both his spoken words and what remains unsaid.

I smile, and this time it doesn't feel plastic.

Damien eyes me, and I see the playful light in his eyes.

"What?" I demand, amused but wary.

He shrugs, then glances again at the painting. "It will be a miracle if I get any work done in this room." He nods toward the stone wall above the fireplace where the painting is to hang. "And I damn sure shouldn't entertain in here."

"Oh?" He has a cocktail party scheduled for this very room in only two days.

Damien chuckles. "I find that it's a social faux pas to host a party with a permanent hard-on."

"Well, then, perhaps you should have planned to hang the painting in the bedroom."

"I don't need the image in my bedroom. Not when I have the real thing."

"And you do," I say, my tone teasing. "Bought and paid for. At least until midnight when I turn into a pumpkin."

His eyes darken, all playfulness vanishing. "Midnight," he repeats, and I wonder at the harshness I hear in his voice. After all, it's not as if I will truly turn into a pumpkin when our game is over. And I certainly won't be going away—to be honest, I don't ever want to go away. All that will change is that there will be no more rules—no more "sir," no more orders, no more safewords. There will be panties and bras and jeans if I want them. And, yes, there will be a million dollars.

But above all else, there will still be Damien.

"Follow me," he says.

Again, I glance at my leg, then give my bound hands a little shake. "Untie me."

He stands for a moment, his eyes on mine, and I can see that we are still playing games. My pulse pounds in my throat, and my nipples are erect. My hands, tied behind me, pull my shoulders back and lift my breasts. They feel full, needful, and I graze my teeth over my lower lip as I silently wait for Damien's touch.

A game, yes. But I like it. In this game, there are no losers.

Slowly, he lets his gaze drift down over my body. My breath is shallow, and small beads of sweat form at the nape of my neck. I can feel the moisture between my thighs, the quivering need, and it takes all of my effort to stand silent and still and not beg for him to please, please fuck me. The bed is just a few yards away, the prop Damien brought in for the portrait. *There,* I want to scream. *Just take me there.*

But I don't. Because I know this man. And most of all, I know that everything with Damien is worth the wait.

Finally, he bends down and untwines the cord from around my leg, but when he gets to my wrists, he stops, leaving them bound together behind my back, the red silk trailing from them like a tail.

"Damien," I say, trying to sound stern, but there's no keeping the amusement—and the excitement—from my voice. "I thought you were going to free me."

"Bought and paid for, remember?"

"Oh." My word is little more than breath.

"Come," he says, and the dual meaning isn't lost on me, especially not when he slides the cord from back to front between my legs, then tugs on the end as if it's a leash. A very erotic, very tantalizing leash. The smooth silk teases my yearning sex, the friction from the cord's braiding making my legs so weak that I'm not sure I'll make it to wherever he's leading.

His tug is gentle, but enticing, and by the time we reach the spalike bathroom, I am weak with desire. Fire courses through my body, and I look with longing at the shower's eight strategically placed jets. The thought of Damien standing behind me, his hands on my breasts, his lips brushing my neck, is almost more than I can bear, and I actually whimper.

Beside me, Damien chuckles. "Later," he whispers. "Right now, I have something else in mind."

My mind whirs through the possibilities. We have already passed the bed. He has resolutely dismissed my thirst for the shower. And as far as I can tell, Damien is paying no heed to the deep Jacuzzi-style tub.

I haven't a single clue what he has in mind—but I don't care. This night is no longer about the destination, but the journey. And considering the touch of Damien's hand upon my shoulder and the tantalizing pressure of the cord against my sex, this voyage is turning out to be very pleasant indeed.

The closet into which he leads me is at least the size of the living room of the condo I share with Jamie in Studio City. This is not the first time I've been in here, but I still feel as though I need a map.

It would take me years to wear all the clothes that Damien has bought for me. And despite the fact that the left side of the closet is full to overflowing, I'm ninety-nine percent sure that at least a dozen new outfits have been worked into the mix since the last time I changed clothes in here.

"I don't remember seeing that one before," I say, nodding toward a silver dress that sparkles in the dim lighting and looks to be small enough and tight enough to leave nothing to the imagination.

"Don't you?" His smile is slow and easy, and it matches the gaze that skims over me. "I can assure you that won't be a problem after you put it on. No one will be able to forget it."

"Least of all you?" I tease.

His eyes darken, and he steps closer, the movement adding slack to the cord and making it drop away from my body. My disappointment at the loss of contact is short lived, however. Damien is right there, only inches from me, and the air between us seems to hum. Every tiny hair on my body stands up, as if I'm standing in a lightning storm with danger crackling all around me. I gasp when his thumb gently strokes the line of my jaw. My lips part. I want to feel his thumb on my lips, in my mouth. I want to taste Damien. I want to consume him as the fire from his proximity is consuming me.

"There is nothing about you that I could ever forget," he says. "You are burned into my memory. Your hair glittering in candlelight. Your skin, dewy and soft, as you step out of the shower. The way you move beneath me when we make love. And the way you look at me, as if there is nothing you could see inside me that would make you want to turn away."

"There's not," I say softly.

Damien says nothing, but keeps his eyes fixed on me. He eases closer, so that my nipples barely brush the soft cotton of his T-shirt. The shock from the contact is electric, and I swallow a gasp. I am tingling all over, and as he gently strokes his fingertips down my bare arm, all I can think is that I want to press against him. I want Damien inside me. Rough, gentle, I don't care. I just need him, right then, right there.

"How?" I say, barely able to force the question past the lump in my throat.

"How what?"

"How can you make love to me with only the whisper of a touch?"

"I'm a very resourceful man. I thought you knew." The corner of his mouth twitches, and I see the hint of a sparkle in his eyes. "Perhaps I should offer you a more imaginative demonstration?"

"Imaginative?" I repeat. My mouth is dry.

"I'm going to make you come, darling Nikki. Without the touch of my hands, without the caress of my body. But I'll be watching. I'll see the way your lips part, the way your skin flushes. I'll watch as you try to control yourself. And I'll tell you a secret, Nikki. I'm going to be fighting for control, too."

I realize that I have taken a step back as he has spoken, and I'm now leaning against the bureau that divides the his and hers hemispheres of this massive closet. It's a good thing, because without that stalwart support, I doubt my trembling legs could keep me upright.

"What are you going to do?" I don't understand why he says that I'm going to try to control myself. I've learned many things during my time with this man, and one thing I know is that with Damien, I am free to go utterly wild. Why then, would I want to rein that in? Why would he expect me to?

He doesn't answer my question, and I find myself biting my lower lip and examining him through narrowed eyes as I try to discern some clue as to his intentions. He steps away from me, and though I am sure that it is only my imagination, the air seems to chill with the increasing distance. The cord that had dropped to the ground now rises. Damien pauses about a foot away from me, but he continues to tug at the cord, taking up the slack so that it lifts between my legs. He moves slowly, but soon I can feel it again. I am so aroused that I gasp from the contact, my body trembling in what is almost, but not quite, an orgasm.

My eyes find Damien's, and I see his victorious grin. "Don't worry, Ms. Fairchild," he says. "I promise there's more where that came from."

He steps toward me, still taking up the slack so that the cord never breaks contact with my body. Each movement makes the smooth braid of silk shift slightly, and I close my eyes, concentrating on not biting my lip and on not grinding my hips. I don't know what kind of game Damien is playing, but I do know that I want it to last.

His fingers brush my neck and my eyes fly open. I tilt my head to look up at him, but he doesn't meet my eyes. He is focused on his task.

He is focused on tying the cord around my neck.

I swallow, my emotions a storm inside me. There's excitement, yes, but it's mingled with fear. Of what, I'm not sure. I'm not afraid of Damien. I could never be afraid of Damien. But dear God, why is he leashing me? And how tight will he make that cord?

"Damien," I say, surprised that my words sound normal. "What are you doing?"

"What I want," he replies, and though the words do not answer my question, a swell of relief washes over me, followed by delicious anticipation.

This is how it began for us, with those three simple words. And so help me, I don't ever want it to end.

2

Damien ties off the end of the cord so that it essentially forms a choker with a very long tail. That tail extends down between my breasts, over my sex, and then back up to where my hands are still bound behind me by the other end of that very same cord. I shift a little. I am antsy and turned on and, yes, a little bit uncomfortable.

Slowly, he looks me up and down. "I'm tempted to commission another painting, Ms. Fairchild. I think I'd like to have you like this all the time."

I smirk. "Are we negotiating, Mr. Stark? I don't come cheap, but for someone of your discriminating taste, I'm quite certain that we could come to terms."

He laughs, and I have to bite my lip not to join in. "There is very little that I'd like more than to negotiate with you. But I'm afraid we're running out of time."

"Time?"

"Places to go," he says. "People to see."

Oh. Suddenly his comment that I will be fighting to keep control makes a lot more sense.

I glance down at my very bare, very bound body. "I don't think I'm dressed for company."

"It's just as well that the traditional morals of our society don't allow me to take you out like this. I'm a very selfish man, and I have no interest in sharing you with the world."

"Believe me," I say, with a wry twist to my mouth, "I have no interest in being shared." My mind turns to the portrait, in which I am bound so similarly to how I am now. A larger-than-life painting that will hang in a room meant for entertaining. In that way, I suppose Damien has already shared me, and I have agreed to be shared. But I am anonymous in the painting. That had been a key term of our deal.

"I'm exceptionally glad to hear that, Ms. Fairchild. Especially since, as you reminded me, you are my exclusive property until midnight. Completely mine to do with as I wish. Isn't that so?"

"Yes."

"To touch, to tease, to tempt."

My body tightens at his words, but I manage to nod.

"To punish and to praise."

"Damien—" My voice is raw, and he silences me with a gentle finger to my lips. Then slowly circles me.

"To clothe, to feed. Mine, Nikki," he says, his breath stroking the back of my neck as intimately as a hand upon my sex. "Mine to protect, mine to cherish." He has finished the circle and is facing me now. "Mine to rule. Tell me, Nikki. Tell me what I want to hear."

"I'm yours," I whisper. I am craving his touch, my body so hyperaware that I feel drugged, done in by the sweet narcotic that is Damien.

"Good girl." His words are low, barely audible. Slowly, he moves behind me again. I turn my head, trying to see him, but I don't know what he's doing until I feel him loosening the knots that bind my wrists.

"I'm surprised," I say. "After what you said, I didn't think you'd free me."

"Who says I am?" His voice is low and sensual. It surrounds and strokes me. "I'm taking care of you, Nikki. Wholly and completely."

I close my eyes in sweet anticipation. Behind me, he finishes unraveling the knots. I sigh and rub my wrists, which have gone a little numb from being in one position for so long. I try to guess what Damien has planned, but it's no use. I am clueless, and I watch helplessly as he moves across the room to the section of the closet that boasts a wider selection of designer tops than the Neiman Marcus back home in Dallas. He chooses a sleeveless black sweater with a cowl neck. Then he returns to my side.

"I'm going to dress you now," he says. "Arms up."

I obey. The knit is soft yet snug, and I can't deny that it fits perfectly. I lift my hand to my neck, enjoying the freedom of movement, and am happy to realize that the high, loose neck covers the cord that still hangs between my breasts under the shirt.

He holds out a tiny leather miniskirt next, and I dutifully step into it, careful not to trip over the cord that still hangs in front of me, and that Damien makes sure remains hidden inside the garment.

"Damien," I say, and though I try to sound harsh, there is no hiding the excitement that laces those three simple syllables.

"Hush," he replies. He moves behind me, presumably to zip up the skirt. Instead, he reaches between my legs for the dangling cord and tugs it toward him. Once again, I tingle from the enticing feel of the silk against my oh-so-sensitive flesh. He pulls it up, threading it under the skirt so that a tiny bit peeks out from the waistband. Then he zips me up tight.

"I don't think that adds much to the outfit," I say, looking over my shoulder at the flash of red that resembles an exotic zipper pull.

"I beg to differ," he retorts, and underscores his words with a slow, yet firm tug on the cord. I cry out in pleasure and surprise, the simultaneous stroking of my sex and ass almost more than I can handle.

"You still need shoes," he says gently, this time crossing to a section of shoe cubbies. He grabs a pair of strappy black sandals with three-inch fuck-me heels. "These will do," he says. "And as much as I like you in stockings, I think we'll skip that tonight."

I can only nod, then sit on the white leather bench to which he leads me. As I sit, the cord tightens, and I am quite certain that Damien intended it that way.

He crouches in front of me and lifts my foot. My knees are apart, and as he slides on the shoe and fastens the tiny buckle around my ankle, his eyes flicker up to meet mine, and then down to the shadow between my parted legs. Unless a red silk cord constitutes underwear, I am naked beneath the skirt. Naked and wet and so needful that I want to slide my hips forward in a silent demand that he touch me. That he take me.

With Damien, however, I don't have to beg. As soon as he has fastened the other shoe, he puts my feet on the ground. Because of the heels, my knees now rise above the bench, which means my skirt has lifted a bit as well, giving the man in front of me an even more intimate view.

Gently, he presses his palm against my bare knee. Then he leans in and brushes his lips over the sensitive skin on the inside of my right thigh. I shiver from the contact, the pressure from the cord making the sensation that much more erotic.

"You're like a drug to me." Damien's voice is low and his breath upon my skin is so tantalizing that I have to close my eyes and clutch the bench even tighter. "I wasn't going to touch you—not yet. But I don't have the strength to deny myself the taste of you."

"Yes." It is the only word I can manage, but right then it is the only word that matters.

His hands ease up my legs as he presses gentle kisses along the insides of my thighs.

"Up," he says, as he pushes at the skirt. I rise off the bench and he lifts the skirt over my rear so that when I sit back down, my bare ass is against the warm leather bench. His hands are still on my hips, and his thumb gently strokes the worst of my scars. The one where I'd cut too deep and been too scared to go to the ER. I'd fixed myself up with duct tape and superglue. I'd survived, but the scar now acts as a hideous reminder of the emotional damage that had put it there in the first place.

Between my legs, Damien's lips brush over another angry scar. "You are so beautiful," he murmurs. "Strong and beautiful, and mine."

I tremble and blink back tears. I desperately hope that he is right, but I still fear that my strength is like a rubber band. Stretch me too far, and I will snap.

I can't worry about that now, though. I can't think about anything except the brush of Damien's lips against my skin and the pressure of his hands upon my legs.

Gently, he urges my thighs farther apart and I comply willingly, almost desperately. I need him now—need to lose myself in his touch—and Damien does not disappoint. I feel his breath upon my sex, and my own breath comes faster, my breasts rising and falling, my nipples tight against the knit sweater.

He teases me, his tongue gently stroking the tender flesh between my legs and my vulva. I squeeze my eyes tight and try not to squirm. I cannot help it, though, and when I do, that wonderful, damnable cord slides over my dripping sex. I am so wet, so turned on, and just that tiny bit of friction is enough to shoot electricity all through me. I curl my toes in the shoes, shifting them so that only the points touch the ground and my knees raise even higher. I want more—so help me, I *need* more—and then, thank God, his tongue flicks gently over my clit and that is all it takes. I shatter, leaning back, my hands gripping the bench so hard I'm afraid I might dent the frame.

He holds me in thrall, his mouth pleasuring me so fully, his tongue dipping intimately inside me. The orgasm that is racking my body seems to go on forever, and I squeeze my legs shut, trapping Damien, not certain if I am trying to ensure that he never stops, or trying to make him stop because I cannot possibly survive such an onslaught of pleasure.

I feel the stubble of his beard against my thigh and gasp, then realize that I have been holding my breath. I lean forward, my senses returning, and twine my fingers in his hair. I don't want him to stop, and yet right then, I need his arms around me. I need to hold him close and kiss him, and I roughly pull him up. I claim his mouth with my own, kissing him fiercely and relishing the taste of me upon his lips.

"Take me to bed," I plead moments later. I've had only a taste of Damien, and like a long-starved refugee, I am nowhere close to having my fill. "Please, take me to bed," I repeat.

"Not yet," Damien says, and his eyes are dark with promise. "First, I'm going to take you out."

I shift on the soft, leather passenger seat as Damien maneuvers the sleek and speedy Bugatti Veyron onto the Pacific Coast Highway. Damien has not actually said as much, but I think that of all his cars, this one is his favorite. It's certainly the one we use the most, and I have even managed—finally—to memorize the make and model. Now it's "the Bugatti," not "that unpronounceable car."

He's smiling, obviously enjoying putting the car through its paces, leading us away from Malibu to God knows where. He hasn't told me, and I haven't asked. Wherever we're going, I trust that it will be fabulous, and I am happily lost in the pleasure of watching him. Damien Stark, my playful, sexy billionaire. I smile even broader. *Mine,* I think. That is what he said about me. That I am his.

But is the reverse really true? Is Damien mine? For that matter, can a man like Damien Stark—a man who holds power close, but his secrets closer—ever belong to anyone?

His attention shifts from the road, and his brows rise in question, creating two horizontal furrows on an otherwise perfect forehead. "Penny for your thoughts," he says.

I force my lips to curve, banishing my worries. "I haven't taken a look at your balance sheets, but I think you're worth more than a penny, Mr. Stark."

"I'm flattered."

"At my assessment of your value?"

"That you were thinking of me," he says, taking his eyes off the road long enough to meet my eyes. "Then again, I suppose I shouldn't be surprised. There isn't a moment that goes by that I don't think of you." His words are as smooth as whiskey and just as intoxicating. "Even at the bargain-basement price of a penny, if I was required to pay each time my thoughts turned to you, my fortune would have evaporated days ago."

"Oh." My smile is soft and ridiculously, foolishly shy. He has, in that Damien Stark way that he has, completely banished my troubled thoughts. "I guess I won't charge you, then. I'd hate to see you destitute." I flash an impish grin as I snuggle back against the soft leather seat. "I like your cars too much."

"I imagine they make putting up with me more palatable."

"Oh, absolutely," I say. "The cars, the clothes, the jet." I'm counting on my fingers now.

"The paparazzi?" He glances sideways at me, and even in that quick flick of his gaze, I see the concern on his face.

I grimace. "They make me want to pull out my Leica and snap pictures of them. Then we'd see how they like it." I frown. "On the other hand, I love that camera." I think back to the day that Damien surprised me with it after I'd told him how I dabble in photography. "I don't want to soil it by taking pictures of them." I say the last word as if there's a nasty taste in my mouth.

"Besides," Damien says, "no tabloid will pay for a picture of one of them. They want you. And because of that—because of me—you've lost a level of privacy."

I shift in my seat to look more directly at him. Is this the source of his concern? Was that what the telephone call was about? His lawyers warning him about some new picture of us that will appear on the cover of a half dozen magazines next week? Mentally, I flip back through the last week, trying to think what image could be so mortifying that it would cause Damien so much consternation.

Already, the tabloids have gotten hold of a half dozen shots of me in a bathing suit, courtesy of the various pageants I've entered over the years. Seeing myself displayed at the grocery store checkout line had been a less-than-fun experience, but I'd taken about a million deep breaths and reminded myself that those pageants had been open to the public and at least two of them had even been televised.

I can't think of anything else disturbing that could be printed about me or about the two of us together. Certainly there's nothing that Damien and I have done in public that I'd be embarrassed for my mother to see. And as for in private—well, if the paparazzi have pictures of us in private, they would have to be very brave indeed to face Damien's wrath and publish them.

But there is the balcony of the Malibu house.

Every day I've stood naked and bound in front of that open

door, and although Damien owns acres and acres, and the distant beach is a private one, surely a resourceful photographer could—

I can't even finish the thought. A wave of fear crashes over me, so palpable that I suddenly feel nauseated. And despite the cold that seems to settle over me, I realize that my armpits are damp with perspiration. "They don't have anything new, do they?" I say, trying hard to make my voice sound normal. I can handle the attention that goes with being Damien's girlfriend. But nude images of me splashed across papers and the Internet? *Oh, dear God* . . .

"It's not like they've stepped it up a notch, right? I mean, it's not like someone's been aiming a long lens at the balcony. Have they?"

"Good God, no." His response is so fast and full of such astonishment that I know my guess completely missed the mark.

I relax, the feeling returning to my body. "Good," I say. "I thought—" I break off, because I need to take another deep breath. I realize my fingernails are digging into the flesh above my knees, and I release my grip and force myself to relax. I don't need the pain to get through this; there's nothing to get through except fear. And besides, I have Damien to hang on to.

"Nikki?"

When I speak, my voice actually sounds normal. "I just thought that since you brought up the paparazzi, that maybe that was what the call was about."

"Call?"

"Earlier," I say. "At the house. You looked so upset."

His eyes widen with what I recognize as genuine surprise. "Did I?"

I lift a shoulder in concession. "I doubt Blaine noticed. But I know you."

"Yes," he says. "Apparently you do. But no, that call had nothing to do with those vultures."

I can almost see a red haze of anger surrounding Damien, but I don't know if he's angry at the original caller or with me.

I clear my throat and continue the conversation as if I'd never even mentioned it. "Besides," I say, "the paparazzi are not one of your acquisitions. More like an infestation. I don't like them, but I'm learning to live with them."

He glances at me, and I catch his worried expression. It had been too much to hope that Damien missed my minor freak-out moment a second ago. Damien, I've learned, misses nothing.

"Really," I say, and I mean it, too. So long as no one has taken a nudie picture of me with a long lens, I am just fine. "They're like fire ants in Texas. They swarm, but the trick is to just not get in the middle of them. And if you do get bit, the sting fades soon enough." I am so firm that I almost convince myself. "Besides," I add with a wicked grin, "your Santa Barbara hotel and your penthouse apartment make it all worthwhile."

He remains silent for so long that I feel sure my ploy to change the subject has failed.

"Don't forget the house in Hawaii," he finally says.

I release a happy sigh. "You have a house in Hawaii?"

"And an apartment in Paris."

"Oh, now you're just trying to make me drool."

"Have I mentioned that Stark International has several divisions in the food industry, as well as a significant share of a company that produces high-end Swiss chocolates?"

I cross my arms. If we're playing Itemize Stark's Assets, this game will go on forever. "You realize that the fact that you have never once offered me one of those Swiss chocolates is grounds for me to hold a grudge for at least two weeks."

"Two weeks?" His hand hovers over the button on the steering wheel that operates the speakerphone. "And would you be withholding sex during that time, Ms. Fairchild?"

I manage a very unladylike snort. "Hardly. The idea is to punish you, not me."

"I see." He moves his hand away from the button. "No need to bother Sylvia this late, then. I'll have her order your chocolates in the morning."

I laugh. "So far the chocolates are in the lead in my assessment of your assets. But I'm also impressed by your fabulous taste in restaurants. That's a hint, by the way."

"I applaud your subtlety."

"I try."

"And I'll reward you with the news that we're almost there."

"Really?" I've been ignoring the world outside the car, but now I look through the passenger side window. We've been on the road almost half an hour, the dark Pacific with the moon-crested waves rippling to my right as we head south. Now I see that we've arrived in Santa Monica, and after a few turns and stops at traffic lights, we are on Ocean Avenue between Santa Monica and Arizona.

Damien pulls up in front of a sleek white building that, as far as I can tell, has no hard angles, only sweeping curves. It's several stories tall and mostly dark, but when I press my nose to the window and look up, I can see that the top floor is brightly lit.

There is a valet stand a few feet away, and a guy not much younger than Damien hurries to my door. Just as quickly, Damien presses the button that locks the car. I look at him curiously, but he provides no explanation. Just gets out from his side and walks around the Bugatti to where the valet stands helplessly.

I'm struck by the difference between the two men. I'm guessing the valet is twenty-six, just two years older than me and only four years younger than Damien. And yet Damien carries himself with such confidence that he seems ageless. Like a mythic hero, his tribulations have strengthened him, giving him a sexy self-assurance that is so attractive it almost outshines the physical beauty of the man.

At thirty, Damien has already conquered the world. The valet, who now stands confused without a door to open, probably has trouble conquering the rent. I don't feel bad for him—he is like so many young people in Los Angeles. Struggling actors or writers or models who've moved to the City of Angels in the hope that the town will make them over. It is Damien who is the exception. Damien doesn't need this town; Damien needs nothing but himself.

Once again, I feel that unwelcome twinge in my heart. Because if my meanderings are true, then what does that say about me? I know he wants me—I see that desire every time I look into his eyes. But I have come to need Damien as potently as the air that I breathe, and I sometimes fear that while our desire is mutual, my need is one-sided.

My melancholy thoughts evaporate the moment Damien opens the door and I see him smiling down at me with such a fiercely protective set to his jaw that I can't help but sigh. He holds out his hand to help me from the car, his body positioned so that there is no way that the valet will get a gander at my private parts, even if my attempts to ease out modestly are foiled by this very low-to-the-ground car.

I manage the maneuver successfully, thank goodness, and Damien releases my hand and slips his arm around my waist. It is summer, but this close to the beach the air is cool, and I lean against him, relishing his warmth. Damien tosses the keys to the valet, who I think is going to weep with joy at the prospect of sliding behind the wheel of that exceptional car.

"Let me guess," I say, as we wait for our rather inefficient valet to get a ticket for Damien. "You own the building." I glance at it as we speak. Only the entry is well lit, and in the shadows, I see clusters of people. Couples talking together. Men wearing everything from swim trunks to business suits. I suppose that's normal. After all, the beach is just across the street.

"This building? No, though I might put in an offer if it comes up for sale. It's an office complex right now, but with this location, it could be converted to a very successful hotel. I'd keep the rooftop restaurant, and not just because I'm friends with the owner."

The valet hands Damien the card, and for the first time, I notice the restaurant name on the valet stand. *"Le Caquelon?"* I ask as we head for the door. "I haven't heard of it."

"It's excellent. Fabulous view, even better food." He grins wolfishly as he looks me up and down. "And the tables are very, very private."

"Oh." I swallow, because there it is—that sensual ping that is Damien. That makes me turn on a dime from calm and collected to a swooning mass of sensual, sexual need. *I'm going to make you come,* he'd said, and dear God I hope that is a promise he intends to keep.

I clear my throat and try to calm my speeding pulse. I'm sure he can feel it beating against him. "What does the name mean?" I ask.

Before he can answer, the clusters break apart, then seem to re-form into a mob. Now camera strobes are flashing and the vultures are shouting their questions. It's happened so quickly that I don't even have time to think. Automatically I wipe all expression from my face, then paste on the tiniest of smiles. For so many years, I've hid behind a practiced, plastic mask. Social Nikki, Daughter Nikki, Pretty Pageant Nikki.

Right now, I am Public Nikki.

Damien's hand tightens around my waist, and though he says nothing, I feel the tension building in him. "Just walk," he whispers. "All we need to do is get inside." Inside, as his attorney

Charles explained to me, we are safe. Inside, they would be trespassing.

"Nikki!" A voice stands out from the din, so familiar in its tone that I want to slug the shouter. I don't, however, react. Instead I face straight ahead and reveal only that tiny public smile.

"The photos that came out last week from the Miss Texas bathing suit competition have gone viral. Is it true you leaked them to promote a new modeling career?"

In my mind, I imagine my hand tightening into a fist, my nails biting into my flesh.

"What about television? Can you confirm that you'll be starring in a new reality show next year?"

No, not a fist. I am holding a razor blade, that tight, sharp line of steel biting through my skin, the cold pain something I can grab on to.

No.

I force the thought of blades and pain out of my mind. It infuriates me that these parasites are a catalyst for my weakness. They aren't worth my time, much less my pain.

"Nikki, how does it feel to have snagged one of the world's most eligible bachelors?"

I breathe in deep as Damien's hand tightens around my waist, pulling me even closer. *Damien.* I don't need the pain—I don't. They are nothing—*nothing.* I am centered. And I have Damien to help keep me whole.

"Mr. Stark! Can you comment on the rumor that you refused to attend next Friday's tennis center dedication?"

For a moment, I think that Damien stumbles, but then we are moving again, and in front of us the doors open and a man who must be seven feet tall bursts through, flanked by two men in suits who move to either side of us. The three form a triangular-shaped barrier, and we move like an arrow through the crowd, over the threshold, and into safety.

As soon as the doors close behind us, my chest feels less tight. My breath comes easier. Damien takes his arm from around my waist, but twines his fingers in mine. He looks down at me, the question clear in his eyes. "I'm fine," I say as we hurry toward the elevator. "Really."

The tall man, Damien, and I enter the car, but the other two stay behind, presumably to make sure none of the vultures try to enter the restaurant pretending to buy a meal. Once the door slides shut, I look up at Damien. His eyes blaze with raw fury, but beneath it there is concern for me that is so potent I almost weep.

Slowly, he lifts my hand, then gently, sweetly, he kisses my palm.

"I am so, so sorry, my friend," the giant says with an accent that I can't place. "A busboy saw the reservation book. It would appear he hoped to make more than just his share of the tips tonight."

"I see," Damien says. His voice is level, but there is a tightness to it, and the pressure of his hand on mine increases. I doubt that I am the only one who can tell that Damien is working hard to control the temper that had been so famous back in his tennis days. The temper that had, in fact, caused the injury that left him with dual-colored eyes. "I'd like to have a word with that young man."

"I've already dismissed him," the tall man says. "He was escorted off the property at the same time I came to assist you and the young lady."

"Good," Damien says, and I silently echo the thought. Because considering the rage that I see etched on Damien's face, if that busboy was still on the premises, he should be very, very worried indeed.

3

Damien says nothing else during the ride to the rooftop restaurant, and the air in the small elevator car is thick. I'm sure our escort—who I've decided is Damien's owner friend—is mortified that one of his employees leaked the news of where Damien would be. And the fact that Damien hasn't formally introduced us is more proof of how much the incident has upset him.

Damien's manners are always stellar.

As for me, I can't help but regret going out at all. The paparazzi were bad, but this cloud of gloom is worse.

I squeeze Damien's hand. "They'll get tired of us soon enough. Some movie star will divorce some other star. Or a reality star will get caught shoplifting. We're boring by comparison."

For a moment, I think my ploy hasn't worked. Then he lifts our joined hands and presses a kiss on my knuckles. "I'm sorry," he says. "I should be the one making you feel better."

"I'm with you," I say. "That's as good as it gets."

He tightens his fingers around mine as he looks up at the man. "Alaine, I've forgotten my manners. I'd like to introduce you to my girlfriend, Nikki Fairchild. Nikki, my friend Alaine Beauchene, one of the best chefs in the city and the owner of *Le Caquelon*."

"It's a very great pleasure to meet you," he says, taking my hand. "Damien has told me so many good things."

"Oh." I'm not sure why, but the words surprise me. I can easily picture me talking about Damien with Jamie, but somehow the idea of Damien chatting with his friends about me isn't something I've contemplated before. I can't deny that the knowledge feels nice. It's one more thread in the tapestry that is Nikki and Damien.

"Thank you for rescuing us," I say. And then, because I can't help but jump all over this peek into Damien's life, I add, "How do you two know each other?"

"Alaine's father practices sports medicine. We got to know each other on tour."

"Two young men crisscrossing Europe," Alaine says wistfully. "Those were good times, my friend."

I am watching Damien carefully. I may not know much, but I do know that his years playing tennis were hardly full of happy, fluffy memories. But when he smiles, it seems genuine. "Those were the best times," Damien says, and I feel an odd sense of relief knowing that his years on the tennis circuit were not total hell. That there had been one or two moments of sunshine peeking through the gloom.

"The two of us and Sofia," Alaine says with a laugh. He glances at me. "Two years younger than us, and the little imp was determined to stick like glue. Have you heard anything? How is she?"

"Fine," Damien says, and I am certain that Alaine catches the curtness of his tone, because his lips curve down in the slightest of frowns before curving back up again in what I can only assume is an attempt to be jolly.

"At any rate," he says as the elevator glides to a stop, "enough about the old days. You are here now for the food, not the memories."

The doors open, and Alaine gestures for me to exit first. I do, and find myself in a reception area that can only be described as spectacular. It's not elegant, and at the same time it's not casual. It is uniquely its own, with a glass roof that is open to the night sky crisscrossed by colored beams of light. The maitre d' station is an aquarium, and the hair of the girl who stands behind it is at least as colorful as the fish in the tank.

The wall to the left is entirely made of glass and reveals a chunk of Santa Monica and the Westside, along with a bit of beach, and the tiniest view of the Pier. The wall in front of us seems to be made up of panels that glow in the same colors as the beams of light crisscrossing the ceiling. I'm not sure if the design is modern or futuristic, but I like it. It's funky and different and so brightly colored that I don't see how the gray fog that has settled over this evening can stay.

"I must get back to the kitchen," Alaine says. "But Monica will show you to your booth. Ms. Fairchild, it has been a pleasure. Enjoy your meal, and I hope to see both of you next Friday at the dedication." His voice rises as if in question, but I can't answer since I have no idea what he's talking about.

"I won't be attending," Damien says. "But I'll call you next week. We should have drinks."

His words are perfectly polite and certainly friendly, but they are spoken from behind a mask. I wonder if Alaine can see it. Does he truly know Damien? Or does he only know the bits and pieces of the man that Damien has selectively revealed over the years?

I have a feeling that it is the latter. I doubt that anyone has ever seen completely beneath Damien's mask, and the thought that I am included in that group makes me sad. I want so desperately to shine a light into those dark places, and I even believe that Damien wants me to. But he's spent so long building walls to protect his privacy that I think he forgot to build a door. And now all I can hope is that we can chip away at the stone together.

We've been following Monica across the room, weaving between the tables to reach a bright green panel of light. She grabs a handle that I hadn't noticed and uses it to slide the panel to one side, much like the walls in Japanese movies. Inside, there is a table between two booth-style benches. But it's not a true booth, because if you slide through or walk behind the bench seats, there is an open area between the table and a window that looks out onto the spectacular, brightly lit Santa Monica Pier.

I follow Damien to the glass, drawn by the allure of both the man and the vibrant colors.

"Your wine is already breathing," Monica says, gesturing to the table, "and you have both flat and sparkling water. Will you be having your usual, Mr. Stark?"

"Just dessert," he says. "For two."

She inclines her head. "It will be right out. In the meantime, please enjoy the wine and the view."

She leaves, the panel closes, and Damien stands completely still beside me. And then, without any warning at all, he lashes out and slams his palm against the glass.

"Damien!" I expect to hear a commotion from the booth beside us, or at least the clatter of Monica's heels as she comes to check on us. There is nothing, though. Apparently we're better insulated than I would have guessed.

"Do you know how much I'm worth?" Damien asks, and I blink at the seemingly random question.

"I—no. Not exactly."

"It's more than the GNP of many countries, and it's damn sure enough to keep me as comfortable as I want to be for the rest of my life and then some." He turns to face me. "But it's not enough to keep those bastards away from you."

My heart melts. "Damien. It's okay. I'm fine."

"You're on the goddamn Internet in a bathing suit because of me."

"I'm on the Internet in a bathing suit because my mother forced me into pageants from the time I was four. And because I didn't have the balls to say no to her when I got older. I'm on the Internet because of those jerks out there. I'm not on the Internet because of you."

"I don't like that something that comes from me hurts you. I don't like it," he repeats. "But I don't know that I have the strength to change it."

"The strength?" I repeat, but he doesn't answer.

I see the shadows cross his face before he turns back to the window. Damien Stark, the strongest man I know, is twisted into knots, and suddenly I am scared. "Damien?"

His palm against the window clenches, and I can see his muscles tighten. "I owned a small, gourmet wine and cheese company once," he says. "Or rather Stark International did."

My mind spins at the shift in conversation. I don't know why he's telling me this, but I trust he has a point. I ease behind him and press against his back. I put my arms around his waist and brush my lips against the nape of his neck.

"Tell me about it," I say.

"It was an old company, family run, good reputation. I loved their products and thought it could be a profitable partnership. And it was—for about a year."

"What happened?"

"The press learned that Stark International was behind this mom-and-pop business and started lambasting them. Didn't matter that we weren't mass-producing the food. We hadn't changed the system. We had simply provided enough capital to let the company grow within its own parameters. But they were called out as Big Business disguised as the Little Guy, a trick designed to fool consumers. All the negative attention stopped growth cold. Suddenly a company that was solidly in the black was in the red."

"What did you do?" I hold my breath, because I am certain I know where he's going, and I don't like it.

"I pulled out. Very publicly and very loudly. Even so, it took a while for the business to get back on its feet. Being associated with Stark International almost destroyed the company whose cheese and wine I loved so much."

"I'm neither cheese nor wine," I say softly. "And I'm not spiraling down. I could never spiral down with you beside me. You hold me up, Damien. We both know it."

He is silent for so long that I think my words haven't touched him. And then, with an abruptness that takes my breath away, he spins us around, so that my back is against the cool glass. He steps away long enough to turn to face me, and then suddenly his mouth is on mine, and he is kissing me. His mouth is hard and demanding against mine, and I am held fast between the glass and Damien, an infinity of night stretched out before me, and the power of his kiss the only thing that is keeping me anchored.

When he breaks the kiss, I see an unfamiliar ferocity in his eyes. "I will do it," he says. "If that's what it takes to protect you, I will leave you. Even if it kills me."

"You won't," I counter, my breath coming hard and fast as my chest tightens painfully in protest and fear. "You won't because it would kill me, too."

"Oh, Nikki."

He lowers his head to close his mouth over mine once again, more gentle this time, but just as possessive. I arch back, losing myself in his touch. I am like a switch, and all it takes is the slightest contact from Damien to send a wild current through me. To light me up and make me shine.

"Do you have any idea what I want to do to you right now?"

"Tell me," I beg.

"I want to strip you bare and press you up against the glass. I want to trail my fingers over you lightly, just enough to make you awaken to my touch. I want to watch the lights of the Pier flash behind you, and I want to watch my own reflection in your eyes as you come."

My mouth is dry, so the little "oh" that I say doesn't actually come out as sound.

"But I can't," he says. "I believe I told you that I wasn't going to touch you."

"I won't hold you to it," I say.

"But that would be breaking the rules."

I have to force myself not to whimper. "You're playing games with me, Mr. Stark."

"Yes," he says plainly. "I am."

"I suppose that's fair, *sir,*" I say. "I'm yours, after all. At least for the night. But tomorrow, I'll be a rich woman and the game's going to have a new set of rules."

For a moment, he is perfectly still. Then he nods slowly. "You raise a good point, Ms. Fairchild," he says. "I need to make sure I get my money's worth."

"Your money's worth?"

"Did you read the article in *Forbes* I sent you?" he asks. "The reporter did a good job of describing my philosophy in business."

"I read it." In fact, I'd read it several times, savoring every tidbit I learned about Damien the Businessman.

"Yes, *sir,*" he corrects.

"Yes, sir," I repeat. "I read the article."

"Then you know that I attribute much of my success to my

ability to extract as much value as possible from every monetary transaction."

I lick my lips. "And I'm a monetary transaction?"

"You are indeed."

"I see. And how do you intend to extract value?"

"I already told you," he says. "If you're not going to pay attention . . ."

"You said you were going to make me come."

His mouth curves into a lazy smile and the corners of his eyes crinkle. "So I did. Good girl. You get an A in class, after all." Then, with a devious gleam in his eye, Damien takes hold of the cord at the small of my back and begins a slow tugging motion.

Oh. My. God.

It's as if he's creating electricity out of friction, and I close my eyes as my breath comes shallower and faster. "Damien," I whisper.

"Do you like that?"

"Yes—oh, God, yes."

"Good," he says. And then releases the cord.

The friction stops and my eyes fly open.

He's looking down at me, his smile a little too smug. "Frustrated, Ms. Fairchild?"

"No," I lie, but even I can hear the petulant whine in my voice.

He laughs, then kisses my nose. "Patience, sweetheart. Right now, I have a treat for you." He presses a button on the table and a light above the panel door shifts from red to green.

I glance at Damien curiously. "The panels lock to allow guests their privacy. When the food arrives, the server presses a button on the outside and the button turns red."

"And green unlocks it," I say. It's an interesting system—and also makes me realize that we would have had complete privacy if Damien had actually stripped me bare and fucked me against the window, just as he'd described.

I imagine the feel of the cool glass against my back. Of Damien's hands on my breasts. Of his mouth on my neck. And of his cock filling me as he thrusts deeper and deeper inside me until I explode in a cacophony of colors that rival the shining lights of the Pier in the distance.

"Nikki—"

My head jerks up and I realize that the waiter is setting a fondue pot on the table and Damien is gesturing for me to sit down. Although the waiter seems oblivious, I am quite certain that Damien knows exactly where my thoughts had wandered.

Naughty, he mouths.

I flash him my most innocent smile, then bat my eyes for effect.

There is a pattern in the middle of the tabletop that turns out not to be a pattern at all. It's a heating element, and onto it the waiter puts a heavy stone pot—*le caquelon*—filled with partially melted chocolate. Another waiter has a basket of all sorts of dippables, ranging from juicy strawberries to tiny squares of cheesecake. I grin at Damien like a kid in heaven. "Chocolate fondue?"

"I had considered cheese," he says, after the waiters have slipped out and shut the panel door again. "But this way will ensure that I'm not punished by the withholding of sex."

I must look confused, because he continues. "Alaine imports the chocolate from the Swiss subsidiary I mentioned earlier."

"Really?" I peer into the pot. "I already know you're delicious. I suppose your chocolate will be, too."

As if to prove the point, I reach for a strawberry, but he gently smacks my hand. "No, no," he says.

I stare at him. "Um, hello? *Chocolate.*"

He laughs. "Close your eyes."

I narrow them but don't close them.

"Disobedience, Ms. Fairchild? You do live dangerously . . ."

I smirk, but I also close my eyes. After a moment, I feel something soft brush my cheek, then cover my eyes. A napkin or a handkerchief? I'm not sure, but whatever it is, Damien is using it as a blindfold.

"What—" But my question is stalled by his finger on my lips.

"I made you a promise, Ms. Fairchild."

I nod, my nipples tightening and my sex clenching as I recall Damien's words. "You're going to make me come."

"That, too," he says, and I can hear the laughter in his voice. "I also said I was going to feed you. Conveniently, I think the two may go together very well."

For a moment, I feel nothing. Then the cord that is still between my legs tightens as Damien tugs gently at it from behind. I gasp, and when I do, something cold brushes my lips. "Open for me," Damien says, and I do. He brushes the mystery item over my lips again. It's soft and rough at the same time, and though I try to catch a scent, the heady smell of chocolate in the room is overpowering.

"Now bite," he says, and I when I do, I moan with pleasure as the sweet strawberry bursts in my mouth. Juice dribbles down my chin, and then there is Damien, the tip of his tongue stroking up, dipping into the corner of my mouth, tasting the juice that escaped and teasing me mercilessly in the process.

"I thought you weren't going to touch me," I say, turning my head to try to find his mouth. I want his kiss. I want his touch.

"Holding me to my promise, after all?" he asks as he once again tugs at the cord. I whimper, my hips shifting on the seat. I can feel how wet I am, how slippery the cord is. It's so close to my clit, but not quite there, and I'm craving that sweet, specific attention.

"No," I breathe. I want to beg him to touch me, promise be damned.

He chuckles. "Ah, but I'm a man of integrity. But let's agree that I'll keep to the spirit of my promise and not the letter. Do you want me to gently press my fingertip against your clit? To feel that hard nub beneath my finger? To tease it, stroke it, to play with it until you come?"

"I—"

"Shhh. You don't speak, Nikki. Not until I say that you can. Do you understand?"

I nod.

"Good. Let's continue to discuss the parameters of my promise. Perhaps you want me to slide my hands between your legs. To spread you wide. To lay you back on this bench and kiss my way up your legs. To breathe in the scent of your sex, and dip my tongue in your sweet folds, more delicious than any chocolate could ever be?"

Yes, I want to say. *Oh, yes, please.*

"Maybe you just want me to fuck you."

I whimper, but Damien ignores the sound.

"To all of those possibilities, Ms. Fairchild, I am saying no. I promised I wouldn't touch you, and I won't. I won't touch your sex, at any rate. As for the rest of you—well, perhaps we shall make one or two small exceptions. Nod if you understand."

I nod.

"Good girl. Now try this."

I open my mouth, and discover a truly decadent treat. Creamy cheesecake that Damien has dipped in chocolate. I moan and swallow it, then lick every bit of chocolate from my lips.

"Naughty girl," Damien chides. "Not even leaving a taste for me." As he speaks, he plays with the cord again. Behind the blindfold, I close my eyes and let the sweet sensations roll through me.

All too soon Damien stops. It's time for another treat. This time, a piece of dipped pound cake. Then a dipped marshmallow. And then—oh, God—it's Damien's finger in my mouth. I lick the chocolate off, then greedily pull him in. I run my tongue over his skin and suck and draw his finger in and out until I hear his soft moan and know that, yes, I've gotten to him.

I wait for the next treat, but instead, Damien tugs at my sleeve. "Pull your arm in," he says, and I do. He repeats on the other side, until both my arms are out of the sleeves and he is able to pull my shirt all the way up to my shoulders. "That looked like such a good idea, I may have to try it myself."

I have no idea what he means—at least not until I feel something warm and wet and sticky on my breast. And then Damien's finger is back at my mouth, and I am once again sucking the chocolate from his skin. But this time, he is doing the same, because as I suck, so does he. His mouth is over my chocolate-coated breast. He licks, he sucks, and with each erotic motion my nipple tightens and my areola puckers. My sex clenches, too, hot and demanding, and wildly stimulated by the cord that Damien plays with, the tempo of the gentle tugs matching the rhythm of his mouth on my breast.

Again and again, the cord slips and slides, sweet friction that comes close to sending me spiraling off.

Again and again, his mouth teases and taunts. Sucking and pulling and biting, not too hard, but enough that I feel it. Enough that the sharp, sweet sensation shoots all the way through me, straight to the cord that is so sweetly tormenting me.

Over and over, more and more, building and building until finally the tremors in my body build to a crescendo that breaks like a wave over me.

I ride it, letting my hips shift as I glide over the cord, concentrating on the feel of Damien's mouth tight on my breast. It is explosive and raw and I gasp as it builds, and then sag with spent pleasure when the orgasm inevitably fades, and I am left grinning in the heady glow.

Slowly, Damien tongues the last bit of chocolate off my bare skin. Then he gently helps me put my arms back through my sleeves. "So tell me, Nikki," Damien says, his voice soft and seductive. "Did you enjoy your dessert?"

"God, yes."

"Do you want more?" he asks, as he tugs off my blindfold.

I blink and breathe in the sight of him, my beautiful Damien with just the slightest smudge of chocolate in the corner of his mouth. I lean in and kiss it away, using the tip of my tongue to taste those last sweet drops.

"No more than that," I breathe. "Now the only thing I want is you."

4

There is no traffic on our return to Malibu, and Damien takes advantage of the empty highway, driving like a demon up PCH and then along the curving roads of the Malibu canyons.

He manages to make the jaunt in less than twenty minutes, which is probably both a record and proof that the folks at Bugatti haven't misrepresented the car's zippiness.

Despite the shortness of our trip—and even despite the thrill-ride quality of the drive itself—it is the longest twenty minutes of my life.

Now we're in the house, and Damien is slowly—achingly slowly—drawing the cord out from under my outfit. The waistband of the skirt is snug, and that provides some resistance, so that as the cord slides between my ass cheeks and over my sex, I have to bite my lip so as to not cry out against the growing power of the sensations building within me.

"Damien," I murmur. It is the only word I can manage. We are standing in the barren foyer of this unfinished house. The room is huge and empty and even my breath seems to echo. Behind us, the front door still hangs wide open.

I'm not really caring about any of that. At this moment, in fact, the hard marble floor is looking pretty damned appealing.

I meet Damien's eyes, and I see my own desire reflected back. This night has been foreplay, and it has been wonderful. But now it's time for more. I want to be fucked.

I want Damien.

"Take off your clothes," he orders as soon as the cord is fully free, though still hanging from my neck.

I nod and silently comply, stepping first out of the skirt and then tugging the top over my head. As I do, Damien goes to the door and slams it shut. When he returns, I'm fumbling at the knot around my neck.

"No," he says. "Leave it."

He bends to my feet and unfastens the tiny buckles around my ankles. I sigh with relief as I step out of each shoe in turn. The marble is cool beneath my feet, and considering how much desire has heated my body, I'm surprised that steam doesn't rise up from the floor simply from the contact.

I am naked now, with only the cord around my neck, and he is still fully dressed, his clothes not even wrinkled. That simple reality only excites me more.

I am aware of everything around and within me. The heat from Damien, standing only inches from me. The quick beat of my pulse in my neck. The quickening of my sex, so desperate for his touch.

Our eyes meet, and I gasp. I expect the desire I see there, but I am done in by the rest of it. By the raw emotion. By the desperate longing that he isn't even endeavoring to hide.

"Nikki," he says, and with one quick motion he grabs hold of the cord and pulls me to him. I stumble, then find myself pressed against him, my hot flesh against the cool cotton of his shirt. I have no time to think about the feel of him, though, because his mouth closes over mine in a kiss that is more of an assault than a seduction. He is claiming, demanding. I can taste nothing but Damien, feel nothing but Damien. At this moment, he is my entire world, and I know with unerring certainty that in that moment there is no world for him beyond the two of us, either.

"I want to go slow," he says when he finally breaks the kiss. "I want to make you moan with anticipation and writhe with need of me. I want you so ready that you beg for me."

I swallow. I want this, too.

"But, dammit, Nikki, I can't wait."

"Then don't," I say, and my voice is hoarse, the words barely able to scrape past the desire.

"God, what you do to me." The words seem wrenched from him, and he closes his mouth over mine almost before he's finished speaking. At the same time, he scoops me up, one arm around my back and the other under my knees. I curl close to him, relishing the feel of his arms around me, but wanting more. So much more.

He carries me up the stairs, then sets me on my feet in front of the now-closed doors that lead to the balcony. I have barely got my balance when his mouth catches mine again in a bruising kiss and we stumble together backward. The bed is right there, barring our path even while keeping us from falling to the ground in a claiming, grasping flurry of lips and hands.

The mattress brushes against the back of my thighs, but before I can even think to sit, Damien breaks our kiss. "No," he says, and then turns me around. "Bend over," he says. "Hands on the bed."

I comply, the cord dangling from my neck like an ornamental leash. I wriggle my ass as coquettishly as I can manage in such a position. "For someone who says he can't wait you're taking an awfully long time."

"Perhaps I'm waiting for an apology. It's not kind to remind a man that heaven is ending in mere hours," he teases sternly. "A young woman with your meticulous upbringing should have more tact than to bring up such a sore subject several times over the course of one evening. Whatever happened to etiquette and decorum?"

"That's a very good question, Mr. Stark. Perhaps I'm not as polite and refined as you think I am."

"Perhaps not," he says as his fingers trail over my back. "I don't like being reminded that the end is near. It was quite unkind of you to mention it so boldly."

"Quite unkind," I agree. "Rude, even. Definitely thoughtless. And certainly not worthy of the Emily Post seal of approval."

He doesn't answer. I'm pretty sure his silence is masking a laugh.

I manage another flirty ass-wiggle. "Maybe you should punish me."

I immediately know that I've said the wrong thing. He is still silent, but now the quiet feels dark and heavy instead of playful and light.

"Should I?" he finally says, his voice low and controlled. "Do you think I didn't see the way you dug your nails into your thighs in the car on the way to the restaurant? We were only talking about the paparazzi then. It was worse when they accosted us. You kept control, Nikki, but you had to fight for it."

I close my eyes, not wanting to remember.

"Nikki, look at me." His voice is a tight command, and though my instinct is to tease him, I know better.

I don't alter my body's position, but turn my head to the right. He steps sideways into my line of sight, and I force myself to meet his eyes. There's fire there, but there's worry, too. I should have expected it. It is one thing when he initiates, surprising me with a sting to my bottom to complement the ache between my thighs.

But when I ask for the pain, he hesitates. It is his way of protecting me, but right then, it isn't protection I want. It's the sensual thrill of his palm against my ass.

"Nikki," he says. That's it. Just my name. But I hear the question in his voice.

I start to answer, but the words don't come as easily as I had hoped. Because the truth is that I know now that I haven't left the cutting as far behind as I had thought. True, I've done nothing but dig my own nails into my flesh tonight. But it's barely been a week since I tossed a knife across my kitchen, angry and scared by how much I wanted to press the blade against my skin and erase my fears and doubts in the consuming rapture of the pain. I'd won that battle, but I hadn't won the war, and my now-short hair is a scar upon my soul as much as the raised ridges on my thighs are scars upon my flesh.

Is that why I want this? Do I crave the sting of his palm because I need the pain? Does the pleasure I feel when I give myself over so completely to Damien flow from the same place that has fomented my compulsion to cut?

The thought twists inside me, dark and unpleasant, and I force it away. It's not true. And even if it is, I am safe with Damien no matter what the source of my desire. He's proven that much to me so many times.

Suddenly I'm no longer bent over the bed. He has me by the arms and he's pulling me up to stand in front of him. "Dammit, Nikki," he says. "Talk to me."

I press my palms against his cheeks and take his mouth with mine, letting the kiss deepen as he pulls me tight against him. I feel his body relax, and the fear that must have been growing in him as my silence lingered now seems to seep out from his pores.

"I need you," I tell him when I break the kiss. "*You*. I don't need that." His eyes are intent, and they seem to see so far inside me that I know I can't keep even the slightest of secrets. I take a deep breath and lay out my heart for him. "I don't need it," I say, "but I want it."

I see the slightest twitch of the muscle in his jaw, as if he's fighting for control.

"Do you?" he says.

I nod, then swallow. My cheeks are warm, which irritates me. I've been more intimate with Damien than with any person in my life, and yet I'm blushing? It's a ridiculous girly-girl reaction, probably instilled by my mother, and that in and of itself pisses me off—and *that* gives me strength.

"I want it," I repeat. "And not because I need the pain. But because I need you."

I need him even more than I can say. I want his hands on me. I want to be the object of his pleasure, and I want to lose myself in the knowledge that there is nothing Damien wants more than to please me, and nothing I want more than to surrender to him.

He swallows, looking humbled by my words. "I need you, too, Nikki. God, how I need you."

I breathe in deep, cherishing those words more than he can possibly know. "Then touch me."

He does—*oh, how he does*—and though I expect the caresses, the passion, the immediate sensual assault, I am jarred off-center by the fervency I see in his eyes, and by the firm line of his mouth. There is nothing else in the world to him except me, and I can see it with every glimpse of him. I taste it in his hard, lingering kiss.

"Bed," he says, once he breaks the kiss. "Bend over. Legs apart."

I raise my brows in question. "Bossy much?"

He slaps me lightly on the bottom, and I gasp, both surprised and excited. "What do you say?"

"Yes, sir," I say obediently, forcing myself not to smile. I turn back to the bed and bend over, my hands firmly on the mattress, my excitement so raw I'm certain that it clings to me like perfume. I no longer question my motives; I am not in an analytical mind-set. All I want is Damien setting my body on fire. Damien thrusting himself deep inside of me.

His hand cups my rear, moving in slow, sensual circles. I feel a momentary wash of cool air on my skin as he breaks contact, and then I cry out in both pleasure and pain as his palm smacks hard against my ass, then presses against the point of impact, the sweet pressure soothing the sting.

Slowly, he slides his hand down between my legs. "Oh, baby," he says as his fingers slide over me. I'm desperately wet, and I tremble from his touch, so close that I have to fight the temptation to take one hand off the bed and touch myself where Damien is so carefully avoiding.

Then again . . .

I keep my weight on my left hand, and dip my right hand between my legs. A shiver runs through me as I brush my fingertip over my clit. I'm swollen and sensitive and so very, very close.

"Oh, you have been naughty," Damien says, as his fingers brush against mine.

I swallow, anticipating another spank, but it doesn't come. Instead he bends me over more, so that I have no choice but to move my hand back onto the bed if I don't want to fall over on my face.

Damien takes his hand away and I whimper at the break in contact. He's not touching me at all, and that's the most keen punishment he can deliver. I wonder for a moment if that's what he has planned. To leave me like this, bent over, naked, my ass in the air, waiting and wanting. He might, I know, and I can't help but smile at the thought. It would piss me off and drive me crazy, but I know that when the punishment is over and he finally does fuck me, it will be all the sweeter for it.

That, however, isn't what he has planned. I hear the tug of his zipper, followed by the brush of denim against skin as he quickly strips off his jeans. I bite my lip, then exhale in sweet triumph as his cock presses against my rear, my body opening to him in sweet anticipation. *Please, Damien. Take me. Please take me now.* I want to cry the words, but I stay silent. I don't, however, stay still. I can't help it. My body is demanding and antsy, and my hips gyrate against his cock, and his low moan of pleasure only makes me more frenzied.

His hands close on my hips and hold me still, and I can't help my whimper of protest. He laughs, and I want to cry out in frustration because he is very thoroughly, very meanly teasing me.

Then I feel the tip of his cock on the slick folds of my vulva and I want to cry with relief. He teases me at first, barely entering, and I bite my lower lip so hard I fear I will taste blood. The anticipation is brutal, but sweet. He is so hard, so ready, and he is tormenting both of us as he controls his thrusts, using my hips to steady himself.

I have none of his control. Every inch of me is desperate and demanding, and my muscles tighten greedily around him with every tantalizing thrust. *Deeper. Harder. Oh, dear God, please.*

"As you wish," he says, and I don't even have time to be surprised that I've spoken the words aloud, because he's inside me now, his cock filling me, his body pressed over me as I keep both hands on the bed to steady myself. One of his hands snakes around my waist, and I am grateful for the support. My rear is arched up, I am on my toes, it is as if my body is doing everything it can to draw him in deeper and deeper. I want to take all of him. To consume and be consumed.

And when he pulls gently out and then thrusts back into me with a single, powerful movement, I am certain that the world will explode around me.

"You're close," he whispers, and I can tell from the tightness in his voice that he is close, too.

"Yes," I say, but my voice is so raw I doubt the word is co-herent.

"Touch yourself," he says.

The excitement that's been building in me seems to shiver through my body like a jolt of electricity. "What?" I ask, then moan as he continues to slowly torture me, as if he knows ex-actly how much pressure will take me to the edge—and just how much more is needed to take me over.

"You heard me."

I lick my lips and swallow. My fingers twitch with the desire to obey. To feel where our bodies are joined, and to stroke the hard length of him even as I tease my oh-so-sensitive clit.

"I—I thought that was naughty," I say, feeling strangely shy.

His response alone almost sends me rocketing into space: "Maybe I like you naughty."

I gasp, then swallow. Then I lift my right hand from the bed. It throws off my balance, but he keeps me steady with the arm around my waist. I slip my hand down, barely brushing over my slick clit. My body clenches, my muscles tightening greedily to draw him further inside me. I feel glorious, full, and so desper-ately close that I know only the slightest touch will be the end of me.

I want it, and yet I also want to feel him. The way our bodies are joined as he slides deep inside me. I ease my hand back along my own slick folds. I feel him there, like velvet steel, and I hear his guttural moan as I gently stroke him.

"Jesus, Nikki, I can't hold back."

"Then don't." I close my eyes, and my fingers have barely grazed my clit when he trembles, tightening his grip around my waist as he fills me. His release triggers my own, and I clench tight around him, dropping my hand back to the bed so that I don't fall, too sensitive to continue touching myself, anyway.

"Nikki," he says when his body stops quivering.

He releases my waist, then immediately catches me when I start to sag, my legs so weak I'm not sure if I'll ever be able to stand again.

"I think you've unraveled me," I say. "If you were going for punishment, though, you missed the mark completely."

"Did I?" His voice rises provocatively. "Sounds to me like you're assuming I'm done with you. I assure you, I'm not."

"Oh." My pulse kicks back up again. "That's a very interesting bit of information."

"I'm glad to hear you're intrigued." He slides a hand down my still weak legs. "But this time maybe you ought to lie down. You seem a bit unsteady."

"You think?"

He scoops me up so that I am once again cradled against his chest. I feel warm and safe and cherished, and when he places me gently on the bed and presses a soft kiss to my forehead, I want to cry from the sweetness of it all. But then his eyes take on a devilish gleam. "Don't go to sleep on me yet," he says as he unties the cord from around my neck—then immediately ties it to my right wrist. He attaches the other end very firmly to the bedpost.

His face is right over mine, his smile undeniably wicked. "I'm going to enjoy this. And, Nikki? So will you."

I lick my lips, all thoughts of gentleness fading under the weight of Damien Stark's decadent, silent promises.

He retrieves the robe from the foot of the bed and pulls out the sash. He trails it lightly over my body, then smiles with purpose. "Left hand."

I comply, raising my hand above my head and gripping the bar of the headboard. My arms are spread wide now, my back slightly arched, and my legs tightly together.

"Nice," Damien says, once he's secured that wrist as well. "But I think we can make it nicer."

With obvious purpose, he slides off the bed, then walks to the door that leads to the patio. It's made of sliding glass panels, and he opens them now, letting the night breeze come in. The air is cool, but my body is so much on fire that I don't even notice. He stands next to the door, his hand running gently over the gossamer white drapes that fluttered against me as I posed for Blaine.

"Remember our first night?" he asks.

How can I not? Those drapes. This bed. And me, lost to Damien's sensual onslaught, my fears and my shame soothed by his kisses and his soft words.

I say none of that now. I only whisper, "Yes."

"So do I," he says, then takes two drapery panels, one in each hand, and rips them off the metal rings that attach them to the curtain rod. From my perspective, I see the muscles in his back flex and then the soft swell of filmy white as the sheer material falls to the ground, set free by Damien's will. A small smile touches my lips; he's set me free, too.

He is back at my side in no time, and as I anticipated, he uses the drapes to bind my legs to the iron bars at the foot of the bed. The result is sweetly, painfully intimate. I am spread-eagled, arms wide, legs open. I can't touch him or myself. I can't roll over. And I certainly can't close my legs to hide my swollen, sex-slick cunt. I turn my head to the side, part of me wishing I could burrow beneath the sheets, and part of me desperately aroused by the knowledge that I am completely wide open to Damien. His to do with whatever he wants.

I wonder what he has in mind, and then whimper when he moves away from the bed instead of climbing on beside me. I bite my lower lip, suddenly worried. I know that no matter what happens, this will end magnificently. But I also know that Damien's a master at manipulating anticipation. If he leaves me like this—wide open and ready—I just might have to scream.

"Don't worry," he says, as if he can read my mind. "I might

have it in me to torment you a little bit, but tonight that would be torturing me, too."

"Sadism, not masochism?" I say archly, then smile when he bursts out laughing.

"Sadism, Ms. Fairchild? Let me see if I recall the definition. I believe that sadism is the deriving of sexual gratification from inflicting pain, suffering, or humiliation on another person." He moves to the small table by the bed and opens a drawer. "I'll admit to the sexual gratification—and I intend to be significantly more gratified before the night is over—but let's explore the rest, shall we?"

I lick my lips as he pulls a box of matches from the drawer. I trust Damien completely, but what on earth is he planning to do with matches?

"So tell me, Ms. Fairchild, are you in pain?"

I swallow. I'm in very dire straits, but I'm a long way from pain. "No."

"I'm very glad to hear it." He crosses the room, then disappears from view. A moment later he returns carrying a thick candle, the flame flickering as he walks. "Candle wax can be very enticing," he says in response to my questioning glance. "The sensation of the quickly changing temperature. The way it tightens when it hardens on the skin. Have you ever experienced that, Ms. Fairchild?"

I shake my head. "No." I'm not certain if I'm scared or excited.

"Mmm," he says, as if marking my words in his memory. "Well, today, I'm interested in only one thing from this candle." He pauses by the bed and tilts the candle so that the wax drips onto the marble surface of the decorative side table. Then he sets the candle in the wax, letting it harden to form a stand. After that, he takes something else from the drawer. I realize only when the sconce lighting begins to dim that it's a remote control.

Soon we are in darkness, bathed only by the flickering orange of a single candle.

"Oh . . ."

"Disappointed?" he asks.

"No," I say. I feel my cheeks heat. "But I might have been a little intrigued."

"Were you? I'll have to remember that. But where were we? Oh, yes. Sadism." He eases onto the bed and kneels between my widespread legs. My breath comes in small gasps as he gently rests his hands on my thighs just above my knees, his thumbs on the soft inner skin. "Humiliation was next, I believe. Are you humiliated, Ms. Fairchild? You're exposed to me, after all. Wide open like a blossoming flower and so very wet. You're beautiful, Nikki," he says, and I hear the raw passion in his voice. "But are you humiliated?"

I've turned my head to the side, because the truth is that I do feel exposed. Exposed and open and decadent and wild. I don't, however, feel humiliated. On the contrary, I feel aroused. And I think it's that odd combination of emotions that heats my cheeks with a ridiculous blush. "No," I whisper.

"Look at me."

I turn my head until I can see his eyes, the amber one shining in the candlelight, and the near-black one as dark as eternity.

"Not humiliated," he says. "And not suffering, either, I assume?"

"No."

"Good." His lips curve into a smile as his hands stroke my inner thighs, the pad of one thumb brushing ever so softly over the worst of my scars. "You are exceptional, Ms. Fairchild," he says. "I could look at you forever. Lose myself in you forever."

I draw in a trembling breath. The muscles of my sex clench with longing, and my breasts are so heavy they are almost painful. I want to move—want to satisfy this sexual itch—but I'm stuck fast and helpless.

"I like that I can make you blush," he says.

I swallow. "Why?"

"Because I know why you do."

"Really? Well, then please, Mr. Stark, share your insight."

"Because I have you spread open. Because you're naked before me and helpless. Because I can do anything to you right now, anything at all. And because that excites you."

His hand cups my sex, and I release a moan so soft it is little more than a breath.

"So tell me, Ms. Fairchild. If you're not in pain or suffering or humiliated, how do you feel?"

"Turned on," I admit, and my cheeks heat even more.

Even in the candlelight, I can see the way his face darkens with my words. I'm not the only one turned on right now.

I start to speak, but he shakes his head. "Hush, now, and close your eyes. I'm going to kiss you."

I comply, my lips parted in expectation of his touch. But it's not my lips upon which he presses his kiss. I feel the rough stubble of his beard on my thigh, then his tongue in the soft crease between my leg and vulva. My breath is coming in little gasps now, and whatever playfulness had been in the air mere moments ago has evaporated, replaced by want and need and quiet desperation.

His mouth closes over me, his tongue laving me in a rhythm designed to drive me completely crazy.

His thumbs tease me, never going so far as to enter, but combined with the erotic power of his tongue against my clit, it is a wonder that my body isn't ripped apart by the force of the sensations rocketing through me.

My back is arched, my hips grinding. Instinctively, I try to close my legs, trying to forestall this tidal wave of pleasure that is so potent it borders on pain. But I can't. I am bound open, and I have no choice but to yield to these amazing sensations.

Damien's hands move to hold my hips, keeping me even more immobile. I feel drunk on lust, intoxicated by desire, and I close my eyes and let my head fall back in complete surrender as Damien's mouth and tongue work some kind of erotic magic on me, taking me higher and higher until that magic culminates in an explosion of sparks and colors and shooting stars that leaves me spent and breathless.

Slowly, reality returns to me, and I gasp, spread-eagled on the bed. My chest rises and falls, my body so sensitive that I can feel every thread of the sheet below me. I feel spoiled and pampered and adored and used. I am certain that all that is left is for Damien to untie me and then gather me into his arms as we drift off into the bliss of sleep. Because what else could be left for this night? He has utterly, sweetly destroyed me.

I should know better than to assume anything about Damien Stark.

His teeth graze my nipple, and I arch up, thoughts of sleep vanishing. I am battered, ripped asunder by his sensual assault, and yet I do not want it to end. The torment is delicious, and I would happily stay like this forever, forgoing food and friends and the world outside if I could simply escape into Damien's arms.

I open my eyes as he arches up, and his self-satisfied smile suggests that he understands just what I'm thinking. Then he glances sideways, and the smile fades, replaced by a blank, unreadable expression.

Worry cuts through me. "Damien?" Instinctively, I turn my head, my gaze following his line of sight. There is a clock mounted to the wall amid a collection of framed photographs, the few personal items that Damien has already moved into this shell of a house. *Oh.*

Automatically, I try to sit up, but I am still trapped, bound spread-eagled to this bed, naked and vulnerable. Somehow, though, in that moment it seems as though Damien is more vulnerable than I.

"Less than a minute," he says, turning his head so that he is looking straight at me again. "Do you turn into a pumpkin or do I?" The words are light, but something in his tone worries me and I am unnerved.

"I don't think I'd like you as a pumpkin," I say, forcing out the teasing words. "And I look terrible in orange."

He laughs, and my worries fizzle away as he straddles me, his weight on his knees and his erection rubbing provocatively on my belly. He traces my lips with the tip of his finger, and I gasp as I suddenly realize that I've forgotten to breathe.

He slides down my body and grazes his finger over the platinum and emerald ankle bracelet he gave me when our game began. He looks at me, his eyes burning with passion. "You're still mine," he whispers. And then, before I can answer, he shifts position and enters me so swiftly that I cry out in surprise and passion. We move together, making love slowly and gently, and when I feel his body shudder above mine, I close my eyes in the feminine satisfaction of knowing that he has found pleasure in my body.

He rolls off me, then curls himself beside me. "Nikki." It is not a demand or a question. It is simply my name on his lips, and I soak it up like warm sunshine.

We lie like that, our bodies touching, until I can no longer stand my immobility. "Untie me," I say.

He lifts his head to look at me. I still see the heat in his eyes, but there is a playfulness, too. He does not rush to release me.

"Hello?" I say, then tap my fingernails on the iron bedframe. "Did you get lost between the middle of the bed and the headboard?"

"I'm considering my options," he says. "Why should I?"

"Because my arms will cramp up soon."

"I'll be happy to massage you."

I aim a scowl at him. "And because you have a cocktail party here on Saturday, and your guests will ask questions."

"Perhaps, but won't it be nice to know that the guests will have plenty to talk about?"

"As much as I hate the thought of depriving your guests of interesting conversation, I would still like my hands to be free."

"Would you?" He trails a lazy finger down my side, and I bite my lower lip to keep from writhing. The sensation is delicious, a cross between a caress and a tickle, and my skin tingles in his wake. "And what is it that you wish to do with your hands, Ms. Fairchild?"

"Touch you," I say boldly. "I'm allowed. After all, we're on equal footing now that midnight has passed. Aren't we, *sir*?"

There is a pause before his head tilts down in a quick, formal nod. "Yes, madam," he says as he leans past me to loosen the knots that hold my wrists in place. "We are."

Once my hands are free, I sit up while he unbinds my ankles. I pull my legs close, enjoying the sensation of moving again. Then I kneel on the bed in front of Damien, who is sitting at the foot of the bed, watching me. It's hard not to look at him. He's even more magnificent by the glow of candlelight. I reach out, wanting to feel him beneath my fingertips. Wanting his warmth against my skin. Slowly, I lay my palm over his heart, then close my eyes as I feel it beat, strong and steady like the man himself.

I lay him gently back onto the bed and straddle him, my knees pressed against either side of his waist. I trail my fingers over his chest and watch the way one small muscle jumps in his jaw, evidence of how hard he is fighting for control. I smile, relishing the power he's relinquished to me. "You make me feel amazing," I say. "I want you to feel the same."

"I do. When I touch you. When I see your skin tremble with desire. When your muscles tighten and draw me in. What is it you think that you're doing to me other than making me feel more deeply than I ever have before?"

"But you're the one in control." I shift my hips a little, silently letting him know that I hold the control now.

"No." He shakes his head. "That's an illusion. It's you, Nikki. You have captured me utterly, and you hold my heart in your hands. Be gentle with it. It's more fragile than you might think."

I swallow, then blink, moved by his words. Gently, I run my fingertip over his jawline, enjoying the feel of his beard stubble against my skin. I lean over, my body pressed to his, and draw his mouth into a slow, deep kiss.

"What do you want?" I ask once I've broken the kiss. "Right now, if you could have me any way you wanted, what would you have me do?"

"Right now, I want you beside me," he says. "I want to hold you."

His words undo me, and my throat feels thick with tears. I am weepy and emotional and don't think I've ever been happier. Gently, I ease off him and curl up next to him. My back is to his chest, and I am looking out at the world beyond the window as he casually strokes my arm. We have lain this way before, and it feels warm and familiar. It feels like us.

"I'm going to miss this bed," I admit.

"I suppose I could keep it here. But it doesn't really fit the decor."

"Well, if you're trying to be all traditional . . ."

I trail off and he laughs, then pulls me tighter against him. It's so comfortable between us, and I cherish the way that I feel with Damien. I roll over, wanting to see his face, and I'm immediately glad I do. He presses a kiss to my forehead and we curl up on the bed facing each other. His hand is on the curve of my waist, and I trail my fingers lazily up and down his chest. He has only the slightest smattering of chest hair, and it feels downy beneath my fingers. I amuse myself by making patterns on his chest, and when I look up at him, the corner of his mouth is twitching.

"What?" I ask.

"Having fun, Ms. Fairchild?"

"As a matter of fact, I am."

"I'm glad. Earlier—the way those bastards upset you. I didn't like it."

"Me, neither," I say, in what is undoubtedly the understatement of the year. "But I'm okay now. And you seem pretty okay yourself."

"I would have happily ripped their heads off at the restaurant," he admits.

"I could tell," I say. "But I didn't just mean the paparazzi."

"Oh?" he eyes me warily.

I lift a shoulder. "I'm still wondering about that call," I admit. "Is something going on?" I blurt, because I've been holding it in all evening and can't take it anymore. "Has Carl done something?"

Damien doesn't answer, and I glare at him, irritated. "Come on, Damien. All that stuff that Carl said—we both know it isn't going to just go away."

"I hope it does just go away," Damien says. "Though I tend to agree."

"Damien!" I sound as exasperated as I feel. "Just tell me straight out. Has something happened that you haven't told me about? Is that what the phone call was about?"

"No." He brushes the tip of his finger over my nose. "I promise."

I frown as I eye him.

He shifts so that I can see him better, then draws an X over his heart.

I raise a brow, and he lifts three fingers in a Boy Scout salute.

I hold back a laugh, and he holds up his pinkie finger. "Shall we pinkie swear?"

That does it—I laugh and hook pinkies with him.

"I swear to you," he says, lifting our joined hands and kissing the tip of my little finger, "that call had nothing to do with Carl Rosenfeld."

I nod. I believe him, but I'm still worried.

Because whoever was on that telephone call had the ability to crack Damien Stark's cool veneer. And anyone who can do that is no one to trifle with.

5

I open my eyes to a blanket of stars hanging beyond the doorway, uncertain as to what has awakened me. I am groggy and I turn toward Damien, automatically seeking the soft comfort of sliding back into sleep in his arms. But instead of his warmth, I find only the rumpled coolness of abandoned sheets. I sit up, confused. I'd slept soundly, nestled safe against him, and it is disorienting to come back to the world and find myself alone.

The candle has burned down, but Damien has turned the sconce lighting on low, and each fixture emits the slightest of glows, just enough to take the edge off the darkness. I glance toward the kitchen, but that area is dark and quiet. Beside me, the sheets are cool. Damien has not been here for a long time.

I slide off the bed and lift the robe off the floor where it has fallen. I put it on, the gentle caress of the material seeming to mimic Damien's touch. I reach out for the bedframe, and untie the sash from the iron bar. I wrap it around my waist, cinching the robe. Then I close my hand over the cool iron ball. I will be sorry to see this bed go, but its purpose is done. It was a prop, an illusion chosen for a specific effect.

I tremble, struck by the sudden and unreasonable fear that everything has been an illusion, Damien most of all.

But those are just ghosts. I know better. At least, I hope that I do. I recall his words in the restaurant—that he would leave me to protect me.

I hug myself, suddenly cold. But I know that I am being foolish. Damien hasn't left me. He's simply left the bed.

"Damien?"

I expect no answer, and I'm not surprised when none comes. The house is large, and over the last week, the workmen have finished painting the interior and even the grounds are almost fully landscaped. There still isn't any furniture in most rooms, but even so, he could be anywhere, and in a house this large, "anywhere" covers a lot of ground.

For a moment, I consider returning to bed and trying to sleep. He didn't wake me, after all, and I wonder if he left the room to find some solitude. He told me the phone call wasn't about Carl's threats, and I don't doubt him. But the call still disturbed him, and I'm selfish enough to want to understand why. I want him to confide in me and turn to me for comfort.

I want him to keep his promise to me about shining light on the shadows that surround Damien Stark.

But is that my only motivation for seeking him out now? If so, I really should crawl back in bed. Promise or not, Damien is entitled to his privacy. And no matter how much it may frustrate me, the promise is his to keep or to break.

My hesitation lasts only a moment, because while I do want to understand the man, I want even more to comfort him. I want to hold him and touch him and silently promise him that no matter what he needs, I am there for him.

I want . . .

Maybe I am still being selfish, but I'm arrogant enough to think that Damien needs me. And, yes, I'm selfish enough to go.

I see that he left his phone beside the candle. I pause, thinking of the text he received, and then the phone call that came soon after. He either recognized the number or the caller's name is programmed into his phone. Should I look?

I hesitate just long enough to be disgusted by myself. If Damien went pawing through my call history, I'd explode into a completely justifiable rage. And yet I'm actually thinking about looking at his phone? Have I been miraculously transported back to high school?

The thought is undeniably unpleasant, and I forcefully push it out of my mind as I pad to the service elevator at the back of the kitchen. It opens on the first floor in a utility room off the main kitchen, a magnificent space filled with commercial-grade equipment that hasn't yet been used. I pass through the kitchen into a sunporch. I expect to find him in the gym that eats up at least a thousand square feet on the north side of the house. But when I get there, there is no Damien.

The room is large and divided into distinct sections. The first one I come to is a weight room, filled with machines, free weights, mats, and a boxing bag. I move quickly across the room to the functional but beautiful polished oak door that separates this room from the larger area beyond. In this second room, there is a running track complete with stations. More free weights, pull-up bars, spin bicycles, another boxing bag, and a variety of other equipment.

As is Damien's style, an entire wall of the track room is made of glass, giving a view of the property and the ocean beyond. The negative-edge pool opens off the living room on the main level, but it is also accessible from the gym, with one of the glass pocket doors opening onto the deck. From where I stand, I don't have a view of the water, but at least one of the pool's dim lights must be on, as I see the greenish-blue light undulating on the deck. For a moment I think nothing of it—Damien has left the light on since the pool was filled three days ago, ever since I mentioned that as a child I loved to sit by the pool at night with my sister and watch the light dance as the wind played across the water's surface.

Right now, however, there is no wind. Even the three drapes that Damien left unmolested had been still when I'd awakened. And the dancing light is moving in a rhythmic, controlled pattern.

I smile, knowing that I have found him.

I head to the glass door, but pause when I see the small table next to the boxing bag. A bottle of water rests atop the table, but that isn't what catches my eye. It's the newspaper that is on the floor. Reviewing the news is like a religion with Damien, but I've never once seen him not fold the paper neatly when he's finished. This section, however, is on the ground. I suppose it could have simply fallen there, but somehow, I don't believe it.

I pick up the errant sheet and immediately realize it's the sports page. Considering Damien's original career as a professional tennis player, this is hardly a shocker. But it's the headline that has me gasping with surprise—and with understanding.

Apparently a new tennis center in Los Angeles is near completion. The dedication ceremony is next Friday, exactly one week away. And the center is going to be named after Damien's former coach, Merle Richter. The man who killed himself when Damien was fourteen years old. The man who, I believe, abused Damien for five long years. The man Damien's father forced him to continue working with even though Damien pleaded to quit tennis altogether.

I remember what Alaine had said about a tennis center dedication. It had meant nothing to me at the time. Now, it means everything.

I leave the paper on the table, then exit the room through the sliding glass door. The flagstone decking is smooth beneath my feet, and the robe flutters around my legs as I move toward the pool. The property is built in the Malibu hills, and the pool's far edge is designed with the illusion of dropping away, as if you could swim over the edge and fall out into space.

Damien is swimming laps along that precipice, and I wonder if he has chosen that spot intentionally.

He is naked, and the pool lighting seems to accentuate his muscles as he glides freestyle through the water. His body is magnificent, athletic and powerful, and I feel a tight curling in my belly. Not sexual—though I would be lying if I didn't admit that there is always an undercurrent of sexual desire where Damien is concerned—but of possessiveness. *He is mine,* I think. But the thought is tinged with fear. Because though I know that the reverse is true—I am most definitely, undeniably his—I sometimes fear that Damien belongs to no one but himself.

I fear, too, my motivations for giving myself so fully to him. Damien fills a need in me, that much is undeniable. But I do not have the best track record in that regard, and as my hand slips almost unconsciously inside my robe to feel the rigid hardness of the scars that mar my thigh, I have to concede that I have often needed things that are not only bad for me, but very, very dangerous.

Right now, though, I don't care about my motivations. I neither know nor care if it's the truth or self-delusion, but I cannot believe that anything about Damien is a danger to me. On the contrary, he is a gift. A rescuer. A knight upon a white steed, though he would scoff at the image and insist that the horse must be a black one.

Perhaps so, but to me there is nothing dark about Damien Stark. There is only the light that he brings to my world. And that is why I feel all the more helpless when I see that he is hurting. And why I feel all the more lost when it is not me that he turns to.

I've been walking slowly toward the water, and now I stand

at the edge of the pool on the side near the house. There are five steps into the water here. Wide steps designed for lounging half-in and half-out of the water. I walk out, holding the robe up around my knees so that it won't get wet.

Damien is at the opposite end of the pool and he has not noticed me. I take three steps, then move down to the next level. The water hits me just below my knees. This is the first time I've been in the pool, and I'm surprised by how warm the water is. Not quite bath-temperature, but balmy, and warmer than the night air that surrounds me.

I walk to the edge of this second level and look out toward the man who has captured my heart. My feet are about twelve inches below the pool deck now, and from this new perspective all I can see is Damien, the water, and the wide night sky. I watch, entranced, as he cuts through the water. His movements are efficient and controlled, just like the man himself. I don't realize that I've moved to the third step until I notice that I am no longer holding up the robe. Instead, the thin material is spread out like the petals of a rose floating on the gently lapping surface.

I am about to take it off and lay it on the decking when Damien stops midway through a lap. He treads water, his body turned toward me, but the shadows and light that play across his face, reflected by the motion of the water, make it impossible for me to read his expression. All I know is that I feel the heavy weight of his gaze upon me, and though I want to cut through the water and go to him, I remain rooted to the spot. It's fear keeping me here. I'm afraid that I have overstepped my bounds. That I'm interrupting a moment when he needs to be alone, and that instead of comforting him, my presence is going to have the exact opposite effect.

The longer he stays at the far end of the pool, the more that fear grows in me, so that when he finally does move toward me, I take an involuntary step backward.

It is only when I see his face that I stop. He is looking at me with such open adoration that it makes my heart skip a beat.

He stops swimming and stands in the chest-deep water. "I didn't mean to wake you."

"How do you expect me to sleep without you beside me?" I've moved forward again, and the robe floats around me. Damien eases closer, cutting through the water, then tugs on the sash at my waist. The robe drifts open, exposing my body. He slips his hands up to my shoulders and slides it off. The damp material sticks to my arms, but I move forward, leaving the robe behind me, until I am no longer wrapped in silk, but wrapped in Damien's arms.

"I think I ruined the robe," I say. "I didn't actually mean to wear it into the pool. I was watching you and got carried away."

"I know the feeling." His hand gently strokes my face while his other arm holds me firmly around the waist, as if afraid I'll float away like the robe.

"Do you mind that I'm here?"

His mouth curves into an ironic smile and he pulls me closer. I feel his erection press against my thighs. "What do you think?"

I swallow and shake my head. But it's not sex that I've come here for, though with Damien standing naked and erect next to me I am having a hard time recalling what my purpose actually was.

But, no, I *do* remember. I tilt my head up so that I can look directly in his eyes. "I was worried," I admit.

"About the phone call? I told you it wasn't about Carl's threats."

I nod, then take a deep breath. "Was it about the tennis center?"

He looks at me sharply. "You know about that?"

"Is that what's bothering you?"

He hesitates, then gives one curt nod. "Yes."

I bite my lip, because though I believe him, I'm certain that's not the full story.

"How did you learn about it?"

"I saw the paper. You left it by the boxing bag."

The corner of his mouth tugs upward. "Perhaps my subconscious wanted you to find it."

"Well," I say with a laugh. "That's a start."

As I had hoped, he laughs as well. Then his shoulders relax and he pulls me closer, his arms closing around me in a tight hug. I sigh and put my arms around his neck, then bury my head against his chest.

"I'm not a fan of Richter," he says. "The idea that a professional tennis facility will bear his name pisses me off."

"Can't you do something?"

"I could buy the goddamned center," he says. "But I won't."

I want to look at his face, but I don't move. I've told him that I suspect abuse, but he's never told me if I'm right or not. I stay very still, wondering if now is the time when Damien Stark will reveal his secrets to me.

"The call that upset me," he begins. "It was from my father."

"Oh." I'm surprised enough that I do move, leaning back so that my weight is supported by his arms as I look into his face. It's hard, and there's something dark in his eyes. I'd been right about his earlier hesitation, and this is the reason why. The topic of Damien's father is never an easy one.

I know they aren't close. I know that Damien's father pushed him to compete the same way my mother pushed me into pageant after pageant.

I know all that, because Damien has told me. But what I suspect is truly vile; I believe that Richter was abusing Damien, and that Damien's father knew. But he forced Damien to stay with the son of a bitch anyway.

I swallow, and then speak the words that I know I shouldn't: "Do you want to talk about it?"

"No." The word is simple and final.

"Right. Okay." I try to keep my voice casual, but I know I've failed when he presses his forehead against mine, his hands firm on my shoulders.

"I know it bothers you," he says. "And I'm sorry."

I start to protest. Every Proper Nikki attribute that was pounded into my head by my mother is ready to burst out and reassure him that no, really, it's fine that he's keeping secrets, fine that he doesn't want to talk to me. Fine that though I now turn to him for comfort, he leaves our bed in the middle of the night to find solace in solitude.

Proper Nikki wants to say all of that, but I mentally shove my heel hard into the blond twit's ass.

I take a deep breath, and this time it's not Proper Nikki or Rebel Nikki or Social Nikki. It's just me, wishing that I had some magic formula to make everything better for Damien, whether he tells me the truth or not. "It does bother me," I admit. "But only because I don't like to see you wounded."

"And here I thought I hid my scars so well." He is only half-teasing.

"You do," I say. "But you're talking to an expert at hiding scars. I see them even if no one else does. And I know how much it helped me to talk to you. To know that I could borrow your strength if my own wasn't enough."

He starts to speak, but I press a soft finger over his lips and shake my head.

"I mean it when I say that I want to be there for you, Damien, but saying it that way makes me sound more altruistic than I am." I take a deep breath because honesty is never as easy as it should be. "The truth is that it feels unfair. I've shared everything with you, but you still keep so many things locked up tight."

"Nikki—"

"No," I interrupt. "This isn't a demand or an accusation. It's an apology. Because it was my choice to tell you, and it's unfair of me to be irritated because you haven't made the same choice. It's not like we're playing Follow the Leader."

"No," he agrees, and I see the faintest hint of a smile touch his lips. "But considering how much I enjoyed our game of Simon Says, perhaps we should add that one to our repertoire."

I cock my head and grimace. "I'm serious."

"I know you are." He pauses. "Thank you."

I look at him, at this man who commands an empire. But right now the power and the fame and the money mean nothing. He is just a man. *My* man. And in that moment I must acknowledge the truth that has gone unspoken and unexamined for so long—I am falling in love with Damien Stark.

The thought doesn't scare me. On the contrary, it makes me smile.

He matches my grin, then brushes his fingertip over my lower lip. I open my mouth, drawing him in, tasting the chlorine and the soft comfort of Damien's skin. "What are you thinking about?"

"You," I admit. "Always you."

"What about me?"

I allow my smile to widen. "Close your eyes, Mr. Stark, and I'll show you."

His brow lifts, but he complies, and I move closer, then stroke my fingers over his slick, wet chest.

"I'm going to make love to you, Damien." My words are so full of emotion they feel too big for my throat.

"I'm going to take your mind off everything that's bothering you. And a lot more effectively than swimming laps." It's late—after three—and I'm tired. I'm a bit sore, too, but it doesn't matter, because I need this moment with Damien. I need to take care of him now, to stroke and soothe him.

I need it—and I desperately hope that he needs me, too.

I press a soft kiss to his temple, then ease down, trailing kisses down his neck, then his chest. We're standing close together in waist-high water, and his erection presses against my thigh as if in silent demand. I want to shift and capture him between my legs, to use the buoyancy of the water to rise up and then sink back down again, impaling myself upon him.

I don't, though—not yet. Instead, I slide my hands down over his back, breaking the surface to cup his perfect ass beneath the water, then continue my oral exploration, lower and lower until I'm tasting the lapping water along with the smooth skin of his tight lower abs.

I tilt my head to look at his face and find that he's cheating—his eyes are open, but he's looking at me so tenderly that I cannot chastise him. Instead, I allow myself one tiny smile, then slip beneath the water.

I hold his hips to keep me in place, and run my tongue along his cock. I've never done anything like this before, and the sensation of moving water coupled with the taste of chlorine and Damien seems sweetly wicked somehow. I want to draw him into my mouth, but I'm afraid of swallowing water, and so I satisfy myself with simply dancing my tongue and lips over his hard, beautiful cock. I can't see him, but I know that the sensations are equally arousing to him. He's becoming even harder under my ministrations, and the tension tightening in his body seems to shoot through him and into my hands as I hold tight to his bare, wet skin.

I rise up, needing both air and his kiss. I break the surface, gasping, and then press my mouth against his. His lips part, drawing me in, his tongue warring with mine as he takes control of the kiss. His lips are hard against my mouth, his tongue hot and demanding and so very thorough that there is no question that I have gone from being the seductress to being the seduced.

I'm only vaguely aware that he has moved us to the side of the pool. Now he breaks the kiss and turns me roughly around. I can feel my ribs beneath his hands and I am struck by how strong he is, and how fragile I am. He possessively skims his hands up to cup my breasts as his erection nestles against my ass. The cool air brushes my damp skin, but I hardly feel it. I am hot; hell, I am burning. I may have started this with the comforting warmth of glowing coals in mind, but I can already tell that Damien's finish will be scorching.

"Tell me you trust me," he whispers.

"You know that I do."

"Tell me I can take you however I want to."

I close my eyes and pull my lips into a smile. "Oh, yes."

"I'm going to make you shatter, Nikki," he says, as he takes one hand from my breast. He slips it between my legs, urging my thighs apart as he teases my sex with his fingers. "I want to feel my hands on you when you explode, and I want to know that I'm the one who gave that to you. Every breath, every ripple of pleasure, every ache in your cunt, every bite mark on your back. *Me*. I did that."

My body shudders simply from the words and the anticipation of their fulfillment.

"Hold on to the side of the pool," he orders, and as soon as I comply, he shifts his position and enters me from behind, gently at first, and then with a hard thrust that makes me gasp as water sloshes around us and my vagina clenches around him. I'm sore, but it doesn't matter. I shift my hips, wanting more and more of him. One of his hands seeks to soothe my need for an additional touch, and it snakes around, finding my breast, squeezing my nipple so hard that it makes my sex clench even tighter around him. And then fingers are teasing their way down, down, until he brushes over my clit and I bite my lower lip in the expectation that, yes, he is going to let me come.

But not yet. This is Damien's show, Damien's game. And he is playing by his rules tonight.

Soon, he has withdrawn his cock from my vagina and his hand from my clit. I am bereft, lost without his touch, and I turn in his arms, intending to beg, then grateful to realize that I don't have to, because he's pulling me to him once again, demanding that I rise up, that I let the water do the work, that I wrap my legs around him and sink down deeper and deeper on his cock.

His hands on my ass support me, and I gasp in surprise and pleasure as he slides one finger down to our connected bodies, then rims my anus with a finger slick with pool water and my own arousal.

"Everywhere, Nikki." There is a rawness in his voice. A need that seems to edge close to desperation, and as he speaks, he thrusts forward with his hips, at the same time pulling me down, impaling me hard against him even as his finger slips inside my ass.

I am impossibly full and the erotic sensation of having both his cock and finger inside me is almost more than I can handle. But Damien is relentless, and the force of his pounding has edged us backward so that my back scrapes hard against the pool's edge and the water is as wild as a stormy sea.

"Forever," he growls. His voice is rough, his actions more so. His thrusts are deep and violent. He is pounding into me, thrusting me wildly against the edge of the pool, my bare back scraping against the stone coping. Between my already sore sex, the assault on my back, and the tender flesh that his finger is so brutally invading, yes, he is hurting me.

I bite my lip because I don't want to cry out. I don't know why he needs this, but I know that he does.

Before he was gentle. Even his spanks were inflicted only for the purpose of pleasing me. This, however, is about Damien.

Damien taking. Damien *needing*. It is me that he needs, and I give myself willingly. I am no stranger to pain. It gives me control, something tangible to hold on to. And I can take Damien's pain and pull it tight inside me like a precious thing.

I think I understand what Damien needs. Not the pain, but the control. He needs to claim me. Maybe he can't grab hold of the ghosts from his past that have returned to haunt him, but he has me. Right now, I am his to touch and possess. His to claim and use.

His. Simply Damien's.

His release comes hard and fast, and I wrap my arms tight around his neck until the last shudder rips through him. He softens and slips out of me, first his cock, then his finger. I ease off him and find my footing, leaning back against the edge of the pool and breathing hard.

After a moment, he opens his eyes and looks at me. One moment passes, then another. And then I see the storm approaching. "Goddammit," he says. "Nikki. I—"

"No." I stroke his cheek. "No," I repeat. "Don't you get it? I want to be there for you. All of you. Whatever you need."

For a moment, he is silent. "Did I hurt you?" he finally asks, his voice flat.

"No." It's only a little lie. Already the sharp pain has passed. I'm sore, yes, but it's a pleasant feeling. A reminder of Damien. "No," I repeat. "You felt wonderful."

I don't think he believes me, but he leads me to the steps and out of the pool. We towel off in silence. When I'm dry, he picks me up without asking and carries me back inside. He places me gently onto our bed on the third floor then gets in beside me.

He doesn't speak, and neither do I. Instead, I move to snuggle against him. I know that he is still disturbed, as much because he thinks he hurt me as because he lost control. I, however, feel the opposite. He's lost control with me. And that is almost like sharing a secret. The thought makes me smile, and I close my eyes and sigh deeply. Sore, yes, but sweetly content.

I'm on the verge of falling asleep when his soft words wash over me.

"My father intends to go to the dedication."

"Oh," I say. It's all that I can manage, though I am fully awake now, and I rise up onto my elbow to face him.

"I won't be there. Richter was a balls-out bastard, and I won't support the decision to honor him, not even in the smallest way."

"Of course you won't go."

"I'm glad you understand."

"I'm glad you have the balls to stand up to your father. I don't think I could ignore an edict from my mother."

"I bet you could," he says. "You're stronger than you think."

I don't answer. Instead, I search his face. "And the tennis center thing is all that's been bugging you? Truly?"

"Yes," he says.

Am I imagining the hesitation? Am I so used to Damien's secrets that I'm seeing them when they're no longer there?

Yes, he said. And I decide to believe him. At the very least, he has opened a door. But Damien Stark, like this house, has many rooms, and I can't help but wonder how many doors remain shut and locked.

6

I wake in the morning to the scent of brewing coffee and fresh baked croissants, and when I peel my eyes open I find Damien beside the bed holding a tray, which I immediately identify as the source of those mouthwatering scents. "What's all this?" I ask.

"A woman heading off to the first day of a new job deserves breakfast in bed," he says, setting the tray across my lap as soon as I've sat up and scooted back.

I take a sip of the coffee, then sigh as the elixir begins to work its magic. "What time is it?"

"Just past six," he says, and I stifle a groan. "When are you supposed to be at work?"

"Ten," I say. "Bruce is having me start on a Friday since it's going to be a day of paperwork and getting my feet wet. Probably the last truly relaxing week I'll have for a long time. Monday, I'll be dragging myself in by eight, I'm sure."

"Don't even pretend to complain. You know you love it." He sits on the bed beside me and takes a sip from my mug. I don't think he even realizes that he's done it, but I can't help but smile at the casual intimacy.

As for loving the work, he's right. I'd moved to Los Angeles less than a month ago planning to take the tech world by storm. My job at Carl's company, C-Squared, turned out to be a bust, but I'm giddy about my new position at Innovative Resources, a company that does equally fine work with a less psychotic boss.

I spread some strawberry jam on the croissant and take a bite, surprised to find that it's warm and flaky and just about melts in my mouth. "Where did you get fresh croissants?" I cannot believe that his morning jog took him into town. And these are not heated-up frozen pastries.

"Edward," Damien says, referring to his driver.

"Thank him for me."

"You can thank him yourself. Unless you're planning to walk to work, he'll be giving you a lift."

"Not you?"

"While I would love to carpool with you, I'm afraid that's not possible today." He leans close and I expect a kiss. Instead, his hand closes over mine and he very deliberately brings the croissant to his mouth and takes a bite. He grins at me, his eyes dancing like a mischievous child. "You're right," he says. "Delicious."

"You owe me now, mister. You can't expect to steal a woman's pastry and get away with it."

"I look forward to your just and severe punishment," he says, standing. He holds out his hand to me. "Or perhaps I could make it up to you in the shower."

"I don't think so," I say archly. "I don't want to be late for my first day."

"I thought you weren't due in until ten."

I nod as I finish the croissant and wash it down with another slug of coffee. "I'm not. But I need to get home and get dressed." I shoot him a wicked smile. "And I need to shower off last night's sex."

"That's a very sad thought," he says. "Of course, if you insist on taking such drastic action, I did offer to share my shower."

I look him up and down. He's clean-shaven and dressed in neatly pressed slacks and his usual white button-down shirt. His jacket is laid across the foot of the bed, and I can even smell the soapy fresh scent of him. "Looks like you managed just fine without me," I say.

"Never." The word is heavy with meaning. "And for you I'm willing to get doubly clean."

"Tempting," I admit as I push the tray away and slide out of bed. The air is cool, but it feels good against my still Damien-sensitive skin. "But don't you have work to do? Things to merge? Cutting-edge technology to acquire? Perhaps a galaxy to purchase?"

He holds a robe open for me to slip on. It's not the red one that I soaked in the pool, and I wonder how many robes he has stocked in that closet. "I did that last week. Apparently there's nothing left to buy."

"Poor you." I twist in his arms and plant a gentle kiss on his chin as he tightens the sash around my waist. "Just like Alexander. No worlds left to conquer."

He slides his hand up my silk-covered arm and I shiver from the touch. "I assure you that I am very content with my conquests." The heated look in his eyes shifts to something more calculating. "Although you are right. I have a day full of meetings in Palm Springs starting at eight."

I gape at him. "And you were offering me a shower? What would you have done if I'd taken you up on that?"

"I would have enjoyed myself very much, I assure you."

"And been late for the meeting."

"I'm rather confident they can't start without me. That is not, however, an excuse to be late."

As if on cue, a loud rush fills my ears and the house seems to vibrate. "What is—"

"My ride," Damien says as a helicopter appears below the roofline and continues its descent below the balcony.

I hurry outside and watch as the helicopter lands on a flat, grassy area of the yard.

I turn and look at Damien. "What?" I say. "You couldn't afford a proper helipad?"

"On the contrary, you're looking at a state-of-the-art, eco-friendly, reinforced turf landing platform."

I blink at him. "Seriously?"

"It's quite revolutionary, I assure you. The ground is prepped with a high-tensile-strength mesh system that creates an anchored root system providing a surface area with remarkable load-bearing capacity. And because the Malibu hills are prone to mudslides, I've taken additional precautions and strengthened the area with a buried grid system into which that root area blends. The result is pretty damned impressive."

"If you do say so yourself."

He smirks. "I'm afraid this isn't one of my projects. Not yet, anyway. I've begun talks with the company that holds the patent on the mesh technology."

"To acquire the company?"

"Perhaps. Or maybe I'll simply be a silent partner." He fixes me with a steady look. "Not all of my business ventures involve my fingers in the pie."

I ignore the unstated message. I want the million that I earned posing for the portrait in order to seed my business—a business I intend to kick into gear once I feel like I'm ready. Damien wants to help me—and he thinks I'm ready now. It's not a discussion that I'm diving back into now, but he presses on.

"You're ready, Nikki. You can do this."

"Surprisingly, I think I'm a better judge of my ability than you are," I say, more sharply than I intend.

"Willingness, yes. Ability, no. That's a much more objective criterion, and I see more clearly than you do. You're too close to the subject in question. Let's examine the evidence, shall we?"

I cross my arms over my chest and scowl at him, but he presses on.

"You already have two reasonably profitable smartphone apps on the market, fully designed, marketed, and supported by you and you alone. You accomplished that entrepreneurial feat when you were still in college, so that in and of itself indicates the kind of self-sufficiency a successful business owner needs. Your degrees in electrical engineering and computer science are only icing on the cake, but your invitation into PhD programs at both MIT and CalTech demonstrate that I'm not the only one who sees your worth."

"But I turned down the programs."

"So that you could work in the real world and gain experience."

I can see that I'm not going to win this argument, so I do the only thing I can do—I ignore it and kiss him gently on the cheek. "Your car pool's here, Mr. Stark. You don't want to be late for homeroom." I turn to head inside, but he grabs my hand and pulls me back. His kiss is long and deep and makes my knees go weak, but Damien considerately holds me up so that I don't collapse in a puddle on the flagstone tiles.

"What was that for?" I breathe when he releases me.

"A reminder that I believe in you," he says.

"Oh." His voice is filled with so much pride and confidence that I wish I could soak it up like a drug.

"And a promise of things to come," he adds with a sexy curve to his lips. "I'll call you when I get back. I'm not sure how late I'll be."

"The helicopter's not as speedy as it looks?" I tease.

"More like my colleagues don't conduct business as expediently as I'd like."

"No prob. I should have dinner with Jamie tonight, anyway. I've been a best friend in absentia lately." I start to pull away, but his fingers tighten around mine. "What?"

"I don't want to go." His grin is boyish, and I laugh with delight. Damien is so many things, and I am falling hard for all of them.

"But if you don't, then how can I spend the day looking forward to having you back?"

"You're a very wise woman," he says, then presses a fresh kiss to my lips. "Until tonight."

7

Edward greets me outside by the door of a gracious silver and burgundy car that looks like it belongs on *Masterpiece Theatre*. "New car?"

"No, ma'am," Edward says. "Mr. Stark rebuilt her about three years ago."

"Really?" I look the car over, wondering when on earth Damien found the time. I try to imagine him under the chassis, his hands dirty and a spot of grease on his nose. Surprisingly, it's an easier picture to conjure than I would have imagined. As I've seen time and again, Damien can do pretty much anything. And look damn good doing it, too.

As for looking damn good, the car certainly fits that bill. It's all soft curves and flowing lines, the epitome of automotive class and grace. It's almost a crime that Edward wears a simple suit instead of livery, and it wouldn't surprise me a bit if his voice took on a British tinge.

He is oblivious to the way my mind is wandering. "We normally reserve the Bentley for formal occasions, but Mr. Stark thought you might enjoy arriving at your new position in style."

As he speaks, the helicopter rises from behind the house, far enough away that it barely kicks up a breeze. It's too far for me to see Damien, but I lift my hand anyway and wave a silent thank-you.

"I need to go home, actually. Not work. But Mr. Stark was right about the rest," I say as I slide past Edward into the car. "I'm definitely going to enjoy this ride."

"I'm afraid Mr. Stark was very clear that I am to see you safely to your office."

"Was he?" I consider pulling out my cell phone and giving Damien a piece of my mind, but that would ultimately change nothing. I consider my options and then nod. "Fine," I finally say, pushing my irritation aside. "But I do have to go home first."

"Of course, Ms. Fairchild." He shuts the door, and I'm snug in a leather and wood cocoon, breathing in the scent of luxury.

The windows, I notice, are not electric but instead operate with old-fashioned knobs that appear to be mahogany and are polished to a sheen. The white leather seat is as soft as butter, and the seat back in front of me actually has a tray table. I defy convention and release it from its full upright and locked position. It eases down to form a perfectly positioned writing surface. I'm suddenly overcome with a longing for a quill pen and parchment.

"What year is the car?" I ask Edward as he maneuvers us down the drive.

"It's a 1960 S2 Saloon," he says. "Only 388 were produced, and I'm afraid there are very few still on the road. When Mr. Stark ran across this one in a junkyard, he was determined to bring it back to its former glory."

I'm not at all certain what Damien would have been doing in a junkyard, but it takes no effort whatsoever to imagine his determination. What Damien wants, Damien gets, be it a classic car, a Santa Barbara hotel, or me.

I run my finger over the varnished surface of the desk, the motion reminding me of my earlier whimsy. "You don't happen to have a paper and pen up there, do you?"

"Certainly," Edward says. He leans over and pulls something out of the glove box, then passes a folio back to me. I open it and find a fountain pen and heavy linen stationery monogrammed with *DJS*—Damien's initials.

I hesitate. I hadn't really expected that Edward would have the things I asked for, and now that I'm faced with the prospect of putting my thoughts on paper, I am suddenly tongue-tied. Or finger-tied, as the case may be.

But this is too sweet an opportunity to squander, so I draw a breath, put the nib of the pen on the paper, and begin to write.

My very dear Mr. Stark,

Before I met you, I never gave any thought to the sensual nature of an automobile. But now, once again, I am surrounded by soft leather, snug in the warm embrace of this graceful, powerful vehicle. It is heady stuff, and I—

I continue to write, pouring out my teasing phrases through the intimate flow of ink onto paper. As I watch my precise handwriting fill the page, I almost regret the tech revolution. How wonderful to have received a letter from a lover. To open it and see his heart on the page, his handwriting bold and strong. There's an immediacy to texts and emails that can't be denied, but the intimacy of a letter really can't be replicated.

By the time Edward pulls up in front of the condo that I share with Jamie in Studio City, I have finished the note. I fold it neatly, slide it into the matching envelope I find in the folio pocket, seal it, and print my return address on the top left corner. I realize then that I don't know the street address of Damien's Malibu house. Odd, considering how much time I've been spending there. But it doesn't matter. The letter will reach him just as easily at his office building, which is also where his downtown apartment is located. I print his name and address neatly across the center of the envelope:

> Damien Stark, CEO
> Stark International
> Stark Tower, Penthouse
> S. Grand Avenue
> Los Angeles, CA 90071

I can't remember the street number for the tower, but under the circumstances I imagine that the post office can deal. I find a stamp in my wallet and affix it to the envelope. Then I slip out of the car and smile at Edward. "I need to shower and change and grab a few things. I might be a while."

"That won't be a problem," he says, and as I head toward the stairs, he slips back behind the wheel.

I feel absolutely no guilt whatsoever about my plan. Edward undoubtedly has an audiobook, and it's not as if he needs to go back to Malibu in order to drive Damien around. By the time he realizes that I have snuck down the back stairs to my own car, I imagine he'll have gotten in quite a bit of quality time with whatever book he's enjoying.

I slide the letter through the outgoing mail slot before I hurry up the stairs to the condo, calculating the time I have to shower and change and get to the office. Traffic was worse than Edward had expected—there was a wreck on the 405—and I am going to be more rushed than I'd intended. I know I could have simply worn one of the zillion outfits that Damien has stocked for me, but this new job is my territory. And silly or not, I want to wear my own clothes and drive my own car.

I expect to find the door unlocked, because Jamie never re-members to lock the damn thing, so I'm surprised to find both the dead bolt and the knob locked up tight.

I dig my keys out of my purse, then frown as I enter the dark apartment. She's probably asleep, and I hope that she's alone. She probably is. Though Jamie drags men home like stray cats, she routinely kicks them out once they've given her bedsprings a thorough shaking. It's dangerous and I worry, because it's almost become a game with her. Unlike the games I play with Damien, though, I don't think there's any sort of safeword for Jamie.

Her door is closed, and I consider passing by. But this is my first day at work, and I want to see my best friend.

I tap lightly on the door, then lean close to listen. I expect either a groan or a startled apology followed by a rush to the door and a hug for me on my first day. But there's only silence.

"James?" I tap harder, but there's still no answer. I take hold of the knob and turn, trying to both look and not look, just in case she finally let the guy she dragged home stay for the entire night.

But the room is both dark and empty. I tell myself not to worry. Jamie probably just had somewhere to be this morning. Or else she crashed somewhere after a night of partying. Except I don't really believe either of those explanations. Jamie's not an early riser, and she rarely stays overnight anywhere. She's not the kind to crash on a couch—she likes the comforts of home too much.

I hope I'm overreacting, but I pull out my phone and tap out a text. Where r u? Do I need to send out a search party?

I wait, staring at the screen, but my phone stays silent.

Well, shit.

I call, but the phone rolls over to voice mail.

Now my stomach really is in knots. I can't call the police—I may not watch much television, but I've watched enough to know that they won't do a thing unless it's been twenty-four hours. I almost dial Damien, but my finger hesitates over his name. There might be nothing that he can do, but if I'm worried, I'm almost positive that he'll cut his meeting short and come to me no matter how much I protest. He may be firmly perched on a white steed in my mind, but I am most definitely not a damsel in distress, and really don't want to be.

Fine. Okay. No problem. Jamie's probably just in the shower, which is where I need to be. I'll shower and change, and if she hasn't called me back by the time I'm ready to head downtown, I'll call and text her again. And if she still doesn't answer, I'll call Ollie. I don't know what he could do, but as my other best friend, I'm allowed to call him in a crisis. And with Ollie, my odds of interrupting a billion-dollar summit are significantly lessened.

Most important though—and as much as I hate to admit it—there's a possibility that they're together. They slept together one time that I know of. And though Jamie swears it was a singular event—and though Ollie has assured me that he's been otherwise faithful to his fiancée—I'm not certain that I really believe either one of them.

My doubts weigh on me, because Jamie and Ollie are my two best friends, and I don't like the way their tryst has clouded up things among the three of us.

I'm frustrated as I head into my own bedroom and toss the phone onto my bed, barely missing Lady Meow-Meow, who has blended in so well with my white duvet I don't see her. She lifts her head in sleepy protest, stares at me until I apologize, and then promptly goes back to sleep.

Apparently our cat doesn't share my concern about Jamie's whereabouts.

Partly because I'm running late, and partly because I don't want to be away from the phone that long, I rush through my shower. I towel-dry my hair until it's damp, then use some gel to twist a few curls into place. I've discovered that it's much easier to take care of shoulder-length hair than the tresses that used to fall midway down my back. Not that I want to repeat my meltdown, but on this small point, I think it worked out okay.

I wrap a towel around me, then open the door to our tiny bathroom. A cloud of steam escapes ahead of me, and I follow it out, then jump about a foot when I hear the sharp *crash* of ceramic shattering against the tile kitchen floor.

For an instant, I'm terrified, imagining intruders and boogeymen and God knows what. But what would have been a scream breaks into a relieved burst of laughter when I hear Jamie's voice cutting sharply through the apartment. "Oh, fuck a duck! *Nikki!* I just killed your favorite coffee mug!"

"I'm right here," I call, hurrying down the two stairs, my back to our tiny dining area as I face Jamie in the kitchen.

She looks at me oddly, probably because I'm still laughing. She holds up the handle of my Dallas Cowboys mug. The rest of the shattered blue ceramic is scattered on the tile at her feet. "Sorry," she says.

"It's okay." I'm still laughing. I don't know why. Relief, I guess.

"It was a ridiculous favorite, anyway," she says, as if I'm giving her grief about the mug. "You don't even like football."

"It was big," I said. "It could hold hot chocolate and marshmallows without the chocolate dribbling over the side when you stick a spoon in."

"Yeah, but what's the point of drinking hot chocolate with marshmallows if you're going to be all prissy about it?"

I can't argue with that, so I don't. Instead I shove my feet into a pair of flip-flops that are by the stairs, then step gingerly into the kitchen to get the small broom and dustpan I put under the sink after I moved in.

"Thanks," she says, then rolls her eyes when I hand the broom to her. "Okay." She sighs. "Fine."

As she squats down, much better dressed for the job in jeans than I am in my towel, I ask where she's been. "I was worried," I admit. "Did you sleep somewhere else?"

"Shit no." She brushes the last of the mug splinters into the dustpan, then tilts her head to aim a cat-ate-the-canary grin up at me. "I may have stayed out all night, but I didn't sleep." Her dreamy grin fades and she peers hard at me. "And you? Because it seems to me your bed's not getting all that much action lately. Pretty soon you're going to have to sign the poor thing up for therapy. Loneliness can lead to depression, you know."

"I'll get right on that," I say dryly. "And as a matter of fact, no. I wasn't here, either."

"Uh-huh."

I hold my hands up in surrender. "I didn't say a word," I point out. "But if I were going to say something, it would only be that when I stay out all night it's with the same guy. You have so many different men you should start a Facebook page just to keep track of them."

"Not a bad plan, actually. Except that I think this guy might be something special."

I gape. "Seriously?"

"Totally. He's not as fuckalicious as Damien-king-of-the-world-Stark, but I wouldn't run screaming from a repeat performance. Or even a triple play, for that matter."

This is as close as I've ever heard Jamie get to discussing a relationship. To say I'm bowled over would be an understatement. "You can't just drop a bomb like that on me when I'm running late. So come on. We can talk while I get dressed."

She follows me into my bedroom and perches at my desk in front of my laptop. It's open, and the screensaver is a slideshow of pictures of Damien that I took in Santa Barbara. Damien with so much light and humor in his eyes that I can't ever look at those photos without smiling. Between that screensaver and the exquisite, original Monet painting Damien gave me that now hangs between my desk and my dresser, I cannot enter this room without feeling cherished. It's a nice feeling, and one that I am not used to. In college, my apartment was simply a place to live. With my mother, my room was the place I wanted to escape. But here, there is Jamie and my newfound freedom. There is excitement. There is potential.

Most of all, there is Damien.

This room is proof that I really have moved on, and that where I am going is where I want to be.

At my desk, Jamie is typing away. "Raine," she finally says.

I'm standing by my closet, debating between a blue skirt and a gray one, and it takes me a moment to realize she's not talking about precipitation.

"*Bryan* Raine," she says, when I turn to face her, as if that will make me understand. Since my face apparently continues to register complete cluelessness, she shakes her head in mock exasperation, and taps the laptop screen. "*My* guy is Bryan Raine."

Despite my rush, I'm curious enough to forgo my wardrobe analysis to see what she's doing, and when I reach my desk, I see that she's pulled up a series of images. They're all of the same man. Gorgeous, mostly shirtless, with a well-fucked quality and the kind of eyes and facial structure and that dirty blond hair a camera loves. Most of the images, in fact, are from advertisements. Cars, men's cologne. Jeans. I have to confess that the man could definitely sell a pair of jeans.

"That's him," Jamie says proudly.

"That's the guy you were out with last night?"

"Yup." She grins mischievously. "Though we stayed in most of the time. Pretty hot, huh?"

"He's incredible," I say as I move to my dresser and rummage for panties and a bra. For a moment, I hesitate. In the game I've been playing with Damien, I've had to follow his rules. And for the last two weeks, I've worn neither bra nor panties. It was odd at first, but undeniably sexy, especially when I was with him, knowing that at any moment he could slip a hand under my skirt. That he could touch me, tease me, even fingerfuck me.

There's something desperately erotic about being naked beneath your clothes, and even when Damien wasn't around, my body was keyed up, and I was aware of every brush of material over my rear and every whisper of a breeze that stroked my sex.

But this isn't a game, it's the first day of a new job and the Elizabeth Fairchild Rules for Living are too ingrained in my life. I might have spent my entire life trying to escape from my mother, but she has still soaked in through the cracks. And in my mother's world, the thrill of sexual freedom doesn't override the necessity of panties at work.

I slip on my underwear, sigh, and return to the closet to continue debating my outfit.

I glance at Jamie to see if she has an opinion, but she's still gazing dreamily at the screen. "Don't get drool on my keyboard," I chide. "So how did you meet him?"

"He's my co-star," she says, referring to the commercial she's about to start shooting. "He mostly models, but he's also done a few television guest appearances and he was even one of the bad guys in the last James Bond movie."

"He was?" I'd actually seen that movie, and I don't remember him.

"Well, he stood around with a gun and looked hot," she amends. "But he was on the bad guy team."

"But you guys haven't started to shoot yet," I say, because I'm still confused. "So why did you go out with him? Which one?" I add, holding up the two skirts I'm considering.

"The blue. And he called me. He said that since the commercial's basically a love story in thirty seconds, we ought to go out and suss out our chemistry."

"I take it the chemistry is good?"

"Sizzling," Jamie agrees, and although I'm still not thrilled about the ease with which Jamie bounces from bed to bed, I can't deny that this morning my roommate looks good. Sparkly, fizzy good, and I figure that the new job and the new guy have a lot to do with that. I feel a surge of protectiveness mixed with relief and tinged with a tiny bit of worry. Jamie's never confided in me about it, but I'm pretty sure that before I moved in she often chose her men based not on attraction but on their willingness to help her make the mortgage. If a real relationship develops between Jamie and Bryan Raine, no one will be happier than me. But if he ends up breaking her heart, I have a feeling that my strong, self-sufficient roommate will shatter.

I glance at her and see that she's frowning. I swallow, afraid that my fears show on my face. "What is it?"

"You're really wearing a skirt? I thought you tech folks were all about the jeans and T-shirts with math equations."

I scowl, because I happen to own several T-shirts with truly funny math jokes. "First day on the job, and I'm not doing the tech side, remember. I'm management. I want to look professional."

I've zipped up the blue skirt, and now I slide my feet into my favorite pair of pumps, then slip on a white silk shell that I top with a darling jacket I found at one of the studio resale shops that Jamie took me to during our Nikki-just-arrived-in-LA shopping spree. It has a classical cut with a muted pattern in gray and blue. The clerk told us that it was worn by one of the characters on some television show I never watched, but that Jamie assured me was great fun.

"I want to hear more about this guy," I tell her as I move back into the bathroom to fly through my makeup routine. "But I have to get going." She follows me and leans against the door as I finish up by carefully lining my eyes and brushing mascara on my lashes. When I'm done, I do a little spin in the tiny area between the tub and the sink. "Do I look okay?"

"When don't you?" she asks. "And if anyone asks, Lauren Graham wore that jacket on *Gilmore Girls*. Trust me, it's cool."

I nod, taking her word for it.

"Want to meet after work? I'll tell you about Raine and you can tell me all about your nights away from home, too. I want to hear everything."

"Sounds good," I say, not bothering to tell her that where Damien is concerned, there is no way that I'm going to be revealing "everything." "Du-par's?" I ask.

"Are you shitting me? I want a drink. Meet me at Firefly," she says, referring to a local bar on Ventura Boulevard that we went to my first night in town.

"I'll text you as I'm leaving work," I say, then pull her into a hug. "I'm really glad about this guy. I can't wait to hear more."

"I can't wait to *see* more," she says with a wicked grin. "Trust me, I could look at that man all day."

I leave Jamie sighing and probably replaying last night's coital gymnastics in her mind, then hurry down the back stairs to the parking area. As I pull out, I see the limo in my rearview mirror. I keep an eye on it until I turn, but it doesn't move from the spot, and as I turn onto Ventura Boulevard, I can't help but smile. After all, it's not every day I manage to outmaneuver Damien Stark.

Despite the fact that my ancient Honda has very little spunk and has lately taken to stalling out at stoplights, I manage to get from Studio City to the Innovative Resources office in Burbank in less than fifteen minutes, completely stall-free. I consider this a stellar beginning to the day. I park next to a red Mini Cooper that I eye jealously, then lock my car and head toward the ugly four-story stucco building that houses the Innovative offices along with a few subtenants.

My phone beeps and I pause in the middle of the parking lot to pull it out of my purse, then smile when I see it's from Damien.

Thinking of you. Be good on your first day. Get along with the other kids. But don't share your candy.

I laugh and tap out a reply. I only share my candy w/ u.

His reply makes me smile. Very glad to hear it.

I answer quickly. Heading into building now. Wish me luck.

His response is just as quick. Luck, though you don't need it. Meeting reconvening, must go. Tonight, baby. Until then, imagine me, touching you.

I always do, I reply, then sigh happily as I slide my phone back into my purse, but not before noticing the time. It's only 9:45, which means that I have fifteen minutes before I'm supposed to report for work.

My phone rings, and I pull it out. Damien again. "I'm imagining," I say, keeping my tone sultry.

"What the hell do you think you're doing?" He doesn't sound sultry at all. In fact, he sounds downright pissed. I grimace. Apparently, he's just spoken to Edward.

"Going to work," I say.

"I'm supposed to be in a meeting right now."

"So why aren't you?"

"Dammit, Nikki—"

"No," I snap. "I'm the only one who gets to say that. Dammit, Damien, I am perfectly capable of driving myself. And if you want to hire out Edward then ask me. It's easy. You walk up to me and say, 'Nikki, darling, light of my life, can I have my driver take you to work?'"

There is a pause, and I hope that he is laughing. "And you would have said yes?"

"No," I admit. "But that's the way you should have handled

it. It's my job, Damien. I want to drive myself. I *will* drive myself."

"I don't want you around the paparazzi without someone there with you."

Oh. I feel a little bit better. I don't agree with what he did, but at least there was a reason for doing it. "Nobody's here," I say.

"But there could have been."

"And I would have dealt with it," I say, probably too sharply. I count to five. "You can't be with me every second of every day. No matter how much I wish you could. I'm going to see them when I'm alone. It's going to happen, and we both just have to deal with it."

I hear him exhale. "I don't like it."

"Me, neither."

"Dammit, Nikki."

I don't answer. I don't know what to say.

Finally Damien speaks. "I'm going to my meeting," he says, but what he means is, *I'm worried about you.*

"I'm fine," I say. "And, Damien?"

"Yes?"

"Thank you. Right emotion. Crappy execution."

That gets a laugh out of him. "We'll have to agree to disagree on that," he says. "It is not an argument I can have from Palm Springs."

I frown. Apparently it is an argument he can have in Los Angeles. Great.

He really does have to go to his meeting, so he ends the call, and I'm left scowling at my phone and the knowledge that I'm going to have to deal with not only the paparazzi, but with Damien trying to babysit me through my day.

I shove the problem out of my head and hurry into the building. I no longer have time to grab a coffee, but that's okay because I don't want to risk spilling it on my white blouse. As my mother's voice in my head reminds me, there are better ways to make a first impression than coffee stains on your outfit.

The reception area is on the fourth floor, and I punch the elevator call button and wait impatiently for the elevator to arrive.

The doors finally slide open and I shift to one side to let the passengers get off. I'm about to step into the car when I hear a throaty, familiar voice behind me.

"Well, look at you, Texas. All dressed up with someplace to go."

I turn and find myself facing Evelyn Dodge, a brassy broad if ever there was one, and one of my favorite people in the world. She's wearing flowing black pants and gold sandals that look like something imported from Morocco. The pants are mostly obscured by a blustery multi-patterned shirt that, as far as I can tell, was created by stitching together dozens of Hermes scarves. She looks a bit like a gypsy with very expensive taste.

"I knew today was your first day," she says, "but I didn't think I'd get lucky enough to see you."

I realize that I'm still staring at her in complete surprise—and blocking the entrance to the elevator. I step to the side so that the small group that has gathered can get on, and force myself to speak despite the grin that is plastered across my face.

"What on earth are you doing here?" I ask. Evelyn lives in Malibu, not far from Damien's new house, and she's not the type to make the trek to the Valley unless the apocalypse is upon us.

"Same thing you are, Texas."

I lift a brow in amusement. "You're going into the tech industry? Designing an iPhone app to feature Blaine's work?"

She taps her nose and points at me. "Not a bad idea, actually, and I just may have to wrangle some advice out of you about that later. But no. I'm here to see Bruce."

"Why?" The question is out of my mouth before I realize how completely rude it sounds.

Evelyn, however, isn't the kind to take offense. "I need one of his keys," she says, then barks out a throaty laugh. "But don't worry. It's not for a tryst. Blaine's more than I can handle in that department—and now he's decided he wants to touch up some of the paintings for Saturday's showing, but apparently they're in the gallery's off-site storage facility."

Now I really am confused. "Can't Giselle let you in?" Giselle is Bruce's wife and the owner of a few Southern California art galleries. Saturday's cocktail party will not only feature the portrait of me—though only a handful of guests will actually know that I am the model on the wall—but also a number of Blaine's other paintings.

"If she hadn't hauled her ass to Palm Springs, sure. But she called me from the road. Apparently she's on her way to get a few pieces from her gallery there, and her assistant doesn't have the spare key to the unit. Why the hell Giselle gave it to Bruce instead of her assistant, I don't know. Sometimes, that woman baffles me."

"Damien's in Palm Springs, too. He went there this morning."

"Too bad Giselle didn't know. She could have dumped the job of bringing the paintings back on him. Would have saved me a trip." Evelyn shakes her head. "Frankly, I would have much rather gone to Palm Springs than Burbank, and I'm sure she knows it, but I think she and Brucey boy are having another tiff."

"Why are they fighting?"

"With those two? Who the hell knows." She brushes the conversation away, as if it is old news, but to me the topic of Giselle is one of unpleasant but undeniable interest. I'd been jealous of the woman for about five minutes when I'd first met Damien at Evelyn's party because it had seemed to me that she was the girl on Damien's arm. Once I'd learned that she was married, however, the jealousy had been shoved into a dark corner where it belonged. I wouldn't say that the jealousy has returned, but my hope that Bruce and Giselle quickly regain a state of marital bliss is definitely more selfish than altruistic.

"And what about you?" Evelyn continues. "I keep hoping you and that camera of yours will take me up on my offer so that I can ply you with drink and wrangle some gossip, but I guess you don't need me now that you've got Damien's view at your disposal."

"It is one hell of a view," I admit. "But I'd still love to come over sometime."

"Anytime. Bring your camera if you want," she says. "Or just come for the liquor and the gossip. Both flow free at my house. Advice, too, if you need it. But from what I'm hearing, you're doing just fine."

"Blaine's been telling stories on me." I can't help my grin. The skinny young artist and the large brassy woman don't seem like a couple at first glance. And while Evelyn will say she only keeps Blaine around to warm her bed, I have a feeling there's a lot more to it than that.

"Hell, yes. What's the point of sending that boy out in the world if he doesn't bring me back the dirt?"

"And?"

"You're boringly dirt-free," she says. "From what I hear, you're swimming in bliss."

I laugh. "I'll go with that."

"Good. Glad I'm not the only one getting hot sex regularly."

My cheeks burn, and I have to press my lips together not to burst out laughing.

"But it's more than that, I take it? From what Blaine says, it sounds like you've tamed the savage beast." I don't reply, but her words please me so much that I'm pretty sure I must be glowing. "So there's no new dramas on the horizon?"

"No," I say warily, because this is neither the time nor the place to tell her about Carl's threats. From her tone, though, I can't help but fear that she already knows. "Why? Is there something I should know?"

She waves an airy hand through the air. "Not a thing."

I narrow my eyes at her. Evelyn may have been a good liar back in her agenting days, but she has lost the knack.

She eyes me, then snorts with laughter. "Aw, hell, Texas. I meant what I said. There's nothing you need to worry about. Not now, anyway."

Several groups of people have gotten on and off the elevator during our conversation, and now the car once again opens in front of us.

"Time to go to work, right?" Evelyn says.

"You are not getting off that easy," I retort, following her on. I have every intention of interrogating her, but there's no time during the short ride up, and when the doors open, there's no privacy. The receptionist, a girl my age who I remember is named Cindy, immediately stands.

"Wow, it's so cool to have you here," she says to me, then blushes. "I mean, you're going to fit in great. We can do lunch if you want."

"Thanks," I say, with a sidelong glance toward Evelyn, who only looks amused. "I think I'm having lunch with Bruce today."

"Oh, right. Mr. Tolley's ready for you. Just a sec, and I'll walk you back." She turns to Evelyn before I have the chance to tell her I'm supposed to meet first with the lady from Human Resources. "May I help you?"

"Evelyn Dodge," Evelyn says. "I called Bruce about picking up—"

"Oh, sure thing, Ms. Dodge." She comes around the desk and hands Evelyn an envelope that presumably contains a key.

Evelyn slides it into her humongous purse and points a finger at me. "We'll see each other tomorrow, Texas."

"Yeah," I say meaningfully. Evelyn is one of the few people who knows the identity of the woman in Blaine's portrait. "You'll certainly be seeing plenty of me tomorrow."

Evelyn guffaws and then steps back onto the elevator. I follow Cindy down the plain gray halls to Bruce's office, Evelyn's laughter still ringing in my ears.

8

We don't even make it to the office before Bruce emerges. When we met during the interview, he'd been the picture of corporate calm. Now he looks undeniably harried. "Nikki, great to see you." He holds out his hand for me to shake. It's firm and no-nonsense, and I think that bodes well for Bruce as a boss.

Cindy returns to reception and Bruce starts down the hallway, easing farther into the bowels of the company. He's moving fast, and I hurry to keep up. If the fight with his wife is weighing on him, I don't see it. He looks like a man with a work problem, not a marital one.

"If this is a bad time," I begin. "I mean, I'm pretty sure Human Resources is expecting me."

"I talked with Trish. She'll take care of your paperwork this afternoon. Right now, I've got something I'd like you to handle." He comes to a stop outside an office, its closed door covered with taped-on cartoons and various band logos. "I hope you don't mind getting thrown to the wolves."

I eye the door curiously. The truth is that I have no idea what he's talking about, but what I do know is that the proper response to such a question from your new boss is "Not at all. What's going on?"

"Calendaring screw up and I'm double-booked. I need you and Tanner to head downtown to meet with the IT team at Suncoast Bank. They're interested in the 128-bit encryption algorithm we've been beta testing. You'll be stepping in to head up marketing on the product anyway, but I had hoped to give you a little time in-house to get your feet wet. Sorry to bring all this down on your first day."

"Not a problem," I say. My voice is calm, but inside I'm doing cartwheels. Bruce told me about Innovative's cutting-edge encryption software during my interview, and I know that it is shaping up to be the company's gold-standard product. I hadn't expected to actually land such a choice assignment right off the bat, but since I have, I fully intend to use this meeting as a chance to prove to my boss that I can do this job, and do it well.

"It shouldn't be too hard a sell," Bruce adds. "The product is exactly what they need, but we're going to want to put our own team on-site to make sure their IT group gets trained properly and that we have eyes on and a fast response to every bug and every glitch."

"Of course."

"That's why I'm sending Tanner in, too," he adds, tapping lightly on the cartoon-covered door. "He worked on the development of the project and, frankly, I think it would be good for him to work six months in-house with a client."

"Why?"

Bruce frowns. "If you don't mind mixing business with pleasure, we can go into that when I see you tomorrow. Right now, I'll just say that when I was talking about the wolves, I didn't mean the client."

"Sure," I say, realizing with a mental head-thwap that of course he's going to be at the party. The first hour will be intimate—just our friends who know that it's me up there on Damien's wall—but then Damien is opening the third floor to a whole slew of Blaine's clients.

A voice filters out from behind the still-closed door. "I said 'come in,' already."

Bruce pushes the door open, and a blond man with a surfer's tan and the air of a salesman looks up at us. His desk is buried under an array of papers, and probably twice as many sheets are splayed out across the floor. He looks up at us and smiles widely. I know I should wait until I have more to go on, but I instinctively do not like this man.

"Bruce!" he says, his voice full of friendly bluster. "Just got off the phone with Phil. He's sending up the information on the Continental Mortgage proposal. I'll make sure he stays on top of it."

"Sounds good," Bruce says, but I have the feeling he's only half-listening. "Tanner, this is Nikki."

Tanner's smile grows even wider and for an odd second I feel as though I'm looking at a mirror of myself. That's not a real smile any more than my practiced pageant smile. Or any more than the Social Nikki smile I paste on right now.

"We've all heard a lot about you," Tanner says. "Everyone's been eager to meet the flavor of the month." He half-laughs as his eyes dart to Bruce. "So welcome aboard and all that."

I meet Tanner's eyes and deliberately let my smile grow wider. "I'll try to live up to expectations." I shift just enough so that I'm looking at both men, then I pull out all the stops, dazzling them with my "what I really want is world peace" pageant-perfect smile.

"I'm sure you will," Bruce says. "We're thrilled you've joined the team." The sincerity in his tone is unmistakable, and I can tell by the look on Tanner's face that he realizes it, too.

"We really should get going," Tanner says, then grabs a messy sheaf of papers off his desk and shoves them into a leather messenger bag.

"Here." Bruce hands me a notebook with *Suncoast* embossed on the cover. "You can bone up on the specs during the drive."

He tells us that he needs to go prep for his own meeting, promises me we'll do our first-day lunch on Monday, then wishes us luck. Before I know it I'm standing in front of the elevator with Tanner beside me. And, yes, I'm a little nervous. Sure, I can do this job. I understand encryption algorithms and I'm more than capable of presenting a good company face to a client. It's not my skill that's bothering me. It's the fact that I'm standing next to a man who, for some inexplicable reason, seems to despise me.

Bruce may not have noticed, but I'm certain I didn't misread Tanner. Suddenly I feel a little sick to my stomach. And that queasiness turns into downright nausea when we step onto the elevator and he leans against the far wall, his eyes on me and his lip curled up as if he's just seen something gross in the road.

I look away, intending to ignore it, but I stop, because suddenly I'm thinking of Damien. To say that he's the most successful businessman I know would be an understatement. So what would Damien do when faced with a recalcitrant, disrespectful colleague? Would he turn away and pretend to ignore it?

For that matter, if Nikki Fairchild met up with some backbiting bitch under social circumstances, would she ignore it?

She would not.

I may be well-practiced in not showing my true face to most of the world, but even Social Nikki wouldn't stand for this kind of shit. Neither would Damien Stark.

And neither will Business Nikki.

I press the emergency stop button, then take a step closer to

Tanner. I'm not enjoying the proximity, but I deliberately put myself in his personal space. The sneer fades, and he actually looks a little uncomfortable.

"Do you have a problem?" I ask, ignoring the bell that's now ringing at annoyingly regular intervals.

His lips thin, and he pales a bit under the tan. For a second I think that this is it. I've made my point and won the alpha dog title.

Then he opens his mouth, and I see his color return. "Yeah," he says. "You're my problem."

I force myself to stay where I'm standing. At least now it's out in the open. "Me? You mean working together?"

"Working together? *Together?* Is that what you call it?"

"At the moment, no," I admit. "I don't think this is working at all."

"We're not working *together*," he says, making air quotes with his fingers. "You're my fucking boss now."

"Yeah," I say. "I am. And I suggest you think before you talk to me like that." Seriously, what the hell is this guy's problem?

"This was supposed to be my job. I worked this encryption package since day one. I know it inside and out. And I've proven to Bruce over and over again that I can head up a team. Then what happens? Some privileged little bitch decides she wants to work for pin money, and suddenly I'm booted back downstairs."

"Pin money?" I repeat. "What century are you living in?"

"What's the matter? Get bored with spending your boy-friend's money? Thought you'd come here and shake things up? Do you know how many calls Cindy's had to field? Dozens of calls from reporters who just want to know if you really work here. It's a fucking waste of her time."

The tempo of my pulse kicks up and I feel beads of sweat rise in my cleavage. How the hell would the press know that I work here? And why won't they back the hell off? Even with Damien Stark in my life, I am just not that interesting.

On the upside, Tanner's enigmatic "flavor of the month" comment makes more sense.

"And you know what really chaps my ass?" he asks, then continues without waiting for an answer. "The fact that you're here just because the boss wants to make his wife happy."

Now my head really is spinning. I haven't got a clue what Giselle has to do with this, but at this point, I'm done playing games.

I reach over and start the elevator up again, then turn back to him once it lurches into motion. "This job requires a certain amount of finesse. An ability to communicate with clients and the public. And most of all a talent for smiling at people that you'd much rather spit on." I flash my brightest Social Nikki smile at him. "Tanner," I say. "I don't think this position is for you."

We reach the lobby, and the doors open. I step out, leaving him to follow. I *am* the one in charge here, and he can damn well deal with it. I may not have a handle on everything he's just said, but I know enough to know that if I don't take control now, he'll do whatever he can to snatch it from me.

As we head through the lobby toward the exit, I see a poised-looking Asian woman sitting at a table outside the cafeteria. She's reading what looks to be a stock report, and in the brief instant when she flips a page, her eyes lift and catch mine. I've never seen her before, but something in her poised, confident manner inspires me. This is my job, and I got it on merit, not because of Damien, and certainly not because of Giselle. I'm in charge here, and I'm damn well going to prove it.

I march to the exit and burst through the doors—and half a second later, my bright, shiny bubble of self-assurance pops as six paparazzi with flashing cameras and rising voices rush toward us from where they were apparently lying in wait in the parking lot.

Before I can even think about reacting, I am verbally bombarded.

"Is it true that Stark is looking to take over Innovative Resources?"

"Nikki, what exactly is your role at IR?"

I fight to keep my composure. To keep my Business Nikki face plastered on. I hate this, but I'm not going to let them have the satisfaction of knowing it.

"Are you reporting back to Stark's company?"

"What do you say to the allegations of corporate espionage?"

At that, I have to force myself not to clench my hands. Not because I want the pain, but because I want to smash my fist into the face of whichever one of these assholes has dared to suggest that Damien would send me in as a corporate spy.

"Is this a ploy to up your value to reality-show producers?"

"Tell us about the real Nikki—is it true your sister committed suicide?"

I stumble backward, my composure knocked out of me by the force of those words.

No. No, no, no.

This time I do clench my fists. I want the pain. I need it to collect myself. To give me strength.

I need it because I have to find the will to put the mask back on. To face these people. And then to get the hell out of here.

Slowly, I square my shoulders. And though it takes every ounce of strength within me, I look at each one of them in turn. Then I flash my million-watt smile. "No comment," I say, before I turn casually around to find Tanner.

He's still in the building doorway, and my eyes locate him just in time to see his smug expression fade. "Hurry up, Tanner,"

I say as I push my way past the paparazzi. "We need to get to a meeting."

"Oh, my God! I can't believe you got paired to work with such a twit!" Jamie says. We're sitting at the polished wooden bar in Firefly Studio City drinking dirty martinis. She eats the final olive out of hers, then points the little plastic sword at me. "It's like you're living a sitcom. No, a movie," she amends. "One of those screwball comedies where the spunky heroine is paired with the completely incompetent idiot and wackiness ensues."

"Except he's vengeful, not incompetent. And doesn't the heroine in those movies always end up with the idiot?"

"Not necessarily," Jamie says, leaning back and looking smug. "Not so long as there's another love interest in the B-story." She swipes her hand through the air. "*A Day with Tanner*. I can practically see the trailer."

I grimace. "Well, you can star in it. Personally, I'd rather have another leading man."

"You do," Jamie says. "And as much as it pains me not to talk about either of our fuckalicious men, I want to hear the rest of this story first. How did the camera-vultures know you were there? Did Tanner tell them? Have you told Damien about the corporate espionage comment? Was he totally livid?"

"I'm going to tell him when I see him," I say. "And yeah, he'll be livid." I bite back a grimace. This wouldn't have been prevented by Edward driving me to work, but I have a feeling that simple fact isn't going to matter when Damien hears what happened and goes ballistic.

"As for Tanner . . ." I trail off with a shrug. I suspect he's the source, but I can't prove it. "Doesn't matter much. They know now. Yay," I add dryly.

Jamie leans closer to me, her brows pulling together as she studies my face. "Are you okay? I mean, really okay?"

I almost put on my practiced smile and nod and say that everything will be fine. But this is Jamie, and she's been my best friend since about forever. More important, she knew how much my big sister meant to me. How much I'd relied on Ashley to survive all the shit my mother put me through. The nights locked in my room with no way to turn on the light because my mother was convinced I needed my beauty sleep. The interminable hours walking with a book on my head. The second weekend of the month when I was allowed only water with lemon so that I would detox and "keep that nasty cellulite at bay." The big things, the little things, and so much more.

I was the one to win the ribbons and the tiaras, but it was Ashley I'd envied. Ashley, who'd been allowed to live a normal life, or so I'd thought. Ashley, who'd tended to her little sister even before tending to herself.

I hadn't thought about how my mother's harping must have been drilled into my sister's head, too. Or, at least, I hadn't thought about it until it was too late and I was holding Ashley's suicide note in my hand and looking at her neat, precise handwriting blaming her husband leaving her on the fact that she must have failed at being a woman and a wife. That somehow, she hadn't managed to be the lady our mother had tried to train us to be.

Bitch.

I close my eyes and realize that my hand is resting on my thigh—right over the scar beneath my skirt. I'd cut before Ashley died, but once she was gone, I'd kicked it up a notch.

There are so many memories tied up in those scars, as if each small ridge of tissue represents an emotional mountain. Mostly, though, there's Ashley.

"No," I finally say in answer to Jamie's question. "I'm not okay. But I was—before they brought up Ashley, I was dealing with it. I didn't like it, but I was coping. And I'll be okay again. I just wasn't prepared today."

"It will pass, you know. That's the good and the bad about publicity. It goes away."

"And like Tanner said, I'm the flavor of the month." I smile, and this time it's genuine. "Maybe next month they'll leave me alone and focus on the rising starlet who's dating Byron Rand."

"Bryan Raine," she corrects. "And don't even try to change the subject. So come on—forget the stupid paparazzi. I want to hear the rest of what happened at the meeting."

"Right," I say, then finish off my martini. I've been telling Jamie what happened once Tanner and I reached Suncoast, and I was up to the actual meeting with the clients.

"I'll field that," Tanner had said when the head of IT asked me a conceptual question. "Ms. Fairchild is coming at this from a purely administrative point of view."

"The little prick," Jamie says when I get to that part of the story.

"No argument from me," I say. "But I probably should have said nothing. I mean, the whole idea was to get the client to take the product and the team. That would get Tanner out of my hair for six months."

"So what did you do?"

"When he finished, I just casually pointed out that while Tanner's overview was entirely accurate, he left out some key information. Then I spent the next fifteen minutes running through ways to tweak the algorithm to give them a huge variety of options. I mean, conceptually, the program is brilliant, but when you get down to the actual coding, then all you really—"

"Okay," Jamie says, lifting her hand. "I get the idea. Techie stuff. You impressed them. Tanner looked like a doofus."

"So sweet and so true," I admit. "But the beauty is that he didn't look like an ignorant doofus. He knows his stuff. He just left out some important details."

"Which is good, because they wouldn't want some bonehead moving in-house for six months," Jamie says.

"Exactly. I think I'd have to quit if Tanner were working down the hall from me. The guy's toxic."

"Well, we wouldn't want you to quit," Jamie says, rolling her eyes. "How on earth would you live? A million dollars just doesn't go as far as it used to."

I toss my napkin at her, but I'm smiling as I do it.

The bartender comes over and Jamie orders another martini. I go with a sparkling water.

"You have no sense of adventure," she says.

I think about the rather adventurous things Damien and I have done together and bite back a very self-satisfied smile.

"So when do you get the money?" she asks.

"It's already mine. But I need to tell Damien where to transfer it."

"Uh, yeah," Jamie says.

I shrug. The truth is, I'm oddly hesitant to invest it. There's so much riding on that money, and after seeing how my mother's horrible investments went spiraling down the drain, I'm nervous about making my own choices. Of course, Mother's failure was about her craptastic running of the family business and her ridiculous over-the-top spending habits, but knowing that I am not my mother and believing that I am not my mother are two entirely different things.

"I've been talking with brokers," I say, which is sort of true. I've talked with two receptionists to make appointments to talk with brokers. From the way Jamie eyes me, I'm pretty sure she's cluing in to my deception. "And enough about the money," I say, as the bartender returns with our drinks. I lift my water. "To you. Today a commercial, tomorrow an Oscar."

"I'll drink to that."

"You'll drink to anything."

"True," she says, and polishes off half the martini. "Would you have believed it?" she asks.

I don't know what she means. "Believe what?"

"When we were in high school and you were doing all those damned Miss Corner Gas Station pageants and I was auditioning for community theater. Would you have believed we'd be in Los Angeles and I'd have a commercial and you'd be on the cusp of starting your own business? Not to mention lassoing the town's most eligible bachelor."

"No," I say. "I never would have believed it."

"So this is for both of us," Jamie says as she holds out her fist, waiting for me to bump it. I do eagerly. "For two Texas girls who moved to LA on their own, we're not doing half bad."

Since Jamie walked to the bar, I drive us both back to the condo. It takes longer than I anticipate since my Honda keeps stalling out at the lights.

"Face it, Nik," Jamie says. "You can't do LA in this car."

I'm afraid she's right, but the truth is bittersweet. The car is the first thing I bought on my own. I'm proud of what it represents, and I can't help but feel a little bit superstitious about the fact that she's starting to die right now when I'm starting to take off.

"I'll take her in for a tune-up soon," I decide. "It's probably just something like spark plugs or a gunked up carburetor."

"Do you even know what a carburetor is?"

"No," I admit. "But presumably the mechanic does."

"Open your eyes and observe the reality, Nik. She's been a

great little car, but she's going to stall out on the highway one day, and you're going to be the lead story on the eleven o'clock news. 'Billionaire's girlfriend squashed like a bug in fifteen-car pileup.' Don't say I didn't warn you."

I roll my eyes, but I don't argue. The truth is, she may have a point.

"Speaking of the billionaire boyfriend," Jamie continues, "who all's coming to the party tomorrow? I'll finally get to meet Evelyn, right?"

"Oh, yeah," I say. "And Blaine, of course. And you and me. We're the only ones who know it's me on that wall, so we're keeping it intimate—"

Jamie interrupts me with a snort, and I curse my choice of words.

"We're keeping it small," I begin again, "until eight. That's when the regular guests arrive to see all of Blaine's paintings and do the mingling thing."

"Cool. And Ollie?" She says it casually, and I can't tell if she's just making conversation or if there's still something going on between the two of them. I know I should simply ask, but I can't bring myself to do it.

"He's not coming," I say.

"Not for the first part," she clarifies. "I know you never told him about the painting." She eyes me sideways. "Did you?"

"No," I say firmly.

"I was wondering if he was coming to the rest of it. The showing, or whatever you want to call it."

"I'm still calling it a cocktail party," I say as I pull the car into my assigned parking space. "And no, he's not coming. I think he and Courtney have plans," I add, referring to Ollie's fiancée. I feel guilty about the lie, but I don't want to tell Jamie that Damien refused to invite Ollie to his home. It bothers me that

Damien and one of my best friends don't get along, but I get where Damien's coming from.

Though they'd started out sniffing around each other like two alpha dogs, they'd ultimately forged a tentative truce. But that came to an abrupt end when Ollie told me some of Damien's secrets—and breached the attorney-client privilege by doing so. Damien understands that Ollie thought he was protecting me, and that's probably the only reason that Ollie is still a lawyer and still working in this town. Or on this continent, for that matter.

But Damien doesn't want him in the house, and I can't say that I blame him. I hope they find a way to get along, because I need both these men in my life. But it's only been about a week since all the shit went down, and things are just too raw between them.

Jamie, however, knows none of that, and I don't plan to tell her. But that's one more wedge between us, even if I'm the only one who realizes it's there.

Soon we're at the door and I'm fumbling for my house key. I slide it into the lock and push open the door—then stop dead on the threshold.

"Holy fuck," Jamie says, looking over my shoulder.

I don't say anything. Jamie has pretty much said it all.

There, in the middle of our living room, is the bed. *The bed.* The beautiful iron bed beside which I'd posed. The stunning bed upon which Damien so thoroughly fucked me last night, and so many nights before that.

I realize we're both standing frozen and take a step into the room. There's a dress bag from Fred's on the bed with a note pinned to the plastic. I only have to glance at the handwriting on the envelope to feel my body tighten with anticipation. Slowly, I pull the folded slip of paper from the envelope, then unfold it and read:

I would appreciate it if you would do me the honor of
wearing this dress tomorrow, Ms. Fairchild. And then
perhaps you will do me the even greater honor of taking
it off.

I realize too late that Jamie is behind me, reading over my shoulder. "How did you get so lucky? The guy is seriously swoon-worthy."

"Totally," I agree, smiling.

She flops down on the bed while I unzip the garment bag, and then laugh. I'd fallen in love with the dress while we were shopping yesterday. It hits mid-thigh and is made out of dusty-blue chiffon. It's not fitted, but the pleated front and flowy design make it fun and flirty, and I cannot wait to put it on with my favorite pair of clunky silver sandals and a matching silver bangle.

I hold it up for Jamie to see. "What do you think?"

"I think you're going to look hotter than sin in that dress," she says. "Can I raid your closet? I'm bored out of my mind with my clothes."

"Jamie, you're a size four. I haven't been that small since I escaped from Mother and learned about the existence of that mysterious substance I like to call food."

She sighs and eyes my new dress lustfully. "I need my own billionaire boyfriend."

"I don't disagree," I say. "I find him a highly desirable accessory."

"Wanna go shopping?" Jamie asks. "I'm serious about my wardrobe crisis."

I glance at my phone. Still no word from Damien. "Sure," I say. "But give me a sec to change and feed the cat. And can we get some real dinner while we're out? Vodka isn't one of the major food groups."

"It's not?" Jamie retorts, displaying her stellar acting skills by putting real bafflement into her tone. She heads to her room as I go to the kitchen. Lady Meow-Meow appears the minute I pop the pull-top on her kitty food, and she head-butts the back of my leg until I finally put the food dish down in front of her.

I'm in my room stripping off my work clothes when Jamie calls to me. "How'd he get in the apartment?"

"Beats me," I say, though I can guess. He probably bribed the manager, who's just wacky enough to have been amused by the thought of a surprise bed delivery.

I change into one of the math T-shirts Jamie maligned earlier—*friends don't let friends derive drunk*—and a pair of jeans. It's the first time I've worn jeans since Blaine started the portrait, actually, and I hesitate before zipping them up, feeling a bit naughty. Like I'm breaking a rule.

I'm not, of course. The game's over. If I want to wear jeans, I can.

And if I want to go pantyless under a skirt? Well, I can do that, too.

I'm grinning as I leave my bedroom, but my mood shifts when I get back to the living room and the giant bed that overwhelms the space. I'd been so happy when I walked in and saw it there, as if I were being bathed in a flood of special memories.

Now that happiness is mixed with a tinge of some unpleasant emotion, though I'm not entirely sure what is troubling me.

I move to the bed and press my palm against the smooth round ball of the footboard. I'm thrilled that the bed wasn't shipped off to a warehouse somewhere or sold to an antiques store, but at the same time, I'm undeniably melancholy.

"It doesn't belong here," I say, when Jamie returns and asks me what's wrong.

"The bed?"

"It's supposed to be at the Malibu house. Not here," I repeat. "It feels like an ending somehow."

I remember the story Damien told me. About how he sacrificed a deal he was passionate about in order to save the tiny gourmet food producer. I didn't like the story then, and I like it even less now.

Jamie is silent for a moment as she stares intently at me. "Oh, shit, Nik," she finally says. "Don't even."

"What?"

"Don't go all Psych 101 on me. You're looking for all sorts of meanings that aren't there. You do this all the time."

"I do not."

"Well, maybe not all the time, but you did it with Milo."

"That was freshman year of high school."

"So maybe 'all the time' was a tiny exaggeration," she concedes. "My point is that you had a crush on him and he was a senior, remember?" I nod, because I remember it well. "And it was cold one day, and he lent you his letter jacket."

"And we spent a week trying to analyze what his underlying motivation was." Oh, yes. I remember.

"Turns out he was motivated by the fact that you were cold and he was nice."

"And your point?"

"Do you like the bed?" she asks.

"I love it," I admit.

"Does Damien know you love it?"

"Sure."

"So there you go. You like the bed. Damien likes you—understatement of the year, but there you have it. I'm sure that when you move in, you can take the bed back there with you."

"When I move in?" The idea is both terrifying and exciting.

"That's what you want, right? Not that I'm trying to kick you out, but a girl's gotta face reality."

Yes, I almost say, but then I close my mouth and start over. "It's too soon to even think about that."

"Shit, Nik. You want it. Own it."

"Fine," I say. "I want it. But leaping into things that we want isn't always the best course of action. Sometimes, a little thought and discretion make a lot of sense."

"This isn't about me," she says, totally catching on to the way I've shifted the subject.

I sigh. "Maybe it should be. You're not exactly one to be giving relationship advice."

"True. But you asked. So which one of us is the idiot here? Besides," she continues as I stifle a grin, "maybe I'm turning over a new leaf. Monogamy can be fun. I mean, I can't imagine getting tired of Raine." Her face turns dreamy. "Actually, after last night I don't think I can imagine Raine getting tired."

I laugh, but have to silently admit that I know the feeling.

"So I keep the bed?"

"Hell, yes, you keep the bed. For that matter, keep it in the living room for a day or so. Margarita sleepover tonight after shopping?"

"With movies?"

"Nothing sappy," she says. "I'm not in the mood to cry. Action. I want to see shit being blown up."

And right then, that sounds like a pretty damn perfect evening to me.

9

After stuffing our faces at Haru Sushi & Roll Cafe and emptying our wallets at the Beverly Center, Jamie and I settle in with a blender full of tequila, frozen limeade, and just a splash of Cointreau. We already had sake with dinner, and we're both tipsy enough to sing along with the Christmas-themed rap song at the beginning of *Die Hard*.

We're right at the point when Bruce Willis is making fists with his toes in the bathroom when Jamie's phone rings. She glances at it, then squeals and jumps off the bed before running to her room for privacy.

Bryan Raine, I presume.

I debate continuing with the movie—for all I know, she's going to stay on the phone with him all night—when my own phone rings. I don't bother looking at the screen; I just tap the button on my headset and answer the call. "Damien?"

"Are you okay?"

It takes me a minute to realize what he's talking about. The paparazzi. "How is it you know every little thing that happens to me? Did you task a satellite? Are there tiny transmitters hidden in the clothes you've bought me?"

"Every person in the world with a smartphone and a social media account saw pictures of you today," he says. "And, frankly, I like the satellite idea. I'll get my aerospace division to look into that."

"Great."

"I asked you a question, Nikki. Are you okay?"

I want to snap at him for not giving me credit for taking care of myself, but the worry in his voice is genuine. So I say simply, "Yes. I'm fine."

"They mentioned Ashley." His voice is as gentle as I ever heard it, and it is that tone as much as the mention of my sister that brings tears to my eyes.

"I know what you're thinking, but it wouldn't have mattered," I say. "No one was around the building when I arrived. They came later. Even if Edward had driven me, he would have been long gone by then."

"We'll talk about it later," he says, and though I know I should argue, I'm happy to shove the topic off into some future neverland. "Tell me about the rest of your day," he says.

"Do I have to?"

"Not good?"

I consider the question. "Not bad, but I spent most of the day with this guy on my team named Tanner who turned out to be a backbiting little prick. Jamie thinks he's the one who called the paparazzi."

"And made a few suggestions about corporate espionage?" I'm surprised to hear amusement in Damien's voice. "I must say you're a most lovely spy."

"You're not pissed?"

"I'm livid," he says. "I don't take those kinds of accusations lightly. If your little prick initiated them, I'll find out."

"Oh. You sounded like you thought it was funny."

"The situation, no. I'm merely anticipating the joy of decimating whoever started a rumor like that. I will stand for a lot of things, but corporate espionage isn't one of them. And suggesting that my girlfriend is my spy makes it that much worse."

I swallow. I tease Damien about the extent of his empire all the time, but sometimes I forget just how wide a net he casts and just how much power he really has. He will find out who started that rumor, be it Tanner or someone else. And I do not doubt that he'll destroy them.

Like Ollie has said—Damien is dangerous. To his enemies, at least.

"This is not my first choice for a topic of conversation," he says.

"Nor mine," I say, relieved. "Tell me about your day."

"I'd rather hear what you're doing right now. Where are you?"

"On our bed," I say. "Thinking of you."

"Are you really? I can picture you," he says. "Lying back, hair on the pillow, your naked body stretched out on top of the duvet."

I can't help but laugh. "As much as I love the fantasy, jeans and a ratty T-shirt are closer to the truth. Jamie's in the other room. Which reminds me—where are you? You're not still in Palm Springs, are you?"

"The day was interminable. I'm in the limo now, getting close to LA. I'm going to send a driver to pick you up. I want you home when I get there." The heat from his voice is enough to melt me, and I make a little sighing noise as I lie back with my eyes closed and let the whiskey-smooth words wash over me.

"I want you in bed," he continues. "I want you naked."

My smile is lopsided and a little drunk. "But the bed's here,"

I remind him. I roll over and stretch my arm out across it, pretending that I'm reaching for Damien.

"The apartment," he says. "The security desk will give you the codes to get inside. Naked, Nikki. Leave your clothes in a pile by the door so I can see them when I get home. I want to know you're inside and that you're wet and that you're waiting for me."

My lips are parted, and my breathing is shallow. Little shivers of electricity race across my skin, and I close my eyes, lost to the power of his words.

"There's wine in the fridge. Pour yourself a glass and sip it. Take it to the living room. You'll be thinking of me, Nikki, alone in my house. Alone in all those places I've fucked you. You'll lie down on the couch with your wine beside you. One hand on the glass, one hand on your breast. Maybe a dab of wine on your fingertips as your hand drifts lazily over your body. You'll be thinking of me, won't you, baby?"

"Yes." I can barely speak.

"Your breasts. Your nipples. The insides of your thighs. I want you wet for me, baby. A little drunk and a whole lot wet."

"Damien." I barely breathe his name. His words have gone to my head like the wine he wants me to drink—like the margaritas I already have drunk. My teeth graze over my lower lip, and I realize that I'm making small, gyrating movements with my hips, the pressure of the seam of my jeans against my throbbing sex taking me so very, very close.

"Do you understand?" he asks.

"Mmm."

"And when you get my text that I'm pulling in to the garage, I want you to go in the bedroom and lie facedown on the bed. Then spread your legs. I'll be there soon, and when I step into the bedroom the first thing I want to see is you wide open and wet for me. I've missed you today, Nikki," he adds, his voice a low, demanding growl. "I need to touch you. I want my hand on your cunt when you come, and I want to hold you tight as you tremble in my arms. Mostly, I want to hear you scream my name."

I can't help myself—I moan aloud.

"What?" Jamie calls from her bedroom. Her voice fills the apartment. And completely erases the sensual haze to which I have succumbed.

I sit up, my head throbbing with both the motion and the realization that I was very close to getting off with my best friend in the next room.

"Nothing," I shout to her. "I'm just talking to Damien."

"Sorry, what?" she says, poking her head out of the door. "I'm off the phone. Ready to start the movie again?"

"I—" I hesitate, drawing in a deep breath. I'm still limp and tingly simply from Damien's words, and I want nothing more than his touch. But I've seen so little of Jamie lately, and now we're in the middle of a girls' night and—

I draw in a breath. "Hang on," I tell Jamie. "I'm on the phone."

"Oh. Sorry." She disappears into the kitchen.

"You still there?" I say into the phone.

"Always."

"Listen, what you just said, it sounds wonderful—"

"I'm very glad you think so."

"But I can't. Not tonight."

There is silence.

"Damien? You there?"

"I'm here." I can tell nothing from his tone.

"It's just that Jamie and I are doing a girls' night, and—"

"It's okay," he says, and this time I hear the emotion in his voice. There is regret, yes. But I think there is also understanding. "I'm disappointed."

"Me, too," I say. "You going to survive without me?" I add, trying to add some lightness.

"It will be hard," he says, "but it's probably for the best."

"Thanks a lot," I say, and laugh.

"I have a stack of reports I need to get through this weekend. If I can get through them tonight, then Saturday and Sunday are yours."

"In that case, I have no guilt whatsoever. Go forth and review, buy, trade, or barter. Whatever it is you do to keep the Damien Stark universe from collapsing."

"I'll get right on that," he says evenly. "And I'll see you tomorrow. You can tell me all about your first day then."

"Okay."

"Until then," he whispers, "think of me, touching you."

"I always do," I say, before we end the call.

I'm grinning as I toss my phone down beside me on the bed, and when I turn and see Jamie come back from the kitchen with a bag of chips and a bowl of salsa, I can't help but smile even wider. "How can you even think about eating more? I'm stuffed."

"Like anyone could be too full for chips." She crawls back onto the bed and nods at the phone. "Did he want you to come over tonight?"

"He wanted me at the apartment when he got home from the desert," I say. And, yeah, I'm still smiling. I may not be going, but the thought is still nice.

"Seriously?" Jamie leans over and feels my forehead.

I shrug away. "What are you doing?"

"Checking for fever. Are you ill? I thought that all Damien had to do was crook his finger and you'd come."

"I told him we were hanging out tonight," I say. And then, because I just can't resist, I add, "And for the record, you're right. He crooks his finger, and I most definitely come."

Jamie rocks with laughter, and after another slug of margarita, I join in. We settle back against the pillows and watch as Alan Rickman joins the party. Soon Bruce is kicking butt and taking names and we're glued to the screen. Since this is Jamie's favorite classic action flick, I've seen it at least a dozen times, but I still jump when Rickman kills the boss.

Naturally, that's when my phone rings again.

It's Ollie.

"Hey," I say. "What's up?"

"Are you with Stark?"

It's an innocent enough question, I suppose, but I stiffen anyway. "No. Why?"

He sighs, and I realize he heard the terseness in my voice. "I just didn't want to interrupt. Swear to God."

"Sorry. No, I'm at home."

"Yeah? That's cool. So would you be up for getting a drink?"

"Now?" The truth is, there was a time when I wouldn't have hesitated. So what that I'm supposed to be in the middle of a girls' night in? Ollie could totally come over and join the movie marathon, or we could all go out and get plastered.

But things have shifted so much between us that instead of being psyched to hang with him, I'm wary. And that saddens me. Lately, every time I see Ollie, bits of my life come crashing down around my ears. And I do not want another piece to get chipped away if I can help it.

Still, this is Ollie talking, and I'm not ready to give up on us. "Do you want to just hang?" I ask. "Or is there something you want to talk about?"

He's silent for a moment, and I know he's also aware of the storm clouds between us. We know each other too well. "Both," he finally admits. "Oh, hell, Nikki. This is bullshit, and you know it, too."

I do know it, but I'm not inclined to admit it. "What is?" I say.

"Charles mentioned the party at Stark's tomorrow," he says,

referring to Charles Maynard, his boss and the attorney who's represented Damien for over a decade. "He just assumed I was invited, too, what with me and you being me and you." He's trying to be matter-of-fact, but I hear the hurt in his voice.

"Ollie—"

Beside me, Jamie shifts her attention from her iPhone to me. Apparently this one-sided conversation is more interesting than clearing out her junk email.

"I think this is the first time you've thrown a party that I wasn't invited to," Ollie says.

"I'm not the one throwing it," I say, but the words are hollow despite their truth. If I'd asked, Damien would have let Ollie come to the party. If it was important to me, I am certain that he would have pushed his disdain aside.

But I hadn't asked, because I understood why Damien didn't want Ollie there. I'd chosen the man in my bed over my lifelong friend, and I do not regret the decision.

He sighs. "It's just—look, I'm sorry, okay? I get that you're with the guy. And, yeah, I have my issues with him, but if this means that we can't be friends anymore . . ."

He trails off, and I squeeze my eyes closed tight. "I don't want to screw up our friendship, either," I finally say, and then I let the thought hang. As far as I'm concerned, Ollie's the one who's built the wall. He can damn well be the one who starts tearing it down.

"So how about it?" he asks. "Let's go get a drink. Hang out. Make up dialogue for the people at the next table."

I smile despite myself. When I was in college and Ollie was in law school, that was our favorite form of cheap amusement. We'd go to Magnolia Cafe or Z'Tejas in Austin and watch people at the other tables. How they moved, how they interacted. And then we'd write their dialogue, turning friends into lovers, crafting arguments, and professing profound love. We never sat close enough to find out what the people were really saying. This was all about the make-believe.

"Tonight's kind of hard," I say, glancing at Jamie. "But hold on a second."

I hit the mute button on the phone and look at Jamie. "What do you think? Want to make tonight a threesome?"

"I'm not really into that kind of kink."

I roll my eyes. "Seriously, Ollie wants to go out for drinks."

"With both of us?" I can hear the disbelief in her voice.

"He only invited me, but if you two can't play nice together then you shouldn't have jumped into bed in the first place. Seriously, James. You need to get past this."

She tosses her hands up in surrender. "Hey, fair enough. But I'm not the only one being weird. You haven't been in the pro-Ollie camp lately, either."

"So maybe we all three need to have an intervention. Go out. Have fun. Pretend like things are back the way they used to be."

I think she hesitates, but it may only be my imagination. "So Courtney's not coming?" she asks, referring to Ollie's fiancée.

"He didn't say. I'm guessing not. She's probably traveling this week. So what do you think?"

"Yeah, sure," she says. "But not drinks."

"Jamie, if you don't want—"

"No, no," she interrupts. "I do. And tonight's fine. I just mean that you and I already have plans later, anyway. Ollie can tag along."

"What plans?" This is totally news to me.

"Raine invited us to a party at The Rooftop and Garreth Todd is going to be there."

"Who's Garreth Todd?" I ask.

"He, my clueless friend, is the hottest thing in Hollywood right now. And we're going to meet him."

"Alan Rickman or Sean Connery, I'd be excited. Garreth Todd, not so much."

"Well, you're going anyway. This is our night to have fun, remember?"

I glance at the television. I was totally looking forward to the airplane version of *Die Hard* next, but I have to admit it does sound like fun. I've never been to a Hollywood party, and just because I haven't got a clue who the latest stars are doesn't mean that the glitz and glam won't be a hoot. Then again, stars mean paparazzi, and that sounds decidedly less fun.

"Won't the press be there? I'm really not in the mood to deal with them."

"Nah, Raine explained how it works. They'll be hanging around the entrance probably, but since they don't expect you, just wear a hat and keep your head down. Ollie and I can flank you. It's totally no big. And once we're at the party, the only photographers are part of Garreth's PR corp. So it'll be a vulture-free night. Swear to God."

My phone rings, and I realize it's Ollie, who apparently decided he'd been on hold for long enough and hung up. "Sorry," I say, then explain the whole Garreth Todd–Hollywood party thing. Unlike me, he doesn't live in a cultural bubble, and he knows exactly who Garreth is, and he's keen to do the party thing. As it turns out, I'm right about Courtney, but wrong about the reason. I'd assumed she was away on business, but Ollie tells me that she's flown to San Francisco to look at wedding dresses with her mother.

He says he'll be over in less than an hour, and we'll all go together. And even though I'm a little nervous about the three of us hanging together for the first time since Jamie and Ollie screwed around, I'm also looking forward to it. These two are my best friends, after all. And, yeah, I miss them.

I pick up my phone to call Damien and tell him I've had a

change of plans. If he's not deep into work stuff already, maybe he can even join us. But my finger hesitates over his name. Damien doesn't want to spend time with Ollie. For that matter, while he was fine with me hanging with Jamie, I have a feeling he'd be less than thrilled if Ollie had been part of that mix. And besides, nothing of what I told him has changed—I *am* still with Jamie. We've just added another person, too.

I drop my phone back onto the bed, then get up and head to my room to find an outfit for tonight. The glow I was feeling earlier, however, has faded a bit, and that frustrates me.

I'm not doing anything wrong. So why do I feel so guilty?

A woman wearing nothing but a bikini and down-covered wings brushes by me carrying a tray of rainbow-colored champagne. As far as I can tell, the champagne has been dyed to match the pool, which is changing color every thirty seconds as the lights rotate through the spectrum.

If I had been held at gunpoint and forced to come up with the most ostentatious Hollywood party imaginable, I do not think I could have conjured anything even close to what now sur-rounds me. The waiters and waitresses wear tiny gold bathing suits that leave nothing to the imagination and decorative wings that make it difficult to maneuver through the crowd. We are on the roof of one of downtown Los Angeles's tallest buildings, and I can only presume the unstated message is that we, the guests, hold such a prominent spot in heaven that the angels themselves must serve us.

Jamie bounces up to me and presses a glass of bright red champagne into my hand. She's wearing an extremely short red skirt paired with a black lace blouse over a red bra. As always, she looks amazing. I'm wearing a black sarong skirt and match-ing black tank, the only color provided by a pink scarf that I have draped around my neck. Considering the outfits that I see walking past us, on the whole Jamie is dressed at least as conservatively as I am.

"Amazing, isn't it?" she asks.

"It's exactly what I would expect a Hollywood party to be," I say dryly. Beside me, Ollie barks out a laugh, and Jamie scowls at us both.

"Don't be cynical," she says. "From what Raine tells me, this is one of the parties of the summer, and it's incredibly exclusive." She gestures vaguely in the direction she came from. "Steve said he's been finagling to get an invite for months."

"Steve's here?" I rise up on my toes and search the crowd. "What about Anderson?" Steve is the first person Jamie met after she skipped out on me during our college years and moved to Los Angeles to find fame, fortune, and near starvation as an actress. I met him during my many pre-graduation visits, but I haven't seen him since I actually moved here.

"He's here, too. I told them we're by the pods," Jamie says, referring to the odd, red waterbed pods near where we're standing. "They're making the circuit."

This doesn't surprise me. Steve is a working screenwriter despite the fact that he's never seen one of his movies produced. According to Jamie this is not an unusual thing in Hollywood. His husband, Anderson, sells real estate. I adore Steve, but unless he takes pity on me and talks classic movies, my eyes glaze over ten minutes into the conversation. But I can always find something interesting to say about houses.

"This really is ostentatious as hell," Ollie says, "but it's also pretty damn cool. I mean, look at this place."

I have to agree that the venue is amazing. It's a clear night, and we seem to be floating among the skyscrapers. I can see the mountains in the distance, looming black dotted with pinpoints of light against a pencil-gray sky. From a booth on the other side of the roof, a DJ is providing danceable music, and many of the guests are taking advantage of the huge dance floor. Drinks are provided by the roaming angels, but can also be had at the poolside bar. And, lest we forget this is a Hollywood party, a series of clips from various films—presumably starring Garreth Todd—are being projected onto a two-story tall screen.

"Okay," I say. "Y'all win. It's pretty cool." I take a long drink and finish off my champagne, because I am here tonight to have fun with my friends. "So where is your guy?" I ask, which prompts Jamie to crane her neck and look around.

"Unless he fell off the roof, he's here somewhere. Let's wait here for Steve and Anderson, then we can go make the circle and find him."

"So are you getting serious about this guy?" Ollie asks her. "I mean, after a guy like me, it's hard to imagine you could want anyone else."

He is clearly teasing, but underneath I think I hear a hint of wounded pride. I hope that I'm imagining it. For his sake, for Jamie's sake, and mostly for Courtney's.

"Yeah," Jamie says, a slow smile blooming. "Emphasis on the 'getting.' We're not there yet. But, well, yeah."

"Good," Ollie says curtly.

I frown, trying to think of something pithy and cutting to say, but nothing comes to mind.

"Now, if you want to talk serious . . ." Jamie trails off, her eyes on me, her eyebrows waggling mischievously.

I smile innocently. "A lady never tells."

"It's too damn soon," Ollie says shortly. "And—" He cuts himself off.

"What?" I snap.

"The whole thing just worries me. *Stark* worries me."

"Jesus H. Christ," Jamie blurts out. "Don't you ever give it a rest?"

I'm grateful for Jamie's interference. I'd thought that the

Ollie-Damien war would be off the table tonight after my talk with Ollie earlier, but apparently two glasses of green champagne have loosened his tongue.

"That's why I love her," Ollie says, hooking an arm around Jamie. "She tells it like it is and doesn't take my shit."

"And what?" I ask. "Courtney doesn't tell you when you're being a prick?" It is bad form for me to play the Courtney card right now, and I know it. But I'm pissed. Besides, I'm supposed to be Ollie's best man at his upcoming wedding, and although I've never actually been a best man before, I'm pretty sure that one of the jobs is smacking down the groom when he crosses the line into being an asshole.

"No," Ollie says seriously. "She doesn't." He bends down and sits on the edge of the water-filled mattress inside the pod. His body shifts and rolls, and he reaches out and grabs the red molded plastic that forms part of the pod's arching roof. "She just waits until all the shit has built up and then she breaks up with me."

I sit down next to him, ignoring the way our seat sloshes beneath us. "I thought you weren't going to let any more shit build up." Ollie and Courtney have been on-again, off-again for years. This is the first time they've made it all the way to an official engagement. I really like Courtney, and I hope it works out. But the more time that goes by, the more I'm afraid that Ollie's going to fuck it up yet again. Or, to be more accurate, that he already has fucked it up.

"I'm like Pigpen," Ollie says. "Shit just follows me around. Not all of us lead the charmed life of a certain billionaire we know."

"Dammit, Ollie!"

He holds his hands up in surrender. "Sorry, sorry, I'm a total prick."

"Yes," I agree. "You are." I suck in a breath. "Look, I'm

sorry you have a problem with Damien, but he's important to me. And if I'm important to you, then you need to figure out a way to deal with that."

"That's the point," Ollie says. "You *are* important to me. And I can deal with Stark. I can even ignore all the shit on him I could dig up in just one hour in the Bender, Twain file room," he adds, referring to the law firm where he works. "It's not the man that's the problem—well, not the big problem. It's what's around him."

"What are you talking about?"

"Come on, Nikki, you practically disguised yourself to come here tonight," he says, referring to the hat that I'd worn, just as Jamie suggested. "Do you want that life? Hell, can you handle it?" he adds, then brushes his hand lightly across my thigh before twining his fingers in mine. "I just worry about you is all."

My throat is thick, and I look down, not quite willing to meet his eyes. I know his concern for me is genuine—Ollie has seen my scars, and he has seen me break, too. More important, he's helped put the pieces of me back together.

"Damien's worried about the same thing," I admit quietly. "But I can stand it," I add, looking up so that I can see his eyes. "I am standing it, and I want to, because Damien is worth it."

His shoulders droop. "Who would have thought I'd have something in common with Damien Stark?"

I laugh out loud, and Ollie grins.

"Seriously," he says. "I may have my issues with Stark, but I also know he cares about you."

"He does," I say. I'm about to add that I know that Ollie cares for me, too, but my words are stalled by the arrival of Steve and Anderson accompanied by two absolutely gorgeous men.

"Thank God," Jamie says. "You guys have perfect timing."

Since I am desperate for a change in subject, I agree wholeheartedly, and allow myself to be hugged and air-kissed and complimented by Steve and Anderson while Ollie shakes their hands and otherwise looks grim. I recognize the guy who has swooped Jamie into his arms as Bryan Raine, and it doesn't take a huge mental stretch to identify the final member of my rescue party as Garreth Todd. After all, his face has been splashed on the movie screen all evening.

"Well, hello," he says, stepping into my personal space. "I don't think we've met."

"Nikki," I say, my mask firmly back in place. I am no longer in a party mood, and right then all I want is to run through the social niceties and get the hell out of here.

"I hope you're having fun," he says, moving even closer. I take a step back, and find myself bumping against Ollie. He puts a steadying hand on my shoulder, and that simple touch makes me want to cry. That's the way it used to be—Ollie reaching out to steady me whenever I felt I might shatter.

"We were going for a celestial theme," Todd says. "Get it?"

"It's very colorful," I say.

"It doesn't even come close to sparkling the way you do," he says. He's only inches from me, and I'm sandwiched between him and Ollie. It occurs to me that if Damien said those words to me, I would probably melt. From Garreth, however, they only irritate.

I hope that Jamie will intervene, but she is lost in her Raine storm, and will not be rescuing me anytime soon. I'm on my own, and I know only one surefire way of regaining my personal space. "You have me at a disadvantage, sugar," I say, with my brightest smile and my thickest Texas drawl. "You know my name, but I don't have even a teensy, tiny clue as to yours."

"Oh." He takes a step back, presumably allowing his hyperventilating ego to get some air. "I'm Garreth Todd."

"Very nice to meet you. And what is it you do?"

Behind me, Ollie shifts, and I can tell that he is going to

explode with laughter. Jamie, thank goodness, isn't paying attention. "I thought we were going to dance," Ollie says, curling his fingers around mine.

"Of course," I say, as he tugs me away. "So nice chatting with you, Mr. Todd."

"You just dissed a movie star," Ollie says as he pulls me onto the dance floor.

"Oh?" I say innocently, then bat my eyes for effect. "Was he a movie star?"

Ollie ignores my silliness. "Jamie is going to kill you."

"I know," I say. As far as Jamie is concerned, anyone who can help her climb the ladder must be treated with the utmost deference. "You have to admit he deserved it."

"I admit nothing," Ollie says, but he's smiling. "So we're here. Are we going to dance?"

It's either that or head home, and right then I'm basking in the detente between Ollie and me. "Sure," I say, then follow him onto the floor and let the music take over. It's loud and heavy on the bass and just what I need to get my mind off everything. Still, I can't help but wish that the song was slow and it was Damien on the floor with me instead of Ollie.

The wish is so fervent, in fact, that my imagination conjures the man. His tall form, cutting through the crowd. His mouth a hard line, his face expressionless, his eyes like a storm at sea. It is only when all eyes turn toward him, drawn in by the pull of Damien Stark, that I realize this is the real Damien striding through the wash of colored lights—and heading straight toward Ollie and me.

10

"Go," Damien says to Ollie, his voice colder and more commanding than I have ever heard it.

I see my friend open his mouth as if to argue, but I catch his eye and nod. He frowns, then shoots Damien a look so full of disdain it makes my stomach curl. Damien doesn't notice. He's paid Ollie only scant attention, and his eyes have never left my face.

"Damien," I begin.

"No," he says. He pulls me roughly to him and wraps his arms around me. He practically trembles with anger, and I press my cheek against his chest, thankful to have this brief reprieve before the storm hits.

The music is still loud and fast with such a heavy bass that the roof beneath our feet seems to throb. I imagine we must look ridiculous, holding each other as if in a slow dance, but I don't care. And soon, to my surprise, the music changes to match our pose. I glance up, curious, and see that a small crowd has gathered around us. Damien Stark is at least as famous as Garreth Todd, and we have stolen Mr. Todd's spotlight.

I can only presume that the DJ is among the spectators, and has decided to match the music to our mood.

Since we do nothing more than sway in each other's arms, interest soon wanes. The crowd either drifts away or joins us on the floor, and I begin to feel less like a fish in a bowl. A chastised fish, ready to be scolded.

He holds me through one song and then another, and though I am happy to spend my entire life inside the circle of his arms, I have reached the point where I can no longer stand the suspense. "Say something," I plead.

He stays silent, and a cold dread curls through me. I am about to beg again when he speaks, so low and so gentle that I have to strain to hear him, and even then I am not sure that I have actually caught his words.

"I'm sorry."

"You're—what?" I step back so that I can see his face, because I am certain that I have not heard right.

"I'm sorry," he repeats. We have stopped swaying and now we stand still on the dance floor.

"Is this some sort of reverse psychology? Because I know you pretty well, Damien Stark, and that wasn't repentance I saw in your eyes when you crashed through the crowd. More like scary megalomaniac fury. Besides," I add with a small grimace, "I'm the one who's sorry."

Damien's expression doesn't change, but for the tiniest of instants, I think I see a flicker of amusement. "First off," he says, "I didn't crash through the crowd. I walked, and quite calmly, too, considering the circumstances."

I swallow. I knew he was pissed.

"Second," he continues, "I believe a megalomaniac is someone who suffers from delusions about their own power. Trust me," he says, and this time I am certain I see mirth dancing in his eyes, "I suffer no delusions about the extent of my power. And finally, you may have reason to be sorry. I, however, have more."

"I—oh." I have no idea what to say. This conversation isn't going at all the way I expected. But he's right; I do have reason to be sorry. "I should have told you that Jamie and I were going out with Ollie."

"So you knew at the time?"

"No. Raine called later and told Jamie about the party. Then Ollie called and ended up coming along. I actually picked up the phone to call you. But then I didn't," I finish with a shrug.

"Because you knew I'd be pissed."

I nod. "And that's why I'm sorry."

"Then we have that in common."

I watch his face silently, waiting for him to explain.

"I don't want to be the asshole who keeps you away from your friends," he says. "And I don't want you to feel like you have to keep things from me in order to see them. And I'm sorry because you obviously felt exactly that way."

Polite Nikki starts to protest, but what he's saying is the truth. Slowly, I nod.

"I won't keep you from your friends, Nikki. But dammit, I don't like the son of a bitch."

This is not exactly breaking news, but I still take a moment to consider how to respond. "I get that," I say. "He hasn't exactly earned your trust. But I've known him forever, and he's one of my closest friends."

"He's seen you naked, Nikki. He's touched your scars."

I blink at him. Surely he's not— "Are you jealous?" The possibility shocks me. I've already told Damien that Ollie and I never slept together. It was never like that between us.

"Hell, yes, I'm jealous. I'm jealous of anyone who comforts you. Who pulls you into his arms and makes the hurt go away."

"I didn't even know you back then," I whisper.

"And I'm jealous of the time that he's had with you that I haven't."

"You're not being fair."

"I'm not being fair at all. But that doesn't change the facts. You're not just friends. You haven't been for a long time. At least not since he got you through the hell with that asshole Kurt." I close my eyes, remembering the boy who'd hurt me so badly years ago that I'd needed Ollie to help me pick up the pieces. "Ollie's in love with you, Nikki. It's the one thing I do respect him for," Damien continues. "He has excellent taste in women."

These are not things that I want to hear. Ollie has only ever been my friend, albeit an extremely close one, at least until recently. I don't like the way things are changing, and I don't want to hear what Damien is saying.

Mostly, I don't want to suddenly realize that I've been foolishly, stupidly blind.

I think of Courtney and feel a little sick. "He's engaged, Damien," I say, but the words are weak, and I cannot help but see Jamie in my mind. Fidelity is not one of Ollie's strong suits.

"I know he is," Damien says. "And maybe he loves his fiancée, I don't know. But I do know that he loves you. And one of these days, that's going to cause a very big problem between him and me."

I manage a weak smile. "Don't go all Wild West on me. Though with all your money, I guess it would be more Stark Manor than O.K. Corral, and a duel instead of a gunfight. But be careful, Damien. Ollie grew up in Texas. He's a good shot."

"I'm a better one," Damien says, and there's none of my light teasing in his voice.

"I really am glad you're here."

"As am I. It's good to hold you. This entire day has been chal-lenging."

I wince, thinking of the paparazzi that accosted me outside of the office and those bullshit allegations of corporate espionage. "Sorry."

He gently strokes my cheek. "No," he says. "Not you. But there are things." He sighs, and I am surprised at the exaspera-tion I hear. "Tapestries that I've woven carefully over the years are starting to unravel. I don't like it when things don't go as I plan or expect." He aims a small smile at me. "You may not have noticed it about me, but I am most comfortable when I am in control."

"I'm shocked, Mr. Stark. Truly shocked."

He ignores my sarcasm, and when he speaks, his voice is low and even. "Actually, I suppose you do fall within those parame-ters. I wanted you at home. You said no. I didn't like it."

I step close to him and slide my hands around his waist. "I suppose if it bothers you that much, you can simply tie me up and keep me permanently at your side."

I can feel the way his body stiffens against mine, and I am glad I'm holding on to him. My own knees are weak. How sim-ple it is to slip into passion with Damien. Even when we quarrel, we're never far away from the fire, and it's so easy to get pulled into the conflagration.

And always, always, there is the need to touch him, to feel him, to know that he is real and that he is mine.

"Why, Ms. Fairchild," he says, "I believe you're thinking naughty thoughts."

"Very," I confirm.

"I may have to take you up on your suggestion," he says. He tugs on the end of my pink scarf. I feel the smooth brush of the material as it slides over my skin. "Tie you up," he says, twisting the end of the scarf around one wrist. "Keep you close." He gives the scarf a tight, quick jerk, and I stumble toward him. He catches me so that I don't fall, and bends down so that his lips are close to my ear. "But first, I think you need to be very thoroughly spanked."

I tilt my head so that he can see my eyes. "I'd rather be thoroughly fucked."

He groans, and I know that I have won this round. "Oh, God, Nikki. What you do to me."

"No," I say, my entire body on fire. "What *you* do to *me*. And please, Damien, do it soon."

"We're leaving," he says, and I can only nod mutely.

"Where are we going?" I ask, as we take the elevator down. There are two other couples in the car with us, and only the tips of our fingers are touching. It is so intimate, though, that I feel like I'm naked before them.

"The apartment," he says curtly.

Thank God. If he wanted to go back all the way back to the Malibu house I was going to lose my mind. Even so, I'm not sure I can make it the few short blocks.

But then the elevator doors glide open and as soon as our companions step off in front of us, we are accosted by the flash of cameras, the press of microphones, and the overlapping queries of a dozen demanding voices.

Now I clutch Damien's hand and move closer to his side.

"Mr. Stark!"

"Damien!"

"Nikki, over here!"

"What can you say about your refusal to speak at the dedication of the Richter Tennis Center?"

"Can you explain your decision, Mr. Stark?"

I hold tight to Damien and keep my head down as we press forward toward the street. I assume at first that these are simply the same reporters and paparazzi that had been hovering about when we'd arrived. But then I see that in addition to the TMZ and E! reporters, there are vans from CNN and even the *Wall Street Journal*.

Apparently someone noticed Damien's arrival, and the word spread like wildfire.

I squeeze Damien's hand tighter, hoping he has a car nearby. It may only be a block to the apartment, but I do not want to walk it with these vultures following in our wake.

"What about the rumors out of Germany, Mr. Stark?" a voice calls, and Damien's hand tightens around mine as he leads us firmly and silently toward the valet stand.

"Nikki, is Damien Stark off the bachelor block?"

"Damien! How will the talk of a possible German indictment affect your holdings in the European Union?"

My mind is spinning. An indictment? I force myself not to look at Damien, and instead look forward, my face a mask of disinterest. There is no way—no way in hell—that I am letting these vultures see that I haven't a clue what they're talking about. Is Stark International in some kind of legal snafu? Is that what he meant by the tapestry unwinding?

"Nikki! Mr. Stark! Germany! Indictment!" The voices blend together into a hideous cacophony. "Richter! Dedication! Damien! Damien! Damien!"

Damien must have summoned Edward without me realizing because the limo pulls to a smooth stop in front of the valet stand, and Edward gets out.

"No," Damien says. "I've got it." As Edward gets back in behind the wheel, Damien tugs me forward, then opens the rear passenger door, his body shielding me from the blinding storm of lights and questions.

I'm just about to slide into the car when Damien pulls his hand from mine, then turns and faces the crowd. A hush falls.

Considering Damien's staunch policy of not talking to the press, I think the paparazzi are at least as shocked as I am.

"I will not be attending the dedication ceremony for the Richter Tennis Center," Damien says, in the firm clear voice he uses during business meetings. "While I fully support the construction and operation of such a center, I cannot in good conscience support its dedication honoring a man I don't respect. As for your other questions, neither Ms. Fairchild nor I have any comment."

Immediately, the air fills with mingled voices, each louder than the next, none discernible. They are shouting follow-up questions, shouting for Damien to turn for a picture, shouting for me to step away from the open limo door. Damien ignores them, turning to face me. I realize that I am still standing frozen, slightly bent midway in the motion of entering the limo.

And then, another voice rises above the noise, this time from the far side of the street.

"Damien Jeremiah Stark!"

I glance at Damien, but his hard expression reveals nothing. I straighten, then peer over the roof of the limo. The reporters have shifted the aim of their cameras, and now their lights are focused on an older man making his way across Flower Street.

"Get into the car," Damien snaps at me.

"We need to talk," the man calls out.

I stand frozen.

"Get in," Damien urges, his voice more gentle.

I comply, but I peer out the far window at the man, and then once more up at Damien. "Who is that?" I ask.

He meets my eyes, his jaw tight, his expression hard. "My father."

11

Damien slides in beside me and tugs the door closed. "Go," he says to Edward, who nods and starts to pull slowly out into the street. Reporters scramble to get in front of the car, taking pictures of the limo and of Damien's father, who is now pounding on the side window and yelling for Damien to stop.

I grab Damien's hand, then look left at the old man's face. "Damien," I say. "Let him in. If you don't, those reporters are going to eat him alive."

Silence.

"Damien," I say gently. "You need to find out why he's here."

Damien's face is tense, his breathing even, and I wish that I knew what he was thinking.

Finally, he squeezes my hand and nods. "Stop," he tells Edward. "Unlock the doors. And as soon as he's in, run those goddamned piranhas over if you have to."

A moment later the old man is inside the limo and Edward is pulling hard to the left and accelerating. I hold my breath, not really caring if a reporter gets squashed, but also not wanting Edward to get into trouble. Then we're clear and the limo is traveling smoothly down Flower Street. "Make the block," Damien says. He looks at his father, who's settled on the seat facing us. "What do you want?"

The old man ignores him, instead focusing on me. "You must be Nikki," he says. "I've seen your picture in the paper with my boy. I'm Jeremiah, but you can call me Jerry."

"What can we do for you, Mr. Stark?" I ask.

"We," he repeats, then looks between the two of us. "We," he says again, then actually guffaws.

I squeeze Damien's hand tighter. I didn't like this man before I met him, and I like him even less now.

"Ms. Fairchild asked you a question," Damien says. "What can we do for you?" I can sense the low bubble of anger rising off Damien, and I hold tight to his hand. I'm certain that this man sitting so casually across from me either abused his son or was complicit in it, and I'm not sure if I'm holding on to Damien to give him support—or to keep from leaping across the limo and slapping the old man's face.

Jerry shakes his head as if in defeat. "Damien," he says, then leaves the name hanging.

My initial impression of him is someone oily and untrustworthy, but as I look more closely, I realize that he's actually attractive, although a little too smooth. Like a man who discovered luxury late in life and has spent the rest of his time trying to play catch-up.

"I repeat," Damien says, "what can we do for you?"

Jerry leans back in his seat, and his face takes on an unattractive, calculating edge. I can see a bit of how this man managed, despite his low income and working-class background, to maneuver his son onto the international tennis circuit. "What can you do for me? What can you do for *me*? Not a goddamn thing now. But this ain't about me. It's about you. And you managed to fuck it up real good."

"Did I?" Damien asks coldly. "Let me explain the situation to you. You are in this car only because the lady insisted. If you want to earn the right to stay, then you speak, and you speak clearly. Otherwise, we are through."

"You want clarity? How's this: You're acting like a damn fool, Damien Stark, and I may be a lot of things, but I am not the father of a fool. You get your high-class PR people to put some sort of spin on that nonsense you just spouted. You write a speech that would make angels sing. And you get your ass to that dedication on Friday, and you smile that photogenic smile, and you write a big, fat check if you have to. Because you need to do this, son. You need to push it through. You need to be goddamn squeaky clean, damn you."

"Don't call me 'son.'"

"Goddammit, Damien!"

I watch the two men, trying to understand what is really going on here. Trying to intuit why Damien's refusal to attend the dedication and his very public announcement as to the reason means so much to the elder Stark. Damien did not outright say that Richter abused him, and he certainly didn't say that his father was involved. Is that what Jeremiah fears will come next? That once Damien spills one truth, the rest will come tumbling out? If, as I suspect, that truly is the rest.

I don't know, and all I can do is hold tight to Damien's hand.

Damien has not responded to the criticisms his father poured out. Instead, he has been staring at the elder man's face, his eyes narrowed as if the older man's features were some sort of equation with a missing variable.

When he finally speaks, I do not understand the context: "How much of this is your doing?"

"I don't know what you're talking about," Jerry says, sitting up straight, his eyes wide as a child getting chastised. Even I can see that he is lying.

"Let's get this straight," Damien says. "I am not interested in your opinion or your help. Now get out. Edward, pull over." We've circled three blocks, and now we're at Pershing Square, two full blocks from where we started.

"I'm not even parked near here."

"I don't care," Damien says. "Out."

Suddenly, Edward is outside pulling the door open. Jerry hesitates, then looks from Damien to me. "Does she know? I wouldn't tell her, Damien," he says, and there's malice in his voice. "If you want her to stay, I wouldn't tell her a thing."

He gets out, and Edward immediately slams the door, as if the driver wants him gone as much as Damien and I do.

Damien runs his hands through his hair and sighs. "I'm sorry," he says.

"So, you've met my mom and I've met your dad. I guess that means we're really dating." I'm shooting for a light moment here, but Damien's expression doesn't change. "Hey," I say. "It's okay."

"Very little about this entire day falls into the category of okay."

"Oh, I don't know," I say. "I rather enjoyed dancing with you."

"Yes," he says. "So did I. Come here." I am already right beside him, but I slide closer and lean against him. His arm is draped over my shoulder and his fingers are idly stroking my arm. I slide down and put my head on his lap. I kick off my shoes and curl my legs up on the seat as Damien strokes my hair. Part of me wants to stay like that forever, warm and safe in Damien's lap. But another part of me has questions—so many questions. I want to understand what Damien's father was talking about— why he cares so much whether or not Damien endorses the ten- nis center. But I don't want to ask—I want Damien to tell me because he wants me to know.

If you want her to stay, I wouldn't tell her a thing.

I shiver. I can think of nothing so horrible that I would walk away from Damien. But is that because nothing exists that is so bad it could rip us apart? Or do I simply lack the imagination to think of it?

Damien holds me calmly for the short drive to the Tower apartment.

He remains coolly collected as Edward pulls into the parking garage beneath Stark Tower.

His composure doesn't break during the ride either to the building lobby or from the lobby to the penthouse fifty-seven floors up that houses his private office on one side and his residential apartment on the other.

It is only once the doors to the apartment slide open and we have entered the residence that Damien's equilibrium shifts and the facade of calm vanishes. There is something desperate in his eyes, and he grabs both ends of the scarf that is still draped around my neck. "What was it you said about tying you up?"

His words are as rough as the anger that still clings to him. "Yes," I say, because I know he needs it. He needs to get lost in the passion that is always ready to burst between us. He needs to forget what just happened—the paparazzi, his father, Ollie, and even my own refusal to meet him here tonight.

He needs to do something about that tapestry of his that is coming undone.

He needs to be in complete control—and right then, I want nothing more than to surrender to him.

"Yes," I repeat, my voice raw. "Yes, please."

He uses the scarf to shift our position until my back is against the wall, and he is against me, and I am breathing hard, my body quickening with excitement and expectation. With one hand, he holds both ends of the scarf while the other hand strokes slowly down my body, over my breast, down my belly, over my hip. His touch is slow, the movements designed to make me melt. It's working. My lips are parted, my skin hot and sensitive. If I was not already leaning against a solid structure with Damien keeping me upright, I think I would sink to the floor, my body too limp and malleable to hold myself up.

He slips his hand inside my sarong skirt, his finger dipping under the string of my thong to find me wet.

I tremble, a small shiver rushing through me, as if a portent of an explosion to come.

"Why, Ms. Fairchild," he says, "I do believe you want me."

I bite my lower lip and say nothing; he doesn't need to hear my answer. He already knows he's right.

Slowly—so painfully slowly—he starts to peel me out of my clothing. The knot of the sarong. The tiny thong panties. The tank he tugs gently over my head. Even the scarf falls into a pile on the floor. I see it there, a lonely bit of pink in a sea of black, and I sigh.

"Trouble?"

"I thought you were going to tie me up."

"Maybe I changed my mind."

"Oh."

"Complaining, Ms. Fairchild?"

"Never with you, Mr. Stark."

"Good answer. For that, you get a reward." His expression takes on a dangerous edge. "Come with me."

I follow him to the bedroom, where he lays a blanket on the floor, then opens one of the leather trunks. He pulls out two lengths of rope and slowly twines them between his hands. I can feel my eyes go wide. We've moved a long way from soft pink scarves.

"What are you going to do?"

But Damien doesn't answer. He just nods at the floor and tells me to lie down. I hesitate only a moment, and then comply, my head near the foot of the bed and my body stretched out on the blanket.

"Hands above your head," he says.

I stretch my arms up, my excitement building along with my curiosity, and he uses the shorter length of rope to tie my wrists together. Then he fastens my bound hands to the center leg of his king-size bedframe.

"I'm going to please you, Nikki," he says, then strokes his fingertip slowly down my arm. He starts at my wrist, then gently teases the soft flesh of my inner arm, then the bend of my elbow, his fingertip finally trailing along my upper arm to the sensitive flesh of my underarm.

I bite my lower lip and squirm. The sensation of his finger upon my skin is exquisite. It is feather-soft, almost a tickle, and desperately, wildly erotic.

"Do you see how you writhe?" he asks. "That movement lets you control the intensity so that you're not overwhelmed by the onslaught of sensations. Do you understand?"

I nod.

"I'm going to take that away from you," he says as he begins to position me. He moves the soles of my feet together, and then slowly wraps the jute rope around them once, twice. I test the bindings and find that I cannot move my feet at all. I am strangely helpless, and it's unnerving and exciting all at the same time.

"There will be no writhing," Damien says as he gently spreads my knees and brings my joined feet up higher on the blanket. "No shifting. No place to hide."

I'm essentially in the butterfly pose from yoga now, my knees spread wide and each only inches off the floor. I'm not particularly athletic, but my mother kept me doing both yoga and ballet long enough that I am sufficiently limber, so that Damien has no trouble positioning me.

My back is arched, the inside of my thighs tight from the stretch. And, yes, my sex is completely exposed. The position is undeniably erotic, and not only because I am so wide open. As Damien has said, there is nowhere to go. Not now, and certainly not when he finishes what he has started. I will be utterly at his mercy—and that, of course, is the point. Damien has lost so much tonight, but these ropes and my body can give him some of it back.

But this isn't just about what Damien needs. I want this, too. I want to surrender to him. I want to abdicate my pleasure to Damien's command. I want to float, with only Damien to tether me.

Damien's eyes meet mine, and when he then trails his gaze down my body, there is so much heat, it is a wonder that he doesn't leave scorch marks on my skin.

He has used the middle section of the long length of rope to bind my feet, and now he takes one of the free ends and begins to encircle the shin and thigh of my left leg.

"I'm giving you pleasure, pain, and beauty combined," he says. "I want to look at you like this, open for me, your legs bent, your body like a diamond shining bright and glistening for me."

He pulls the rope tight so that it both marks my flesh and ensures that my legs stay at the proper angle. Then he ties it off. I am now half-bound—and completely turned on.

"You're like the portrait," he says. "A vision of erotic beauty. But a portrait isn't flesh, and its beauty can't feel pleasure."

He closes his mouth over my breast and sucks and I feel a fast, electric trill race from my nipple to my cunt. My sex tightens, as if begging for attention, but Damien is in no hurry, and he suckles and teases, his teeth grazing my tender nipple, his mouth drawing against my flesh until my areola is tight and puckered. His tongue teasing my skin, and he is right—I am desperate to move beneath him, to escape even slightly from the overwhelming sweetness of this onslaught. But I am trapped and the sensual assault continues, edging me high and higher until I am certain I have no choice but to fall.

Just when I am certain that I will scream if he doesn't relent, he trails kisses down my belly until he reaches my navel. He takes a quick, playful nip, then sits up and returns to the task of tying me down. He takes the rope again, and this time moves to my other leg. Before he does, though, he gently strokes my sex. I'm hot and needy, and a tremble runs through me. I want him to do it again, another stroke, his mouth, his fingers deep inside me. I want that tremble to turn into a full-blown explosion. I want that—and Damien damn well knows it.

He does nothing about it, though, except focus on my other leg. "You're wet, baby. And every quiver, every sign, every dewy hint of your arousal is on display for me. Tell me you like it, Nikki," he says as he finishes binding me. "Tell me you like being open and ready for me."

As he speaks, he trails his finger up and down my leg, then traces the rope that binds me. My body trembles and shivers run through me, sparked in the wake of his touch. I can barely breathe, much less talk. I want to tell him everything that's bubbling inside me. That there is an exquisite joy in surrendering to him. In giving myself over for his pleasure and trusting that he will see to mine.

I want to tell him that "like" doesn't even come close to describing how I feel, and it is certainly a poor measure of the extent of my arousal.

I want to pour my heart out to him, but I can manage only one simple word: "Yes."

He has finished binding me, and the ropes are tight. They cut into my skin just past the point of pleasure and into the realm of pain. I close my eyes and draw it in, idly wondering if other women need time to get used to this. I do not. I simply lie back and revel in it. After the night we've had, I want this; I want everything that Damien is willing to give.

I want the pain and the pleasure and everything that comes between.

Slowly, methodically, Damien places his hands on my shoulders, then traces his fingertips down my body, over my breasts, along my waist, down my inner thighs.

I bite my lip, fighting against the painfully sweet sensation, but he's right; bound like this, there is no escaping—and the pleasure crescendos, leading toward the edge of pain.

When he finally stops touching me, I exhale in a burst, only then realizing that I've been holding my breath. I gasp, my chest rising and falling, my eyes wide open as I watch Damien rise and stand near my own bound feet.

Slowly, so painfully slowly, he takes off his clothes. His cock is hard and thick and I inhale, my breath shuddering in my chest, the desire pooling in my wide open sex. Then, with slow deliberation, he comes to me and kneels over my bound feet. Gently, he places the pads of his thumbs on each of my inner thighs, then slides his hands upward. I shiver, my body primed to explode, but he still doesn't touch me where I crave him most, and I am left hanging on a precipice.

"You're a cruel man, Mr. Stark."

"Am I?" He leans farther in, and those hands that I want so desperately between my legs move up to cup my breasts. I gasp as he pinches my nipples, once again sending hot threads of desire all through me. I bite my lower lip and squeeze my eyes shut. I swear if he does that again I really will come, and I silently beg him to do just that.

Naturally, he doesn't, and I teeter there on my imaginary cliff, so very ready to leap into the chasm, but quite unable to take myself there.

"Cruel?" he whispers. "Or am I being very, very good to you?"

"Cruel," I say very firmly, then smile when he laughs.

He slides his hands off my breasts to curve around my sides. I can feel the fragile bones of my rib cage beneath his strong hands, a reminder once again of how much I am his in this moment. Bound. Helpless. His to tease, to torment, to command.

Tenderly, he kisses the tiny scar above my pubic bone. I feel the rough brush of his beard stubble against my sensitive skin.

"Tell me what you want," he says. "I want to hear you say it."

I open my mouth, but no words come. "You," I finally manage. My voice is rough. "I want you inside me."

"Why, Ms. Fairchild," he murmurs, his lips grazing my pubis and his voice so low I can barely hear him. "Are you saying you want to be fucked?"

"God, yes."

"I like your answer." He gently cups my needy sex. His skin is hot, but not as hot as mine. "But I don't think you're quite ready."

It is entirely possible that I will die from frustration. I suck in a breath and find my words. "Mr. Stark," I say sternly, "if you can't tell how ready I am, then I'm afraid you're not as skilled a lover as I had thought."

"On the contrary," he whispers. "I'm an exceptional lover. You just need to be more patient and let me prove it to you, slowly, methodically, and very, very thoroughly."

I say nothing. Every sensation in my body, every ounce of feeling and desire has rushed between my legs. I feel heavy and swollen and desperate.

I need him inside me. If he doesn't fuck me soon, I'm one-hundred-percent certain that I will implode. "Damien, please."

"This?" He slides two fingers inside my vagina, and I gasp as my body tightens hungrily around him. My hips gyrate without me even thinking about it, and it's an odd, amazing sensation with my legs bound open like that, because he is right. Not even the slightest shimmer of my desire can be hidden.

"Yes," I manage, forcing the word to my lips. "But more. *You.*"

He adds another finger and begins a slow, sensual in-and-out. I tilt my head back, letting the pleasure build. I'm close, so very close, my muscles constricting to pull him in, harder and deeper. And then, finally, he gives me what I really want. He shifts his body over mine and holds himself up with one hand near my waist. The other he slides under my ass, lifting me just slightly. It feels strange because I cannot help. My knees and feet are not my own, but it's not something I'm particularly worried about—for that matter, I'm no longer worried about anything, because Damien penetrates me now, his hips thrusting forward, his cock hard inside me as he holds my hips with his hands and pulls me toward him to meet his thrusts.

His movements are steady, even, and the tingling sensation in my body is like electricity building to a thrumming, steady power. But that's the thing about electricity—it can surprise you, and when Damien changes the rhythm, I cry out, my body shuddering as a powerful, unexpected orgasm bursts through me, sending vibrant sensations throughout me like ripples from a rock in a pond.

Damien doesn't stop. He thrusts again, harder and faster, again and again, until he, too, explodes. And, more than that, I explode again with him.

"Oh, baby," he says, as his body melts against mine.

"That was spectacular," I say, surprised that I can actually manage to form words.

He leans up on his elbow and looks at me. "Are you okay?"

"Mmm." I moan in satisfaction. "More than okay. But just a little stiff," I add.

He chuckles, then kisses me softly and tells me to wait. A moment later he is carefully cleaning me, then slowly unbinding me, massaging each place where the rope cut into me, and gently stretching out my limbs.

He picks me up and carries me to bed, then eases up to spoon behind me, his arms around my waist. I sigh, lost in the pleasure of being so well attended to. I feel spoiled and cherished. More than that, I feel safe.

For a moment, we are silent, but as my mind drifts back over the evening, I cannot keep my question in any longer.

"Damien?"

"Yes?" His voice is tired. Sleep will soon be upon both of us.

"What was your father talking about? Why do you need to be squeaky clean?"

He is quiet for so long that I hold my breath.

"He's yanking my chain," Damien finally says. But that is not the truth, and I'm certain that Damien realizes I know it.

"Damien—"

He rolls me over, and something about his eyes tells me that this is it. If I press, he will tell me.

I swallow. Because this isn't about learning the truth, it's about Damien willingly sharing the truth with me.

I begin again. "How did you know where to find me tonight?"

For a moment his expression reveals nothing. Then I see the smile light his eyes, though it does not reach his lips. He cups my head with his hand and looks at me with an expression of such adoration it takes my breath away.

"Don't you know, Nikki? No matter where you go, I will always find you."

12

My legs are deliciously sore when I wake Saturday morning. I roll over, searching for Damien, but he isn't there. I consider staying in bed—after all, at some point he has to come back—but the lure of coffee wins out and I head for the kitchen.

The man knows me well, because the note he left for me is taped to the coffeepot.

A few things came up. At the office. Loved last night.
The image of you naked and bound, spread wide for me,
is burned into my mind. I expect that I will find it
difficult to concentrate. I may just have to spank you
later for distracting me so . . .

I smile and tuck the note into my purse. Then I shower and change before heading through the door in the back that connects the apartment to the office. When I finish navigating the maze of hallways and find myself in the reception area, Ms. Peters greets me with a smile.

"Good morning. He and Mr. Maynard are on the phone. Would you like to wait?"

"That's okay. He's obviously busy." I think about the reporters and what they said about an indictment. If Charles is here, there must be some legal wrangling going on with one of the Stark International divisions.

Edward isn't working until later, but Ms. Peters arranges another car for me. Only the cat greets me when I come through the door. Jamie, I assume, is with Raine.

I haven't been alone that much lately, and it's nice to be in my room with my things. Especially since so many of my things now remind me of Damien.

I look over at the Monet he gave me—haystacks at sunset. It's stunning, and thank God it's insured. I'm still nervous, though, but at the same time, I don't want it anywhere else except the room in which I sleep. Well, the room in which I sleep when I'm not with Damien, anyway.

I settle in front of my computer and start looking through my image files. I should be doing work stuff, but I so rarely have time to spend on the gift I'm making for Damien—a scrapbook filled with mementos of our time together. A snapshot of the Monet. Dozens of pictures of sunsets, and lots and lots of images of the two of us together. As much as I hate the paparazzi, I have to admit they've captured a few nice candid shots.

I work on organizing the pictures and writing captions for a few hours, then decide I ought to tackle cleaning the apartment before I shower for tonight. Weirdly, "cleaning" includes making up the bed in our living room.

As I vacuum, the sound of grunts and moans comes from next door, loud enough to be heard over the machine. I close my eyes, silently thankful that Jamie is not still sleeping with Douglas, our too-loud, too-fucked by too-many women, neighbor.

Mostly, I wish she hadn't fucked him in the first place, especially since he's been making hints about wanting her again.

By the time Jamie gets home, Douglas's latest fuck buddy has gone and I've moved on to the kitchen counters.

"Wow," she says. "You're hired."

I lift a brow. Jamie's idea of cleaning is to let the place get completely trashed, then spend an entire day complaining about how much she hates cleaning. It drives me nuts.

"Will there be food tonight?" she asks.

"Appetizers and drinks," I say.

"Wanna grab a late lunch?"

I shrug. "Sure. Edward will be here at six to get us, so we want to leave time to come back and change."

"In the limo?" Jamie perks up.

"I don't know," I say, tossing her a sponge. "But if you go wipe down the bathroom counters, I'll text Damien and tell him that's what we want."

And that, I think as she trots off to clean, is how to manage a roommate.

"Holy architecture, Batman," Jamie says as one of the staff that Damien hired for the party opens the door for us.

I follow her inside, and stop just over the threshold. Apparently Damien has house elves, because the huge room that was bare just yesterday is now furnished in a manner that is both welcoming and opulent. The white marble tiles, which extend through the entrance hall all the way to the back of the house, gleam, a perfect stage for the equally white furniture that now fills the space, the only color provided by the vibrant artwork decorating the two walls to the left and right. The far wall is glass and is constructed like the door to the third-floor balcony so that the panels can be thrust aside and the room opened to the pool deck and the negative-edge pool that extends beyond. The ceiling extends up all four floors to a glass skylight, giving the room an atrium-like feel.

The two focal points—the pool outside and the massive marble staircase—complement each other, as if each is beckoning the visitor to come exploring, promising all sorts of delights no matter which direction the guest chooses to go.

"This place is fabulous," Jamie continues in a stage whisper that probably carries all the way to the third floor.

"I know," I say as a kind of proprietary pride swells through me. I have had nothing to do with building or decorating this house, and yet there is no denying the simple truth that it feels like home. "Want a tour?"

"Drink first," she says. "Tour later."

"Come on, then." I lead her to the marble stairs and we climb up to the third floor. The second floor is really more of a balcony or mezzanine and has no enclosed rooms. Instead, it is an area that is accessed from either a set of stairs near the kitchen or from the small service elevator. What makes the floor unique is that it serves as a library, and as our climb takes us even with that level, I hear Jamie suck in air. "Wow," she says.

"Amazing, huh? The workers just finished the shelving a few days ago. I have no idea where Damien was storing all those books." From our perspective on the stairs we appear to be completely surrounded by cherrywood bookshelves filled top to bottom with every volume imaginable, ranging from rare first editions to spine-broken sci-fi paperbacks that Damien has read over and over again.

Like the rest of the house, one entire wall is made of glass and looks out over the ocean. This glass, however, is especially designed to block damaging rays that could harm the books. Four leather armchairs make up the focal point of the reading area.

They are a deep, chocolate brown and they are covered with a buttery soft leather that I happen to know feels wonderful against naked skin.

Even with no enhancements, the library would be awe-inspiring. Tonight, though, it is magical. Damien must have had a crew working all day, because the intricate iron railing now sparkles with strings of white lights. They glow softly, invitingly, and when we ascend the stairs and pass by them, the twinkle of lights gives the illusion that we are passing by the stars and entering heaven.

I've brought my Leica tonight, despite the fact that my camera bag does nothing for the stunning blue dress that Damien bought me, and I pause on the stairs long enough to take a photo of Jamie with the lights shining behind her.

I tuck the camera back into the bag and we continue up to the third floor, then step out onto the landing. Beside me, Jamie gasps. I do, too.

Because the first thing I see is me, my naked body, standing strong and bound for the world.

"Not a bad way to greet visitors, eh, Texas?" Evelyn smiles broadly as she hurries over to envelop me in a very un-LA-like bear hug. Evelyn is not an air kiss kind of woman. "You are as gorgeous in that painting as you are in real life," she says, adding another squeeze to the hug.

She releases me and turns to face Jamie. "And you must be Jamie."

"I guess I must be."

"Well, then, turn around and let me have a look at you."

I've never seen Jamie intimidated, but I think she's a little bowled over by Evelyn because Jamie spins without complaint, showing off the red sheath dress she purchased for the party.

"Good ass, nice tits. Definitely got the face and the hair."

"What?" Jamie asks, deadpan. "Is there something wrong with my legs?"

Evelyn snorts and looks at me. "I like her." She turns back to Jamie. "Texas tells me you're an actress."

"Trying to be," Jamie says.

"Well, assuming you can actually act, you've got the right equipment to make it in this business. And between you and me, your assets are good enough that you can probably even make it without that pesky talent thing."

"I can act," Jamie assures her.

"You find me later. We'll talk. I may not be in the business anymore, but that doesn't mean I don't still have a hand in the pic."

"Sure." If Jamie smiles any broader, she's going to injure her facial muscles. "Thank you. That would be great."

Evelyn turns to signal one of the waitresses, and as she does, Jamie faces me. *Wow,* she mouths. *I know,* I reply.

When the waitress arrives with a tray topped with wine and champagne, Evelyn hands a glass to each of us. "Come on in, girls. No point in standing here on the landing all night." She indicates the room, which is now sparsely furnished in the same style as the first floor. Considering the care that Damien took in decorating the library, I assume that these furnishings are for tonight only, probably leased from a company that stages real estate for sale.

Scattered among the tables, chairs, and small sofas are easels displaying Blaine's work. Unlike my portrait, those canvases are actually on sale tonight. The artist himself fidgets with one easel, adjusting the angle of a small canvas featuring a nude on an Oriental rug. Evelyn lifts her hand in a wave, but Blaine doesn't see her.

"Come on," she says, taking my friend's arm. "I'll introduce you to the man of the hour. Nikki, if you're looking for Damien, he said he was going to go change. By the way, looks like great minds think alike. Turns out he did help Giselle get the paintings back from Palm Springs. Edward was bringing some in from the limo yesterday when I was finishing up."

"Oh." Her words surprise me, because Damien hadn't mentioned that he'd seen Giselle, and I feel a little finger of irritation start to claw at me. I force myself to shake it off. I'm just sensitive because Giselle is suddenly, inexplicably in my orbit, what with Palm Springs and Tanner's strange comment. And now past jealousies are poking up their little heads. But I don't want to be that girl, and I smack down their green-eyed little faces.

As Evelyn leads Jamie to Blaine, I head into the kitchen, planning to drop off my camera bag and continue to the closet.

I don't get that far, however, because as I'm hooking the Leica strap over my arm and putting the bag in one of the cabinets, I see Damien coming down the hallway from the bedroom area. I stop what I'm doing, and stand frozen, simply staring at him. He's wearing pressed black pants and a collarless black jacket over one of the starched white shirts I love so well. It's unbuttoned, and the open shirt paired with the jacket gives him the quality of a powerful rebel. He looks so breathtakingly sexy that I have a hard time believing that he is real, much less that he's mine. On the contrary, he must be a fantasy that I have conjured. A dream in which I'm now living. A perfect dream from which I do not wish to wake.

He's holding his phone and speaking low, so that I can only make out a few words. But from his tone, I can tell that the subject is urgent, and that he is bothered.

I think about last night and wonder if this is more fallout. Maybe it's his father. Or maybe it has to do with Stark International's legal troubles in Germany.

After a moment, he frowns, ends the call, and slides the

phone into his pocket. For a fleeting instant, I can see the irritation on his face. Then it is wiped away, as if he has willed the universe to behave, and the universe has no choice but to agree. Damien Stark is a man who gets what he wants, however he wants.

When he looks in my direction, I see in his eyes that what he wants right now is me.

His smile is as potent a greeting as any kiss could ever be. It is like something inside me has come undone and I rush to him, then throw myself in his outstretched arms. He pulls me close, and the last wisps of jealousy disintegrate under the touch of this man.

When I've had my fill of him—though, really, I can never have my fill of him—I ease back and smile. "Missed you."

"Missed you more."

"Is everything okay?"

He eyes me oddly. "Of course. Why?"

"I saw you just now. On the phone, I mean."

For a moment, the irritation is back. "It's nothing," he says. "Something I thought was under control has turned out to be more volatile than I expected. Nothing to worry about, though." He tilts my chin up and gazes into my eyes for so long that I feel as though I am going to fall in. Then he smiles, so slowly and sweetly that I cannot help but sigh. "You look beautiful," he says, after we've stood like that, lost in each other, for what feels like a lifetime.

"Thank you for the dress." I do a small turn to show it off. "And for the bed." I'm looking right at him as I speak, so there is no missing the shadow that crosses his face. "Damien? What is it?"

He hesitates, and I see the ghost of a frown before it fades into a smile. "I'm just very pleased you like them."

"Of course I do." Worried, I look in his eyes, the dark

one seeming to draw me in and the amber one bathing me in a warm, loving glow. Whatever hesitation I thought I'd seen has faded, but I am not soothed. There are things he wants to say to me, and yet he is not saying them. I start to press, but hold back. Now is not the time.

"We should join the party," I say.

"In a minute." He pulls me closer to him, so that my breasts are pressed against his chest and my chin is tucked onto his shoulder. I breathe deeply, memorizing the scent of him, all musk and masculine spices.

"How is it that I can miss you so much when you're not beside me?" he asks.

"I don't know," I whisper. "But I could ask the same question."

"Oh, Nikki." The last sound of my name is cut off as his mouth closes roughly over mine.

My body melts against him, and I feel myself opening up. I want him. I want him now. Here. On the goddamn stove if we have to, but I want to know that this man is mine. I want to claim him. I want to fuck him.

And I'm frustrated as hell because none of that is going to happen. Not now, with our friends on the other side of this wall, just a few feet away.

Reluctantly, I break the kiss, then extend my hand to him.

"Are we observing formalities, Ms. Fairchild?"

"We are, Mr. Stark."

He laughs, then presses a soft kiss to my palm that makes my thighs tremble and my nipples tighten almost painfully.

Damien eyes me, a smug smile on his beautiful face. "Me, too, Ms. Fairchild."

I aim a prim smile at him. "I don't know what you're talking about. But I will say that you look dashing as usual." I nod toward the next room. "Shall we mingle?"

We leave the kitchen and join the other three, who have moved to the balcony. Evelyn is entertaining Jamie with stories about her television and movie deals back in the day, and Blaine presents a mock frown of frustration as Damien and I approach. "We've lost them," he says. "Once she starts talking Hollywood, she never stops. And I think she's found the perfect audience."

"She has," I agree, lifting my camera to take a few shots of the two women deep in animated conversation. "Jamie can talk classic television and old movies for days, but she's just as happy if the conversation shifts to current sitcoms."

"In other words, they're going to keep each other occupied all night," he says.

"Not all night," I say. "I need some Evelyn time, too." I say the words lightly, but I'm completely serious. It feels as if it's been years, but it was only yesterday we spoke at my office. Evelyn knows about something that's going on with Damien. Something she says I don't need to worry about. But I am worried. And I intend to get answers.

I focus on Blaine and force a smile. "Right now, I want to see your other paintings," I tell him. "Will you show us?"

"Sure." The three of us head back inside and Blaine leads us around the room, pausing at the various canvases so that he can describe what he was going for in a particular scene. There is a similarity in all of them, both in color and in theme. Blaine has bound each of the models in some way, and though the images never cross the line into what I consider bad taste, some do display an intimacy that I would never have agreed to. Some even remind me of the pose Damien had me in last night.

There is one that particularly catches my eye. The model is on a chaise, her legs draped over either side. Two black ribbons bind her legs in position. Another ribbon ties one arm up above her head. Only one hand is free, and it is draped between her legs in such a way that it is clear she is touching herself. Her nipples are erect, her areolae puckered. The muscles in her belly are taut. Though her face is partly turned from view, there is no hiding her arousal.

I don't bother to ask Blaine what he intended with that image; I know only too well. There is an excitement to being bound. To being helpless. A sensual thrill that comes from trusting fully and abandoning modesty at the command of your lover.

Damien presses his hand lightly against my back, and I shiver, imagining that it is me touching myself, and Damien who is watching. I tense, my skin suddenly too sensitive and too damn hot. I feel tiny drops of perspiration bead at my hairline and take a step forward, needing to either break contact with Damien or beg him to take me right there on the floor.

As I move away, I catch his eye.

Yes, he mouths, and his smile holds so much wicked promise that I go weak in the knees.

Honestly, it's a miracle that I don't just melt.

Blaine, thank God, is so caught up in his procession of art that he doesn't notice our near tryst. We move from canvas to canvas, Blaine pointing out details about the composition or the color, telling stories about the models and how they came to him. Most were simply girls looking to make a little extra money. Some posed for free because they wanted the experience. And at each portrait, there is Damien's hand on my back, and my body becoming increasingly, desperately needy.

My nipples, now erect and sensitive, rub provocatively against the soft chiffon with every step I take. My sex feels swollen, begging to be touched. I am wildly turned on, and there's not a thing I can do about it.

It's torture, but as torment goes, it's pretty damn sweet.

Evelyn calls Blaine back out onto the balcony just as we've moved to another canvas, and I cannot help my sigh of relief.

Damien steps behind me and puts his arms around my waist.

"This feels like the night we met, Ms. Fairchild. You and I surrounded by erotic art, and me unable to think of anything but fucking you."

My breath is shaky. "We met six years before that, Mr. Stark."

"So we did," he says, his lips brushing my ear. "I wanted to fuck you then, too."

"Do you always get what you want?" I tease.

"Yes," he says, easing closer behind me so that I feel his erection pressed against my rear. "I thought you knew."

"Why Mr. Stark," I say. "I thought you told me it was bad form to host a party with a hard-on."

"True," he says. "Perhaps we should escape to the powder room. I can think of a rather pleasant way to prevent a social faux pas."

"Keep talking," I say. "You just might tempt me."

His hand grazes over my skirt, and I feel the material snaking very slowly up my thigh.

"Stop it," I say, my voice low as I push his hand down. I shift a bit in his arms, then freeze at what I see on the far side of the floor—Giselle stepping into the room through the kitchen. I tense, because Giselle is not one of the people who knows that I am the girl in the portrait, and I don't understand why she's here early. I tell myself that she owns the gallery. That it's not like she hasn't seen nude paintings before. And surely she doesn't know it's me. That was part of our deal, and Damien is a man of his word.

I tell myself all that, and I've almost convinced myself, too. But then Bruce steps into the room behind her, and I freeze, my body like one solid block of icy mortification. *My naked portrait hangs on the wall, and my boss is looking right at it.*

"You're very tense," Damien teases. "Again, I can suggest several ways to loosen you up."

I realize that he hasn't noticed them and that he doesn't know why I've gone still. Nor can he see my face, or the confusion that must surely be rising in my eyes. *Do they know? How could they know?*

His thumb grazes over the filmy chiffon. "Tell me, Ms. Fairchild," he murmurs. "What will I find if I slide my hand under your skirt? Did you wear panties tonight?"

"Why are Giselle and Bruce here already?" I ask.

His body goes tense. "What?"

I pull out of his arms and turn to face him. "They don't know it's me in the portrait, do they?"

He's not looking at me, but I can see that his eyes have found the couple. His jaw is tight, but that's the only reaction that I see. "They're not supposed to be here," he says, his voice calm and even.

"No," I say. "Because they don't know. Right?" I shift a bit so that I'm standing in front of him. I feel strangely frantic, as if I'm precariously balanced and if I'm not careful I'll be tumbling without a net. "Damien? Did you tell them?"

For a moment, his face goes hard. He's the businessman, the negotiator. The man Ollie warned me was dangerous. The man Evelyn told me is an expert at keeping secrets.

And then his expression softens, and it is as if all he sees is me. "Yes, but, Nikki—"

That's all I need to hear. "Oh, God. How could—" I clap my hand to my mouth and breathe in hard through my nose. I'm tumbling now, and I was right—there is no net to catch me.

Anger bubbles through me. Anger and hurt and humiliation, all black and cold and desolate.

My anonymity was a vital part of our deal. I'm naked up there. And not just naked, but revealed, so that anyone who sees the portrait—who sees the scars—also sees my demons.

How could Damien be so cavalier? He saw me melt down at

the first session with Blaine. He's the one who soothed me, who I thought understood me.

And now it feels like he's the one who's slapped me.

I blink, because I am not going to cry. Instead, I concentrate on the fury that is cutting through me like a knife, giving me both strength and a weapon. Because so help me, I want to wound Damien as he's wounded me. This cut is deep, all the more so because he is the one person I trusted most to never hurt me.

He reaches for me, his face now as gentle as I've ever seen it. "Nikki, please."

"No." I hold up my hand and shake my head as I choke back a little sob. "And for the record," I say, coolly meeting his eyes, "of course I wore panties. Game's over, remember? The rules no longer apply."

I see the hurt in his eyes, and feel it cut sharply through me. For a moment, I regret the lie. I'm overcome by a desperate longing to lose myself in his arms. To hold him and comfort him, and to let him comfort me.

But I don't. I can't. I need to be alone, and so I let my sharp words hang in the air as I lift my head and walk steadfastly away.

But my exit doesn't give me any satisfaction. Our game may be over, but I don't want the relationship with Damien to end.

I think about the bed and my fear that it was a portent. About Giselle and Bruce and the trust that has cracked like a mirror. I think about the secrets that I know Damien keeps from me, and about the depths of this man who is still so much a mystery to me.

All of that haunts me. And, yes, I'm afraid.

Not of the ghosts of his past, but of the possibility that we will have no future.

13

"Nikki!"

I'm trying to escape down to the second-floor library, and Bruce is the last person that I want to see right now. Well, almost the last. At the moment, I don't particularly want to see Damien.

I can't, however, continue toward the service elevator without appearing incredibly rude. So I pause and wait for him to catch up with me. I try to plaster on my Social Nikki mask, but honestly, I just don't have the energy. And I'm sure that the smile with which I greet my boss is thin at best.

"I wanted to thank you for doing such a great job at Suncoast yesterday," he says.

"Oh." I wasn't expecting business chitchat. "Thank you. I was pleased you gave me such a challenging assignment on my first day." Over his shoulder, I see myself looking down upon us. I wonder if, having seen me nude before the world, Bruce's assessment of my professionalism has been knocked down a notch. Or twelve.

"Challenging because of the work, or because of your partner?"

"A little of both," I admit.

"I promised you that we'd talk," he says. "Is now a good time?"

It's not, of course. But I'm curious. And so far, I'm only getting a business vibe. Maybe Damien only told Giselle that I'm the girl in the portrait, and Bruce has no idea. After all, it's not like there's a neon arrow over my head saying, *She's the One.*

"Sure," I say, relaxing a little. "Now's great." There is a seating area surrounding the fireplace, and he leads me in that direction. As we walk, Damien catches my eye. He has moved to the balcony, where he now stands between Evelyn and Giselle.

I look away, then smile at Bruce as I sit. "So why is Tanner the wolf?"

Bruce draws a deep breath. "Listen, before we get into all of that, I think I owe you an apology."

Now I'm confused. "Because of Tanner? It wasn't that bad," I lie.

"No. Because of tonight. Giselle told me that it's you in the painting."

I nod, too dumbstruck to speak. So much for my shiny new theory that Bruce was clueless.

"To be honest, I didn't think anything of it. But once we arrived, I realized that you didn't know that I knew."

"It's fine," I say, though it is a very long way from fine.

"No. It's not. Giselle had no business telling me. I don't think she meant anything by it, but sometimes she just doesn't think."

He looks at me, but I say nothing. It's still not fine, and I am not capable of repeating the lie again.

"I wanted to talk to you now, though, because I don't want you to think that this affects our working relationship."

"Of course not. Why would it?"

He must know that I'm bullshitting, because he doesn't even

bother to answer me. Instead, he seems to change subjects altogether. "Did Damien tell you about my sister?"

"Um, no."

"As brilliant a woman as you will ever meet. She does mathematical equations in her head that I can barely do with a calculator. She teaches at MIT now."

I cock my head. "Jessica Tolley-Brown?"

"You know her?"

"Of her," I say, not bothering to hide my excitement. "I almost entered a PhD program at MIT just so I could study under her. But what does she—"

"Do you know how she put herself through school?"

"No. Scholarships, I assume."

"Mostly," he says. "But my sister has expensive taste, and she supplemented her income with modeling."

"Oh," I say. I have a feeling I know where this is going.

"I don't have a problem with the female body," he says. "And I don't think any less of a woman's intellect just because she poses nude. Considering my sister's portfolio, and the fact that she can trample me in just about any contest of wits, it would be pretty hypocritical of me, don't you think?"

"I suppose it would." Embarrassment still lingers, but he has managed to soothe the mortification. "And thank you for pulling me aside to tell me. It—well, I appreciate it."

"Good." He pats his hands on his knees. "As for Tanner, again, I'm sorry. I imagine he gave you a bit of grief. He didn't make it a secret that he wanted your job. Now he doesn't have one."

"What?" I feel whiplashed by his words.

"I've put up with him for a long time, probably too long, but he was with me when I started Innovative, and he stuck with me even when I couldn't pay him a salary for months on end." He frowns, then rips off a thread dangling from a seam in the lining of his jacket. He drops the thread on the small table between us, then continues without missing a beat. "I always thought he had the company's best interest at heart, but this morning I learned that he's a backbiting sack of shit."

"Oh." I try to think what to say next, but nothing seems quite appropriate, so I wait.

"Damien made some calls after you told him what happened yesterday, and he confirmed that our boy Tanner is the one who told the press you were coming to Innovative. That's bad enough—making you deal with that shit—but he also planted that bullshit about corporate espionage."

"Oh, no." My words are barely a whisper. "He's an idiot."

"Yes, he is," Bruce says cheerfully. "And now he's an unemployed one." He points a finger at me. "Don't be mad at Damien for interfering."

"I'm not," I say. All Damien did was find and report the truth. Bruce is right; Tanner screwed Innovative and he screwed me. And Damien protected us both.

The cold fist around my heart loosens a bit.

"Tanner seemed to think that you gave me the job as a favor to your wife." The statement is out of my mouth before I can think better of it.

Bruce looks at me sharply, and I can't help but wonder what sort of quagmire I've stepped in. "Did he?" Bruce says. "That's odd."

"I thought so, too. What did he mean?"

The corners of Bruce's mouth turn down. "Not a clue," he says, but he doesn't meet my eyes.

"Oh, well," I say lightly. "Probably just Tanner being Tanner."

"I'm sure that's all." He stands up. "We should probably mingle. I think the rest of the guests are starting to arrive."

He's right. In the time that we've been talking, a steady

stream of people has been coming in. A few I recognize from a similar party at Evelyn's just a few short weeks ago. There's even a Damien-approved photographer from the local paper, snapping away for what will undoubtedly be a spread in tomorrow's Sunday edition.

I find Jamie talking with Rip Carrington and Lyle Tarpin, two sitcom stars Evelyn must have invited. Since Jamie considers them each utterly drool-worthy, I know that no matter what else happens, this party will rate a full ten on the Jamie-meter.

My score? Not nearly so high. Bruce has soothed my embarrassment, but I'm still irritated that Giselle knew my identity in the first place. And I'm troubled and confused by Tanner's strange comment—and Bruce's even stranger response.

Bruce has gotten washed away in the crowd, but I'm still standing by the fireplace. I bend over and pick up the string off the table, then twist it between two fingers as I look around this room that has been transformed from someplace warm and familiar into a cold, polished place in which I don't feel comfortable, especially without Damien by my side.

I search the crowd, looking for him, but all I see are strangers. The third floor is full now, bright shiny people with their bright shiny smiles. They all look polished and fresh, and I can't help but wonder if any of them feel as raw inside as I do at this moment. Between my thumb and forefinger, I am still twisting the string, rolling it this way and that so that it wiggles as if it were a snake. It has given me something to occupy my hands, but that is not why I picked up the string. I tell myself I should set it back down on the coffee table and walk away, but I don't. I plucked it off the white melamine tabletop for a reason.

Slowly, methodically, I wrap the string around the tip of my finger. I tug it tight, and the skin around the thread immediately turns white, while my fingertip turns a deep red that quickly shifts toward purple. With each revolution, the pain increases. And with each revolution, I am a little more grounded.

I am like a windup doll, and each twist of the key focuses the pain—focuses *me*. I will keep turning and turning, taking as much as I can, and then, when the key is just about to snap, I will let go and Pretty Party Nikki will perform, moving in and out among the guests, smiling, laughing, and focusing on that one shining spot of dark red pain to guide her back home.

No.

Goddammit, no!

I jerk my left hand away from my right with such ferocity that I stumble and upset the small table beside me. A young man in a purple sport coat is standing nearby, and he takes a step forward as if to help, but I turn away, frantically scraping at the string, too upset to calmly unwind the thread. Instead, I claw at it, my heart pounding wildly, and when it finally falls off my finger and onto the floor, I leave it there, then back away as if it is something poisonous, like a scorpion determined to strike.

I push past the guy in purple then lean against the stonework that surrounds the fireplace. The stones press against my bare shoulders uncomfortably, but I don't care. I need something to hold me up. And until I find Damien, the wall will have to do.

"Are you okay?" the guy in purple asks.

"Yes," I say, though I'm not okay. I'm not okay at all.

The guy still stands by me, but I barely notice him. Instead, I'm searching for Damien, and the swell of relief that rushes through me when I find him is so forceful that I have to reach back and hold tight to the stones. He is standing to the side, away from the bulk of the crowd near the hallway that leads to the bedroom. He is alone except for Charles Maynard, his attorney, who stands beside Damien looking harried.

I can't see Damien's expression, as his back is to me. He has one hand in his pants pocket and the other holds a glass of wine. It's a casual position, but I see the tension in his shoulders, and I wonder if he is thinking of me, just as I am thinking of him.

Damien.

As if my thought calls to him, he turns, his gaze finding me immediately. I see everything on his face. Worry. Passion. Need. I think that he is fighting hard to give me space. But I no longer want the distance, and I take a step toward him.

As I walk, I see Maynard reach out for Damien's shoulder and hear his voice, suddenly raised in frustration. "—not listening. This is Germany we're—"

Damien turns back to his attorney, and I stop cold, as if the connection between us has been broken. I consider continuing on my way, but then rule it out. I am, after all, the one who is mad at him. So why am I so desperate to run to him?

I glance down at my left forefinger. The indentations from the string are still visible, and the tip is still slightly purple. That pain satisfied a need. It grounded me and kept at bay my anger, my fear, my humiliation. It gave me strength and focus, and once again I wonder if Damien gives me the same thing. Is he a new kind of pain?

The thought makes me shiver, and I want nothing more than to erase it from my mind.

A waitress passes in front of me and I signal for her to come over. Right now, I need a drink.

I've downed the glass and have just grabbed another when Jamie rushes up. "Those two are so funny. And they told me what's going to happen on the show next week." She grabs my elbow. "If you forget to remind me to set the DVR, I will never forgive you."

"Fair enough," I say.

"You're getting pictures, right? I want to post them on Facebook. Sorry," she immediately adds. "I know you're avoiding social media."

It's true. I've never used it much, but once all the gossip and speculation about Damien and me started, I took all the social media apps off my phone and have been doing my damnedest to avoid anything that smells of tabloid. As for the photographs the paparazzi take of Damien and me, I rely on Jamie to find those and either email them to me or cut them out. *Without* the accompanying text.

"It's okay," I say. "And, yeah. I've taken some," I add, though I've taken very few.

She narrows her eyes at me. "You okay?"

I almost smile brightly and reassure her that of course I'm okay. Why would I not be okay? But this is Jamie, and even if I could, I don't want to deceive her. "It's been a strange evening," I admit.

"Want to talk about it?"

I lift my glass. "Hell no."

"Where's lover boy? Or is that the part we're not talking about?"

"He's doing the host thing." I look around for him and see that he's left Charles, and is now at the center of a small cluster of guests.

"So who is she?" Jamie nods toward the group, and I see that the people have shifted, revealing a lithe brunette at Damien's side.

The muscles in my face suddenly seem uncomfortably tight. "That's Giselle," I say. "She owns the gallery that sells Blaine's work."

"Ah. The hostess to Damien's host. No wonder you're in a pissy mood."

"I am not in a pissy mood," I say, but of course I am. And

although the whole Hostess Giselle thing hadn't occurred to me before, it is now at the top of my list of affronts and irritations. *Gee, Jamie. Thanks so much.*

"I know how to cure your not-pissy mood." She grabs my hand and gives it a tug. "Rip and Lyle really are funny. You're going to love meeting them. And if you don't love it, then at least pretend like you do, okay?"

I stare her down, because she knows damn well that if there's one thing I know how to do, it's put on a good face at a party.

I don't bother to remind her that I've met Rip and Lyle before and since all they speak is Hollywood, I couldn't make sense of a thing they were saying. This time, though, I'm seeing them through Jamie's eyes, and she's right—it's actually fun.

Armed with my best party girl facade, Jamie and I make the circuit. I am smiling and bubbly, and it's easy to slide into conversations, easy to pull out my camera and tell people to smile or laugh or cluster closer together.

How simple to fall back into my old habits. To hear my mother's instructions in my head. "A lady is always in control. Never let them see that they've wounded you. Because once you do, they'll know your weaknesses."

Mother's words are calculating and cold, but I cling to them. As much as I've run from my mother and my pageant days and the hell of my life with her, I can't deny that there is comfort in turning back to the familiar. Because my mother is right. They can't hurt you if they don't see you. And right now, all I'm willing to show is the mask.

Throughout all my mingling, though, I've felt Damien's eyes on me. Watching me. Burning into me. Making me aware of every little movement. Of the brush of my dress against my skin. Of the feel of my shoes on the curve of my foot.

He's frustrated with me—possibly even angry—but that doesn't change the fact that his desire is palpable.

For that matter, so is mine.

My fears and frustrations can wait. All I want right then is Damien.

I've made up my mind to go join them at the canvas when Evelyn sidles up beside me. "I don't know if I need to wring Damien's neck or Giselle's for only having wine and champagne," she says to me. "Come on, Texas, you must know where the secret stash is."

"As a matter of fact, I do," I say. Probably not the best display of manners to lead Evelyn back into the kitchen area, but the truth is that I could use a shot of bourbon myself.

We maneuver around the hired staff that is now using the kitchen to refill drink and appetizer trays, and park ourselves at the small breakfast table.

"So spill it, Texas," she demands once we're seated and I've poured two neat shots. "Something's on your mind."

"I'm slipping," I say. "I used to be able to hide my troubles better."

"Or maybe it's putting on a good face that gives you away."

I consider that, and decide that in addition to everything else, Evelyn is a very wise woman.

"Come on. Tell Auntie Evelyn."

"Tell you?" I smile. "I seem to recall there was something I wanted you to tell me."

"Oh, hell," she says, then tosses back the drink. She slides the glass back toward me and I top it off again. "I was just running my mouth off. Don't listen to me."

"I do listen," I say. "And I don't believe you. What's going on that I don't know about?"

The corners of her mouth turn down and she shakes her head in exasperation. "I just hate it when I see a shitstorm coming and know there's not a damn thing I can do about it."

"Carl?"

She bats the name away. "Carl can go piss up a rope. No, Damien's managed to keep his business private for almost two decades. But that's about to end, and I'm not sure if he even realizes it."

"Not much gets past Damien," I say, both because it's true and because I'm loyal. "But what on earth are you talking about? He's already done damage control on the Padgett scandal," I say, referring to recent attempts by a disgruntled businessman named Eric Padgett to implicate Damien in the death of his sister. Damien, thankfully, stopped that rumor cold. "So what else is—" I sit back, suddenly realizing the truth. "The tennis center."

Evelyn's head cocks warily. "What has he told you?"

"Pretty much what he told the press. That Richter is an asshole and he's not going to the dedication ceremony. He didn't tell me why," I add, watching Evelyn's face. "But I have my suspicions."

Evelyn's brows lift almost imperceptibly. "Have you told Damien what you believe?"

"Yes." I shrug. "But he hasn't told me if I'm right." I watch Evelyn's expression closely as I speak. I know that she represented Damien back in those days, before and after Richter's death. If anyone knows whether Richter abused Damien as a child, it's Evelyn.

Her face remains passively blank. "But he hasn't told you you're wrong, has he?" She doesn't wait for an answer, but she meets my eyes straight on. "He really has fallen for you, Texas, and I couldn't be happier. For both of you. I don't think I've ever seen that boy looking so good. But goddammit, I wish he'd just show his face at that damn dedication. And I could kick the boy in the nuts for that stunt he pulled last night. He deserves better than to have the press all over his ass like a piranha with a hard-on."

"Is it really such a big a deal?" I don't understand why both

Evelyn and Damien's father think that Damien's statement was such a horrible idea. "Maybe it wasn't the best move to share with the world that he doesn't like Richter, but all he's doing is not showing up to an event. The way he's being hounded, you'd think he turned down an invitation from the Queen and then insulted her."

"All I'm saying is that sometimes you have to play the game to avoid a shitstorm," Evelyn says. "And now I'm afraid the storm will hit dead-on."

I am completely clueless. "What shitstorm?"

"You ask Damien," Evelyn says. "As for me, I hope I'm wrong. But I bet I'm right."

I almost say that I will talk to him again and try to convince him to recant the statement and go to the ceremony. But it's not true. I would never ask him to do that, and I would never expect him to change his mind. Richter's memory doesn't deserve even the tiniest bit of support from Damien, and if a world of shit falls down on Damien's head, I'll stand at his side and help him fight it.

"But that's not what's been on your mind," Evelyn says after polishing off the rest of her drink. "Come on, Texas. I've been watching you and Damien all night—and most of the time I haven't been watching you together."

I conjure a practiced smile, but I know that it must look as false as it feels. "As far as the cocktail party is concerned, I'm simply a guest. Damien and Giselle are doing the host and hostess thing."

"Uh-huh." She leans back in her chair, then pushes her whiskey glass toward me with the tip of a finger. I fill it once again. I almost top off my own, too, but considering the way Evelyn is looking at me, I think I need a clear head.

Evelyn ignores the glass, but leans forward on her elbows and peers at my face until I start to feel uncomfortable.

"What?" I finally demand.

"Not a thing," she says. "Just that I could've sworn your eyes were blue. Not green."

I sag a little. "I'm a bit discombobulated where Giselle is concerned," I admit. "She's coming at me from all sides lately, and it's messing with my head." I am amazed that these words come so easily. I am much more comfortable living behind my mask, and with the exception of Damien and Jamie and Ollie, that is where I usually stay. With Evelyn, however, it's far too easy to talk, and I find myself revealing things that I would normally keep locked up. I suppose that should make me uncomfortable around her, afraid that one day she will see too much. But it doesn't, and I am glad.

"Damien didn't tell me he was helping Giselle bring the paintings back," I say. "And I know that's no reason to be jealous. But—"

"But now she's at his side instead of you?"

"Maybe. But that's not really fair of me since I'd be at his side if I hadn't gotten mad and stormed away. Damien's giving me space."

"Ah, a lover's quarrel. That's okay, Texas. The drama always increases in the second act. What dastardly deed did he do to bruise your heart?"

Her words resonate, because that is exactly what he's done—bruised my heart. "He told Giselle it's me in the painting." The words sound as heavy as they feel. "And she told Bruce."

"I see."

Something in Evelyn's tone makes me take notice. "What? Do you think I should just get over it? I've been telling myself it's not that big a deal, and maybe it isn't. But Damien—"

"—broke his word. Yes, of course that would upset you. Would piss me off, too. But in this case, I think you need to forgive the boy."

I can't help my ironic half-smile. "I will. I honestly can't imagine staying mad at Damien. But not right now. I'm feeling a little fragile."

She keeps speaking as if she hadn't heard me. "You need to forgive him because he didn't break his word. Blaine did."

"What?" I play her words back in my head, but I still don't understand.

"Blaine told Giselle," Evelyn says matter-of-factly. "He didn't mean to. He was mortified. They were talking about model releases for the gallery and somehow the conversation turned to the portrait. He doesn't even remember what he said, exactly. You know how he gets when he starts chattering. And the next thing you know, he'd told her. He rushed home and told me the whole story. Didn't sleep that night—took all my harassing to keep him from calling Damien right then and there, but it was two in the morning, and I told him it could wait. Poor kid looked green until he finally got Damien on the phone at five the next morning."

"When was this?" I am flabbergasted.

"Four days ago."

"But—but I asked Damien point-blank if he told Giselle, and he said yes. He was lying for Blaine? Why?"

"Aw, honey, it wasn't Damien that Blaine was green in the gills about. It was you. He fucked up, and he hurt you, and he fully intended to come clean. He wanted Damien's advice on how to tell you, and Damien told him not to. Damien said he'd talk to Giselle and make sure it didn't go further, and that if need be, he'd take the blame."

"But why?"

"You already answered that one, Texas," she says gently.

For a moment, I don't understand. Then I recall my words. *I honestly can't imagine staying mad at Damien.*

"He's protecting Blaine," I say, more to myself than to Evelyn. "He's protecting our friendship." Suddenly, my hand is over my mouth and I'm blinking back tears.

"You want me to tell Blaine that you know?"

I shake my head violently. "No. No. I don't want him to worry that it bothers me or that I'm mad at him. Maybe someday I'll tell him, but right now, no."

"I wasn't sure about telling you myself," she says. "I'm glad I did."

"Me, too," I say.

"To be honest, I was surprised as hell to see Giselle here. Blaine told her that he didn't mean to say anything. She must know that showing up would embarrass you and piss off Damien. Hard to believe she'd go out of her way to piss off her best client."

"No kidding," I say, but I've realized now what Tanner meant. If Damien is Giselle's best client, then the accusation that Bruce hired me to make his wife happy makes sense. Keep the wife's best client happy and keep the galleries making money.

"Maybe I had it wrong," Evelyn muses. "Maybe Giselle's the one who's jealous."

"Of me? Why?"

"You're with Damien," Evelyn says. "And she's not. Not anymore."

This is a night of revelations. "Damien and Giselle used to date?"

"Years ago. They were an item for a few months before she and Bruce tied the knot. Now there's an interesting story."

"Damien and Giselle?" That's a story I'm not sure I want to hear.

"Giselle and Bruce," Evelyn says with a small shake of her head. "But that's dirt for another day." She tosses back the last of her drink, then slams the glass onto the tabletop. "Ready to head back into the fray?" she asks, standing.

"No," I admit, though I stand as well. Because it's not people that I want right now. It's just Damien.

14

I wait a moment after Evelyn has gone, then make a quick circle through the party. A few people smile or nod at me, moving a step to one side as if silently inviting me to join their conversations. But I pass by; I have no time for anyone but Damien, and I move through the crowd with singular determination.

When I finally see him, I stop short. He stands in a small group, listening to a story told by a stout woman with curly brown hair. As if he feels me looking at him, Damien turns. His eyes find me, and suddenly everything around me seems to melt away. The people are nothing but blurs of colors, the conversation little more than white noise. We are the only two people in the room, and I stand transfixed, my body tingling, mouth suddenly dry. It is as if this man has cast a spell over me, and I am a willing participant to the enchantment.

I want to bask in the heat that radiates between us. I have been so cold today, my body battered by icy winds and drifting tides. I want to stay here, lost in time. Lost in Damien.

But I cannot. There are things to do—things to say. And so I force myself to move. I take a single step forward, and the world around me rushes back into focus, people moving, couples talk-ing, glasses clinking. But my eyes have not left Damien's face, and I smile in apology and forgiveness. And also in invitation.

Then, with my heart beating wildly in my chest, I turn and walk away.

It takes remarkable strength not to turn and look behind me, but I manage the task. I head back into the kitchen, then follow the short hallway that leads to the service elevator. I get in and descend one level to the second-floor library. That floor isn't available to the party guests. It is Damien's private space, and though I am feeling decidedly on edge, I know that I belong there, too, and I smile as I step off the elevator and into the small alcove that houses a computer workstation. This area cannot be seen by anyone climbing the stairs, but neither can I see those magical, sparkling lights. And magical and sparkling is exactly what I need right now.

I move out of the alcove, passing the dimly lit shelving until I come to the open mezzanine. The lights twinkling on the railing are no less impressive from this angle, and I take my camera off my shoulder and focus in close, so that nothing but dots of dif-fused light fill my sight, each pinpoint radiating out into vibrant prisms of color.

I snap, then snap again, and soon I'm lost in the world that I'm capturing on camera. The perfection of the angles of this house I love. The tattered cover of a Philip K. Dick novel that Damien has left on a side table. Even the cocktail party guests, or what little I can see of them, as they seem to float above me. From here, I cannot make out voices. And I can see only the head and shoulders of the few who venture close to the landing.

Nor can I see my portrait, and right then, I am glad. I am so happy to know that Damien didn't breach my confidence, but I still feel exposed and raw.

I know that Damien is behind me even before he speaks. Perhaps I subconsciously heard his footsteps. Or maybe I caught the scent of his cologne.

More likely we are simply so attuned to each other that it is impossible to be in close proximity without my body crying out for the touch of his hand.

"I hope this means you aren't still mad at me," he says.

I am standing at the railing, my back to him, and I feel the whisper of a smile touch my lips. "Should I be?"

I hear the rustle of his clothes as he moves closer to me. He is right there, right behind me, and I can feel the air thickening between us. "I'm truly sorry," he says. "I didn't mean for Giselle to know. And I certainly never expected her to tell Bruce."

I close my eyes, thinking of Blaine and the secret Damien kept. "You are an exceptionally good man, Damien Stark," I say.

For a moment, he is perfectly still behind me. "No, I'm not. But every once in a while I do a good thing." He slides his hand gently over my bare shoulder and I draw in a trembling breath. "Evelyn told you?"

"Yes." I hear the need in my voice. I am certain that he hears it, too.

His hands close around my waist and he pulls me close, then presses his lips into my hair. "I wish she hadn't done that. I didn't want you to be upset with Blaine."

"I'm not. I might have been if I'd learned first that it was him, but you deflected that." I turn in his arms, then tilt my head to look at him. "Like I said, you're a good man."

"I'm still sorry. And even sorrier that Giselle came early. She wasn't invited, and I know it embarrassed you."

"I'll survive," I say, and then, because I think Evelyn might be right about Giselle's motivations, I add, "Why didn't you tell me that you and Giselle dated?"

He looks truly baffled by the question. "You never asked."

"You knew I wondered," I say. "That night. Our first night."

He thinks for a moment, and then his mouth quirks up as if my question is amusing him.

"Dammit, Damien," I say, smacking him lightly on the arm.

"Giselle and I went out a few times, but it was long before she and Bruce got married. And if I recall correctly, at the time Giselle came up, I was in the process of seducing you. I didn't think that outlining my dating history would be conducive to the tone I was trying to set."

I have to smile. The memory of that ride in Damien's limo is beyond delicious.

"After that," Damien adds, "the topic never came up again. And there's no reason it should. There is only one woman I'm interested in," he says, with such fervency that my legs go weak.

He tilts my chin up. "Better?"

"Yes." My scowl is more for myself than for him. "I don't like feeling like a jealous harpy," I confess. "But suddenly I'm being bombarded by Giselle. The painting, the trip back from Palm Springs, what Tanner said, and then finding out that you two actually used to date."

"I have no idea what Tanner said or what Palm Springs has to do with anything, but I can assure you that as far as the painting is concerned, Giselle has promised me again that she won't tell anyone that you're the model. She can be flighty, but she won't break her word."

"You talked to her tonight?"

"I did."

"Oh. Well, I'm very glad to hear it," I admit. "And I don't think Bruce will tell anyone, either."

"Do you want me to talk to him? I haven't yet."

"No. I trust him."

Damien nods, satisfied. "What about Tanner?"

I tell him about Tanner's theory that I was hired to make Giselle happy, and I see the anger light in Damien's eyes.

I laugh. "He's already been fired—thanks for that—but don't do anything else."

"What would I do?"

"Oh, I don't know," I say, thinking of my old boyfriend Kurt. "Sic the Yakuza on him. Task a satellite to blast him with a laser beam from space. Honestly, what couldn't you do?"

"I rather like the laser-beam-from-space idea."

"Promise me."

"I promise. He's out of Innovative and away from you. End of story."

"Good," I say, even though, honestly, I wouldn't be too upset if a space laser took out Tanner.

"And Palm Springs?" he asks. "I've always found it to be such a relaxing place. I'm curious how such a benign location made it onto your list of suspects."

"You're teasing me."

"Only a little."

"You should have told me you were giving Giselle a ride back in the limo."

"Oh," he says, and nods solemnly. "Yes, I can see your point. I should have. I would have. If I had given her a ride back in the limo."

He's patronizing me, of course, but I don't care because I'm still caught up on the whole he-didn't-drive-her thing. "But you came back in the limo. I assumed that was because you were giving her and the paintings a lift. But if you weren't, then why not just come back in the helicopter? Wasn't that your plan?"

"It was. But my meetings ended surprisingly early, and as you've noted so many times, I have a universe to run. It's difficult to conduct business from a helicopter. The noise level makes dictation tricky, and I've found that international clients get touchy when they think I'm shouting at them. Plus, it's much easier to make unscheduled stops along the way from a ground vehicle, and when I realized I had the time, I scheduled a few stops in Fullerton and Pasadena."

I cross my arms over my chest and cock my head to the side. "The point, Mr. Stark?"

"The point is that when I realized my schedule was going to change, I called my office to arrange to have the limo sent. My assistant told me that Giselle had called, hoping that I could suggest a transport company in Palm Springs that could arrange the delivery of some paintings for the show. Apparently she decided to bring back more than could fit in her car."

"And since you were right there, you offered to bring them back yourself."

"The paintings," he acknowledges. "Not the woman. As you said, I can be a very nice man."

I laugh. "Yes, you can."

"I wonder if I might make a suggestion?"

"Um, sure."

"Next time you have a question about whether or not I'm transporting other women in the limo, simply pick up the phone and ask."

"Right," I say. "I'll do that." I shake my head in exasperation at myself. "I really am sorry. I've been out of sorts."

"As have I," he says.

I think of the storm clouds that I've seen in his eyes. Of the legal troubles that seem to be brewing. "Will you tell me why?" I ask softly.

He looks at me for such a long moment that I'm afraid he's not going to answer. "I don't want what is between us to end."

"*Oh.*" His response is not what I expected, but I cannot deny the relief that almost swallows me. "No," I say, my skin already warming from the heat in his voice. "I don't, either."

He searches my face. "Don't you?" he finally whispers, and I see in his eyes the same vulnerable melancholy that I saw last night.

"Damien, God, of course not." I draw in a breath, trying to articulate to him how I've been feeling. "Everything feels skewed tonight, as if nothing is the way it's supposed to be. This house, even. I'm so used to coming here. To standing up in front of that balcony and posing for Blaine, and knowing that you're watching and that when Blaine leaves it will just be you and me in this house, on that bed." I flash a watery smile. "I love that you thought to give it to me, but it felt so final. As if we were closing a door."

"The bed was only a gift," he says. "Something for you to have, to lie on, to think about us. But tonight I thought you wanted to close that door. What was it you said? No rules, no game?"

"I was angry," I admit.

"I don't like the thought that I've hurt you or upset you."

"You haven't," I say. "Not really."

"Haven't I? I wonder . . ." His brow furrows, and his eyes search my face, but I don't know what it is that he's looking for.

"Damien?"

"I watched you tonight," he says, and his words are measured, the vocal equivalent of walking on glass.

I say nothing, just stand there, unsure of where this is heading.

"I couldn't help it," he continues. "When you're in a room, I have no choice but to watch you. You draw me in. You compel me. And I fall willingly under your spell." His eyes light with a smile, but even that doesn't hide the worry I see there. "I saw you with Jamie. I watched you talking with Bruce. I heard your laughter as you chatted with those ridiculous television stars. I saw the hurt on your face when you escaped the party with Evelyn. And each smile, each frown, each laugh, and each flash of pain in your eyes were like wounds to me, Nikki, because I wasn't the one sharing them with you."

I press my lips together and swallow, but still I do not speak.

"But this is what wounded me most of all," he says, and he reaches for my left hand.

I blink, and a single tear escapes and slowly trickles down my cheek. "You saw?"

My fingertip has returned to its normal color, and there are no indentations left. Even so, it seems to throb in memory of the pain. A pain that Damien now soothes with a single, gentle kiss.

"Will you tell me why?"

I want to tip my head down, but I force myself to look straight at him. With Damien, I do not feel weak or broken, but I am ashamed, because he asked me to come to him if I ever needed the pain again. And this is twice now that I have broken that promise. My finger, at least, survived my assault with more aplomb than my hair.

"I've told you most of it already," I say. "It's just been a hell of a day."

"All right. Now tell me the rest." His voice is easy, conversational, and it soothes me.

"This party," I admit. "Seeing Giselle as the hostess. Looking around at unfamiliar furniture." Now that I am articulating these things, I realize how much they've been bothering me. "I didn't even recognize the third floor. That room, this house—for so long, they've been ours. But tonight they weren't." *And I wasn't yours.*

I think the last part, but I don't say it out loud. Instead, I shrug, a little embarrassed, because I have just spilled so many things. I feel vulnerable and fragile, and I do not like feeling that way. And so I wait for him to say something to calm me.

It takes a moment for those words to come, and when they do, they surprise me. "Come with me," he says with an enigmatic smile. He holds out his hand, then leads me to a reading area tucked away against the east wall. It's the most private area of the mezzanine, and there is no line of sight to the third floor. It is dark here, the only illumination coming from the twinkling lights upon the railing.

"What are you doing?" I ask as he pulls me to the wall, then flips a switch. Immediately, soft light fills the long, glass-topped display case in front of us. There are only two things inside, as if this case is meant for treasures, and only two have been located.

They are battered copies of *Fahrenheit 451* and *The Martian Chronicles*, both by Ray Bradbury. I'm confused, but I trust that Damien has a purpose.

"Bradbury's one of my favorite writers," he begins.

"I know." He's told me about his love of science fiction as a child. In a way, it was his weapon against his father, his coach, and his life. I understand; how can I not when I'd relied on weapons of my own?

"He lived in Los Angeles, and one day I heard that he was going to be signing books at a store in the Valley. I begged my father to take me, but he'd scheduled an additional practice with my coach, and neither one of them was willing to cut me a break."

"What did you do?"

His grin is slow and wide. "I went to the signing anyway."

"How old were you?"

"Eleven," he says.

"But how did you get there? Didn't you live in Inglewood?"

"I told my dad I was going to the courts, hopped on my bike, and headed for Studio City."

"At eleven? In Los Angeles? It's a miracle you survived."

"Trust me," he says dryly. "The trip was much less dangerous than my father when he learned what I'd been up to."

"But that's an insane distance. You rode all that way?"

"It's only about sixteen miles. But with the hills and the traffic, it took me longer than I thought it would. So when I realized that I'd be late, I hitched a ride."

My chest is tight, my mother's warning to avoid strangers and never, ever, ever pick up hitchhikers ringing in my ears. I am terrified for the boy he was, taking horrible chances because the father that he was supporting was too much of a shit to grant him the one small request that could make him so happy.

"It was close," he says. "But I made it on time."

Obviously I already know that he survived the journey, but even so, my shoulders sag with relief. "And you got the books," I say, with a nod to the case.

"Unfortunately, no. I got there during the scheduled time for the signing, but they were all out of books. I decided to ask Bradbury to sign a bookmark instead, so I told him my story and he told me he could do better than a bookmark. Next thing I know, his driver is putting my bike in the trunk of his car and we're off to his house. I spent three hours chatting with the man in his living room, then he let me pick two books off his shelf, signed them, and had his driver take me home."

I feel ridiculously weepy at this story and blink back the threatening tears. "And your dad?"

"Never told him. He was pissed as hell, but all I confessed to was taking my bike and riding along the beach. I paid for it," he adds darkly, "but I had the books. I still have the books," he adds, nodding toward the case.

"You do," I say. "Bradbury sounds like a really nice man."

"He was."

"This is a wonderful story," I say, and I mean it. These are the kinds of tidbits from his life that I want inside me. Bits of Damien, to fill me up. "But I'm not sure why you're telling it to me now."

"Because the things in this house mean something to me. Not the props I had brought in for the party, but the real things. There's not much yet, but it's all precious to me. The art. Each knickknack. Even the furniture." He looks at me, and I see passion in his eyes. Not sexual, though. This is deeper. "You are no exception, Nikki. I brought you to this house because I want you here, just as I wanted your portrait."

I lick my lips. "What are you saying?"

"I'm saying that I don't think you could have made me happier than to say you felt jealous watching Giselle act as hostess of the party. But let's be clear. She's not the hostess in this house, and she never could be. Do you understand?"

I nod awkwardly. I am breathless. I am overwhelmed. And I want desperately to be in the circle of his arms.

The air between us crackles as Damien moves forward. He is close, so close, and yet he is not touching me. Not yet. It is as if he is punishing both of us. As if he is reminding us of why we should never be apart—because the coming together is just too damned explosive.

"Damien," I say. That is all that I can manage.

Slowly, he strokes his fingertips down my arm. I bite my lower lip and close my eyes. "No," he says. "Look at me."

I do, my eyes meeting his as his fingers slide farther down, lower and lower until his hand is over mine, both resting lightly on my thigh over the hem of my dress. His palm is flat, his hand completely covers mine. Slowly, he slides our joined hands up so that I am lifting my skirt until it is at the juncture of my thighs and my ass. "You belong here," he says. "Wherever I am, you belong. You're mine. Say it."

"I am. I am yours." My breath is coming harder as his hand eases off mine, then begins to creep even higher, slowly, slowly, so goddamned slowly.

"I need you." His raw voice sends ripples of desire through me. My sex clenches, and it takes all my self control not to grab my own damned hem and yank my skirt up around my waist. "I need you now."

"God, yes," I manage, forcing out the words. "Damien, oh, please."

Roughly, he pushes me backward until I am wedged into the corner. The glass case is beside me, and I reach out, clutching the polished wood for support as his mouth closes over mine. Our kiss is wild, fevered. I am starved for him and I take greedily everything he has to give.

His fingers continue their upward climb as I hungrily take his mouth with mine, my tongue thrusting against his, my teeth grazing his lip. And then, suddenly, his fingers stroke my sex and I cry out, my sound of pleasure muffled only by the renewed assault of his lips against my own.

"No panties," he says, sliding a finger deep inside me. "You said—"

"I lied," I admit, though I am not certain how I am able to form words. "Shut up and kiss me."

"Kiss you? Ms. Fairchild, I'm going to do more than that."

"The party?"

"Fuck the party," he growls.

"If someone comes down—"

"They won't."

"But if—"

"Nikki?"

"Yes?"

"Hush."

It's an order that I can't disobey, because he closes his mouth over mine, his tongue filling me, and I open to him, wanting to taste him, to lose myself to him.

Roughly he lifts my thigh. I bend my knee and hook it around his leg. My skirt slides up again and he pushes it up even farther until I am fully exposed. He breaks our kiss long enough to look down at my naked sex, and his groan is low and almost painful. I cannot touch him—I need my hands to steady myself between the wall and the case—and I am tormented by the desire to feel his cock beneath my hand. To stroke him and feel how much he wants me, and to know that his own desire matches mine.

His hand cups me, his fingers sliding over me, making me tremble. I am desperately wet and the feel of his hand upon me is making me crazy.

"Damien, please—"

"Please what?"

"Please, please fuck me."

"Whatever the lady wants," he says, and as he slowly, teasingly slips a finger inside me, I close my eyes and tilt my head back, smiling at the musical sound of his other hand tugging down the zipper of his trousers.

I feel his erection, hard against my leg. Then the head stroking me, teasing me. His hands edge down, one cupping my rear and lifting me just slightly, then releasing me so that I sink down as he thrusts into me. Once, twice—deeper and deeper until we are in a frenzy and he is slamming his body against mine and I want more, so much more, and the sound of my body thrumming against the wall must surely be shaking the house, and how can the guests at the party not hear, when the sound of our passion is ringing so loudly in my ears?

I gasp, clutching the case as a flurry of electric sparks seem to concentrate inside me, tighter and tighter, until they threaten to explode. And then I'm close, so very close and—

I start to cry out, then feel his hand close tight over my mouth. I tilt my head back and swallow the scream of pleasure, my muscles throbbing around him, pulling him in tighter and harder as he thrusts into me again and again.

I open my eyes, and see that he is looking at me, his eyes searching my face with an expression of such unabashed passion that I think I will come again merely from the look in his eyes.

"Damien," I whisper, and it is as if his name is a trigger. I see the rapture cut through his body, I feel him tighten against me, his body going tenser and then the warm release as he comes inside me.

He exhales, then sags against me.

"Nikki," he says.

"I know," I whisper.

His lips brush softly over mine, a tender kiss that contrasts the wildness of our coupling, and is just as perfect.

He is soft now and slips out of me. My thighs are sticky, and though I know I have to, I don't want to wipe away the feel of him on my skin.

"Here," he says. He has a handkerchief in his hand, and he gently cleans me up, then adjusts my dress. "Good as new," he says.

"Better," I say.

He strokes my hair, then traces the line of my ear, then brushes his thumb over my lip. It is as if he is trying to prove to himself that I am real. "I didn't like the way I felt today," he finally says. "Seeing you like that. Knowing you were angry with me."

"I didn't like it, either," I admit.

"I suppose there's something to be said for makeup sex."

"Definitely."

He takes my hand. "I meant what I said, Nikki. I don't want this to end. I don't want us to be over."

I look at his face, at the chiseled expression and the firm, demanding eyes, and I am confused. "I know," I say. "I don't, either."

He strokes my cheek, then curls a strand of hair around my finger. "No," he says. "I need to be clear. I don't want our arrangement to end. You're mine, and there are rules. And I want our game to continue."

15

Our game.

The force of these unexpected words crashes over me, and I take a step backward. He reaches out, and though I take his hand without hesitation, I find that I am shaking my head. Not necessarily in protest, but in confusion.

"I—I don't understand."

"I think you do. And I think you want it, too. Tell me, Nikki, did you leave your panties at home because you like the way it feels, or because you like knowing that you're open to me? That I can touch you—that I can fuck you—whenever and wherever I want?"

I swallow, because he is right. More than that, I understand now the melancholy I saw in his eyes Thursday night, followed by the possessiveness when he claimed me after midnight.

He is right—I am his. How can it be otherwise when he is inside my heart now?

But this?

He is watching me closely, examining me with the same implacable analysis that he uses to vet a business transaction or a financial report. But I am a woman, and my emotions don't follow the line of a ticker tape. He knows that, too, of course, and beneath the hard, logical intellect, I see the soul-deep vulnerability.

He wants this. Maybe he even needs it. And he has handed all of the power of this moment to me.

My heart twists, because the truth of it is that I want it, too. Isn't that why I've felt lost all night? I discovered a new side to myself when we played our game, and despite being "his," I felt more liberated than I ever had. More in control of myself and my emotions. More centered, I think, as I brush my thumb over the finger that I had so tightly bound only moments before.

I am still holding tight to the side of the glass case. As I glance down and see the two Bradbury books, I cannot help but shiver as I think of the story Damien told me. I picture him, young and strong, riding his bike to escape his father. Riding to meet his hero, a man who crafted worlds out of ink and imagination. Insubstantial, but real enough to a boy who needed to escape.

Is that what he's doing now? Crafting a false reality out of smoke and mirrors and tempting me into the fantasy with him? But it's not fantasy that I want with Damien. I want the reality. The moments, like the Bradbury story, when Damien lets me in enough to see a bit of his past and a piece of his heart.

My chest tightens as I shift my gaze from the glass case to Damien's equally transparent eyes. He is awaiting my answer, and I want to melt against him and whisper *yes, yes, of course, yes*. But I stand still, frozen by the fear that if I do, I will be letting myself get pulled into something that isn't and never can be real.

"Why?" I ask. "Before, you said that you wanted me. But you have me now, with or without the game." I lift my leg and point toward the emerald ankle bracelet. "I'm still wearing it,

Damien. You know I'll always wear it. So why? What difference does it make?"

He tilts his head toward the glass case. "You say you want me to open up more," he says, and I marvel at the way he always knows what I am thinking. "I want that, too. I don't want secrets between us, Nikki."

"You told me about the tennis center," I say.

"Not everything," he replies.

I stay perfectly still, because I know that is true.

"I need parameters, Nikki. Especially now. I need to know—" He cuts himself off and looks away, his jaw clenching as he wrestles with the words. "I need to know that you will be here, with me, no matter what."

He looks so vulnerable, and I am humbled that I have so much power over a man with strength such as Damien.

"Don't you already know that? I do."

There is something dark in the eyes that look back at me. "How can you, when there are still so many things you don't know?"

He is not saying anything I haven't thought of, but for a moment, I am afraid. What dark secrets does Damien have that still remain buried?

The thing is, I understand better than anyone why he wants the facade of the game in place if he's going to try to open up to me. I cut myself in order to cope with the horrors of my childhood, but what did Damien do? Nothing except conquer the world and learn to bury his secrets deep.

I glance down at the books in the glass case, and can't help the smile that touches my lips. Even the little things are a big step for Damien. But the shit in his past—the things like Sara Padgett and the guilt he felt over that poor girl's suicide—those are the kinds of things that Damien needs to say with a net.

The truth rips through me. *The game is his net.*

And once that net is in place, doesn't it make sense that the physical between us can strengthen the emotional?

Maybe I'm manufacturing a justification, but there's no denying that I want what he's offering. That desire, however, doesn't quell the lingering fear that still bubbles inside me.

Damien must see my hesitation, because he reaches for my hand. Only then do I realize that I have been unconsciously twisting my once-abused left finger between the thumb and forefinger of my right hand.

"Can you tell me?" he asks gently.

I swallow and try to will the words to come. "I'm scared," I confess.

"Of what?"

"Of you," I say, then immediately regret the words when I see confusion and hurt flash in his eyes. "No, no, not like that." I move closer and press my palms against his cheeks. "You are the best thing that has ever happened to me."

"That does sound terrifying."

I grin, grateful to him for putting me more at ease. "Sometimes I'm afraid that I'm using you." I pause, waiting for him to make a joke about how he would be very happy for me to use him any way that I like. But he remains silent, watchful, and I realize that he understands how hard this is for me. "Like a crutch, I mean." I think of the scars that mar my thighs. Of the string wrapped tight around my finger. Of the weight of a knife in my hand and the ecstasy of that first fiery sting when the blade slices through skin.

Most of all, I think of how much I've needed all of those things, and of the scars I now bear as testament to my weakness.

I swallow, then look down, not wanting to meet the eyes of this man who already sees so much inside me. "I'm afraid that you're a replacement for the pain."

"I see," he says, but there is no emotion in the words. Not anger or hurt. Nothing.

And then there is silence.

I draw a breath, but I don't look up. I'm too afraid of what I will see on his face.

Only seconds pass, but they are heavy, full of the weight of unsaid things. Then he tucks his fingertip under my chin and tilts my head so that I must either close my eyes or look at him.

I look and immediately have to blink back tears. Because it isn't anger or hurt or pity that I see. It is adoration, and possibly even a little bit of respect.

"Damien?"

"Oh, baby." He takes a step toward me, and I see the force of will that pulls him to a stop, staying just far enough from me to give me space, but close enough to give me strength. "Tell me—tell me what the pain does for you."

"You know," I say. I've told him all this before.

"Humor me."

"It grounds me," I say, as a tear rolls down my cheek. "It centers me. It gives me strength."

"I see." He brushes his thumb across my cheek, wiping away my tear.

"I'm sorry," I say.

"I'm not." There's a flicker of a smile at the corner of his mouth, and I find that my fear is fading. That I am, in fact, softly hopeful.

"You humble me, Nikki. Don't you see that?" It must be clear from my expression that I do not, because he goes on. "If I do all those things for you—soothe you, center you, give you strength—then that is worth more to me than every penny I have earned building Stark International."

"I—" I start to speak, but words don't come. I haven't thought of it that way before.

"But, baby," he continues, "it's not true. The strength is in you. The pain is just your way of mining it. And as for me? I like to think that I am a mirror for you. That when you look at me, you see the reflection of everything you really are."

I am crying openly now, and he moves to a nearby coffee table and brings me a box of tissues. I wipe my nose and sniffle, feeling overwhelmed and foolish, but blissfully happy.

"You talk as though you love me," I say.

He doesn't answer, but his slow smile lights his eyes. He steps closer, one hand cupping the back of my head as his lips close over mine in a kiss that starts out sweet and gentle, but ends up so deep and demanding that it curls through me all the way down to my toes.

"Say yes, baby," he says, breaking the kiss. "Say that you are mine."

"How long?" I ask, breathlessly. But he doesn't answer. He doesn't need to. I see the answer in his eyes—for as long as it takes. For as long as we want. For as long as I consent to be his.

He says nothing, merely stands in front of me. So much rides on my answer, and yet his eyes are calm, his stance casual. Damien is a man who shows nothing he doesn't want to show. And yet there is so much he wants to show to me, and so much that I want to share with him.

I hesitate only a moment longer, and only because I want to look at him. I want to drink in this man who has more strength than any human I have ever met, and yet is willing to humble himself before me.

How can I have thought that he has shared too little with me? Not specific events, maybe. But Damien has shown me his heart.

"Yes," I say, holding out my hand. "We have a deal, Mr. Stark."

The smile that spreads across his face is slow and wicked, and I laugh out loud.

"Oh, dear," I say.

"Sweetheart, you have no idea." He gives my hand a tug. "Come on."

Considering we'd both been MIA from a party that he is hosting in his own home in part to celebrate a portrait of me that now hangs on his wall, I assume that the reason we ascend back up the service elevator is to slide seamlessly back into that party.

The first person we see when we step into the small hallway that leads to the kitchen is Gregory, Damien's distinguished, gray-templed valet. "Ms. Fairchild and I are going out." I blink in surprise. Gregory shows no reaction at all.

"Of course, Mr. Stark. I'll take care of supervising the cleanup and closing out the house."

"We're leaving?" I whisper once Gregory has moved away and Damien is propelling me into the main area.

"We are," he says.

I consider arguing. Emily Post and Miss Manners flow in my blood, not to mention the even stricter social rules of Elizabeth Fairchild. One does not leave one's own party. There are rules. Proprieties that must be observed and social niceties that must be respected. Whatever Damien has in mind can wait, and I should say as much. I should put my foot down and insist that we stay here, mingling and making polite conversation.

Instead I mentally bitch-slap my mother's rule book and stay blissfully silent.

We make three additional stops. First at Giselle, who seems baffled, but doesn't argue. I wear my practiced plastic smile as she and Damien talk. I'm not as put off by her as I was earlier, but neither do I intend to enlist her as my new best friend. Next, we track down Evelyn and Blaine to say both congratulations and goodbye. I'm in the middle of a very proper handshake with Blaine when we both look at each other and laugh. "Come here," he says, and pulls me into a hug.

The hug I receive from Evelyn is even bolder, and as she holds me close I hear her whisper. "Glad I'm not the only one getting a little tonight."

"Only a little?" I reply, then smile as she laughs wickedly.

"And there it is, Texas," she says, releasing me. "That's why I like you." She aims a finger at me. "This week," she says. "Photos and wine and talking trash, and not necessarily in that order."

"It's a date," I say. Then realize my camera's downstairs in the library.

"Leave it," Damien says, when I say as much. "I promise you won't need it."

"I don't know," I counter. "I can't think of a more beautiful sight than you standing naked in front of a window."

"Are you under the impression there will be nakedness involved tonight?"

"I'm hopeful, Mr. Stark. I'm very, very hopeful."

Jamie is the last person we seek out, and we find her at a table on the balcony deep in conversation with a tousle-haired guy in a Hawaiian print shirt.

Oh, no, Jamie, I think. *Not another one. Not after going on and on about Raine.*

"Hey, you two," she says, looking up at us. "Louis, this is my roommate, Nikki. I'm guessing you already know Mr. Stark."

As Damien and Louis do the meet-and-greet, Jamie's eyes dart to me. *Everything okay?*

I nod. *Everything's fine.* I glance at Louis. *Are you—?*

She wrinkles her nose and gives the slightest shake of her head. "Louis is a director," she says breezily. "We were talking television. Great house," she adds, turning her attention to Damien. "Greater party."

"Glad you think so. Nikki and I just came by to say our goodbyes."

"Oh." She gives me a knowing look. I paste on my most innocent smile.

"Edward will take you home whenever you're ready," Damien tells Jamie. "Enjoy yourself."

"Cool. Thanks." She gives me a goodbye hug and Damien and I sneak back through the kitchen to the service area so that we aren't waylaid by anyone catching us leaving by the stairs.

"So where are we going, Mr. Stark?" I ask as we step out into the cool night air. "Do you fancy a walk?"

"Actually, I fancy a drive."

Usually Damien parks in front of his house. Tonight, however, the driveway has been taken over by a valet parking team called in to handle the party traffic.

I follow him around the house, frowning as we pass the attached garage. "Where are we going?"

"Someplace you haven't seen yet."

"Uh-huh." I'm intrigued, and as I take his hand I glance around the property. We're in an area north of the house, away from the lights of the party. It's dark here, with the exception of soft landscaping lights cleverly hidden among the plants and stonework.

He's right; despite the amount of time I've spent on the third floor, I've done very little exploring of the rest of the house or the grounds. Of course, the landscaping near the structure has only recently been completed, and beyond that perimeter of flower beds and walking paths and picnic areas, the plants still grow wild, though I see that Damien has hired someone to cut away some of the brush and install soft lighting to mark footpaths through the undergrowth.

"It's so pretty out here," I say as we follow a flagstone path that twines away from the house.

"It is," he agrees, but his eyes are on me.

"Watch the path, Mr. Stark," I say.

"I'd rather watch you."

I grin as he wraps his arms around me and pulls me into a bone-melting kiss. The fire he set inside me only moments ago has not been fully extinguished, and now those embers burst back into flame. "Here?" I whisper, pressing my sex hard against his thigh, then moaning softly at the sweet torment of the returning pressure. "Outside? On these hard, cold stones?" My words may sound reluctant, but I know that my tone does not. Right then I think I want nothing more than the press of stone against my back and the feel of Damien, hot and hard, inside me.

His voice is low and sultry with just a hint of a tease. "What exactly do you want me to do to you, Ms. Fairchild?" His fingers brush my shoulder, sliding the spaghetti strap down my arm so that it hangs loose. "This?" he asks, as he bends to brush his lips over the swell of my breast.

I gasp, my chest heaving, the chiffon that still clings to my now erect nipple rubbing provocatively.

"Or maybe this?" He traces his fingers up my leg, higher and higher until he grazes the soft skin between my thigh and my sex.

"Maybe," I whisper.

"It would be sweet, wouldn't it?" he asks as his hand moves up again, tracing the trimmed line of hair on my pubic bone, then dipping down to tease the same soft spot on my other leg. "Here, under the stars. My hands on you and only the night around us. My tongue on your breast, the cool air grazing your erect nipple. A whisper of cool wind brushing over your hot cunt."

My legs grow weak, and I close my arms around his neck to keep from melting beneath his words and his touch.

"Is that what you want?"

"Yes," I say.

His smile is slow, and I draw in a ragged breath as he leans close. His lips graze the corner of my mouth, then my temple. Then my ear. I feel his warm breath, and then the softest whisper of a word. "No."

I am not aware, but I must make some sort of noise in protest, because he chuckles.

"No," he repeats. "I have something else in mind."

And then he gently frees my hand from his neck and straightens my dress and tugs me forward onto the path. I follow, irritated, turned on, and very, very eager.

A few moments later, he points out a flat area tucked in between two brush-covered slopes. "I'm thinking of putting in a tennis court there."

I glance sharply at his face, but it is carefully blank. "Really?" I say, working hard to keep my voice casual. I know how long it has been since he's played tennis. More, I know why he walked away from the game.

"Maybe. I haven't decided. It's been so long, and I'm afraid—"

He cuts off his words, his forehead creasing into a scowl.

"—that it won't be fun?" I suggest, trying to finish his thought.

He doesn't answer, but I see the affirmation in his eyes.

"Well, if you do install a court, you can teach me how to play." I speak lightly. "That will ensure that you have fun. I promise. Playing with me will be quite amusing."

"Amusing?" he repeats, and I'm happy to hear the teasing note in his voice. "I'm imagining you in a tennis dress. Amusing isn't the word that comes to mind."

"And will our rules apply then, Mr. Stark? I'm not sure how much tennis will get played if I'm wearing one of those outfits and no underwear."

"I'm intrigued, Ms. Fairchild. I think you may have made up

my mind for me. I'll start interviewing construction companies in the morning."

"Very funny," I say.

"You laugh now," he says. "But wait until I take you by the ball cage."

"Now you're just talking dirty to me."

He laughs and grabs my hand, and I hurry to keep step beside him. My mood is light, and I'm glad we escaped the party. Whatever drama had been clinging to me has dissipated. It is just me and Damien and the wide night sky.

"What?" he asks.

I shake my head. "I didn't say anything."

"You're smiling."

"Maybe I'm happy."

"Are you?" he asks, his eyes roaming over my face. "So am I."

"Damien." I move closer, craving a kiss, but it's his finger that my lips find. "Ah-ah," he says. "Start that up and we'll never get where we're going."

"So we are going somewhere? I was beginning to think we were simply taking a hike to Ventura County."

"Actually," he says, "we're here." We've stopped in front of a vine-covered hill.

"Lovely," I say. "But if you're planning to ravage me in the flowers, I should say that I would have been just as happy on the stone path."

"I'll make a note for future reference," he says. "But this isn't our final destination."

"Oh?"

He doesn't answer my question. At least, not with words. Instead, he pulls out a key fob, presses a small red button, and a set of wooden doors—camouflaged with vines—begins to rise.

Light from the interior emerges, spreading wider and wider as the door lifts higher. I feel as though there should be a soundtrack—"Ode to Joy," perhaps—as this secret room is revealed.

At first I can see nothing because my eyes haven't adjusted to the abrupt change in lighting. But as Damien leads me toward the now open door, I see that this is a garage. A huge garage, to be precise, and as I stand in the doorway and look up and down the long, narrow structure, I count no less than fifteen classic cars all lined up and polished.

The walls are white, as is the concrete flooring. The lights overhead are glaring white as well. For a moment, I feel like I've died and gone to car heaven. I turn and gape at Damien. "You have got to be kidding me. You've barely finished the actual house, and yet you have a fully tricked out, fifteen-car garage hidden in the hillside?"

"I didn't want a detached garage to mar the landscape," he says. "Although to be fair the garage has been on the property long before the house. I built this three years ago while my architect was working out the plans for the residence. And just to clarify, it's a twenty-car garage."

I shoot him a bored look. "All this space in the hills and only twenty? And detached from the house? Seriously, Mr. Stark, what happens if it's raining?"

"I use the tunnel access," he says nodding toward the far side and a metal door over which is neatly printed the word "Residence" in red block letters.

"You really are a walking cliché," I say, but I'm laughing.

"Not at all," he says. "I'm a driving one." He looks giddy, like a boy playing with his favorite toys on Christmas morning, and the mood is infectious.

"What kind of car is this?" I ask, pausing by the one closest to the door. It is old-fashioned and open, and I can imagine women in flapper gowns riding with the top down, waving at boys and feeling smug in their daring.

"A Gardner touring car," he says. "But come here, this is my real prize." We walk down two stalls to an ancient model, so polished and shined that it seems to glow as bright as the room itself. "A Baker Electric car," he says. "Thomas Edison actually owned this very automobile."

"Seriously?" I am duly impressed. "That should be in a museum."

"I offer it on loan quite often," he says. "But not permanently. I don't see the point of owning extraordinary toys if I can't have them around to enjoy. Just as I don't see the point of having money and not using it to acquire interesting things, if not for myself, then for the people I care about."

I think about the Monet and the camera and the clothes and all the other gifts he's showered upon me. "Fortunately for those of us who are the recipients of your magnanimity, you have excellent taste."

"Indeed I do, Ms. Fairchild." He holds out his hand. "Come on. I'll show you our ride for the night."

We move down the row of cars and stop in front of a low-slung forest-green two-seater with a hood that seems longer than the car itself.

"All right," I say, unable to stop smiling. "Tell me all about it."

It's as if I've given him permission to sing. "Jaguar E-Type Roadster," he begins, then starts to itemize all of the intricate details of this fine automobile that, he assures me, will transport us to our destination in luxury and style.

"I hope there won't be a pop quiz," I admit. "Because I didn't catch anything but the name and the fact that I'm very impressed."

"That'll do," he says.

"Did you rebuild it?"

"What makes you think that?"

"Edward told me about the Bentley. I can't quite imagine you all covered in grease and oil."

"That's funny," he says with undeniable heat in his voice. "I have no trouble at all imagining you naked and slick with oil, spread out on a bed just waiting to be fucked."

"Oh," I say. "Oh."

He chuckles, then opens the door for me. The car is so low that it is almost impossible to enter and exit modestly in so short a skirt. A fact that Damien clearly picks up on, as his hand slides up the back of my thigh, then slides between my legs. My body trembles from his touch, and I moan as he slowly thrusts two fingers inside me. I grip the side of the door, my balance awkward, my entire body quaking with desire. I want to close my thighs, but I can't. One foot is on the floorboard, the other on the concrete. Shift my position and I will fall.

But then again, I don't really want to shift my position.

"Yes," he says. "This is how I want you. Hot and wet and on fire for me. I want you fuckable, Nikki. Anytime, anyplace, I want you ready."

"I'm always ready for you," I whisper, both because he wants to hear it, and because it is true.

"I should fuck you now," he says, moving his fingers slowly in and out of me. My sex clenches, drawing him in, wanting more and more. Wanting all of him. "I should bend you over the hood of this car and lift your skirt and spank your ass until it's red and throbbing. Then I should thrust my cock into your sweet, wet cunt. Is that what you want, Nikki? You can tell me. Tell me all the things you want me to do to you, Nikki. Tell me how you want me to fuck you."

My eyes are closed, my breasts are heavy. I am so wet and I feel so full. He has three, no, four fingers inside me now, and my hips are gyrating, wanting him harder, faster, deeper.

"Tell me," he repeats.

"I want you to fuck me," I say. "I want your hands on my tits and your cock deep inside me. I want you, Damien. Please, please, I want you so badly."

His fingers slide out of me, and he traces slow circles over my clit while his palm rubs lightly at my sex. I can smell my arousal, and I am shameless, shifting this way and that so that the feeling grows. I'm close, so close, and I want to come in his arms. I don't care that we're in his garage, that I'm bent half in and half out of his car. All I want is Damien. All I want is for him to take me where I want to go.

"Thank you," he whispers as he pulls his hand away.

"Damien," I moan. "Dammit, Damien, please."

"Frustrated, Ms. Fairchild?"

"You know I am."

"Good." The satisfaction in his voice makes me smile despite my state of abject frustration. "Now, into the car."

I do as he says, then sit with my legs pressed tightly together in the hopes that the pressure will quell some of my rising, desperate need.

He circles the car and gets in beside me, then looks over, his amusement obvious. "Legs apart, Ms. Fairchild. You don't get off until I say you get off."

I shoot him a sour glance, but I comply.

"I'm sorry, but I didn't hear you."

"Yes, sir."

"Good girl."

As I sit, lost in a haze of sexual frustration, he starts the car and maneuvers it out of its slot. I expect him to go back the way we came in, but he continues in the direction we were walking, which seems odd to me as all I see is a wall. As we get close, though, he presses a button on the dash and a section of the wall slides away.

Suddenly, we are in a dark tunnel lined with endless arcs of light that provide illumination all the way down, each arc lighting only as we approach it, giving the illusion that we are heading off toward infinity. I feel a bit like a Bond girl chasing down the bad guys. "Where are we going?"

"Just wait," he says. In front of us, no lights appear and for a moment I'm afraid that something has gone wrong with Damien's billionaire escape route. But it turns out that we've simply reached the end of the hill. We've emerged onto a private road—Damien's, of course—and after following it for a while we turn onto a twisting Malibu road and maneuver the hills until, finally, we reach the Pacific Coast Highway.

"You're really not going to tell me?" I ask. I am still sweetly on edge. The car is low to the ground and powerful, and I can feel the thrum of the engine against my ass, and the vibration is more than a little enticing. My breasts feel heavy and swollen and though chiffon is soft, my nipples are so stimulated that they are painfully erect.

Damien stays quiet, but he eyes me sideways, and I see the amused smile playing at his mouth.

"Are we going into LA? It's almost eleven."

"I'm afraid I'm going to keep you up past your bedtime, Ms. Fairchild."

I could protest, but it would be for show only. So I settle back in the soft leather and watch the ocean go by on my right. I feel Damien's eyes on me, though, and I turn to him, my expression stern. "Eyes on the road, Mr. Stark."

"I'd rather watch you," he says, but he turns back to focus on the road ahead. He reaches up and adjusts the rearview mirror. "That's better," he says, and his mouth tugs into a lazy grin.

"Like the view?" I ask. My legs are apart as he'd instructed, the hem of my dress hitting about mid-thigh.

"I'll like it even better in a minute."

I glance sideways at him, suddenly suspicious. "Oh?"

"I saw the way you were admiring Blaine's work," he says conversationally.

"He's very talented."

"The way he can portray arousal, shame, sexual longing. There are some at the gallery that show a woman in the throes of an orgasm. Spectacular, really."

"I haven't seen those," I say.

"Which one was your favorite this evening?"

"I liked them all," I say.

"Did you? I thought I saw a note of particular interest on your face when you looked at the woman on the chaise. Do you know the one I mean?"

"Yes," I say. My pulse has picked up its tempo. I'm remembering the painting . . . and I'm anticipating where Damien is going.

"What was she doing?" he asks.

"Touching herself," I whisper.

"Her lover off to one side. Her legs bound open."

"Yes." I have to force the word out.

"Take your shoes off," he says, and I bend down to tackle the small buckles. "Lift your skirt up around your waist. I want you bare against the leather. Oh, God, Nikki, yes," he says as I comply. The leather is smooth and cool against my red-hot skin. The vibrations beneath me seem even more erotic and I feel wanton and wild.

"Spread your legs, baby. Just like the woman in the painting."

His words—along with all they portend—are as erotic as his

touch, and my already hyperaware body kicks into overdrive. I'm aware of every movement, every brush of air against my skin, every beat of my heart, every tiny drop of perspiration that beads between my breasts. I work to control my breathing as I lift one leg and wedge it between the door and the dashboard. Then I take the other and hook my ankle over the gearshift box. I'm spread as wide as possible, and when I reach down to recline the seat, the motion shifts my hips up a bit. I make a small, strangled sound. My entire body tingles, but I am most aware of the heavy throbbing between my legs.

"She lies there, silently begging for her lover. Her cunt is slick, her breasts tender, her nipples begging to be sucked."

"Damien, please . . ."

"He doesn't touch her, though," Damien continues, and I bite back a frustrated moan. "He leaves her like that, a breeze blowing on her aching cunt."

He leans over and adjusts the air conditioner so that a stream of cool air blows right between my legs. It's soft and decadent and it makes me ache.

"If he were kind, he'd let her touch herself, but if you look closely at the painting, you see that her hand is in the air, wanting, but not reaching. Did you notice that, Nikki?"

"No," I say firmly. "I'm certain she was touching herself."

"Are you? Well, that's the thing about art. It's different for everybody. Shall I tell you what I see?"

I swallow and nod.

"I see the man who is not in the portrait. The woman means everything to him. And nothing can please him more than to bring her pleasure. And not just a quick fuck and a fast orgasm, Nikki. No, he wants to create their own nirvana. To build pleasure upon pleasure until the lines cross and neither is sure if it's torment or delight."

I lick my lips, my mouth dry. I'm hyperaware of my body. Of the motion of the car. Of my breasts, so tender now beneath the thin material.

"He wants his lover to trust him. To surrender herself to him completely. To let him orchestrate the pleasures of her body. But he leaves the ultimate choice up to her. He lets her have one hand free, and that is the moment Blaine captured on the canvas."

He turns and looks briefly at me before returning his attention to the road. "And so the question is, does she touch herself or does she trust him?" His voice is as warm and soft and intimate as the caress I crave. "You tell me, Nikki. What does the woman do?"

"She trusts him," I whisper.

And then I close my eyes and lose myself to the motion of the car and Damien's promise of what is to come.

16

"We're here," Damien says, after a journey that must have been a thousand miles.

"Here?" I repeat. I glance out the window and see that we're pulling into the driveway of the Century Plaza hotel.

"Tug your skirt down, baby," he says. "Unless you want to give the valet a treat."

I shift in the seat and cover myself, then bend even farther and put my shoes on. My body is achy and needy, and I am having trouble switching over to this new reality. "We're checking into a hotel?" The prospect is undeniably enticing.

"You are," he says, as he pulls up to the valet stand.

A young man in a red uniform hurries to Damien's side of the car. "I'm just dropping off the lady," he says.

Now I'm completely confused. "What are we—"

"Go register," he says. "Don't worry, you already have a reservation. And I suggest a drink. Take a seat at the bar. It's a beautiful venue and the bartender makes an excellent martini."

I am still in the car, and the valet is holding my door open. I wait for Damien to say more, but he has pulled out his phone and is scrolling through his text messages. I'm still not certain what the game is, but at least I've figured out that it is a game.

"Yes, *sir*." I slip out of the car, then remember my purse. "Wait a minute," I say, then I lean back in, making sure that the dress gapes enough in the front to give Damien an enticing view of what I wear underneath this dress. Which is absolutely nothing.

"Tip the young man, darling," I say, once I'm standing upright again. Then I turn and head into the hotel, making sure to swing my hips so that the skirt swishes as I walk.

I've not been in this hotel, and it's stunning. It takes me a moment to get my bearings, but I find both the registration desk and the lobby bar. I go to register first, smiling at the clean-cut man who greets me. "I'm checking in. Nikki Fairchild."

He taps at the computer screen, then looks up at me with an even wider smile. "I see that you're in our penthouse suite. Can I have someone take up your luggage?"

"Thank you, but no." I don't bother mentioning that I have no luggage.

"One key or two?"

"Just one," I say. I am, after all, a woman alone.

I consider going up to the room and lying naked on the bed, but Damien has told me to have a drink, and I am intrigued by both his plan for the evening and the thought of an excellent martini.

Mostly, though, I don't want to give Damien any cause for punishing me. Because I am certain that my punishment would be abstinence, and that is not something that is on my radar tonight.

It's late, but the bar is full. There are very few women, and the men are mostly in suits. Considering the business attire, I'm guessing that there is a conference going on, because almost every table is full. I take a seat at one of the bar stools as Damien said and order a dirty martini. As I wait for the bartender to fix it, I glance out across the lobby, but so far, there is no sign of Damien.

I'm not sure what to expect, and I have to fight the urge to pull out my phone and call him. Instead, I tell myself that patience is a virtue. Not necessarily one of my virtues, but a virtue nonetheless.

"You look distracted. Anything I can help you with?"

The voice belongs to a nice-looking man who sits one seat over from me at the bar. I finally see Damien, and am about to tell the man that no, I'm fine, when Damien meets my eyes, then very deliberately takes a seat at a nearby table with three other men.

"No, thanks. I'm fine."

The bartender puts the martini in front of me. I take a sip, confused, and wonder what happens next.

The man moves to the stool next to me, then leans even closer into my personal space. I consider sliding one stool over myself, but decide to remain put, my posture rigid, my body language very, very clear.

Apparently, though, the guy is illiterate in the body language department.

"Here for the conference?" he asks, and I can smell the liquor on his breath.

"No," I say. "I'm looking for some time alone."

"Lucky you," says the man who cannot take a hint. "Insurance regulations. Hours and hours of continuing education."

"Hmm," I say. I have my Coldly Polite face on, but he's apparently blind as well.

He leans in closer still, and now he's at such an angle that he has to grip the bar itself or risk sliding to the floor. I give in to temptation and lean in the opposite direction. "I can think of better ways to spend a late night," he says, his voice low and his intent unmistakable. "And we are in a hotel. You do the math."

"I was never particularly good at math," I lie. I consider moving to a table, but Damien specifically told me to stay at the bar. And no matter what else, I am following his rules tonight.

"You look like you'd be good at a lot of things," the man says, staring at my tits.

I turn back to the bar to find the bartender sliding a new martini in front of me. "From the gentleman," he says, nodding toward Damien.

"How nice," I say, then smile at Damien, which seems to irritate my companion.

Damien rises, says something to the men at his table, and strides to the bar. He stands right beside me, and as is always the case when Damien is near, I am suddenly hyperaware—of him, of my own body, of the rotation of the earth beneath us.

I smile at him. "Thank you for the drink. Sir."

I see the muscle in his cheek tighten when I say the last word, and I have to smile. He wasn't expecting that. "I hope you like dirty martinis."

"The dirtier the better," I say.

"Hey. You want to get lost? I was chatting with the lady."

Damien turns to him. "No," he says. "I don't think so. I want her."

The guy's eyes go wide, but he recovers fast. "The lady wants to be alone." Apparently, he's now all about chivalry.

"Does she?" He looks at me, then speaks very slowly and very clearly. "Did you come here to be alone? Or to be fucked?"

"I—" I have no idea how I'm supposed to answer. Beside us, the guy is apparently shocked into silence. "I guess that depends on who's doing the fucking," I finally say.

"I like your answer," Damien says. "What's your name?"

"Louise," I say, my middle name coming unbidden to my lips.

Damien grins. "Nice to meet you, Louise. I want you to come with me now."

I gasp, embarrassed, but also incredibly, undeniably turned on. "I—"

"Now." He holds out his hand and I hesitate only a moment before taking it.

Beside us, my companion stares with his mouth gaping open.

Damien helps me off the stool and aims a friendly nod at the insurance dude. "Maybe next time," he says, as the guy looks at Damien as if he's pulled off some kind of magic act. At least we're leaving him impressed and not pissed.

I am giddy as I follow Damien. I want to laugh. I want to take his hand and twirl in the lobby. I want to slam him hard against the lobby wall and claim his mouth with my own. I want his hands on me. I want him inside me.

I want him to fuck me, just like he said. And I want it now.

Apparently, so does Damien. As soon as the doors close on the elevator, Damien backs me against the wall. His mouth is hard against mine, his hand under my skirt, two fingers inside me. I grind my hips against him, wanting him, craving more of him than I can get in an elevator.

"God, Louise," he says, and we both laugh.

"I thought someone might recognize us. It's my middle name."

"I know," he says. "And I think they were all too tipsy to care. And too out of town."

"Could have been some paparazzi around."

"Fuck the paparazzi," Damien says, his words as harsh as sandpaper.

I ease my body against his. "I'd rather fuck you."

He kisses me again. Hard.

"That man was very disappointed," I say, when he breaks the kiss.

"Just claiming what's mine. And adding in the public service of giving that man a fantasy to keep him occupied this evening." He easily thrusts a third finger inside me, and I bite down on my lower lip to stifle a scream of pleasure. "Don't tell me you didn't like it."

"I liked it," I say as the elevator doors begin to slide open. "I liked it very much."

He withdraws his fingers, then directs me out of the elevator, punctuating the movement with a light pat to my ass. Our room is at the end of the hall, and I am in awe when we step inside. The suite has a living area and a dining area and a separate bedroom.

The door closes with a thump behind us.

"For a woman who likes to be mine, you were certainly doing an excellent job of flirting with that man."

I am still gawking at the room, but at these words, I turn, ready to defend myself, because I absolutely, positively did *not* flirt with Mr. Pushy.

My words die on my lips, however, when I see the humor in Damien's eyes. But there's something else, too, and I know where this is going.

I give a careless little toss of my head. "What was I supposed to do? You were ignoring me. I was just making conversation."

"He wanted more than conversation." He takes my hand and pulls me into the dining area so that we are standing by the large, round table. He turns me around so that he is behind me, then slides his hand up my leg under my skirt.

"You need to understand how completely you belong to me. Mine to pleasure," he says as his featherlight touch on my clit sparks a flurry of shudders within me. "Or mine to torment." He lands a hard spank on my rear, and I cry out, the sound wrenched

from my throat on a wave of pleasure. "You like that?" he murmurs.

Dear God, yes. I lift my rear, giving him better access.

"Spread your legs."

I comply eagerly, anticipating the feel of Damien inside me. I
hear the metallic sound of his zipper, then the soft brush of material against skin as he takes off his slacks. He keeps his shirt on,
and the starched cotton hem brushes against my skin when he
leans over again in a way that is probably unintentional, but
comes close to driving me crazy.

His hand returns between my legs, the other one going to cup
my breast. I start to rise, but hear his sharp censure telling me to
stay as I am, bent over and ready for him. "You want to be
fucked, don't you?"

"Yes," I moan. It's good that my hands are on the table. I
don't think my legs alone could hold me up. I am little more than
sensation. I am need and longing and sexual energy, and if he
doesn't let me come soon, I fear that I will collapse from the
pleasure of it all.

He slides two fingers in me, and I groan as my body tightens
around him. I'm close—so very close—and I bite my lower lip in
expectation of a soul-rocking explosion.

It doesn't come.

For that matter, neither do I, and I whimper in protest as he
withdraws his fingers, his hands going to a relatively chaste position on my hips.

"Turn around, baby," he says. "I want to see your face."

I turn, and his eyes say more than words ever could. I melt
under the desire I see there. The need and the hunger. It rips
through me until the only thing that I know in the world is
Damien. "Kiss me," I whisper.

He does, and it is a violent, hungry kiss that bruises my lips
until I taste blood. He pushes me back onto the sturdy table,

then grabs the dress at the bodice and rips it down, baring my breasts. I cry out, arching up to meet him, my hands going to his head to pull him down as his mouth closes over my nipple, his teeth biting just enough that I suck in air, cresting on a wave of intense pleasure that borders on pain.

"Now," he says, and what remains of the dress is up around my waist. The table is hard against my back, but I don't care, and I spread my legs wide for him then cry out as he thrusts deep inside me. I arch up, meeting his thrusts, feeling frenzied and wild and wicked and *his*.

Damien's.

He explodes inside me, my name on his lips. And then, spent and soft, he slides his hand down to where I am slick with his semen. I gasp as he strokes me in small circles, faster and faster until I again cry out and my body bucks from the orgasm that rips through it, then finally calms as exhaustion and bliss take over.

"Wow," I say, and curl up next to him.

"Indeed," he says.

We stay like that for a moment, still in each other's arms.

"This table is really uncomfortable," I finally say.

Beside me, Damien laughs.

"I think we need to clean it up, too. I'm not sure the maids will understand."

"I'm sure they've seen it all before," he says.

I turn and meet his eyes, my brows raised.

"Right," he says. "We'll take care of it. But now, I'm taking you to bed."

He holds out his hand, and I follow him into the spacious bedroom, with a bed that looks much more comfortable than the table. "A mattress," I say. "How novel."

"Come here." He tugs me to the bed and we abandon what remains of our clothes before sliding under the covers. I curl up beside him and we lie like that for what feels like hours, talking and flipping channels and watching snippets of old movies.

This is yet another thing I love about Damien—that shift from frenzied passion to these soft moments when I feel safe and warm and cherished beside him. It's as smooth and satisfying as a glass of port after a truly decadent meal.

"I'm not tired," I say, when I notice that the clock reads four A.M. "I'd say that I'm going to regret this in the morning, but it already is morning."

"Will you?" he asks.

I shake my head. "Not a minute of it," I say.

"Thank you."

"For what?"

"For indulging my fantasies."

I laugh. "Why, Mr. Stark. Haven't you heard? I'm yours to command."

He kisses me lightly. "And I'm very, very glad."

For a moment, we just lie there quietly. Then Damien says, "That phone call you asked about earlier. It was bad news. From a friend."

"Oh," I say. "I'm sorry." I remember what Charles Maynard said. "Is the friend in Germany?"

He gives me a sharp look. "Why would you say that?"

I shrug. "Charles's voice carries."

"So it does. No, Germany's something different."

"An indictment? One of your Stark International subsidiaries or something?"

The line of his mouth is hard as he answers. "Or something."

"Are you worried?"

"No." The word is firm. "Charles is handling it."

I nod. Since I know nothing about the laws of international trade and finance, I can't go far with this conversational thread. "Do you want to tell me about your friend's bad news?"

For a second, I think that he's going to say no. Then he speaks, his voice steady and even, as if he's fighting for control. "It's Sofia."

It takes me a moment to place the name. "Your friend from childhood? The one Alaine mentioned?"

He nods. "She's gotten herself into some trouble. It's not the first time, but it's frustrating. I keep hoping she'll get her shit together, but she keeps screwing up."

"I'm sorry. I hope it gets better for her."

He kisses my forehead. "Me, too."

I wait for him to tell me more, but he doesn't. That's okay, though, and I take his hand. "Thank you."

He doesn't need to ask what I mean. "I am trying," he says.

"I know you are." I spoon against him, feeling warm and safe. "And I appreciate it."

I'm facing away from him, and as I close my eyes, he strokes his fingers over my bare skin. The minutes tick away, and when he speaks, I have already begun to drift off, so that his words have the quality of a dream. "I never used to sleep naked."

"Why not?" I am only half awake, and I like that he is sending me to sleep with images of a naked Damien.

"Because when we traveled, Richter would come into my room. Somehow, I was always assigned a room of my own, even though the other boys had to share."

My eyes are open now, but I don't roll over. I'm afraid that if I look at him, he'll stop talking. "What happened?"

"He would come in. And he would touch me." His voice is strained. Hard and measured. "He would threaten me and swear that if I told anyone, that everything I had would be ripped away. And my father would have no money, and we'd starve on the street. But mostly, I would have the reputation of a little boy who told nasty, nasty lies."

"Bastard."

"Yes."

I stay quiet, wondering if he will say more. But he remains silent. I don't mind. He has told me two truths tonight, and I know that this is only one small part of something larger that is growing between us.

"I thought so," I say after a moment. "But I guess I was wrong about your dad."

"What do you mean?"

"I assumed he knew that your coach was abusing you. I realized in the limo that he didn't."

For a moment, there is only silence. When Damien speaks, his words are ice cold. "He knew."

I roll over, shocked into motion. "What? But . . . but why on earth would he expect you to be at the tennis center dedication if he knows what that vile man did to you?"

"I don't know," Damien says. He hesitates, his face drawn into hard lines.

"No," he amends. "I do know. The tennis center is owned by a sports conglomerate based out of Germany. Powerful company, powerful people on the board."

"I don't understand. Is your father involved with the conglomerate?"

"No. And my father couldn't care less whether I endorse a tennis center or a pet store. It's all about trading favors. I lend my name to the tennis center, and maybe those powerful people will pull a few strings in Germany."

"The indictment I keep hearing about?"

"Right. Charles agrees with my dad, actually. He's pissed as hell at me for making that statement outside Garreth Todd's party, even though I reminded him that the longer the whole thing drags on, the more billable hours he earns."

He smiles without humor. "To be honest, I should have kept my mouth shut. I'm not accustomed to acting rashly, and it was rash to make that statement."

"Why did you?"

"Because it's the truth. Because that center shouldn't be named after him. And because I'm tired of the world thinking that I admired that son of a bitch."

"Then you did the right thing."

"Maybe. But sometimes even the right thing has unpleasant consequences."

"It's that bad?" Worry snakes through me. "One of your companies is in that much trouble?"

Damien hesitates. "It has the potential to be very bad," he finally says. "But I don't think it will get that far. I still have a few strings left to pull."

I nod, somewhat appeased. If Damien isn't worried, I won't be, either.

"Come here," he demands, and I comply eagerly. I slide into his arms, and let the strength of his embrace push out the remaining wisps of worry. All I want is Damien, and I drift off to sleep in the comfort of his arms.

17

The shrill buzz of a doorbell startles me awake. I sit up, confused. I didn't even know that hotels had doorbells, but apparently the I'm-richer-than-Midas executive suites do, because that is definitely a bell—and it is definitely not being answered.

"Damien?" I expect to hear his reply from the bathroom, and when it doesn't come, I slide out from under the downy spread and stand up, my body both languid and sore, as if it's not entirely sure how it's supposed to feel after last night's adventure.

Another buzz makes me jump, this one followed by a brisk voice announcing, "Room service!"

The thought of coffee gets me moving. "Just a sec," I call back, then cast about for something to wear. I spy a robe draped neatly over the back of a chair, which is good considering the state of my dress. Damien put it there for me, of course. But where the hell is he?

I hurry out of the bedroom and through the dining area to the door. Although the waiter must have been out there for at least five minutes, he's not in the least bit ruffled. "Good morning, madam," he says as he wheels the cart in and starts to distribute the food to the now clean-and-tidy dining table. Damien really has been busy this morning.

The waiter is uncovering each plate as he moves it from cart to table, and I realize that I am starving. There's coffee, orange juice, eggs, toast, a waffle, fruit, and enough bacon to feed a small army. There's not enough silverware or cups for an army, though. In fact there's one coffee cup, one juice glass, and only one bundle of silverware wrapped in a black cloth napkin.

I may be slow this morning, but I've finally clued in on reality—Damien has skipped out on me.

"Will there be anything else?"

"No," I say. "Thank you. Do I need to sign a check or something?"

"No, ma'am. But I do have this for you." He reaches into the breast pocket of his jacket. He pulls out a small envelope and hands it to me. "Mr. Stark asked that this be delivered with your breakfast."

"Oh." I take the note, surprised but pleased. "Thank you."

I hold on to the envelope until he's gone. The paper is thick linen, and the name of the hotel is embossed on the back flap. It's sealed, and I unroll the silverware and use the knife to loosen the flap. I pull out a small sheet of the same linen paper. It's folded over, and when I unfold it I see Damien's neat, precise printing.

My darling Ms. Fairchild,

Enjoy your breakfast. If there's something you would prefer, simply call room service. I didn't know what you were hungry for. Personally, I woke up hungry only for you, but as you looked so lovely, I thought I would let you sleep. I need to be in San Diego for a six o'clock breakfast meeting with a troublesome business partner, but I'll be back in LA

by eleven. Stay in the room. Shop in the gift store.
Utilize the spa. Whatever you want.

  I will see you in a few hours, and the rest of
Sunday will be ours. I look forward to a delicious next
encounter.

  I must confess that I have never picked up a
beautiful woman in a hotel bar before. Having now
met you, I wonder what I've been missing all these
years . . .

  I will see you later. Until then, imagine me,
touching you.

Yours,
Damien

P.S. I suggest you wear something other than the
   shredded blue dress. Check the closet.

I am smiling so wide it hurts, and I hug the letter to my chest
and sigh, then collapse onto the bed and replay every decadent
moment of last night. Then I spend the rest of the morning doing
as Damien suggested. There's a darling floral-print sundress for
me in the closet, along with a cute pair of Yellow Box flip-flops.
I wear those downstairs and have a mani/pedi at the spa. Once
my nails are dry, I wander the lobby and buy both Damien and
myself oversized Beverly Hills T-shirts and matching baseball
caps.

After that, I sit by the pool with a magazine and drink two
Bloody Marys while I read all about the latest celebrity antics in
what will surely turn out to be a futile attempt to impress Jamie
with my Hollywood knowledge. The magazine has only one
small picture of Damien and me, and I immediately decide that
this particular publication is a million times more responsible
than its competitors.

At eleven, I still haven't heard from Damien, so I go back to the room to wait. The vodka goes to my head and I must drift off, because the next thing I know the mattress is shifting, and I'm opening my eyes and seeing the most gorgeous sight ever.

"Hi," I say.

"Hi, yourself. What have you done so far today?"

"Very little," I admit. "It's been heaven."

"Would you object to going out? I have someplace I'd like to take you."

"Yeah? Where?"

"Rollerblading on Venice Beach," he says, and I burst out laughing—at least until I realize he's serious.

"Really?"

"It's fun. Have you ever done it?"

I have to admit that I haven't, and Damien tells me that it's high time I tried.

"In that case, I have the perfect accessories." I unwrap the shirts and caps, then pull my shirt on over the dress and shove my hair into a cap. "The more we look like tourists, the less anyone will recognize us."

"Not to mention the fact that you look pretty damn cute."

I look at myself in the full-length mirror and decide it could be worse. It's not a fashion statement, but I look like a girl having a lazy, touristy Sunday afternoon.

Damien, of course, looks hot as sin in the gray T-shirt that hugs his body and the black baseball cap that accentuates his chiseled jaw and brilliant smile.

He has a leather backpack, and he offers to hold my wallet and phone. "Leave everything else," he says.

"Don't we have to check out?"

"It's my room," he says. "Well, the company's. We keep this suite permanently leased for visiting clients and execs from out of town."

Not a bad deal, I think, as we head down to the valet stand. Soon we're in the Jaguar and heading west down Santa Monica Boulevard.

Damien knows the small streets of Venice well and soon he has the car settled in an attended garage and we're sitting on a bench strapping on rented Rollerblades, kneepads, and helmets.

Twenty minutes later, we're back on the bench, taking them off and returning them to the little rental stand.

"I told you I'd be horrible," I say.

"You were pretty bad," he acknowledges. "I'm not sure how someone so graceful can actually have no balance whatsoever."

"I can balance," I say. "Just not on tiny little lines of wheels. What about bicycles?"

He eyes me dubiously.

I cock my head and raise my brows. "Yes. I can ride a bike."

We find a rental stand and then I spend the next two hours proving to him that I have in fact retained this childhood skill. Although, to be honest, it's not a childhood skill at all. My mother was too worried about potential scrapes and bruises. So I didn't learn to ride a bike until college.

"Another missing piece of your childhood," Damien says, when I tell him as much.

"That's okay. I'd rather one day biking with you on the beach than an entire summer as a kid."

"For that, I'll buy you an ice cream."

We park the bikes by a bright-blue painted ice-cream stand and order single dip cones with sprinkles. Then we put our flip-flops in Damien's backpack and walk down to the water's edge. Since it's the Pacific, the water is freezing even in the summer, and I am amazed that the people actually playing in the water haven't turned blue.

We walk in the breaking waves, letting the sand slide out

under our feet, holding hands and eating ice cream. A teenage girl is tossing a stick for a big yellow dog, and I tell Damien how I always wanted a puppy and how, surprise surprise, my mother repeatedly refused. He tells me how he brought a stray Lab home one night, but his father wouldn't let him keep it.

"Considering how often I traveled, it was for the best," Damien says. "The poor dog would have been kenneled all the time."

"But wasn't that the point? You were telling your dad you wanted the dog because you wanted off the circuit. You wanted home. You wanted the dog. And you didn't want the traveling."

Damien looks at me with a curious expression. "Yes," he finally says. "That was it exactly."

"Did you ever get a dog? Once you quit tennis and became Mr. Business Dude, I mean."

"No," he says, and his brow furrows. "No, I never have." He nods playfully toward the girl. "Think she'll sell me hers?"

"I'm gonna say no."

We return to the bikes and head in the opposite direction, toward Santa Monica. We take it slow, watching the tourists and locals, talking, enjoying the day. When we reach the mall, we lock up the bikes and walk down the Promenade toward the Coffee Bean & Tea Leaf. Armed with frozen mochas, we continue to stroll the shopping street until Damien says he's starving for real food and it's time he buys me dinner.

He suggests The Ivy, which even I know is a see-and-be-seen kind of place. "One, I don't think they'd even let us in dressed like this," I say. "And two, it's not exactly the best place to avoid the paparazzi."

"Pizza by the slice it is," he says, and we end up eating foldable slices of pepperoni pizza at tiny metal tables.

"There's no way The Ivy could be better than this," I say, and right now, for this day, with this man, I absolutely mean it.

I glance at the sky once we finish our pizza. "It's getting dark. Should we take the bikes back?"

"Soon," Damien says. "I want to show you something."

What he wants to show me is the Pier, though I tell him that I've been before. "But have you ridden the Ferris wheel?"

"No," I admit. "Is that where we're going?"

"Man of mystery, remember? I can't share my secrets."

"I'll take that as a yes."

"That's one of the things I most admire about you. Your cunning intellect."

I grin as we walk the rest of the way, then get in line for the ride. It's surprisingly short, and we only have to wait through two rounds of passengers before we're shown into our own little basket. Then the attendant shuts the door and up we go.

I laugh, delighted. Not only have I never been in this Ferris wheel before, I've never been in any Ferris wheel. It moves slowly, but the basket sways, which would be unnerving except for the fact that it's Damien beside me, Damien with his arm around me. And now—as the basket stops at the very top—Damien reaches for the backpack he set on the floor beneath his feet.

"What are you doing?" I cry. "Don't let go!" I glance out at the world around us. The sun is down now, and the lights from the Pier glow. It's like living inside a fairyland. A little too high up in a fairyland, actually. "Why aren't we moving?" I ask.

"Passengers are loading and unloading below," Damien says. He's upright now and holding two wrapped presents. One about the size of a pack of index cards. The other slightly bigger. More like the size of an external DVD drive.

"You brought me gifts?"

"I did," he says.

I am speechless. "I didn't get you anything."

He points to the hat and the shirt.

"I charged those to your room."

"It's the thought that counts. But if you don't want the gifts . . ." He bends over, pretending to put them back.

"No, no," I say. "It's all good."

We grin at each other. "The small one first," he says, handing it to me. As he does, the Ferris wheel starts to move again. I carefully peel back the paper to reveal a small gold box. When I pull off the lid, there are four chocolate truffles inside. "You've had the fondue," he says. "But the truffles are our specialty."

"Your company?" I ask. "The one in Switzerland?"

"I told you I'd have Sylvia order some for you."

I can't help the wide grin that tugs at my mouth as I pull one out. "Want a bite?"

He shakes his head. "They're all for you."

I take a bite and moan with ecstasy. These are easily the chocolate equivalent of nirvana.

I finish the truffle and hand the box back to Damien to carry in his pack. "Thank you," I say. "You really do amaze me."

"Because I bought you chocolates?"

"Yes," I say sincerely. "And so many other reasons as well."

He kisses me sweetly, then passes me the larger package. "Now this one."

I unwrap it carefully, then gasp when I see what it is. An antique brass frame with a stunning picture of the two of us in evening wear. Damien had taken me to the opera, and the paparazzi had been buzzing all around. This picture ran in the paper—I have a digital copy in my scrapbook file. But this looks like the original.

"Oh, Damien. It's amazing," I whisper. My eyes are locked on the image of the two of us together. "How did you get the picture?"

"Called the paper and bought a print," he says. "You look exceptionally lovely in that photo. I suppose that means the paparazzi are good for something."

"I wouldn't go that far," I say, wrinkling my nose. "But this, this I will always cherish." Emotion squeezes my heart. I've been at Damien's side hundreds of times, and at least as many images have been splashed across magazines and websites. But this—a picture in a frame—it feels permanent and real. It feels like the future.

I blink, suddenly weepy, but very happy.

"I thought you could put it on your desk at work," he says.

"I will," I say. "Then I can look at us every day."

The Ferris wheel stops up top again, but I don't mind. I clutch the framed photo against my chest with one hand and lean in close to Damien.

"It's the best gift ever," I say, and I mean it. "And it's been a great day, too."

Monday morning at Innovative, Trish dumps about a pound of paperwork on me, and I write my address and sign my name until I'm certain my hand is going to cramp up and surgery will be required. After that, she walks me around the office and introduces me to everyone, and I smile and nod and pretend like I'm going to remember all the names she's throwing at me. I've had the tour before, but it's nice to see the place from the perspective of an employee. We end up at my office, a tiny space on the south corner with a view of a parking structure.

It is, however, all mine.

I am organizing my desk when Bruce enters. "Welcome to your second day. All settled in?"

"All I need now is access to the network and I'm good to go." I glance at my phone to check the time. "Carla said she'd have me in the system by the end of the hour, so I guess I'll be official soon."

Bruce nods, then gives me the rundown of what I'll find on my calendar today, which basically boils down to internal meetings and getting familiar with the various company products. By the end of the day, I'll have met my team and have a handle on the products I'm managing. I've got a lot to learn—both product specs and staff names—but on the whole, I'm pleased with the plan for the day.

Bruce stands. "I know I promised you a first-day lunch, but it turns out I have to meet with my attorney. Would you mind if we postpone?"

"Don't worry about it. To be honest, I'm pumped to get caught up with all this reading."

He looks relieved, and I flash my best Cooperative Employee smile. A moment later, his expression shifts, and I fear that my smile has missed the mark. But his thoughts have moved past work. "I feel like I should apologize again for Saturday night."

"No," I say, because I really don't want to go there again. "It's not necessary. Truly."

He peers at me, then nods slowly. "Well, I hope that's not why you and Damien cut out early."

I can't help the heat that rises to my cheeks. "It's not. And please tell Giselle that it's okay. I promise I'm not upset."

His expression hardens. "If I see her, I'll tell her," he says, and I'm left wondering how to shift the conversation, because I have clearly stepped into something unpleasant. As it turns out, though, it is Bruce who changes the topic. He tosses a copy of *Tech World Today* on my desk. "Have you seen this week's issue?"

I haven't, but I immediately recognize the image on the cover of the tabloid-style newspaper. It's the logo of an Israeli company watermarked over a screenshot from some cutting-edge 3-D imaging software. I scan the article and then look up at Bruce. "This has been in the works for a while. Looks like they got it out of beta testing earlier than they anticipated."

"I heard through the grapevine that you were working on

something similar at C-Squared," he says, referring to Carl's company.

"I was," I say, then decide to take the plunge and tell him the truth about what happened. It pisses me off, but it's not as if I'm the one who did anything wrong. "I was on the team that pitched the C-Squared product to Damien."

"Is that how you two met?"

"No," I say. "We actually met years ago in Texas. We reconnected at one of Evelyn's parties." I don't mention that Carl had sent me into the party with the specific goal of attracting the attention of Damien Stark. That had been my first clue that Carl was an asshole. And many more clues followed in quick succession. "At any rate, the pitch went great, but Damien declined to invest because he knew about this Israeli product, though he didn't say his reason at the time. By then, he and I had gone out." Once again, my cheeks heat, because "gone out" doesn't even begin to describe the things I had done with Damien.

Bruce, thankfully, doesn't appear to notice my blush. "And Carl blamed you."

"And fired me," I say with a thin smile. "He's not high up on my favorite people list."

"To be honest, Carl Rosenfeld isn't high on anyone's favorite people list."

I smile, immediately more at ease.

A moment later, Cindy steps into my office with an envelope from a local messenger company. There is no address. I, of course, am certain it's from Damien. Considering the way Cindy hovers by my desk, she must think the same thing, and she's curious about what the world's sexiest billionaire sends to his girlfriend.

I'm curious, too. But since this is Damien we're talking about, I'm not opening it with Bruce and Cindy standing there. I set it firmly on the corner of my desk right next to where I have put the framed picture of Damien and me. "Insurance paperwork,"

I say nonchalantly, before turning back to Bruce and rattling off the first relevant thing I can think of about the Suncoast meeting last week.

Finally they are both out of my office, leaving me to, supposedly, settle in to work. I immediately reach for the envelope.

I open it, peek inside, and find my own pink scarf.

Okay . . .

Then again, at least now I have an excuse to call him. Not that I actually need an excuse.

Unfortunately, I only get his voice mail. "Hey," I say. "It's me. Thanks so much for the scarf. It suits me perfectly. How on earth did you know? I had a great time yesterday," I add, then hesitate a moment before continuing. "And I thought you might want to know—I'm wearing a denim skirt, a purple T-shirt under a denim jacket, and absolutely nothing else."

I'm grinning when I end the call, and it takes some doing to focus on the specs that I pull up on the laptop I've been issued by Innovative. After a while, though, I get into a groove, and it's not until one of the guys on my team pokes his head in my door that I realize I've been engrossed for hours.

"I'm going down to grab a sandwich," he says. "Want anything?"

"Alex, right?"

He nods.

"Mind if I tag along?"

"Oh. Well, sure. Okay. Yeah. I mean, I'm just gonna get something downstairs and bring it back."

"Sounds perfect to me." I grab my purse and follow him to the elevator. He's tall and so skinny that I'm guessing I have at least ten pounds on him. His hair is cut short, almost into a military buzz, and he's wearing a T-shirt announcing that Pluto is still a planet. On that, I agree wholeheartedly, and I tell him so.

It is as if I have opened the conversational floodgates. By the time we reach the lobby, I know everything about him except his Social Security number and have been invited to join his World of Warcraft guild anytime.

"So you're dating Damien Stark," he adds, as we cross the lobby to the small cafeteria. "That's cool."

"I think so," I say politely, but I can't help but cringe a little. I am starting to realize that by being Damien's girlfriend I have taken on more than just Damien. I have parked myself under a microscope. For someone who has lived most of her life behind a mask of polite indifference, it is not the most comfortable place to be.

"Yeah, so the sandwiches here are pretty good," Alex says, and I am grateful for the change of subject. "The pizza kind of sucks, though."

"Salads?"

"Beats me," he says. "I don't do rabbit food. Meet you back here?"

I nod, then head toward the rabbit food area. I'm waiting for the server to put together a Cobb salad for me when a familiar-looking Asian woman steps into line behind me. I'm trying to place where I've seen her before when she points at me and says, "Innovative, right? You're the new girl."

"Nikki Fairchild," I confirm. "I'm sorry, I've been introduced to about a million people, at least it feels that way. I don't remember your name."

"No, no, we haven't met. I work in the building. Lisa Reynolds. I'm a business consultant, and I've known Bruce for years."

I suddenly remember where I've seen her. "You were in the lobby on Friday," I say. "At one of the tables."

"I usually am at least once a day. I can't live without coffee, and I like to get out of the office. Here," she adds, then digs in her purse for a business card. "If you ever want to sneak downstairs for a latte, give me a shout."

"Thanks," I say, genuinely pleased. I haven't met that many people since I moved to Los Angeles, and I'm psyched to have a potential friend in the building.

I promise Lisa I'll give her a call this week, then head upstairs with Alex. I want to get back to work, but I also know I should get to know my team. I suggest that we eat in the break room, but I have to confess that I am relieved when he tells me that he's going to eat at his desk so that he can play WoW.

I've finished the salad and am deep into an analysis of some troublesome code when Damien calls. "Hey," I say. "Did you see that article in *Tech World*?"

"Talking shop, Ms. Fairchild?"

I laugh. "What else should I talk about? The scarf you sent me? Your skill at picking out gifts has become a little rusty, but I guess there is some logic. If I already own it, I probably already like it."

"You make a good point," he says. "I'll keep that in mind for future gifts, too. At the moment, though, I was hoping to talk about the very interesting piece of correspondence I received this morning."

For a moment, I have no idea what he could be talking about. Then I remember the drive in the Bentley. *Oh my.*

"Are you in an office or a cubicle?" he asks.

"An office," I say. I swallow, recalling all the things I wrote in that letter.

"In that case, my dear Ms. Fairchild, I think you should close your door. For that matter, I think you should lock it."

"Damien, I'm at work," I protest, but I do as he says.

"What a coincidence. So am I. Imagine my surprise as I'm reviewing my morning mail. Requests to speak at business conferences. Investment opportunities. Real estate proposals. All intriguing opportunities, but none so enticing as what I find when I open a simple letter sent on my very own stationery."

"Damien . . ."

"You have a way with words, Ms. Fairchild. I was quite relieved that my assistant was at her desk when I read your letter. I don't know that I would have been able to hide my erection. You really are quite a little minx."

My brows lift. "A minx?"

"*I can still remember the sound of your voice,*" he quotes, "*so smooth I almost came just from the sound of it. And the cool leather against the hot skin of my ass. Even then, I wanted your hands on me, your cock inside me. I barely knew you, and yet I wanted to submit to you utterly.*" He says, "Yes, I think minx is a very accurate description."

"Oh." Hearing my own words read back to me, I have to silently agree. "I was inspired."

"I'm very glad to hear it. When I ran across the scarf in the apartment this morning it reminded me of you, and after I got your letter, I thought that I should return it right away. You see, we didn't really let that scarf live up to its potential."

"We didn't?" My mouth is dry.

"No," he says, softly. "But I intend to make up for that. There are a lot of things one can do with a scarf. A lot of things one can do with fringe. The delicate brush over your erect nipple. A teasing stroke over your hot cunt. I promise you that we'll fully explore all of the various possibilities."

"Um." I swallow.

"Wear it today and think about what I'll do with it tonight."

"Tonight?" I ask, as I drape the scarf around my neck.

Damien laughs. "I'll pick you up at seven," he says. "I'll have you naked by eight."

I float through the rest of the afternoon, though I do manage to partition off my Damien thoughts so that I manage to accomplish some work. My head is down as I step off the elevator at the end of the day. I'm reading a text from Jamie detailing exactly how amazing Raine is, so I don't notice Carl until he steps right in front of me.

"Nikki."

I freeze, momentarily caught off guard. Then I regain my senses and start walking again. "We don't have anything to say to each other."

"Wait," he calls. "Please."

Maybe it's the "please," but I pause just before the exit. I don't turn around, but I hear him hurrying up behind me. "Two minutes," I say, then step out the door and wait under the building awning.

He slides in with the exiting crowd and joins me outside. I don't say anything. I just stand there, my face blank, my arms crossed over my chest.

He has a paper tucked under his arm, and he holds it out to me as if it's an apology. I don't take it, but I glance down and see that it is the same issue of *Tech World* that Bruce brought into my office earlier. I meet Carl's eyes, and remain silent.

"Dammit, Nikki, I didn't know there was any other company in that market."

"What is it you want, Carl?" My voice is icy.

"I just—well, I may have acted rashly."

Ya think? I want to shout the words and slap his face. With effort, I remain quietly stoic.

"It's just that, I thought you were fucking Stark."

I am on the verge of boiling now, and I want nothing more than to get away from this toxic little man. But I force myself to conjure a thin smile as I lift my chin just slightly. "I am."

Carl actually looks embarrassed. "Right, right. I mean, yeah, I've seen the pictures of you two and all that. It's just that, well, I thought you had a fight. Or that maybe Stark thought that you and I had a thing going."

"I promise you he thinks much more highly of me than that."

"Dammit, Nikki, I'm trying to apologize here."

"Is that what this is about?" I'm genuinely surprised.

"I fucked up, okay? I was stupid and I blew the whole thing out of proportion." He runs his fingers through his hair, making it stand on end and giving him an even more harried appearance. "I acted rashly, and I'm sorry."

I cock my head, trying to hear the part that he's not saying. "We're talking about more than firing me, aren't we?" My skin prickles with worry. "What did you do, Carl?"

"Oh, hell. Other shit. You know."

"I don't know," I say. "All you said was that you were going to fuck Damien over. So what did you do?" My left hand is closed into a tight fist, my nails biting into my palm. It is only through a supreme force of will that I am remaining calm. "Dammit, Carl. What other shit are you talking about?"

He stays silent, his expression unreadable.

"For Christ's sake, Carl, why did you come here in the first place?"

He sucks in a gulp of air. "You know how Stark paid Padgett off, right? And now Padgett has to keep his mouth shut."

"How do you know that?" Eric Padgett was threatening to go public with his theory that Damien had something to do with his sister's death, and Damien actually wrote a check to shut the worm up. It's not something I like to think about. More than that, the terms of the settlement were supposed to be confidential.

"I know a lot of things. Padgett did a lot of talking before he got Stark's money. And most of his talking was to other people with an ax to grind against Stark. Trust me when I say that I realized pretty fast that Padgett was the least of Stark's worries. There are a lot of people who want to see the shit fly."

"You included," I snap.

"Not me. Not anymore. That's why I'm here. I get it. I got the whole thing wrong and I screwed Damien and I screwed you. I'm saying I'm not the only one."

"Who, then? And what shit?"

He shakes his head. "Just tell Stark that he may not see this one coming." He makes a rough noise in his throat. "I was blown away when I learned who Padgett had lined up with an ax to grind against your boyfriend."

I stand very still. He's scaring me more than he probably knows. "You won't tell me who?"

"I've said everything I'm going to. I've played my part, and now I'm getting out of this mess. Whatever happens isn't coming from me, I can promise you that."

"Then why did you come here at all?"

"Because telling you is like telling Stark. It's a small world, and I burned a bridge I shouldn't have."

"And you think this is going to fix it?"

"No, but I think it's a start." He meets my eyes. "Tell Stark to watch his back."

"I'll tell him," I say, proud of myself for keeping my voice from shaking. "But he always does."

18

I am actually wishing for the paparazzi as I walk toward my car. At least then I could be pissed off at them instead of worried for Damien.

The second I get in my car, I reach into my glove compartment for my phone charger so that I can call Damien, but the damn thing isn't there. I forgot to put one in my briefcase, so my phone hasn't charged at all today, and it's almost dead. I dial anyway, figuring I can talk fast, and am relieved when Damien picks up immediately.

"I ran into Carl," I say without preamble.

"Ran into him?" His voice is low and measured and very, very ominous.

"As in he came to Innovative and waited for me in the lobby."

"Are you okay? What did he do?"

"I'm fine," I assure him, because I can hear both the worry and the temper. "He wanted me to tell you to watch your back."

"Did he? Tell me everything he said, exactly how he said it."

I comply, relating the conversation in as much detail as I can manage.

"And he wouldn't tell you any more?"

"No," I say. "Do you have any idea what he's talking about?" I hold my breath, wondering if Damien will cite the thing going on in Germany. Or the tennis center. Or even the Eric Padgett settlement. There are so many things that this could be about, and though I haven't got a clue, I am certain that Damien does.

But when he speaks, he tells me nothing. "I think this is Carl's way of blowing smoke."

"Why would he do that?" I ask.

"You said he wants to rebuild burned bridges. What better way to do that than to warn me about some upcoming danger?"

"Because there's always some sort of danger for a man like you," I say, picking up the direction of his thoughts.

"An angry competitor. A fired employee. A stolen patent. And then Carl comes along and tells me to be on guard, and when I next notice some nefarious deed, I will think, oh, isn't it lucky that Carl warned me. I guess the little prick isn't so bad after all."

I laugh, because Carl is a little prick and nothing is going to change that. But the laughter doesn't erase my worry. "So you're really not worried?"

"I make it a point not to worry," Damien says. "There's no profit in it."

"Damien—"

"Stop," he says gently.

"Stop what?"

"Stop worrying about me. You're wasting precious energy."

"What else am I going to do with it?" I ask airily. "It's not as if you're here beside me."

He laughs. "Good girl," he says. "Where are you?"

"The parking lot. I'm going to hit the grocery store and go home."

"Good. Can you do me a favor and pick up some—"

And that is when my phone decides to die. I curse it, but at least I got to talk to him about Carl.

Even though Damien isn't troubled, I am, and it stays on my mind as I poke through Ralph's, grabbing coffee and ice cream and other staples of living. I'm sure I'm forgetting something, but as my list is on my dead phone, I'll just have to wing it.

I end up with two plastic bags full of various essentials, and after I park my car at the condo, I leave the parking area and follow the sidewalk around to the front stairs. There's a crowd gathered there, and it takes me a second to realize that they are waiting for me.

Shit.

I may have been in the mood to confront them earlier, but that has passed. All I want now is to get inside, eat ice cream, and wait for Damien.

I square my shoulders, make sure every trace of emotion is wiped off my face, and soldier on.

Immediately, they swarm me.

"Nikki! Nikki, look over here!"

"Was the portrait completely nude?"

"Does it have the usual Blaine elements like bondage?"

I'm breathing hard, and my body feels suddenly cold and clammy. I don't understand where these questions are coming from, and I'm afraid—so very afraid—to think too hard about it.

"Why did you do it, Nikki? Was it for the money or the thrill?"

"Nikki! Can you confirm that you accepted a million dollars from Damien Stark to pose nude for an erotic painting?"

I freeze, too horrified to take another step, as camera flashes burst around me. I feel sick, and I am certain that any moment now I'm going to throw up.

"Have you ever posed nude before?"

"Is the painting a reflection of your sex life with Damien Stark?"

"Why did you agree to be tied up?"

They're all around me, circling me, and I reach out for Damien's hand, but of course he's not there. My knees feel weak, and I have to force myself to stay upright. I will not fall, I will not react, I will not give them the satisfaction of knowing they've gotten to me.

But they have. And as variations of the same questions are thrown at me—as I try to get to the stairs but can barely move even an inch—I know that I'm going to scream soon, just for the shock of it. Just so I can get away.

A loud squeal cuts above the din, and for a moment I think that I *have* screamed, because suddenly the crowd is parting, and I look up and gasp.

Damien. He's running toward me from the street, his black Ferrari left idling in the road. And if I have ever been uncertain about Damien's capacity for murder, I no longer am. I see it in his eyes. In the line of his jaw. In the tenseness that fills every muscle of his body. Right then, in that moment, he would kill to protect me.

He reaches out and grabs my arm, and I'm so relieved he's here I almost cry. He pulls me roughly to him, and hooks his arm around my shoulder, holding me close as he shoves us through the crowd toward the car.

He tosses the groceries onto the floorboard, then gets me settled in the passenger seat. As he straps me in I see something break inside him. "Baby," he says, and though the word is barely loud enough for my ears, I hear the apology and the bone-deep regret.

"Please," I whisper. "Let's get out of here."

He's in the car and accelerating toward Ventura Boulevard before my mind even catches up. His right hand is on the stick, but once we're on the freeway, he reaches for me. "I'm so sorry. The painting. The money. I never thought—"

"No." The word comes out sharper than I intend. "Later. Right now, I want to pretend that it didn't happen."

The look he gives me is heartbreakingly sad. For a moment, we are silent. But the stillness is broken by Damien's single hard smack of his hand against the steering wheel.

"Who did this?" he asks. "Who the fuck leaked this?"

I shake my head. It still feels like cotton. I realize from somewhere outside of myself that I am not coping well.

I slide my right hand down so that it is between my body and the door, and then I clench it tight into a fist, letting my manicured nails dig deep as I squeeze and squeeze.

I bite my tongue, drawing blood.

And I wish—oh, how I wish—that I still had that tiny knife I used to keep on my keychain.

"Look at me," Damien snaps.

I comply. I even smile. I'm starting to get some control back.

I take a deep breath, relieved that I'm functioning. But oh god, oh god, this isn't going to stop. It's out there, and they're going to keep coming, and it isn't going to stop.

"Carl," I whisper. "This is what he was warning me about."

"Maybe, but I don't think so."

"Who then?"

"Does Ollie know about the painting?"

"No!" The word comes fast and hard, but then I immediately falter. Could he have found out somehow? "No," I say again. "And even if he did, he'd keep quiet. I'm not the one he wants to hurt."

"Don't be so sure," Damien says darkly.

I swallow, because Damien has to be wrong. Even if he's right about Ollie being in love with me, surely Ollie wouldn't do this just to get back at me for being with Damien. Would he?

I close my eyes because I can't stand to think about it. "Who doesn't matter," I say, tightening my fist again. "It's out there."

Damien doesn't answer, and we drive toward downtown in silence, Damien's anger so thick it fills the car.

"How did you know?" I finally ask.

"Jamie. She's home. Apparently she had to push through them, too, and they were asking her about the painting. She pretended not to have a clue, then called you."

"My phone's dead," I say numbly.

"I know. She called me when she couldn't reach you, and I tried you, too. When I couldn't get you on the phone to tell you to stay away—"

"You came to rescue me yourself."

"Fortunately I was in Beverly Hills and you made a stop before going home."

"Thank you," I say.

He turns just long enough to glance at me, and his smile is sad. "I will always protect you," he says. "But this—"

He cuts himself off sharply and I see his knuckles turn white as he grips the steering wheel. I understand. He can't protect me from this, and he hates that.

Frankly, I'm not crazy about it, either.

Damien stays quiet until we enter the apartment. But the moment we do, he lashes out. In one fluid motion he grabs and hurls the ornamental vase that holds the floral arrangement that is the focal point of the foyer.

"Goddammit!" he shouts, the crescendo of his voice underscored by the tinkle of shattering glass hitting the floor and the splash as water flies everywhere.

I do nothing but stand there. I know how he feels. I want to lash out and break something, too.

No, that's not true. I don't want to lash out, but I desperately wish that I did. I wish that I could grab a glass trinket and throw it hard against the floor and take comfort in the fact that it is my hands and my power that have caused it to shatter.

But that is not what will satisfy me. Those shards of glass would not be an end for me, but a means to an end. And I would not be comforted until the glass is cutting a line in my flesh, and I have latched on so tight to the pain that it erases all the other horrors around me. Those horrible camera flashes. The jeers from the reporters. The embarrassment, the humiliation, and the knowledge that no matter what, for the rest of my life, this is never going to go away.

I shiver, feeling so very fragile, and I imagine the weight of a knife in my hand.

No.

With effort, I force myself not to cross the room and pick up a piece of the broken vase. Instead, I look at Damien, who stands with clenched fists and real anguish on his face. "It will be okay," I say, because that is the kind of platitude that people say, even if they don't really believe it.

"Screw okay," he snaps. This is the temper that was so famous in his tennis days, and that has fueled his reputation for being dangerous. A sharp brittle breaking point that got him in too many fights and left too many scars, including the dark eye that is now looking at me with a bitter, resolute anger.

"None of this should be happening," he says. "I should be able to protect you. I should be able to keep my bastard of a father out of my life and out of my car. I don't want him or his shit near me, and I sure as hell don't want it near you. And as for the rest of it all over the goddamn globe—"

He cuts himself off, and for a moment I think that it is out of his system.

It isn't. "I should be able to keep your secrets as well as my own. But then again," he adds with a mirthless laugh, "that's crashing down, too. God*dammit*." He lashes out so fast and hard that he puts his fist through the drywall.

I gape. "Well," I say. "That's going to need more than a broom and a dustpan."

He stares at me for a moment, and then his shoulders begin to shake. It takes a moment for me to realize he's laughing. Not because it is funny, but because he is overwhelmed.

I want to hold him; I want to help him. But I can't even help myself.

I draw in a trembling breath, and realize that my hand is curled around the end of the pink scarf that still hangs around my neck.

Slowly, I tug the end of the scarf until I have pulled it free. I wrap one end tightly around my wrist, then hand the other end to Damien. He takes it, though I see the question in his eyes.

"Tie me up," I whisper. "Spank me. Tell me exactly what you want me to do. Do whatever you want. You want to lash out? Lash out against me."

"Nikki—"

"Please, Damien. You can't control the world? So what? Control me." I meet his eyes. "Please," I say, and I hear the tremor in my voice. "Please," I whisper. "I need it, too."

"Oh, Nikki." He cocks his head, looking inside me to where all my secrets lie. "Need?" he clarifies. "Or want?"

I lick my lips, as if that will make the words come easier. "You told me once that if I ever needed the pain that I should come to you. I've broken that promise twice." I point to my hair, and then the tip of my finger. "So yes, Damien. I need it. I need you if I'm going to get through this. And I think you need me, too."

For a moment, he says nothing. Then he runs the scarf through his fingers. "I believe I told you on the phone that I had plans for this."

"Yes," I say.

He stands still, and looks me up and down. His gaze starts at my feet and travels oh so slowly up my body. He does not touch me, but still my body burns merely from the passing of his glance. I let myself go, surrendering to his power over me. Over my body. I want this. I want Damien and his strength. I want his touch.

Mostly I want him to make the rest of the world go away.

He continues his heated inspection, his face as dark and hungry as a wolf, and just as dangerous. He will consume me, and so help me, I want to be consumed. I want to disappear—I want to go somewhere that only Damien can find me.

My legs are weak, my sex throbbing in anticipation. Tiny drops of sweat form between my breasts, and my nipples strain against my T-shirt.

I keep my eyes on his, and my mouth goes dry, my pulse kicking up its tempo. He is no longer the Damien who jokes and teases, who holds and soothes me. This is not a man who will reveal his secrets to me or to anyone, and he is certainly not a man who will explode outward into a fiery rage.

No, the man standing before me is grace and control personified. There is power in his touch, power in the slightest look. He is a hard man who commands a billion-dollar enterprise, and right now I am simply one more thing that he owns.

I bite my lower lip. I am not disturbed by the thought. On the contrary, my body is tingling with awareness. To be owned by Damien Stark is heady stuff.

"Take off your clothes."

I comply, shedding my jacket, then pulling the T-shirt over my head. Because we're playing the game again, I am not wearing a bra, and when he sees that, the tiniest of smiles touches his mouth. I unzip the skirt next and let it fall around my feet. It is as if the hundreds of times he has seen me naked are forgotten. I feel shy and awkward. But when I see the way his eyes take me in, I feel beautiful.

"Spread your legs," he says, and when I do, he goes down on his knees. He holds my hips, then presses a soft kiss just above my navel, and that simple touch sends shivers running through me. My body is on fire, alight with anticipation. I reach down to bury my fingers in his hair.

"No," he murmurs. "Cup your breasts. There you go, baby," he says when I comply. "Stroke your nipples. Are they hard?"

"Yes," I whisper.

"Good," he says. "I want them harder. I want them so tight that just brushing a fingertip across your nipple shoots fire all the way down to your cunt. What do you say?"

"Yes. Yes, sir."

He smiles up at me, a smile of praise and promise, and then he turns back to my bare abdomen. His lips brush over me, lower and lower until he is tracing the neatly trimmed line of my pubic hair. And then lower still until his tongue laves my clitoris and I have no choice but to break Damien's rules and grab hard to his shoulder, because if I do not, I will certainly topple over.

His tongue is merciless. Teasing me, fucking me, hard and demanding until I explode, my body a storm of sensation.

He is kind enough to keep me from falling, urging me down to my knees in front of him. "You taste amazing," he says, then kisses me as if to prove the point. The kiss is deep, but all too short.

"I'm going to fuck you, Nikki," he says. "Right here, right now. Hard and fast, until pleasure rips through you like a cyclone. And then we'll start again, slow and easy, letting it build and grow like a tiny seedling into a massive tree. Do you know how long that takes, Nikki? Can you imagine a pleasure that lasts for an eternity?"

My mouth is dry, but I manage an answer. "With you, yes."

He chuckles. "Good answer. Now unfasten my jeans."

"Yes, sir."

I'm so turned on that my fingers actually fumble with the button fly of his jeans, but I manage, then spread the denim and stroke my fingertips over his cock, still trapped behind the cotton of his briefs.

I hear Damien suck in air, and I relish the knowledge that as much power as he has over me, I have the same over him.

"Good girl," he says. "Now take it out and turn around. On your knees, Nikki."

"Yes, sir," I say, but I have another plan. I slide my hand into his jeans and over the bulge of his briefs until I find his fly. He is thick and hard and as soon as I shift him, his cock bursts out as if desperate to play, too. I know I'm supposed to turn around— and I know that I'll undoubtedly be punished, but I can't resist the temptation.

I lean forward and draw my tongue up the velvety length of his cock. He tastes salty and male and delicious, and when I hear him groan and say my name, my body seems to open up. I close my lips over the bulbous head, tease him with my tongue. Slowly, I take more of him into my mouth, then pull back, letting my teeth graze ever so lightly over him.

I rest my hands on his hips, and I can feel his body start to shudder. I raise up higher on my knees for a better angle. I want to take more of him; I want to make him come.

I am, however, thwarted in my plan, as his hands grasp me under the arms and he gently pulls me to my feet. "Minx," he teases.

I smile innocently.

"Oh, no," he says. "You are not getting off that easily." The scarf that I had wrapped around my wrist has come loose, and now he picks it up off the floor and knots it securely above my right hand. He gives it a tug and then leads me to the bedroom. The headboard on his bed is a solid piece of wood, and dead center is a large metal eyebolt. I'd noticed it before, but had never thought much about it. Now, he tells me to lie on my back on the bed with my hands above my head. I do, and he threads the scarf through the eye, then ties off the loose end on my other wrist. My arms now make a triangle above my head. I expect him to bind my feet as well, but he doesn't, and when he sees my curious look, he grabs my hips and flips me over onto my stomach. The maneuver both surprises me and explains why he wants my legs free.

I realize with a jolt that I am surely not the first woman who has made the acquaintance of this eyebolt. The thought doesn't disturb me, though, because I know two things. I am the first woman Damien has brought to the Malibu house. And more than that, I believe with a bone-deep certainty that I am the last.

"On your knees," Damien says. I comply, and he leaves me there, my ass in the air, my arms forward, and my head bent down and turned to the side so that I can see what he's doing.

He's at the side of the bed, opening the door to the ornamental cabinet he uses as a bedside table. He pulls out a case that is similar to one I remember well from a delicious night at my apartment. This one, however, is bigger. He opens it, and I'm pleased that from this perspective, I can see the contents. Metal handcuffs. Candles. A cat-o'-nine-tails. A blindfold. A string of beads. And a few other things that I do not recognize.

"Handcuffs?" I tease. "Are you going to arrest me?"

"Maybe." He takes out the cat-o'-nine-tails, a small whip with many strands of leather at one end. "But not yet."

He moves behind me so that I cannot see his face. Just his legs and his very hard cock, and that only when I drop my head and look down between my own legs.

I don't look for long, because he dangles the soft leather ends of the whip over my shoulders and back. "Want?" he asks. "And need?"

"Yes," I say as the horror of the evening rushes back. I want to banish those memories and those emotions. I want to claim them and destroy them. I want to survive them. And I want Damien to be the one to help me do that. "Yes," I say again, but my word is drowned out by the snap of the toy against the soft skin of my ass.

It stings, and I cry out, closing my eyes as I draw in the pain and cling to it. I want it, yes. And I need it, too. But with Damien delivering the blows, I can't deny that I am getting off on it as well. "Again," I say, as his hand rubs the spot where the whip connected. "Please, Damien, again."

He complies, bringing it down hard again and again, then rubbing my soft skin, which I imagine is now red. This is better than a knife. Safer, yes, but also more real. I'm turning something horrid into something good. Somehow, being with Damien turns it all around.

"Spread your legs," he demands. I comply, and the end of the whip dangles over my sex. I am more wet than I can ever remember being, and Damien's moan of pleasure only makes me more excited. "I'm going to spank your cunt, too," he says. "And then I'm going to fuck you, because dammit, Nikki, I can't wait."

The whip snaps lightly between my legs, and I tremble from the fast shock of it against my clit. I discovered recently with Damien how much I enjoy this particular sensation, and that feeling hasn't lessened in the slightest. Again, then again, and I am crying out from the spectacular intensity of the pleasure.

I am on fire. I am burning up. I am a blaze burning free, and only Damien can quench this heat.

"Please," I beg. "Please, Damien, now."

He doesn't hesitate. His hands take my hips and I feel the head of his cock at my vagina, and then he is inside me, deeper and deeper until I almost feel as though I cannot take it anymore. He holds me by one hip, the other hand beneath me, his finger stroking me in time with the thrusts so that I am lost in an over-load of sensations.

"Come for me," he demands, and my body tightens around him.

"Come for me," he repeats. "Dammit, Nikki, I want to feel you come."

And then, as if my body really is abiding by his will, a deep, quaking orgasm rolls through me. My body quivers. My muscles clench, bringing him even tighter into me. And my arms go limp. I collapse down onto the bed, breathing hard as waves and waves of violent pleasure continue to crash over me before finally set-tling down into the soft glow of immense satisfaction.

Damien shifts, pulling out of me and then lying beside me, his fingers stroking lazily up and down my back. "Turn over," he says after a moment. "I want to show you something."

Curious, I roll over. He brings the box back onto the bed, and this time, he pulls out a red taper candle.

"Damien?" I say warily. "What are you doing?"

"Something new."

He straddles me at the waist so that I cannot move my legs, and as my arms are still bound, I am essentially immobile.

"Do you trust me?"

"Yes," I say, but as he strikes a match and lights the candle, I can't help but bite my lower lip.

"Liar," he says. "Close your eyes."

I do, and I'm certain I must look ridiculous. My eyes squeezed tight and my teeth grazing my lip.

"Relax," he says.

"Easy for you to say."

"Tell me what this is."

I feel a gentle stroke along the swell of my breast. "Your finger?"

"And this?"

Soft and slightly wet, this time at my cleavage. "Your tongue."

"This?"

It is rough and soft at the same time. "I don't know."

"A feather," he says, though he doesn't say where he got it.

"And this?"

At first I feel nothing. Then there is a sharp, hot *ping* on my nipple that quickly shifts to something cool and tight. It's not painful, and it is more than pleasure. It is, in fact, exquisite. "I— the candle?"

"Very good. Now hold still." I feel it again, only this time the *ping* lasts longer and is not confined to one place. I arch up to meet the sensation as what feels like long fingers tighten on the skin of my breast. Then the feeling repeats and repeats and now I am biting my lower lip not from nerves, but because of the glorious rapture that has sparked inside me, spreading out like electric shocks from my breasts to my sex. And then shooting sparks out through my fingers and toes.

"Open your eyes," he says.

I do, and I see long strands of red crisscrossing my breasts. The skin beneath the wax is puckered and tight, and with my breasts and nipples already so sensitive, the sensation is beyond incredible.

Damien still straddles my waist, but now he slides down and gently spreads my legs. Slowly, he enters me, then he leans forward and, as he thrusts in and out, he tightens his hands over my breasts in time with his movements.

The wax cracks as my orgasm builds, and when I finally do

come, my body clenching around him to draw him farther in, Damien tightens his grip and the last of the wax cracks.

I cry out, lost in the exotic sensations that shoot through me, arching up as if I could keep the feeling from ending.

And then, when my body quits quivering, I close my eyes and succumb to the lure of sleep as it tugs me under.

19

I wake to the smell of bacon and discover that not only are my arms free, but I am snuggled under the covers. I smile and stretch, feeling well fucked and well taken care of.

I slide out of bed, find a shirt in the closet, and follow the scent to the huge black-and-steel kitchen. An electric skillet sizzles on the granite island, while Damien stands at the stove holding an omelette pan. Diced avocado, cubed cream cheese, and something else I don't recognize neatly cover a small cutting board off to one side.

Two flutes of champagne are half-filled, and beside them sits a carafe of orange juice.

"Are we celebrating?" I ask, coming up behind him and peering into the omelette pan.

"We are," he says. "After the day we had yesterday, I thought we should celebrate the important things."

"The day?" I repeat. My body is still deliciously sore and aching. I stretch and smile slowly. "What about the night?"

"That was a celebration in and of itself," he says. His eyes skim over me. I am wearing one of his button-down shirts, and it hangs to mid-thigh. The sleeves are rolled up, and the unfastened buttons reveal more than a little cleavage. The desire in his eyes is as unmistakable as his slow, sexy Damien smile. I'm pretty sure I melt a little.

He traces his finger down the open neck of the shirt. "I like you in my clothes."

"Me, too," I say.

"I like you out of them as well."

I laugh, and dance back out of reach of his fingers. "Don't even get ideas," I say. "I'm starving."

He laughs.

"So what exactly are we celebrating?"

He brushes a quick kiss over my lips. "Us."

That single word sends a thrill running through me. "I'll drink to that," I say.

"Good. You can pour the OJ into our glasses. Then go sit." He points to one of the stools at the breakfast bar. "If you stay back here you'll only distract me, and while that might lead to very interesting kitchen sex, it would also undoubtedly burn the omelettes."

"I am hungry," I concede as I pour the OJ and hand him a glass. I take my own with me and go sit at the bar that is attached to the island. It gives me a nice view of Damien looking deliciously domestic. "I didn't know you could cook."

"I'm a man of many mysteries," he says.

"I'm a terrible cook," I admit. "There's not much point in learning when your mother is convinced that all you really need to eat are carrots and iceberg lettuce."

"After my mother died, my father would drag us out to restaurants for every meal," Damien says. "I couldn't stand being that close to the man for that long, so I told him that if he expected me to be more competitive, I needed to eat better. I cooked, then took my plate to my room and he took his to the television. Worked out great."

"And you learned a valuable skill." I'm smiling, but my heart is breaking. My childhood had been seriously less than stellar, but at least I'd had Ashley during the years when my mother doled out calories as stingily as free time. Damien had no one except a vile father and an abusive coach. "Did you have friends?" I ask. "When you were competing, I mean. Did you make friends with the other players?"

"Other than Alaine and Sofia? Not really." He spoons the cheese, avocado, and mystery food into the omelette, then expertly folds it onto a plate.

"Tell me about Sofia."

His smile is sad. "We had a lot in common. Both our fathers were assholes."

"Are we talking friend or girlfriend?"

"Friend, then girlfriend, then friend again."

I nod, greedily soaking up these bits of Damien's past.

"Was she your first?" I ask.

His face darkens. "Yes. But it wasn't a moment of joy and bliss for either one of us. We were young, and we definitely weren't ready."

"I'm sorry. I didn't mean to bring up a difficult subject."

"It's okay," he says with a flicker of a smile that takes the edge off the flatness of his words. "Really." He takes a sip of champagne, adds some bacon to the plate, then slides it in front of me. "Well?"

I take the fork he offers, sample a small bite, and moan with pleasure. "This is amazing. What's in it?"

"Lobster."

"You just happen to have lobster in your fridge?"

"Sure," he says, deadpan. "Don't you?"

"Not hardly. Apparently the cars, hotels, jets, and chocolate factories aren't the only perks of being filthy rich."

He laughs and I dig into my breakfast while Damien stands at the stove keeping a close eye on his own meal. I'm surprised when my cell phone rings until I see that Damien has plugged it into a charger and left it on the breakfast bar. I consider letting it roll to voice mail, because I am not interested in having the real world intrude. But it's Jamie, so I answer.

"Holy fucking crap," she says, not bothering with the traditional "hello." "Douglas just came over to tell me that you're all over the Internet," she says. "Like I didn't already know. *Douglas!*" she adds, as if that is the worst affront of all.

I want to tell Jamie that if she's so irritated by our one-night stand of a next-door neighbor, then she shouldn't have slept with Douglas in the first place. But I stay silent. We've been over all that before.

"So it's really everywhere?" I ask. "I haven't wanted to look."

"Sorry," she says, her voice thick with sympathy. "Your mom even called me."

"You?"

"Lucky me, huh? She said she was too upset to talk with you yet, but that she—oh, fuck, Nikki. What the hell do you care what she thinks?"

"I know what she thinks," I say. "That I'm a disappointment. That I've ruined the family name. That she didn't raise a whore."

I can tell from Jamie's silence that I'm right. Damien is watching me carefully. He doesn't come to my side, though. I have a feeling he's afraid I'll shatter.

I won't. Just thinking about my mother—about the fact that she cares more about what the tabloid press says than about what really happened—pisses me off and makes me strong. Well, *stronger,* anyway.

"So it's all over everywhere?"

"Yeah," Jamie says. "They don't waste any time. The tabloids, social media, even the legitimate news, too. You get a million dollars from a guy like Damien for posing nude and even CNN is going to be reporting it. I mean, talk about the ratings."

"*Jamie.*"

"Sorry! Sorry! So, are you okay? I mean, what are you going to do?"

"I'm okay," I say. My cheeks heat as I glance at Damien and think about exactly how I went from being a complete wreck to feeling relatively normal. "For now, anyway." I haven't turned on the television. I haven't even checked my email. Considering what might be in my inbox from my mother, I'm certain I don't want to.

I catch Damien's eye and I know he's wondering the same thing that I am—will I still be fine once I step back into the world?

"You're staying in today, right?" she asks.

"I can't. I have to go to work."

Damien shakes his head. "Take the day off. Bruce will understand."

"I heard that," Jamie says. "Listen to Damien. He's smart. And you need to call Bruce before you go to the office, anyway. He called here looking for you."

"I'll call him, but I'm going in."

Except, apparently, I'm not. Because when I call Bruce, he tells me that he thinks it would be in the best interest of the company if I took a leave of absence. "I'm sorry," he says, "but this is more than a few photographers looking for a photo of Damien Stark's girlfriend. They're swarming around this story. And I can't have the press hanging around the building trying to get a shot of you. Not now."

"Now?" I repeat. "What's special about now?"

I hear him exhale loudly into the phone. "Giselle and I are getting a divorce. I haven't wanted to mention it before, but the point is that I need to be squeaky clean, and my lawyer thinks that—"

"I get it," I say. "I'm fired."

"Leave of absence," he says. "Please."

"It's shaping up to be a crappy day, Bruce. Can we at least call it what it is?"

There's a pause, and then, "I really am sorry, Nikki. It's a lovely portrait and it's unfair you're getting this kind of blow-back. And I really could use a talent like yours here at Innovative. But you're going to land on your feet."

"Yeah," I say, looking at Damien. "I know."

"I think I'm going to take the day off today," Damien says when I put my phone down.

"You don't need to coddle me." I point to the back of the apartment where there is a private door to his office suite. "Go. Earn money."

"I'm in the fortunate position of having made enough excellent investment choices that I don't have to actually do anything in order to make money." He cocks his head to the side as if listening. "There. Did you hear that?"

"What?"

"The clink of coins as I just earned a few thousand more."

I roll my eyes. "I'm serious. If you take the day off, I'll just feel like a burden."

"Maybe Switzerland. Or Greece."

"Damien."

"Hawaii's nice, too, and I actually have a house there. We talked about getting sushi the other night. We could go to Japan."

I'm laughing now. "I think if I want sushi we can just go to that little place on Sunset that we like."

"Fair enough. But I'm serious about the vacation. Reporters

are like sharks. Once the chum is out of the water, they go away. There will be a new scandal by Monday, and you can come back to a much calmer Los Angeles."

I can't deny that it's tempting. But no. I don't want to be the girl who runs. "I ran from Texas to get away from my mother," I say. "I ran to LA because this was the place I wanted to start a new life. I picked it. I'm here. I'm staying." I shrug. "Like you said, it'll blow over. I'll keep a low profile."

Damien is looking at me with an odd expression.

"What?"

"You've been tossed in with the sharks, and yet you're digging in your heels and facing them. If you ever tell me again that you're not strong, I'm going to turn you over my knee and spank you."

"Promises, promises," I trill, then slide off the barstool. "If you're determined to take time off, too, then I thought of something we can do today."

There is undeniable hunger in his eyes. "I can think of all sorts of things we can do today," he says.

"Not that," I say. "Although I have a feeling what I have in mind gets you hard, too."

"How you tease," he says. "So tell me, how are we spending our day?"

"Well," I say, "I was hoping we could talk about money."

"It really depends on your goals," Damien says to me, tapping the end of his pencil against the figure-covered sheet of paper.

I nod, wanting to learn as much as he can teach me. As it stands, I'm currently without income, but Jamie's right. I do have a million dollars. And if I'm going to be gawked at and gossiped about because of it, I'm going to damn well use some of it.

"The million is for my business," I say. "You already know that, but I want to make sure we're clear. I don't want the million to go away."

"The principal," he says.

"Yes. The principal needs to be there—and liquid—when I need it. But if I'm going to be out of a job, then I want to be able to live on the interest and dividends. I've got a little bit of money coming in every month from my smartphone apps, and I've got a couple more that are almost ready to go." I grimace. "I haven't launched them because I haven't had time, but I guess that's not an excuse anymore."

He reaches for my hand and squeezes it. "You're going to be fine."

"I am," I say firmly. I've decided that the only way to deal with this is one step at a time. I'm not entirely sure what the step is that will get me past the mortification of being front and center in the tabloids, but at least I can take care of the rest. And if I'm going to be vilified for making a million, then I'm damn sure going to protect that million.

"So you can help me set this up? I want to know what percentage of the money I should put in stocks or bonds and all that kind of stuff."

"I'll teach you whatever you want to know," he says.

I nod slowly, hesitatingly, and Damien eyes me warily.

"Brokers get paid with the trades, right?" I may be brilliant at math, but I've never wrapped my head around investment strategies. I've never tried, honestly. I've always been afraid that I'd do the same crap job as my mother, and the idea of being like my mother is far too disturbing.

"Right," he said. "We could also interview financial managers. They take a percentage, but if they know their stuff, the money grows enough to cover the cost."

"That's where my mother screwed up," I say. I don't mean to speak aloud, and when I look at Damien's face, I see soft understanding in his eyes.

"She made bad choices," he says. "You won't."

"I'm not so sure. I've made plenty of bad choices in the past."
I don't do it intentionally, but I realize that my thumb is idly
stroking the scar on my inner thigh.

"Just the fact that you're being so careful and asking so many
questions proves to me that you're going to be fine. And so is
your money. I work with several brokers and managers. If you
like, I can have Sylvia set up some meetings, get them into the
office today if you want."

"That would be great," I say, then immediately take it back.
"No. No, never mind."

"All right," he says slowly, but I can see the hurt in his eyes.
"Whatever you want."

"That's the thing," I say. "I already know who I want." I take
a deep breath. "Will you manage it for me? I can't imagine there's
anyone I would trust more than you."

There is no trace of the hurt left on his face. Instead, there is
only something soft and tender. His smile is slow, and the shake
of his head is even slower. "No," he says, and I gasp in surprise.
"That's not what I do. But I do oversee my own managers with
such microscopic interest that I imagine they consider me among
their most irritating clients. Fortunately, the percentage they earn
off the growth is sufficient to quell that irritation. I won't manage your money, but I will babysit it. I'll introduce you to my
manager, we'll get you set up, explain your goals, and then I'll
watch over your nest egg. Sound good?"

"Will you explain the investment choices to me?"

"I'll explain anything you want. We'll do this together, okay?
And who knows. Maybe next you'll be asking me to help with
your start-up."

"Don't push," I say. I've explained to him why I want to take
it slow, though I think he is on Jamie's side of the equation.
Damien would simply jump in and do brilliantly. I want to wade
in slowly and do brilliantly.

He holds a hand up as if in self-defense. "I'm not pushing. Why would I push you to go out on your own when I'd much rather get you set up as a division of Stark Applied Technology?"

I laugh. "Once I'm out there on my own and raking in the dollars, then you can buy me out for some obscene amount of money. But I'm starting on my own."

"Fair enough," he says. "I just want to see you actually start. I'm waiting, you know. I fully intend to license some of your software for use in my offices. The cross-platform note system you told me about could come in quite handy."

"All the more reason not to jump in before I'm ready," I say firmly. "I don't want to let you down."

"You could never let me down," he says. He pulls me in for a quick, firm kiss. "And, Nikki? Thank you."

"For what?"

"For trusting me to help you with the million."

I nod slowly. Have I made this decision because a man I trust happens to be brilliant with money? Or am I following the pattern of last night, surrendering control to Damien instead of coping for myself?

He's told me more than once that there is strength inside me. And though the words are a comfort, I'm not sure I believe them. I didn't feel strong last night. And every time I think about the press going apeshit over my personal business, nausea crashes over me.

But Damien is looking at me with such tenderness that I say none of that. "I've trusted you with my heart," I say, because that is an undeniable truth. "Why wouldn't I trust you with my money?"

I speak the words lightly. His expression, however, is serious. "You do know that I trust you, too?"

"Of course," I say.

"Just because it takes me time, doesn't mean I trust you less."

"I know that," I say, because in my head, I do get it, and I have to admit that he's already told me so much. In my heart, though, I want him to spill out everything still locked inside. But do I want that so that I can be strong for him as he is for me? Or am I simply being selfish, looking for a tangible confirmation of how he feels about me, even though I already know from every glance and every touch that I am cherished?

For the rest of the afternoon, we do little more than laze about in bed, our arms touching, our legs crossed over each other. Damien reads various reports that Sylvia emails to his iPad. I flip through magazines, folding down pages with clothes that I like or that I think might look good on Jamie. Sometimes I see an interesting piece of furniture and show the picture to Damien who tells me to mark the page, then promises me we'll go to the Pacific Design Center soon and try to find some of these pieces for the Malibu house.

"I thought decorating your house was something you did on your own," I say.

"No. I said everything in the house is special to me. And if we pick something out together, it will be even that much more precious."

His words are as tender as a caress, and I scoot even closer, leaning in as he hooks his left arm around me and holds his iPad with his right.

"I thought you were taking the day off," I say.

"Do you have a better suggestion?" he counters, a delicious deviousness in his voice.

"As a matter of fact, I do."

I don't think that Damien is expecting my suggestion that we make popcorn and more mimosas, then lounge in bed for the rest of the afternoon watching old *Thin Man* movies, but he takes it in good grace. And I'm surprised to learn that he actually knows the movies as well as I do.

"William Powell is brilliant," he says, "but I think I have a crush on Myrna Loy."

"I have a crush on her wardrobe," I admit. "I could have lived back then. Fitted dresses and flowing evening gowns."

"Maybe we need to take you shopping."

"I'd love it," I say. "But you've already filled up a closet for me in Malibu, and the house itself is sitting empty." I toss him the copy of *Elle Decor* I'd been skimming earlier. "If we go shopping, it's for furniture."

"All right," he says. "It's a date." But neither one of us says when. I know it's ridiculous to hide in Damien's apartment; if I wanted to hide, I should have taken him up on the offer to leave the country. I've never been to Switzerland, after all. But right now, lounging casually beside Damien, it's not the horrors of the press that's keeping me here, it's the sweet pleasure of the man beside me.

We've just finished the first movie and started on *After the Thin Man* when my cell phone rings. I don't recognize the number, and I hesitate to answer, but if I ignore calls, then I really am hiding away, and I don't want to be that girl. "Hello?" I say tentatively.

"Nikki? It's Lisa. We met in the cafeteria."

"Oh!" I'm surprised to hear from her. "If you're looking to do coffee, I'm not in the office today." I don't mention that I won't be in the office ever again.

"I know," she says. "Listen, I heard what happened, and I just wanted to say that I'm sorry. The press are a bunch of vultures, and it sucks that they're shitting all over you."

"Thanks," I say.

"I dropped into the office to see you, and after I learned what happened, Bruce gave me your number. I just wanted to let you know that my offer for lunch or coffee is still open. Anytime. Just call me."

"I will," I say, and I'm not just being polite. I'd thought when I met her that it would be nice to have a few more friends in LA. And I'm happy to know that this one isn't going to run screaming now that I'm the object of ridicule.

Blaine and Evelyn also call, equally horrified, equally supportive. Blaine tells me he feels guilty—after all, it's the erotic nature of his art that has the press all hyped up.

"It's not," I lie. "It's all about the money."

I don't think he's appeased, but I promise him that I'm okay, and that Damien and I will come see them both soon.

I hang up, then realize that the only person I care about that I haven't yet heard from is Ollie. I almost mention that to Damien, but I don't. As far as he's concerned, Ollie is at the top of the list of suspects in the leak, and the lack of communication would only fuel that fire.

Then again, considering how brilliant and observant Damien is, I'm quite certain that he's already noticed that Ollie hasn't made the effort to check on me.

I don't think Ollie is the leak, but I can't deny that my feelings are a little hurt.

"Do you want more popcorn?" Damien asks.

I roll sideways to face him, and just stare, drinking in that gorgeous face and the eyes that see me better than anyone. "Damien," I say.

"What?"

"Nothing." I smile. "I just like saying your name."

"I like hearing it." He reaches over and strokes my neck above the collar of his shirt.

"Damien," I say again.

"Yes?"

"Would you mind very much if we skipped the movie? I have something else in mind."

"Do you?"

I get out of bed and hold out my hand, then put a finger to my lips. "No talking," I say. "Not until we get back in the bed. Those are my rules. Okay?"

In the spirit of the game, he nods. I grin, take his hand, and pull him to the bathroom.

It's at least as impressive as the one in Malibu, but I'm not interested in the multi-jet shower or the humongous closet or even the heated towel rack. All I care about is the insanely large tub. I turn it on and let it start to fill. Then I return to Damien and slowly, wordlessly, I begin to undress him.

It's a delightful process, because I allow myself a kiss with each tiny bit of skin that is exposed. His shoulder. His arm. His pecs. A tongue flicking across his nipple. A long lick above his navel.

And then there are the jeans that come down so slowly, and I brush my lips over his hip. Over those tight, sexy muscles of his lower abs. And his penis, erect and ready for my kiss when I peel down his briefs.

He doesn't break the rules, but when I close my mouth over the head and taste the salty, musky flavor of him, his fingers clench in my hair, and that is as potent a reaction as him crying my name aloud.

I taste and tease and explore his cock. I stroke and lick his balls. I explore every inch of this man whose body I have come to know so well, and who knows mine with equal intimacy.

And I take immense satisfaction at his hand clutching the glass shower stall, because I know that without that support he would topple over, and that it is me who has brought him there.

I don't let him come, though, because that's not part of my game. Not yet. But I continue my exploration of kisses until the tub is full and Damien's eyes are so heated that I know I will be thoroughly fucked.

The thought makes me smile.

I have added some bubble bath to the water, and now I step in, then hold out a hand to him in invitation. He follows me, and though this is clearly my game and I have been calling the shots, I realize soon enough that Damien has reached his limit. It's his turn now, and when he grabs me by the waist and pulls me toward him, the violent movement sloshing water out of the tub, I do not protest.

On the contrary, I spread my legs in anticipation, and I'm rewarded when he settles me on his lap. I shift a little, using my body to stroke him, then cry out in surprise when he grabs my hips and settles me firmly and deeply on his cock. He grins, then lifts a finger over his lip. Gloriously wet and incredibly turned on, I lean forward, relishing the pressure of his cock inside me and the sensation of his pubic hair against my clit.

I begin a slow, steady rocking, the movement designed to drive us both crazy, and if the expression on Damien's face is any indication, my plan is working to perfection.

Again and again the pleasure builds and the only noise is the sloshing of the water and the slick sound of our bodies meeting. That sound alone is a turn-on, and it makes me that much hotter, that much more excited. And as I ride him, Damien's hands on my hips and his strong arms helping me to piston my body on his rock-hard cock, I drink in this sexual symphony, and I look deep into his eyes as we both silently, quietly, explode in each other's arms.

The next morning I wake up alone and immediately slide out of bed, planning to go find Damien. The sound of voices, however, makes me pause, and I double back to the closet in search of something to wear.

As in the Malibu house, Damien has filled a closet for me. I pull on a black T-shirt and a denim skirt, then head toward the living room to see who's here.

What I see makes me stop short. Damien stands shirtless in the center of the room. He wears gray sweatpants tied loosely around his hips. He's balanced on one leg, his arms outstretched. I am behind him, and I can see the muscles in his back as he moves his arms in slow, controlled motions. He is power and grace and it is only after my chest starts to feel uncomfortably tight that I realize I am actually holding my breath.

I suck in air, and Damien puts his foot down, then turns and smiles at me. "Tai chi," he says, without waiting for me to ask. "It keeps me flexible. Come on in. Go ahead, Charles. You were saying?"

The sight of Damien had given me tunnel vision, blocking out everything else around him. But now my vision expands and I see Charles Maynard on the steel and leather couch, an array of papers spread out on the coffee table. The room is flooded with light from the wall of windows and that—along with seeing Damien—makes me smile despite all that has happened.

"We managed to keep all images of the actual artwork out of the more prominent venues," Charles says. "I'm somewhat surprised that the various editorial staffs caved to yesterday's demand letter, but I'll attribute that to your reputation and deep pockets. No one wants to get in a battle with Damien Stark."

"They probably know that if they push me on this, I'll just buy them out."

"If you mean that, I'll certainly share that information if I get any pushback."

"I mean it," Damien says. "If that's what it takes to make this go away, then that's what I'll do." He's looking at me as he speaks, his expression so fiercely protective it makes my knees go weak. I cross to the sofa and sit on the arm.

"Blaine faxed back his affidavit yesterday," Charles continues, "so we filed the Application for Temporary Restraining Order first thing this morning."

"You can actually keep them from talking about this?" I ask.

Charles turns to me, his expression compassionate but businesslike. "I'm afraid we can't do that. We could sue for defamation, but that requires a false statement, and Damien assures me that the rumors are true."

My cheeks heat, but I nod. "Then what are you doing?"

"We want to stop the publication of the painting itself. Or any other of Blaine's works. It's his style that's partly fueling the fire. The idea that the image is dark and erotic."

"Oh." My cheeks burn even hotter. "But how can you keep them from printing photographs? I saw the reporter taking pictures at the party. And there must be dozens of Blaine's paintings in Southern California. Anybody could invite a reporter in to take a few snaps if they want some extra cash."

"The owner of the painting doesn't own the copyright," Damien explains. "That remains with Blaine. So that's how we're handling it."

"Of course, they can still print photos of you," Charles says, and I know that there are many, many photos of Damien and me together.

"I understand," I say. "I suppose every little bit helps. But how on earth did you pull all this together so fast?"

"I'm sure you realize that Damien is one of my most important clients—"

"One of?" Damien interrupts indignantly.

"My most important client," Charles corrects with a laugh. "When he sends me a text outlining an urgent matter, I set the wheels in motion."

I glance at Damien, realizing that sometime last night, despite everything else, he actually found the time to do this for me.

"Thank you," I say. "Thank you both."

"It's only a start." Damien looks at Charles. "Did you bring the footage?"

Charles pushes some papers on the coffee table aside and comes up with a DVD. "Everything that's aired so far, and as much of the raw footage from outside Nikki's condo as we could obtain."

"Why?" I ask.

"Someone leaked this story," Damien says. "I intend to find out who."

"But you just said that if it's the truth there's nothing you can do legally."

"No," Damien says with a thin, dangerous smile. "There's not a damn thing I can do legally. But I want to know who did this to you. Don't ask me to stop, Nikki. Because I won't."

"I'm not going to ask," I say. The truth is, I want to know, too. "But how is looking at the footage going to help?"

"I'm going to identify all of the reporters asking you questions," he says. "And then Charles or I will have a little talk with each of them."

It is probably very wrong of me, but I can't help but wish that I could be a fly in the room during *those* conversations.

"Anything else?" Damien asks.

"Not about this." Charles glances toward me. "But Germany is heating up, Damien. They have the janitor now. We need to expect the worse."

"I always expect the worst," Damien says. "It's how I've survived so long."

"There are other issues in Europe," Charles says. "You really should—"

"I know," Damien says, with a quick glance toward me. "But I'm tied up here at the moment."

"Wait," I say. "I may not know the details of what's going on, but if the company's having legal trouble overseas and you need to be there, then go. I'll be fine."

"She's right," Charles says. "You're needed in London."

I'm surprised that Charles has mentioned London and not Germany. "Sofia?" I ask, and can't help but notice the surprised look that Charles shoots at Damien.

"There are financial problems I need to take care of," Damien says.

"You can handle everything in a few hours," Charles adds. "But you need to be on-site."

"Fine," Damien concedes. He crosses to the window and looks over the city spread out beyond the glass. "I'll leave Friday night."

"That's the tennis center dedication," Charles says. "Damien, you should go."

"But I'm not going. I've already said why. That's final."

I look between the two men. It's a standoff, and my money is on Damien.

Soon enough, I'm proven right.

"Fine," Charles says. "You'll leave Friday, then. If you're out of the country, that's another excuse we can throw to the press."

"I don't give a damn what you say to the press," Damien says, his voice sharp with irritation. "There and back again, Charles. And if you can't get me in and out quickly on commercial flights, then tell Grayson we're taking the Lear."

"I'll arrange it."

He turns to me. "You're sure?"

"There are a lot of things on your resume," I say. "But I'm pretty sure babysitter isn't one of them. Yes. I'm sure."

"Fine, but I want you to stay here while I'm gone."

I cross my arms over my chest. "I'll be fine at home."

"They'll hound you," he says. "And they'll hound Jamie," he adds, because he knows me well enough to know that matters. "Mostly, it will make me feel better. Please, Nikki. Right now I'm asking. Don't make me demand."

It's his way of saying that he's the one making the rules in this game I agreed to continue. I nod in acquiescence. The truth is that I'd rather stay here, too. I want to be strong enough to say that I really don't care if they accost me on the stairs up to the condo. I want to—but I'm not.

"Fine. I'll stay."

"Thank you. Besides, I want to install better security at your place. Charles, on your way out, tell Sylvia to make arrangements for that and to let Ms. Archer know when the installation will happen. What?" he demands, noticing my smile.

"Nothing." Fortunately, I don't think Jamie is going to mind having a security team swoop down on her. And Damien is just being Damien.

As usual, he reads my mind. "Correction," he says to Charles. "Tell Sylvia to ask Ms. Archer if she's amenable to a security system and, if so, when would be a convenient time for the install. Better?"

I nod. "And thanks."

We walk Charles out, and as soon as the door closes behind him, I move closer to Damien and press my palms against his bare chest. "London, huh? I miss you already."

"Just so we're clear, I don't want you to stay in my apartment because I'm worried about you."

"No?"

"I want you here because I like the idea of you in my bed."

"That works out well, then. Because I like being in your bed, too. Mostly, though, I like being in your arms."

20

By mid-afternoon on Friday, I'm craving traffic jams and smog. I want to go out in the world, and damn the reporters and paparazzi and plain old gawkers.

At the same time, I'm enjoying this bubble of domesticity I'm sharing with Damien. He's kicked back on the sofa, his bare feet on the coffee table, his iPad in one hand and a sparkling water near the other. He's wearing a Bluetooth headphone in his far ear, so from my perspective it looks as if he's mumbling to himself. I've long ago tuned him out. As fascinated as I am by Damien in general, I do not need to know the ins and outs of the labor problems that one of his subsidiaries is having in Taiwan.

As for me, I've just finished reading a downloaded copy of *The Martian Chronicles,* and though I'd started the story with a picture of a young Damien in my mind, by the end, I'd been sucked in by the plot and the characters.

Now, though, I'm feeling at loose ends. I don't have my laptop, so there's not much actual work I can do. I'm not in the mood to start another book, and the television doesn't interest me in the slightest. I consider putting on a fashion show for

Damien featuring the clothes he's stocked in the closet, but I can't quite bring myself to do it. I've been dominating his time lately, albeit unintentionally, and though he makes light of his need to oversee his empire, I know that the world of Damien Stark will unravel if he is not actively at the helm.

I go to the kitchen to brew a cup of green tea, since it's supposed to be calming and I feel so antsy. I'm actually not freaking out about the press, but I can't decide if that's because I'm dealing so well with this new crisis in my life, or if it's simply because Damien and I are locked up here in his castle in the sky, and the problems of mere mortals are really not our concern.

I have a sneaking suspicion that it's the latter and that when I go out into the world or log on to the Internet, this smug sense of control is going to blow away like so much dandelion fluff. As evidence of my theory, I have only to look at my phone. My mother has called twice, and each time I've let it go to voice mail. I have not listened to the messages. I have not called her back. Honestly, I'm not sure I ever will. My mother has the ability to push me over the edge where even a Hummer full of paparazzi could not.

Despite a world filled with paparazzi and Elizabeth Fairchilds and other unpleasant beings, I am so antsy that I consider testing the waters of the outside world by taking a walk down to the Museum of Contemporary Art. It's only a few blocks away, and I doubt that there are reporters waiting to ambush me there. It's also close enough that Damien won't worry. Or he won't worry as much, because if I start to freak he is less than five minutes away by foot.

Besides, I really want some fresh air.

I take my tea and a fresh water for Damien and head back into the living room, arriving at the same time as Sylvia, who is coming in from the back entrance that connects to the office of Stark International.

"Ms. Fairchild," she says. "How are you?"

"Good," I say. "How's life on the outside?"

Damien grins at me. "Going a little stir crazy?"

"Not that I don't love this fairy palace, but—"

He makes a noncommittal noise, then turns to Sylvia, who appears to be hiding a smile. "What have you got for me?"

"Just a few signatures," she says, handing him a clipboard and several documents. She glances at me. "And this came for you," she adds, then holds out a plain white envelope. It's addressed to me, care of Stark International. There's no return address, but the postmark is from Los Angeles.

"That's weird," I say, as Damien tosses the clipboard onto a cushion and comes to my side.

"Open it," he says.

I do. There's a folded piece of paper inside. I pull it out, unfold it, and immediately feel sick.

Bitch. Slut. Whore.

"Mother*fucker,*" Damien breathes, plucking the letter and the envelope from my hand. He takes a magazine from the coffee table and puts them both between the pages, then hands the magazine to Sylvia. "Get this to Charles. Don't get fingerprints on it."

"Of course, Mr. Stark. Ms. Fairchild, I'm so sorry. I didn't know."

"No, of course you didn't," I say.

"It's okay, Sylvia." Damien's words are a dismissal.

She nods. "I'll just come back for those documents later." She starts to leave, then pauses and turns back to me. "I apologize if this is out of line, Ms. Fairchild, but I just wanted to say that I saw the painting when I was at the Malibu house coordinating with the decorator before the party."

I've been staring blankly at the magazine in which the vile note is hidden, but now I look up at her face with interest.

"It's a beautiful portrait," she says. "Stunning and engaging. Frankly, I think Mr. Stark got a bargain. As far as I'm concerned, it's worth at least two million."

I've been blinking back tears as she speaks, and now I burst out with a laugh that is choked with tears. "Thank you," I say, then sniff. I shoot a wry grin toward Damien. "I like her."

"Yes," he says dryly. "She's very capable." His mouth is thin, but I can see the hint of amusement, not to mention the silent nod of thanks when he tells Sylvia, "That will be all."

She nods, then slips out of the apartment.

"There are a lot of fucked-up people in the world," Damien says to me. "Don't let them get to you."

"You're never going to be able to track who sent that letter."

"Maybe not, but I'm going to try. By the way, I figured out which reporter originated the story."

"Did Charles go see him?"

"He refused to reveal his source. I may pay him a visit myself, but I thought I'd go the more civilized route first. I've hired a private investigator. I'm guessing he met in person with the source. With any luck, my guy will learn something."

I nod, but I don't expect much. Honestly, I'm not sure I care. I'm certain it wasn't Jamie or Ollie, and they are the only two who could truly injure me by being duplicitous. Other than that, it's the information alone that hurts, and no matter who revealed it, there's no putting that genie back in the bottle. Not now, not ever.

"I want to go out," I say to Damien, who stares at me for a second, obviously trying to digest my sudden change in topic.

"Any place in particular?"

"I was thinking about the MoCa," I say. "I figure there aren't many reporters lying in wait there."

"All right," he says. "Let's go."

"But then I changed my mind," I continue. "I want to go shopping. Let's go look for things for the house. There are all sorts of cute stores on Melrose. Or anywhere in West Hollywood. Doesn't that sound like fun?"

"I always have fun when I'm with you," he says. "But that area is crowded, and it only takes one person who gets off on tabloid news calling TMZ or some other rag before we'll be surrounded by the vultures."

"I know," I say. "But I don't care. I want back in the world. It's not like they can't get me in here, too. Didn't one of them just send me a letter?"

He winces, but nods. "All right, then," he says. "I guess we have a date."

We're not looking for anything in particular other than each other's company, and that makes wandering the stores pleasant, especially since no one seems to be paying any attention to us.

A new store has opened on Fairfax selling high-end antiques, and a massive bed with a head and footboard that is intricately carved from oak immediately catches my eye.

"A bed, Ms. Fairchild?" Damien asks.

"I don't know," I say. "It's worth considering. After all, the house is currently without a bed." I lie down on it, then roll onto my side and pat the mattress, making a point to smile suggestively. "Shall we test it out?"

His lips twitch. "Careful. You're subject to my rules, remember? Who knows what I might make you do?"

"Good point," I say, moving to sit up. I reach out and hook a finger through the belt loop of his jeans, then tug him toward me. He stumbles and falls forward, knocking me back a bit before he blocks his fall with a hand on the mattress.

"Well, hello," he says, then kisses me. "I swear I didn't orchestrate that."

I laugh, and am about to steal a kiss of my own, when I notice that the girl at the counter is staring at us. It's possible she's simply amused or annoyed by the customers who are playing on the furniture. But I don't think so.

I stand up abruptly, pushing past Damien. "Let's go," I say, my cheeks burning. "This bed isn't nearly as cool as our old one, anyway."

The clerk says nothing as we're leaving, and I think I must have been imagining things. I'm proved wrong fifteen minutes later when we exit the next store.

We'd been shopping in ignorant bliss, looking at decorative candles and pretty vases made of ornamental glass. But the moment we step out onto the sidewalk, we're accosted by cameras and microphones and a screaming mass of reporters that I can only assume must have popped up en masse out of the sewers.

Damien is already holding my hand. Now he squeezes tighter, and I squeeze back, letting the pressure of his hand around mine focus me.

"Nikki! Is it true that you were fired from Innovative for violating a morals clause?"

"The tennis center dedication begins in four hours, Mr. Stark. Can you elaborate on your previous statement regarding Merle Richter?"

"Damien! Have you been informed about the content of Mr. Schmidt's affidavit? Is it true that he was paid to keep quiet?"

I don't know who Mr. Schmidt is, but I make it a point not to glance at Damien. There's no way that I'm letting these bastards catch my ignorance on film.

"What are you going to do with your million dollars, Nikki?"

I almost answer that one. Surely, if I explain that the money is going to fund a business, they'll find me less interesting.

A thin-lipped reporter in a neatly pressed suit steps forward and shoves a microphone in my face. "Can you comment on the rumors that you've slept with men in the past for money? Is Mr. Stark your most lucrative client?"

The words strike me like a blow, and I stumble backward, suddenly nauseous. Worse, I'm caught off guard, and my facade has dropped. Tomorrow, all the tabloids will have a shot of my horrified expression. And I know damn well that the captions will suggest that I'm horrified that my secret has been revealed—*not* that the story is bullshit.

I don't even realize that Damien has released my hand until I hear the sharp *crack* of his fist intersecting with the reporter's jaw.

"Damien! No!"

He turns to me, and I see the fire in his eyes. And I know that right then, his violent, fiery temper is one hundred percent aimed at vindicating me.

"No," I repeat, grabbing his hand before he can take another swing. "Do you want to get arrested? They'll take you away from me, and even if it's only a few hours until you post bail, I'll be alone until you get out."

That calms him somewhat, and he takes my hand and yanks me back into the store. He has his phone out, and I hear him telling Edward to bring the limo around.

The salesgirl had been watching through the window, and now she turns to Damien. "Um, mister? Tell him there's an alley in the back." She nods toward the throng still gathered in front of the store. "Unless you want to go through those creeps again."

Damien looks at her, and the slow smile erases the last remains of his fury. I want to give the girl a hug.

Damien keeps his arm around me for the ride back to the apartment, but he says nothing until we are back in the penthouse. His eyes go quickly to where the mirror once hung. He does not have live-in help, but the crew from the office also cleans the apartment, and they'd swooped in quickly and removed all the glass. Even the drywall is now repaired. There is no evidence of Damien's fury left, and yet he and I both know it is there.

"I should have smashed his face in," Damien says.

"No, you shouldn't have," I say. I draw a breath, because I have been thinking about this. "Besides, in a way he's right."

Damien's sharp glance almost halts my words, but I press on. "That million wasn't just a modeling fee and we both know it."

He opens his mouth, then shuts it again and rubs his temples. "I've done this to you." The words are soft and filled with pain. "I swore that I would never hurt you. That I would be the one you could hold tight to. And yet I'm the one who has done this to you."

"No." My tone is harsh. Vehement. "You've never done anything to hurt me. Ever. And I took the money because I wanted it. And I took your deal because I wanted you. To be honest," I add with a wry grin, "I would have said yes for a lot less money."

"Really?" He lifts a brow. "Now I really do feel like a fool. Come here," he adds, then kisses me.

My words, however, have not soothed him enough. I can feel the tension coming off him, like a spring wound too tight.

When he looks at me, his face has the dark intensity of a hunter, and I feel as vulnerable as his prey.

"Come on," he says. "You know what I want. And what we both need."

I follow him to the bedroom, wanting nothing more than to forget the outside world once again, and when I see what he has in mind, I know that in a few minutes I'll be thinking of nothing but Damien. He has pulled out his box of toys and is dangling the metal handcuffs from his index finger.

"It occurs to me that this is the most surefire way to keep you in my apartment—and in my bed—while I'm in London."

"You wouldn't dare," I say, and scoot to the other side of the bed.

"Wouldn't I?"

He leaps onto the bed, then rolls to the side, cutting me off as I try to break for the door. I squeal as he pulls me down on top of him, then very quickly fastens one cuff to my wrist, and then that cuff to the eyebolt.

"Don't you even think about it," I laugh, even though I know he's joking. Or, at least, I'm pretty sure he's joking . . .

"No?" he asks, as he starts to push my skirt up my body. "You don't want to stay like this, in my bed, constantly ready to be fucked by me?"

"Now that you put it that way," I say, and then close my eyes with pleasure as he starts to kiss his way up my thigh. It is sweet torment, because Damien knows exactly how to drive me crazy. His breath teasing my sex, his lips making me wild.

I struggle under his ministrations, as with each touch he finds some new sensation, some new way to make me writhe and beg. Even the way his finger strokes my ankle and his tongue licks the back of my knee sends ribbons of pleasure curling through me.

I twist and turn on the sheets, but the cold metal that surrounds my wrist prevents me from escaping the sensual onslaught that is coming so near to driving me out of my mind.

The cuff digs into my skin, and with each turn, with each motion, I tug hard at it. I want the pain. I want the pressure. I want a bruise to rise there. And not because I want to escape the horror of this afternoon—that, in fact, is the least of it.

No, I want it because it represents *now*. This moment, with Damien's mouth on my naked body. With his fingers exploring every inch of me, finding all sorts of erogenous zones and erotic secrets.

I want the bruise because it is a physical reminder of how Damien makes me feel.

A bruise will be proof when he is London that I was in his bed—and a reminder that he will come back to me.

And so I struggle against my bonds, not because I want to get free, not even because I want the pain. I want what it represents. That I am Damien's.

Bound to him. Marked by him. Claimed by him.

And right now, that is all I want to be.

21

It's the middle of summer, but with Damien gone this might as well be a cold, wet Saturday in December. I know that he will be back Sunday afternoon, and that the trip is a quick one, but on my end it doesn't feel quick at all.

I am restless and lonely. Damien texted me when he landed. He'd asked how I was, and I'd smiled and gently rubbed the bruise that now rings my wrist like a bracelet. "Thinking about you," I'd said. "Missing you." All true, but what I didn't tell him was that I was bored out of my mind. Knowing Damien, he'd hire Cirque du Soleil to come into the living room and entertain me.

Jamie texted me cyber-hugs in response to my SOS, but she is roller-skating in Venice with Raine. I hope she manages to fall on her ass less than I did. I consider calling Lisa, but I don't know her well enough yet, and I think we should start with a simple coffee before I hit her up to provide me with entertainment on a lonely Saturday evening.

I'm left with either work or photography, and since my camera is still at the Malibu house, I decide to go with work. Now is as good a time as any to finish the coding on my two smartphone apps that are almost ready to market. That, of course, means a quick trip to my condo. Since I have no car at Damien's apartment, that's not as easy as it sounds.

The phone in the kitchen acts as both a regular phone and an intercom to Damien's office. I've seen him use it a dozen times, and I press the button to operate the speaker. "Hello?" I say tentatively.

"Yes, Ms. Fairchild? Can I help you?" I grin. This really is pretty cool.

"Um, yeah. Is this Ms. Peters?" I ask, scraping my memory for the name of Stark's weekend assistant.

"How kind of you to remember. It is. What can I do for you?"

"I don't have a car and I need to go pick up something at home. Could you arrange a taxi or—"

"I'll have Edward bring the limo around. If you take the elevator to parking level C, he'll meet you right there."

"Oh. Okay. Thanks." I end the call and shimmy happily in the kitchen. Yes, there are definitely perks to having money.

As Ms. Peters had predicted, Edward is waiting for me.

"Thanks so much," I say.

"Not at all, Ms. Fairchild. Where are we going?"

"My condo," I say. "I just need to run in and pick up something. And I really wish you'd call me Nikki."

"Right away, Ms. Fairchild," he says, but he grins as he says it.

I slide into the limo and curl up in the corner, thinking about that first night I met Damien. Or re-met him, I suppose, since our first encounter six years ago doesn't really count. I close my eyes and remember the way Damien whispered to me. How turned on I'd been by the words he'd spoken into the phone, and how shocked I'd been by what I'd so willingly done in the back of a limo.

By the time we reach the condo, I've played back that entire evening in my mind—and I am very much missing Damien.

"Will you be long?"

"Not too long. I need to download a couple of things onto my laptop, but that's all. Are you listening to a book?"

"Decided to try a classic," he says. "*The Count of Monte Cristo*. Not bad, so far. Not bad at all."

I smile at his assessment of one of my favorite books, then hurry up the stairs.

I can hear the loud bangs coming from our neighbor Douglas's apartment, and I wince. I know it's not Jamie in there burning up the sheets with him, but I still scowl at his door.

Inside, I toss my purse on the bed that still looms in the living room, head for the two stairs that lead up to the bedroom, then scream as the door to the bathroom jerks open on my right.

Ollie.

"Jesus Christ!" I shout. "You almost gave me a heart attack. What are you doing here?" He looks like hell. His eyes are bloodshot, his skin splotchy, and his hair hangs limp around his face. I take a step toward him. "Are you okay?" A horrible thought occurs to me. "Oh, shit," I say. "You and Jamie didn't—I mean, she's out with Raine right now." The idea that he and Jamie had been doing the nasty only hours before she went out on a date with her new boyfriend bothers me almost as much as the idea of Ollie cheating on his fiancée.

Actually, the whole thing makes me ill, and I'm not thrilled about finding Ollie in my apartment. I don't want to think about their drama. More than that, I'm still stinging from the fact that Ollie hasn't called since I saw him at The Rooftop. Sure, he could be busy, but once the million-dollar-painting news broke, surely he could have at least texted. Yet days have passed, and he hasn't said even one word to me about all the gossip that's been swirling around me like leaves in a windstorm.

Or, as Damien would say, like sharks smelling blood.

"I didn't do anything with Jamie," he says sullenly. "Courtney and I had a fight."

"Oh. I'm sorry," I say, though I am not surprised.

"Yeah, me, too." He sighs, then checks his watch. "We're meeting for dinner. Patch things up. At least I hope so."

"So do I." I don't mention that I am dubious. Ollie doesn't have the best track record, and though he is my friend—at least I think he is still my friend—I can't help but think that Courtney deserves better.

Ollie runs his fingers through his hair. "Jamie let me crash here. I slept in your room." He shoots a questioning glance at the bed that fills the space between the dining table and the door. I say nothing, and after a moment, he shrugs and continues. "I didn't figure you'd mind if I slept in your bed."

"I do mind," I say, the words snapping out before I think about it. I see the hurt on his face, but I don't care. I'm pissed, and it's all just spilling out of me. "You just grab my bed like everything is like it always was? It's not. I've needed a friend, and you haven't even called."

"Maybe I didn't call because you didn't tell me about the painting," he says. "A million dollars. Is it true?"

"It's true," I say.

He shakes his head. "Stark's bad news, Nikki."

"No," I say firmly. "He's not. And did you ever think that that's exactly why I didn't say anything about the painting to you?"

"Why the hell are you so fucking obstinate? Are you afraid to learn the truth about him? Or are you afraid I'll learn the truth about what you do with him?"

He's spewing words at me, clearly as pissed off as I am. Then, without warning, he grabs my arm and tugs it toward him. He jabs a finger hard on the bruise around my wrist. I jerk my arm back, blushing, and undoubtedly erasing any possible question in Ollie's mind as to the cause of those marks.

"You're being an idiot," he says. He reaches out and tugs a lock of my hair, then looks pointedly toward my thighs. "How long will it be before Stark does something else that makes you take a knife to yourself?"

I don't even realize I've moved until I feel the sting of my palm intersecting his cheek. "Get the hell out of my house," I say.

He stands perfectly still, his mouth hanging open, his breath coming hard. "Oh, shit," he whispers. "Oh, shit, oh, shit. Nikki, I'm sorry."

"No, you're not," I snap. "You'd be thrilled if Damien and I broke up. I don't know why you dislike him so much—"

"And I don't know why you're so blind."

"I'm not," I say. "I see him perfectly clearly."

"You see what he wants you to see. But you forget where I work. You forget that my boss is his attorney. There is shit raining down on Stark," Ollie says, "and I don't want to see you get hurt." He sighs. "I warned you, didn't I? You're in the spotlight now, and that's not where you want to be. It's not where you should be."

My blood feels as though it's moving too fast through my body, and I feel a little sick to my stomach. "Just go."

"Fine, whatever. I'll get my stuff and get out of here." He returns to my room, then emerges with his briefcase. He marches for the door, then stops. "No, you know what? I get that things are bad between us now, and I'm sorry. But I can't just let this slide. Do you even know where he is now?"

I cross my arms over my chest. "In London."

"Why?"

"Business."

"Yeah?" He digs in his briefcase for his iPad, then pulls up a page from *Hello!* "Here," he says, shoving the tablet at me.

It's a picture of Damien with his arm around a woman. Her head is down, she's wearing sunglasses, and a hat shields most of her face. I don't know who she is, but I can guess. Apparently *Hello!* can't even do that, because the caption reads

Did Damien Ditch the Delicious Darling? Is it the end for Damien Stark and Texas Beauty Queen Nikki Fairchild? Our sources say Stark looked quite cosy with this uniden-tified woman as they strolled the Hampstead Heath ear-lier today. Stark arrived in London without the woman whose portrait he paid a cool million dollars for. Buyer's remorse, perhaps?

I hand the tablet back to him, feeling smug. "She's a friend."

"I thought he went on business."

"He's not allowed to see a friend while he's doing business?"

There's a loud bang on the wall Jamie and I share with Doug-las, followed by a very loud, very satisfied groan.

Ollie and I meet each other's eyes and, as if on cue, we both laugh.

For those few seconds, we are Ollie and Nikki again. But the seconds pass all too quickly.

"I don't want to screw us up," Ollie finally says.

"You already have," I say. "All you can do now is try to fix it."

For a moment I think he's going to snap something back at me. Then he nods. "Yeah. I guess so." He glances toward the door. "Should probably fix things with my fiancée first. That's all I do, lately. Piss people off and then try to patch it up."

"Ollie . . ." Sadness envelops me as he leaves. I think about what Damien says—that Ollie is in love with me. But I don't think it's true. I think that he's grieving. Through our lives, I've always been the more damaged, and Ollie has been my rock. But I'm healing, and I have found a new rock in Damien, and I think Ollie wonders how our lives will fit together.

It's not a question that I can answer for him. Not now. Not when he attacks Damien every time we come together. But I hope there is an answer, because I don't want to lose him. And I know that if I am forced to make a choice, I will go with my heart. I will go with Damien.

I realize that Edward's probably halfway through *The Count of Monte Cristo* by now, and so I hurry to my bedroom and get my laptop and the files I need. I pause at the door, then return to my closet for my old Nikon, since the fabulous digital Leica Damien gave me is still in Malibu. And as much as I love the Leica, the Nikon was a gift from Ashley, and I refuse to give up using it entirely.

"Back to the apartment?" Edward asks as he opens the limo door for me.

I close my hand tight around the camera. "Actually," I say, "there's one more place I want to go."

"How you holding up, Texas?"

"Okay, I guess." We're on Evelyn's balcony, looking out over the beach. Blaine is out with friends, and Evelyn had been enthusiastic when I'd called from the limo to invite myself over.

I've only been here once—the night that Damien and I met in Malibu—but it feels like home. I attribute that more to the woman than the location. "When I'm inside and away from it all, I do great. But when I see a paper or am accosted by a reporter, I feel like I'm going to crumble. Honestly, I don't know how celebrities do it."

"They have the fame gene," she says. "You don't."

"There's no such thing as bad PR?" I say dryly.

"For some people, it's a truism. Have you watched reality television?"

I have to laugh. I don't watch it regularly, but I've caught enough episodes with Jamie to understand what she's saying. Some people don't mind being the train wreck that other folks watch. Me, I mind.

"Pretty soon you'll be last week's news. Until then, hold your head up and smile."

I flash a brilliant pageant smile. "That's one thing I know how to do."

In front of us, the sun is beginning its descent toward the horizon. I take out the Nikon and snap shot after shot, hoping that when the prints are developed, I'll have managed to capture even a fraction of that beauty.

"You're going to show me the shots you took at the party, I hope," Evelyn says. "The more snapshots there are of me, the better my odds of finding a picture that's actually flattering."

"Do not even try fishing for compliments with me," I say, laughing. "You're gorgeous and amazing and you know it."

"It's true," she says, then taps out a cigarette and lights it. "I just hope Blaine keeps remembering it."

"I think you've got him hooked." Despite their age difference, they really do seem like the perfect couple. After the drama with Ollie, it's nice to know that some of my friends have relationships that are actually stable.

I'd been spurred to come here after the bullshit with Ollie, but now that I'm here, I find I don't want to talk about it. Instead, I'm enjoying just hanging and chatting. We've already covered the scintillating topics of male models, Botox, and the current summer blockbusters. The conversation was so scattered in fact, that I'd been surprised when she raised the specter of my personal tabloid hell.

"Blaine's still mortified, of course," she adds. "Thinks it's his fault."

"That's ridiculous," I say. "I'm the one who accepted money to pose nude, and then I consented to be tied up. If it's anyone's fault, it's mine."

"We didn't have any idea how much Damien paid you," Evelyn said, "but now that we do, I have to confess that I agree with Blaine. You sold yourself cheap."

I laugh, remembering that Sylvia said the same thing. At times like this, when I'm with friends and people who don't have shark's blood running through their veins, I feel almost proud of what I did. I negotiated a deal. I got my start-up money. And what the hell is wrong with that?

"Aw, hell, Texas. I see it on your face. Now I've gone and got you thinking about it. We can't have that. You want some wine?"

"Love some," I say.

She disappears inside, then returns a moment later with a chilled bottle of Chardonnay and two glasses.

She sits at the wrought-iron table then indicates the chair opposite with the tip of her cigarette. "So tell me the rest of it," she demands.

"The rest of it? The rest of what?"

"What's going on in your life, Texas. Fired twice—excuse me, once was a layoff. Dating one heck of a fine catch if I do say so myself. Your roommate's got a commercial in the works. Lot of life crammed into not very much time. You've certainly made quite the landing in our fair city."

Put that way, I have to agree. "Despite the firings and the tabloid stuff that we're just going to ignore, things are great. I'm going to take some time to get a couple more apps on the market."

She points at me. "An art app for Blaine. I haven't forgotten."

I grin, not sure if she means it or not. "I'm ready when you are. But that's my short-term plan. Long term is still in the development stages."

"And Damien? You said he's in London? On business?"

"Yeah, but I think he took some time to visit a friend. Sofia. I guess she's in some sort of trouble."

"That's too bad," Evelyn says. She props her hand on her fist and looks at me seriously. "He say what kind of trouble?"

"No."

"Hmm," she says. "What about Jamie? What's she up to?"

I hesitate before answering, wondering about the shift in conversation. Does Evelyn know Sofia? Does she know what kind of trouble she's in? It's possible, I realize. Sofia is from his tennis past, and Evelyn was Damien's agent when he was a young sports icon endorsing tennis shoes and God knows what else.

I think about asking, but hold my tongue. Evelyn has become a solid friend, and I don't want to muddy the waters by using her as a conduit between me and Damien's past.

"Jamie's in heaven," I say, focusing on the original question. "She's really hit it off with the guy she's doing this commercial with. Bryan Raine. You know him?"

"I do," Evelyn says, and she doesn't sound pleased. "I like your friend. Nice girl. A little green, but she'll get there. Bryan Raine, though . . . That one's a climber, and I'm not sure your friend is tough enough to deal with the shit he'll eventually throw her way."

My heart is sinking. "You're serious?"

"Afraid so. He won't be happy until he's banging the next big thing. And while he'd prefer a female, I think he'll fuck anything that moves if he thinks it'll ease his climb to the top. Male, female, or small farm animal." She looks at me hard. "Your friend got the skin to make it when he ditches her?"

I open my mouth to say that Jamie's as tough as they come, but I can't speak the words. They aren't true. She's got a tough veneer, but inside she's soft and vulnerable.

"I hope you're wrong," I say.

"So do I, Texas. So do I."

22

The nice thing about limos is that they have a driver. I take full advantage of that knowledge, and I arrive back at Damien's apartment more than a little tipsy after downing half of Evelyn's very excellent bottle of Chardonnay.

I am interested in nothing but sleep, and I make my way to the bed, hesitating only long enough to feel a pang of regret that I am in it alone.

I've dropped my phone on the bedside table, and I reach for it, then tap out a text: In your bed. Drunk. Wish you were here.

I have no idea what time it is in London, and have had too much wine to bother with the math to figure it out. So I'm not sure if Damien is even awake. But only a few seconds pass before I get his response. Wish I were, too. At airport. Coming home to you. Tell me you're naked.

I smile and tap out a reply. Very. And wet. And wanting you. Hurry home. I have been Damienized, and I don't think I can last long without you. [Damienized, v. To be needful of Damien, especially in the sense of fucking and dirty talk. See, e.g., Nikki Fairchild.]

His answer is almost immediate. I like the new addition to your lexicon. And now I'll be hard for all of a long flight home. Plane boarding. See you soon. Until then, imagine me, touching you.

I don't know if he will get the text, but I send one final message. Yes, sir, I type. And then I hug my phone, and drift off to sleep.

When I wake, it's because my phone is buzzing against my cheek. I roll over, confused, and realize that it's already past noon, and that I've missed a call. I quickly check to see if it's from Damien, but it's only a voice mail from Evelyn telling me I forgot my camera. I curse silently and open my email, planning to send her a quick note telling her I'll get it soon.

That's when I see that there is an email from Damien waiting.

Nikki, on a quick layover in Amsterdam. Arriving LAX five P.M. Do you mind if we go to a charity fashion show tonight? Starts at nine? Would much rather stay in with you, but Maynard's firm sponsoring. Swears press access limited. They'll get the boot if they even think about harassing you. Jamie invited, too. Let me know. Missing you . . .

I read the message twice, trying to decide why I'm smiling so broadly. It's only as I start the third read that I realize—he's asking me, not telling me. I take that knowledge and hold it close to my heart. Then I tap out my reply, though I know he won't get it until he lands.

Of course, sir. But how you do tease, pretending to ask my consent when of course you know that I will do whatever you want, whenever and however.

I hope you're spending your time in the plane thinking of interesting "howevers" . . .

P.S. I have the perfect dress at home. Pick me up at the condo at eight? Will check Jamie's social calendar . . .

As it turns out, Raine has told Jamie that he's having a night out with the boys, so she's completely keen to be a third wheel with me and Damien.

I'm not entirely sure what to expect from a fashion show hosted by a law firm, but it turns out that Bender, Twain is just one of many sponsors for a function that is raising money for juvenile diabetes. The event is being held in a restaurant in Beverly Hills, but the place has been so transformed that it's hard to believe that it has ever been anything other than a fashion venue. A long runway bisects a giant room, and that is surrounded by chairs. The perimeter is lined with tables providing research, raffles, and gift bags. Jamie and I both snag a bag and are pleased to find them filled with cosmetics, hair brushes, and even a darling tank top.

"This is great," Jamie says to Damien. "Thanks for bringing me."

"Happy to have you along," he says. His mood has been light since he's returned from London.

"So the trip went well?" I ask once Jamie skips off to do the circuit.

"It did," he says.

"Sofia's okay?"

"She's settled," he says. "For her, that's about as good as it gets. And I heard from Charles. He's been working with my attorneys in Germany, and with any luck, that problem is going to go away as well."

"You mean they won't indict?"

He cocks his head to look at me. "That's my hope."

"That would be great," I say. "And even though I don't have a clue about international business or what kind of regulations the Germans think you mucked up, you know you can talk to me about that kind of thing. I may not get it, but I promise I'll be supportive."

The expression on his face is surprisingly guarded. "Someday when I'm ready, I will." He pulls me in for a quick, chaste kiss. "And yes, I believe that you would understand."

A smile flickers on my lips. I'm pleased, but I can't help but think that we're talking about entirely different things.

I don't have the chance to ask, though, because the show is starting. We take our seats and watch the models parade down the runway in skimpy, sexy outfits, with Damien whispering his opinion as to exactly which outfits he wants to see me in. Reporters and photographers are at the base of the runway, and I realize that Charles has made good on his promise—the press is leaving me and Damien alone. Some weight inside me lifts a little, and I lean back in my chair and enjoy the freedom of knowing that, at least for a moment, I am not a bug under a microscope.

When the show is over, the guests are encouraged to mingle and imbibe from one of the many cash bars while the crew sets up for the charity auction. I look around for Jamie, but she has already disappeared into the crowd, presumably to jump all over that imbibing thing.

Instead, I see Ollie, and I suck in a tight breath. He is talking with a woman who looks somewhat familiar, but I can't place her. Damien hasn't seen him yet, but I know the exact moment when Ollie's glance finds us.

I'm not sure why I'm surprised that he's here. After all, he works with Charles Maynard. The crowd shifts, and I see a pretty, dark-haired woman coming toward him with two drinks in her hands. *Courtney*. And then Ollie and Courtney and the other woman are all heading our way. I grab Damien's hand and smile my Social Nikki smile. It is the first time I've felt the need to be so armed against Ollie, but I know that I need both the mask and Damien's strength, and that knowledge makes me sad.

"Nikki, Damien, it's good to see you here."

"Ollie," Damien says politely. He glances at the two women.

"Courtney," I say, "it's so good to see you again." I give her a little hug, then formally introduce her to Damien.

"Great to meet you," Courtney says, then turns her attention to me. "I'm planning a destination wedding shower, but I haven't decided where yet." She shifts toward Damien, including him as she speaks to me. "Tell me you two will come? And Jamie and Raine, too."

Automatically, my eyes dart to Ollie's, but his expression is too guarded to read.

"I'm looking forward to hearing all the details," I say diplomatically. The truth is I'm not sure there is going to be a wedding, much less a shower. Courtney, however, doesn't seem the least bit worried.

The other woman with Ollie is introduced as Susan Morris. I keep my polite smile plastered on, but inside, I'm frowning, trying to figure out why her name is familiar.

I'm about to ask, when Ollie continues. "Susan is directing the fashion show."

"I got my training in pageants," Susan says, "although it wasn't formal training. More like an apprenticeship."

"Susan Morris?" I say, finally clueing in. "Alicia Morris's mother?" Susan Morris was almost as much of a stage mother as mine.

"I was hoping you'd remember me," she says. "Ollie said that Damien Stark was here with his girlfriend, and I just had to see you."

"I'm so glad you did," Social Nikki says. The real me isn't at all interested in this relic from my past. I can tell that Damien sees the real Nikki, because he squeezes my hand in support.

"Your mother and I have stayed close. In fact, since I moved to Park Cities, we lunch together at least once a week," she adds, referring to the affluent Dallas neighborhood where I grew up. "I talked to her just this morning, as a matter of fact." Her voice is strangely tight, and I want nothing more than to get away from this woman who reminds me too much of my mother.

"How nice," I say. I flash my wide pageant smile. "I should really go check on my friend Jamie. It was lovely talking to you."

She takes a step sideways and blocks my departure. "Your mother is so mortified she can't even hold her head up in public. And you haven't been any help. You haven't returned her calls or her emails. It's terribly ungrateful, Nichole."

Ungrateful. What the fuck?

Damien steps closer to me. "I believe Nikki has already said that she needs to go check on her friend."

But Susan Morris is not taking the hint. She aims a finger at Damien. "And you! Elizabeth told me how you shipped her home just when Nichole needed her."

My mouth falls open. Needed her? *Needed her?* All I'd needed was for her to be gone.

"And now you've dragged her into this . . . this . . . degrading lifestyle!" Susan Morris is speaking machine-gun fast, and with as much damage. "Posing nude. Erotic art. And accepting money like a common whore. It's contemptible." She literally spits the last word, and I see the tiny droplets of moisture fly from her mouth.

I can only gape at her, my Social Nikki facade having shattered under this unexpected onslaught.

Damien is not so frozen. He takes a step forward, his expression like thunder. I think vaguely that he will hurt her, and that I should hold out a hand to stop him. I don't. All I can think about is the nausea and tightness and clammy coldness that has settled over me.

"Get the hell out of here," Damien says, his hands pressed firmly against his sides.

"I will not," she counters. "You think you can buy anything?

Even a girl like Nichole in your bed? I know your type, Damien Stark."

"Do you?" He takes another step toward her, and she has the sense to look scared. "In that case I think you would listen when I tell you to get out. And for the record, Nikki is a woman, not a girl. And the choice she made was her own."

Her mouth drops open, but she doesn't reply. Instead she turns back to me. "Your mother expected better things from you."

I can do nothing but stand there. I'm frozen, my body chilled to the bone. And, goddammit, I'm starting to shake. Deep, trembling shudders that I cannot control, and that I do not want Susan Morris to see.

Throughout all of this, Ollie has stood stock-still, Courtney's hand tight on his arm. But now he, too, takes a step forward. "Do what Mr. Stark says and get the hell out of here or I will have you fired from this pageant right here, right now."

"I—" She shuts her mouth, gives each of us a hard look, then leaves.

I do not remember sliding into Damien's embrace, but that is where I am, and it feels warm and safe, and my trembling starts to subside. I don't want him to open his arms, because I don't want to face the world. I want to be home with him. Back in the penthouse where ghosts from my past don't pop up. Where I'm not accused of being a whore. Where my personal life isn't gossiped about by people who don't know me and know even less about the choices I've made.

"Are you okay?" Courtney asks.

"No," I say. "I'm not."

I see Ollie shoot Damien a vitriol-filled look. He may have sided with me against Susan Morris, but it's clear that he's still not on Team Damien.

"I'll take you home," Damien says.

I nod, then hesitate, then shake my head. "No. I want to stay."

"You're sure?"

I hesitate only a moment, then nod. "I just need to go to the bathroom. Then I want to find Jamie. We haven't looked at all the booths yet." I am proud of myself. I sound so steady even though I'm anything but.

Damien's phone buzzes and he glances at the screen, then types out a quick response before sliding it back in his pocket.

"Not important?"

"Charles," he says. "He's at one of the cash bars and wants to have a quick talk. I told him I was with you, and business could wait until morning."

"Can it?"

He looks right into my eyes. "Right now, the only thing I care about is you." He takes my arm. "It looks like the ladies' room is over there."

While Damien waits, I go in—then immediately clutch the counter. I've been working so hard not to let Damien see my cracks. Susan Morris. My mother. The rumors of sex for money, of being a whore. It's all tied up in my head like so much noise and I want to sort it out. I want Damien—but I know he blames himself, and if I can just gather myself a little. If I can just make one tiny inroad on keeping myself collected . . .

I look around for something sharp, but there is nothing. Only the granite counter, the mirror, and the ceramic soap dispenser.

I remember the apartment and the glass vase that Damien shattered. I close my eyes, feeling the imaginary shard in my hand. Glass cuts on all sides. It's perfect. It's like a tiny miracle biting into the palm of your hand.

Wildly, I open my eyes and look around for something with which to break the glass. I snatch the soap dispenser, stand back, and start to hurl it.

That is when I see my reflection. *Oh, God. What am I doing?*

My fingers go slack, and the dispenser crashes to the ground—and in the back of the room, from behind a closed stall door, I hear someone yelp.

I jump—I hadn't realized anyone was in there—then immediately relax when I see it is Jamie. Her face is splotchy and her makeup is smeared, but I must look worse because she takes one glance at me, looks down at the ceramic shards on the floor, and says, "I'm finding Damien."

"Jamie!" I call, trying to get her back, but it's too late. She's out the door, and only moments later, Damien is in the ladies' room.

"I didn't," I say immediately. "I just dropped a soap dish. That's all. Jamie overreacted."

He is looking at me with such intensity that I am certain he can see the lie inside my head. "All right," he says slowly. "Now tell me the rest of it."

I sigh, then drop my gaze. I count to five, and then look back up to him, my composure restored. "I was going to," I say. "But I talked myself out of it. And then, really, I dropped the dispenser. It's slippery."

"You talked yourself out of it." It's a statement, not a question.

"I saw my reflection in the mirror. I was going to break it with that," I say, nodding toward the gooey mess on the floor.

"You were going to break a mirror in a public restaurant instead of talking with me?"

I graze my teeth over my lower lip. I don't answer.

"I see."

"I didn't want to make it worse for you. But I guess I did that, anyway."

"But you're okay now?" He is speaking very carefully.

"Yes. Just a momentary glitch. System completely reset now. It was just that woman. That horrible woman."

"All right," he finally says. He takes my hand; his is warm and reassuring. "Let's go. We'll let the janitors worry about the mess."

I nod and follow him. Already I feel better, just knowing that Damien is at my side. In the restaurant, I search for Jamie, but I don't find her anywhere. "I'm worried about Jamie," I tell him. "She was a mess."

"Do you know why?"

"No, she was just—oh, shit. Is that who I think it is?" I point into the crowd, and Damien's low whisper of "Well, hell" tells me I'm right. Bryan Raine is at the event, too, and he's arm in arm, lips to lips, with a svelte, sexy blonde.

"That's Madeline Aimes," Damien says.

I remember Evelyn's words. "A movie star? On her way up?"

He gives me a quizzical look. "When did you start paying attention to Hollywood?"

"I don't. Lucky guess." I look around the room again, suddenly worried. "Now I really want to find Jamie."

I find Ollie, but he hasn't seen Jamie, either. Whatever detente we'd reached earlier when Susan Morris attacked me seems to have shattered, because he is quiet and distant and keeps shooting Damien angry glances. I, however, am too worried about Jamie to call him on it.

It takes another twenty minutes before we learn that Edward took Jamie home.

"I'm so sorry, Mr. Stark," Edward says when we meet him in the parking area behind the restaurant. "She assured me that she'd cleared it with you."

"Don't worry about it," Damien says. "How was she?"

"I understand there was some trouble with a young man she's

been seeing. You might have to restock the limo's supply of Scotch."

Damien grimaces. "Shall we go check on her?" he asks.

I nod. It's already after midnight, and now that Jamie's gone AWOL, I'm ready to go home. I start to move toward the limo, but Ollie's words hold me back. "Raine was just stringing her along."

I turn back to him. "Well, yeah. Obviously."

"Obviously?" He jabs a finger toward Damien. "He's doing the same thing to you."

I grab Damien's hand, as much because I want his touch as to keep him right here beside me. "What the hell are you talking about?"

"He keeps you around, but it's not real." He holds up his hands and flexes his wrists. "It's just kink and fun and when he's tired he'll toss you aside."

"You little shit," Damien says.

"I'm wrong? Really? You know damn well it's just a game to you. That's why you never tell her shit. That's why you haven't even told her that you've been indicted in Germany for murder."

23

Murder!

I look from Ollie to Damien. Ollie looks smug. Damien looks confused.

"There's no indictment," Damien says.

For a moment, Ollie appears scared, then he rallies. "No, apparently they were just stalling. The indictment came in just a few minutes ago. You didn't know?"

"Wait," I say. My head is spinning and I'm having a hard time figuring out exactly what I'm feeling. Anger? Hurt? Fear? Confusion? They are all jostling for position inside me, and at that moment, it feels a bit as though my head is going to explode.

I think about those ceramic shards, and I wish to hell I'd pocketed one.

No. Just breathe. You can do this.

I take a deep breath and turn to Damien. "All this time I've been assuming that the German indictment is some business violation, and it was actually a murder investigation?"

His hesitation seems to last a lifetime, and throughout his silence, his eyes look only at me, as if he's trying to find the answer to the question hidden deep inside me somewhere.

"Yes," he says.

And there it is. The biggest secret of all, and one I gave him about nine billion opportunities to reveal. I think about the times I mentioned German regulations. About the times he let me go on believing that it was just a business thing. Just Stark International dealing with the kind of problem huge corporations deal with.

"I thought your company had broken some regulation about zoning codes or paid too little in taxes or something. This is—"

"Worse," Damien says. "Much worse."

I wait for him to say more. To explain. To lie. Something. Anything.

He stays silent.

I suck in air through my teeth, then press my fingers to my temples. I need to think. Mostly, I just need to be alone. "I'm going," I say. "I need to check on Jamie."

"All right," Damien says, his voice a little too calm. "Edward and I will drop you at home."

"I'll get home on my own. Thanks."

"I'll drive you," Ollie says.

"The hell you will," I snap. With Damien, I'm lost in a maelstrom of anger and sadness and confusion and God knows what else. With Ollie, I'm just plain old pissed. "I'll take a taxi."

I turn once as I walk away, and my eyes find Damien's. I hesitate, expecting him to call after me, but he doesn't, and I fight the urge to hug myself to ward off a coming chill. Slowly, I turn my back to Damien and I continue toward the street. I'm hurt and I'm confused, but right now I just need to focus on one thing. I just need to get home.

It's an easy shot over the hill from Beverly Hills to Studio

City, and I'm home in no time. I hurry inside, expecting to find Jamie in tears on her bed.

She's not home.

Okay, okay. I just have to think. Where could she be?

I know Jamie well enough to know that she may try to soothe a bruised ego by banging some other guy, and I mentally start running through the single men in our complex that she hasn't already gotten horizontal with. That's one thing about Jamie— she rarely goes in for repeat performances.

As if to underscore the brilliance of my thinking, a series of moans and groans floats in from next door. Douglas, once again getting lucky.

At least I can cross him off my list. Although Douglas has made it clear he'd be up for round two, Jamie has repeatedly said no.

I pace the apartment, wondering where she could be. I call the divey bar on the corner near our condo, but she hasn't been there in days. I call Steve and Anderson, but they haven't talked to her. They give me the names of a few other mutual friends. I call them, but nobody's heard from her tonight.

Shit, shit, shit.

Even though I know it will do no good whatsoever, I call the police. I'm coherent enough to forgo 911 and call the station directly. I speak to the officer in charge, explaining that my roommate came home plastered, but she's not here now and I'm worried that she's dead in a ditch somewhere.

He's nice enough—but he's also not sending anyone to help. Not until she's been gone for a hell of a lot longer than a few hours.

I close my eyes and think. Maybe she said something to Edward? That she was going to change and go clubbing? That she was going to visit a friend? That she was going to LAX to splurge on a red-eye to New York?

I don't have a number for Edward, and my finger hesitates over Damien's name. I'm not ready to talk to him, but I have to know. I suck in a breath, count to three, and call.

He answers on the first ring and, damn me, I can't even get the words out because of the tears that are clogging my throat.

I'm still on the phone with him, choking out the story, asking him if I can speak to Edward, when he walks through the front door. I blink in confusion as he walks to me and very gently takes the phone from my hand and ends the call.

"How did you get here so fast?"

"Edward is parked at the end of the block. I was planning to come over anyway, but I was giving you time."

"Oh. Did you ask him?"

"She didn't say anything to him," Damien says. "And he walked her to the door and heard her lock it after he left. He assumed she'd be asleep in minutes."

I press my hand against my forehead. I need to figure out what to do next, but it's all blank. I don't know what to do. I am completely lost—and I'm scared to death.

"She's drunk and she's pissed and she's going to do something stupid."

"Did you check for her car?"

"*Dammit,*" I say. "I didn't even think about it."

"She could have taken a taxi or had a friend pick her up, but if it's still here, it's a start. I can get one of my security guys calling the taxi services to see if there was a call, and then—"

I've been sprinting for the front door as he speaks, ready to go look at her parking space. I yank it open—and freeze at the site of Jamie standing there, her clothes askew, her hair a mess, but otherwise looking none the worse for the wear.

"James!" I pull her into my embrace, then back off long enough to inspect her for hidden injuries. "Are you okay? Where were you?"

She shrugs, but for just a second her eyes dart to the wall we share with Douglas.

"Oh, James," I say, but she looks so damned miserable that I don't say anything else. The lecture can wait. Right now, I need to put my very drunk, very upset best friend to bed.

"I'm going to go help her," I tell Damien. I hesitate for a moment, then add, "I'll be right back."

He nods, and I help Jamie to her room, then out of her clothes. She slides into bed in her bra and panties. "I fucked up, didn't I?" she asks.

"Bryan Raine is the fuck-up," I say. "You just need to sleep."

"Sleep," she repeats, as if it's the most wonderful thing in the world.

"Night, James," I whisper. I start to leave, but she grabs my hand. "You're lucky," she says. "He loves you."

I close my eyes tight to keep the tears at bay. I want to tell her everything, but my best friend is only half-conscious, and the man who might love me—but who has most definitely lied to me—is waiting for me in the living room.

I'm not ready for this, but I leave Jamie's room and return to Damien.

He's ending a call as I return. "That was Edward," he says. "I'm sending him home. I'm staying here tonight."

"I don't think—"

"I'm staying," he says. "In your bed, on the couch, in the goddamn bathtub. I don't care, but you're not getting rid of me. Not tonight."

"Fine. Whatever." I can hear the exhaustion in my voice. "But I'm going to bed." I eye the bed that fills the living room—*our bed*—and the sadness that washes over me is almost enough to bring me to my knees. "The bed in my room," I clarify. "There's a spare blanket in the hall cabinet. Help yourself to whatever's in the fridge."

And then I turn around, go to my room, and shut the door behind me.

Five minutes later I'm in bed, eyes wide open, when there is a soft tap at my door. I could pretend to be asleep. For a moment, I consider it. But while part of me is still hurt and angry, the other part craves Damien.

It's that other part that wins. "Come in," I say.

He enters with two mugs of hot chocolate. I can't help but smile. "Where did you find that?"

"Your cupboard," he said. "Okay?"

I nod. I am not in the mood for wine or liquor, but chocolate comfort is definitely welcome.

He puts mine on the bedside table, then sits on the edge of the bed. Silence hangs heavy between us. "It's Richter," he finally says, breaking the stillness. "I'm being charged with Richter's murder."

I try to process this information, fitting it in with what I know of Damien and what I know about Richter's death. "But it was suicide," I say. "And years ago."

"They're relying in part on the fact that I inherited his money."

"You did?"

He nods. "My first million. It was kept out of the press. I paid Charles a good portion of that money to make sure it stayed out of the press. My enemies will argue that a million dollars is a strong motive."

"That's what they're arguing? But you were just a kid." Everyone in the world heard the story at the time it happened. Young tennis superstar Damien Stark's coach committed suicide by leaping to his death from a Munich-based tennis center. "And you were already making money."

"Most people with money want more."

"It's still a ridiculous argument," I say. "He probably left you the money for the same reason he killed himself. He felt guilty for being an abusive slimebag."

"I'm not sure Richter ever felt a moment of guilt in his life," Damien says. "At any rate, I believe they're putting more stock in the witness than into the money."

"So who is this witness?"

"A janitor. Elias Schmidt. He actually came forward right after Richter died, but my father paid him off and he disappeared before he said anything to the police. Evelyn was around during all of that. So was Charles. There was a tell-all book in the works that was going with the hypothesis that I'd killed my coach. They got it shut down and the rumors locked up tight."

I'm trying to follow all of this. "So the janitor was paid off, but he came back?"

"No," Damien says. "He didn't come back. The German police found out about him and they went to him."

"How?"

"I don't know," Damien says calmly. Everything about him is calm, and I realize that he's gone into corporate mode. He's relating the details of the transaction, but he's not getting emotionally involved. "But I think my father tipped them."

I am beyond shocked. "What? Why? Why on earth would he do that?"

"To punish me for not giving him any more money."

I can't help the shiver that rips through me. My relationship with my mom is fucked up, but this is out in the stratosphere.

The truth is, I'm scared. "But they'll cave once you put on your defense. It'll be fine. I mean, it will cost you a boatload of money, but you have about a billion boats of money, right? And you're innocent, so eventually they'll drop the charges."

"Money helps," Damien says, "but it's not a guarantee. And innocent people get convicted all the time. And besides," he adds, his voice as level as I have ever heard it. "I'm not innocent."

24

I stare, certain that I could not possibly have heard his words right. "No. No," I say. "Richter killed himself. He jumped off a building and committed suicide." If I say it enough, it will have to be true.

"He fell to his death, yes."

I stare at Damien's face, this man that I have fallen for so completely. Does he have it within him to kill a man?

The answer is not long in coming—I know that he does. He would kill to protect me, I am certain of it. And he would kill to protect himself.

Suddenly, I no longer doubt his words. I shiver, but not because I am horrified. No, I tremble because I fear that I will lose him. That he will be convicted for protecting himself against a man who was truly a monster.

"Nikki," he says, his voice infinitely sad. "I'm sorry. I'll go." He starts to get up off the bed.

"*No.*" The word seems ripped from me, and I grab hard to his hand and pull him back down. "Don't leave me. You did what you had to do. What your father should have done, the bastard. I swear if I'd been around back then and knew what that son of a bitch was doing to you, I would have killed him myself."

Slowly, Damien closes his eyes. I think that it is relief that I see on his face.

"Tell me exactly what happened," I say gently.

Damien lets go of my hand and stands up. For a moment, I'm afraid that he is leaving anyway, but then I realize that he just needs to move. He walks around the bed, then pauses in front of the Monet. Haystacks in a field and the splendid colors of sunset.

Sunset.

That is our safeword. The word that Damien told me to pick that very first night that I was his. Mine to use if he went too far.

I look at him, and I hope that he will not invoke the word now. I know that it must be hard to go back, to tell me what happened that night. But I need to hear it. More, I need for Damien to tell me. And I fervently hope that the secrets he is so used to keeping won't tie his tongue now.

"Damien?"

He doesn't turn around. Doesn't even move. But I hear his voice, low and steady. "It started when I was nine. The touching. The threats. I won't tell you the details—I don't want those memories in my head, much less in yours. But I will tell you it was horrible. I hated him. I hated my father. And I hated myself. Not because I was ashamed—I was never ashamed. But because I had no power to stop him." He turns to me. "I learned how important power is. It's the only thing that can truly protect you, and back then, I had none."

I barely nod, afraid that if I speak or react too much, he will stop talking.

"It went on for years. I grew bigger and stronger, but he was a huge man, and as I got older he added more threats to his repertoire. He had photographs. And there were—". He pauses and takes a deep breath. "There were other things that he threatened."

"What changed?" I say gently. I don't want him to relive all those years. I just want to know what happened the night that Richter died.

"All that time he never—he never raped me." His voice is so low and monotone that it gives me chills. "When I was fourteen, we were in Germany at a tennis center in Munich. I went up to the courts on the roof one night—I don't remember why. I couldn't sleep, I was antsy. Whatever. He came up, too. He'd been drinking. I could smell it on him. I tried to go back down, and he blocked me. He tried—for the first time he tried to take his sick games further." Damien meets my eyes. "I didn't let him."

"You pushed him off the roof?" I can barely hear through the pounding of my pulse in my ears.

"No," he says.

I'm confused. "What happened?"

"We fought," he says. "I hit him with my racquet. He grabbed it out of my hands. Smacked me across the back of my head with it—I'm lucky the wound wasn't visible, or the police might have been more interested in me at the time. But it was a nasty fight—and we were at the edge of the roof, an area without the fencing that was by the courts to keep stray balls from going over. I don't remember exactly what happened. He lunged for me, and I got a good shove in. He stumbled backward and then tripped over something, I'm still not sure what. He was drunk, so maybe it was his own two feet. He went over, but he managed to grab the ledge. He was hanging there, and I was frozen to the spot. I couldn't move. He called for me to help him."

I realize that I'm holding my breath.

"I just stood there. He screamed for me, and I can remember the way my head was still throbbing from his blow, but I took one step toward him. One step, and then I stopped. And then he fell." He closes his eyes, and I see the tremor that shakes his body. "I went back to my room, but I didn't sleep. The next morning the assistant coach burst in with the news that Richter was dead."

"They can't possibly convict you," I say. "You did nothing wrong."

"There was a moment when I could have saved him," he says. "I could have moved faster. I could have reached him."

"Don't you dare feel guilty for 'could have,' " I say.

His eyes are hard when he looks at me. "I don't. I don't regret it for an instant."

"Damien, don't you see? You just need to tell the police all of this."

"All of what? All of the abuse?"

"Yes," I say.

"No."

"But—"

"Nikki, I said no."

I draw in a deep breath. "So what happens now?"

"I called Charles from the limo. We're going to Munich tomorrow. The legal team is already in place. I'm hoping that we'll be able to present a decent defense."

"You have a decent defense."

"Don't push me on that, Nikki. I'm not making that aspect of my life public. Richter took a lot from me, but he's not taking my privacy, too."

I nod, because there is no point in arguing this right now. "So the tennis center bigwigs in Germany," I begin. "Charles and your dad were hoping that if you endorsed the Richter Tennis Center here that those folks would pull strings with the cops?"

"That's right."

"But you said your dad started it all."

"I said that I think he did," Damien clarifies. "I don't know everything that goes on in my father's head, but I do know that before I settled with Padgett, he had at least two meetings with my father. Considering your conversation with Carl, I think he may have been involved, too. I think my father must have told Padgett about the janitor—Schmidt apparently witnessed our fight, though he left before Richter went off the roof."

"That was how Padgett was going to hurt you before you settled?" When Carl said the shit was going to hit the fan, he must have meant the janitor. "He was going to get the janitor to go public?"

"I think so. He'd request more money for himself and for my father, who was pulling the strings. But then when Padgett settled, my dad was frustrated that the plan went awry. So he tipped the German police. I don't think he expected it to go this far. The case is very cold, after all, and was never officially treated as a murder. The threat was really to get my attention—and my money."

"But the German police heated it back up again."

"Yes. And so my father wanted me to appear squeaky clean. His house, his car, and much of his bank account are actually in my name. I get convicted—or I need funds for my defense—and all of that might go away. Worse for him, the public might find out that he was complicit in what Richter did to me."

"Your father is a son of a bitch," I say harshly.

"Yes," Damien says. "He is."

"But you're going to come out of this just fine." I cannot even conceive of the possibility that he will be convicted.

"I'm not so sure," he admits. "But right now, I don't want to think about it anymore."

I pull the covers back and hold out my hand. "Then don't."

He meets my eyes. "I should have told you."

"Yes," I agree. "But you've told me now."

For a moment all I can see is sadness in his eyes. Then he smiles, and it is as if light is filling my dim bedroom. "Don't ever forget how much you mean to me, Nikki," he says as he moves to my side.

"I won't. But nothing's going to happen to you."

He is busy removing the T-shirt that I wear in lieu of pajamas, but he looks at me, his expression serious. "You know that I will always protect you. That I will do whatever it takes to protect you."

"Stop," I say firmly. "You won't be convicted. You aren't going to jail. You're staying right here. With me."

He says nothing, just leans in and presses his forehead against mine. My shirt is off now, his breath on my bare skin is magic. "I'm going to make love to you tonight," he says. "Slow and sweet and as long as we can stand it."

"That will be a very long time," I say, as he begins to trail kisses down my neck and over the swell of my breast. Already my body is tight with desire for him. Already I can feel his erection straining against his slacks. "Take them off," I say. "I want to feel you. I want you against me. I want you so close that I can't tell where I end and you begin."

He raises off me long enough to look at me. Slowly, his mouth curves into a smile. "Yes, ma'am," he says, drawing a laugh from me.

He rolls off the bed and slowly unbuttons his shirt. I watch, enjoying the show. Enjoying even more the knowledge that this perfect specimen of a man is mine. He folds the shirt and puts it on my desk. He toes off his shoes and eases his pants off. His briefs are gray, but even in the dim light, I can see his erection straining behind the cotton. He takes them off, and I realize that I am licking my lips. Damien notices at the same time, and his soft chuckle makes me blush.

"What exactly does the lady want?" he asks.

"I want to touch you," I say. "I want to taste you. I want to take you to heaven."

"What a coincidence," he says, as he climbs in beside me. "I want exactly the same thing."

He is on his knees, and he pulls me up so that I am kneeling in front of him. Slowly, he strokes my face, his eyes hard upon me. "I want to memorize you," he says. "Every line, every curve. The way you smell, the way you taste. I want to lock you in my memory so that I will never be without you."

"You never will," I say.

"Nikki—"

I expect him to say more or to kiss me, but my name hangs in the air. For a brief, odd moment, I feel a twinge of fear, but I shove it away. He will not be convicted; he will not be taken from me. I believe it. I do. But as I lie back, I reach for him and pull him down onto me, because I cannot stand him being away from me for even a second longer than necessary. "No toys," I say, then brush my lips over his. "No kink. No games. Just you inside me. That's all I want tonight, Damien. That's all I need."

His hands stroke me, his lips dance over me. "That's all I need, too," he says. "You, Nikki. You in my arms. You burned into my memory. You, drawing me in deep. Keeping me, claiming me."

My hands are on his back, on the curve of his ass. My legs are parted, my knees up. I bring my legs closer so that his body brushes my skin as we move together, body against body, skin against skin.

I do not want the sweetness of this moment to end, but I am wet and ready and I have to have him. I have to feel him inside me. I have to know that he is mine and that I am his and that we are really together—and that we always will be.

"Damien," I beg. "Now. Please, please, I need you now."

He shifts on the bed, easing my legs apart, opening me up for him. Then the tip of his cock is at my sex, and he's moving slowly, thrusting slowly, so maddeningly slowly, until I am certain that I shall lose my mind.

"Now," I beg. "Damien, *now*. I need you now."

"I need you too, Nikki," he says and thrusts hard inside me, filling me, making me arch up with the pleasure that rockets through me as if we are a circuit and our joining is sending electricity spinning round and round between us.

He works a magical rhythm, and I rise to meet each thrust, my body drawing him in, my muscles tightening, my orgasm building until I feel as though I am not lying on the bed, but floating above it. Until I am no longer a woman but an explosion of stars.

Until all I am is Damien's, and that is all I ever want to be.

25

Damien leaves early the next morning to go meet with Charles at the Tower apartment so that he can pack for Germany. I peek in on Jamie, but she's dead to the world. I'm bummed, because I'm worried about Damien and I want someone to talk to, but I also know she needs to sleep it off.

My worries can wait.

I putter around the kitchen for a few minutes, debating between eggs or a bagel, and end up having black coffee. I can't shake this sense of foreboding that has settled over me, and I finally decide that I have to see Damien. I don't care if he is getting ready to leave for Munich, I need to see him one more time. I need to hold him and tell him in the light of day that everything he told me last night changes nothing. That I believe in him.

I need to tell him that I love him.

I change quickly into a peasant skirt, a pink tank top layered over a white one, and flip-flops, then limit my hair and makeup routine to lip gloss and mascara. I don't know what time their plane is scheduled to leave, and I cannot risk being late.

Since I don't know if the paparazzi are clinging like leeches to the front sidewalk, I use the back route to the parking area. Yes, they might swarm my car as I exit the gate, but with any luck I'll be down the street before they realize it's me.

As it turns out, I'm lucky. There is a lone photographer camped out on the sidewalk in a lawn chair. I manage a tight grin. As far as I'm concerned, he's in league with the devil, and I can think of little that is more hellish than sitting outside during a sweltering summer in the San Fernando Valley when the beach and cool ocean breezes are only a few miles away.

My thoughts, however, don't remain long with the paparazzi. Instead, I'm concentrating on only two things: getting to Damien, and working the clutch exactly right so that the Honda doesn't stall out on me.

By some miracle, I get to downtown stall-free, and then it is only a few blocks before I pull into the underground parking structure that serves Stark Tower and the adjacent building.

I grab the closest parking place, yank my purse out of the passenger seat, and sprint to the elevator.

Joe is working the security desk and I wave at him as I jog by in the lobby. "I'm going to the apartment," I call. "Buzz me up?"

"Of course, Ms. Fairchild." Yes, there are definitely perks to being the boss's girlfriend.

The elevator is open for me when I get to the proper bank. I step inside, press the button, and tap my foot for the entire ride to the top. I still feel antsy, and despite being an express, the elevator can't move fast enough to suit me. The doors open onto the apartment side of the penthouse, and I step out into the foyer. I don't hear Damien or Charles, but I assume that they have not left for Germany, since surely Joe would have told me.

"Damien?" I call softly.

I hear a thump from the back of the apartment and hurry in that direction, hoping that it is Damien and that he is alone.

I find him in the bedroom, a suitcase open on the bed. His

back is to me, but flip-flops are not quiet shoes, and he turns as I enter the room.

I start to go to him—I want nothing more than to lose myself in his embrace—but something in his expression stops me. There is pleasure and surprise, yes. But there is also wariness. And something darker, too. Something I don't recognize, but that I fear is . . . regret?

"Damien?" I am scared now, and for no reason, and the rising of this unpleasant emotion bothers me. This is *Damien*. The man who would never hurt me. Who would move mountains to protect me. So what the hell am I afraid of?

There is, however, a tiny part of me that knows what I fear—and hopes with a desperate fervency that I am wrong.

"Nikki." The smile that touches his lips is so warm and genuine that I am emboldened. Whatever gloom has settled over me is simply wrong, and I shove it away and hurry toward Damien.

"I had to come say goodbye again," I say.

"I'm glad you did," he says. "I shouldn't have left without saying goodbye to you. I'm going to miss you more than you can imagine." There is nothing strange about his tone, and he is looking at me with such familiar adoration I think that my heart will burst. Even so, the sense of dread returns.

I press on anyway. "I wanted you to know that what you told me last night changes nothing. I don't care if you pushed Richter off the roof on purpose. What he did to you was reprehensible, and I will stick by you, Damien. No matter what, I am not running."

He looks at me with steady eyes and a sad smile. "I believe you," he says.

"Do you remember when you asked me to play our game again? You said that you wanted to know that I couldn't leave you, no matter what I might learn about you. That you were afraid I'd leave if I knew your secrets. Well, I'm guessing I know pretty much everything now, and I'm not going anywhere. I love you, Damien Stark. And I'm staying right by your side."

He draws in a sharp breath, and the expression on his face looks almost pained, which really isn't the reaction that I was hoping for. "I know you won't leave."

"I won't," I say, warily. His mood is definitely off, but then again he's about to fly to a foreign country to be tried for murder. I should probably cut him a little slack. "I won't ever go."

"Which is why I have to be the one to leave you."

I freeze, then play back his words in my head. That can't be right. Surely, he didn't say what I think he said.

"I'm sorry," he says. This time the words are slow and clear and so gentle they bring tears to my eyes. "I'm breaking up with you, Nikki. It's over."

A roaring fills my ears. I must be hallucinating. Dreaming. This is a nightmare. Because there is no way—no way in hell—that Damien Stark just said those words to me.

And yet I am standing here, and I am looking at him, and the chill that has settled over me doesn't have the quality of a dream. It is reality. It is desolation. I remember its cold harshness from my childhood, and that is not a reality to which I want to return.

I realize that I have been slowly shaking my head, and I force myself to speak.

"I—No. No, it's never over. I'm yours, Damien. Forever. You said so yourself."

He winces and turns his head away as if he can't stand the memory of those words. "I was wrong."

"The hell you were. What the hell is going on here?" I'm angry now, and I'm glad of it. Angry Nikki won't cry. Angry Nikki will demand some goddamned answers.

"I told you that I would leave if that was what it took to protect you." His voice is so calm and even that I want to smack him.

"Protect me? Damien, we're doing fine. I'm doing fine."

"You're not fine. You're a mess with all the press about the portrait, Nikki. Don't try to deny it. I saw the way you looked in the bathroom. You wanted to slice deep into your flesh. You were ready to break the mirror to get at the glass. You wanted blood, Nikki. You wanted pain."

I am silent. I can't argue, because what he says is true. I can only say simply, "But I didn't go there."

"It will get worse. It already has."

I don't know what he's talking about.

"The press, Nikki. They're not focusing on me. Damien Stark indicted for murder. You'd think that would be interesting, right? Apparently not as interesting as his girlfriend. Who, according to those assholes, isn't really his girlfriend at all. Just an opportunistic little whore who'll sleep with anyone who can help her get ahead, murderers included."

My stomach twists violently, and I'm grateful I only had coffee this morning. "I don't care," I lie. "I can deal."

"You shouldn't have to."

"Dammit, Damien, I'm not a mom-and-pop food company. Pulling out isn't going to save me. You're going to destroy me. I need you. *You*. Don't you get that?"

"I can't bear to see you broken. Not when I'm the one who is breaking you."

"You *are* breaking me!" I shout. "If you walk away from me, you're going to snap me in two."

"No," he says simply.

I only realize I am crying when I taste the salt of my tears. "I thought you said I was strong. Or was that just bullshit?"

"You are," he says, his voice maddeningly calm. "Strong enough to stay despite me dragging you into hell. I'm the one who's weak, Nikki, because I kept you in the spotlight for too damn long. I couldn't leave you, and that hurt you. But I'm fixing it now."

He zips up the suitcase and hefts it off the bed. For a moment, he stands there, just looking at me. I am scrambling for words, trying to figure out the magic formula to make him take it all back—but this is not a fairy tale and I am learning the hard way that there is no happily ever after. Then he walks to the door.

He is leaving me. Damien Stark. The man I trusted above all others to never hurt me. He is walking away from me, and he's ripping my heart out as he goes.

Cold fury whips through me, laced with desolation. Tears trail down my cheeks as I bend and unfasten the emerald ankle bracelet. I take a breath and hurl it at him. "Damn you, Damien Stark," I whisper. "Damn you for giving up on us."

He pauses and I see the pain on his face. He glances down at where the bracelet has landed on his feet. He starts to reach for it, then stops. I watch his face, expecting words of comfort. But they don't come. Instead, I hear only the two words I wish were silenced: "Goodbye, Nikki."

And then he is gone.

I am not sure how I manage the drive to Malibu, but I do. And when I pull into Evelyn's drive, I can barely see, what with the tears swimming in my eyes.

"Good God, Texas," she says as she pulls open the door. "What happened to you?"

"He left me," I say, choking the words out between sobs. "He thinks he's protecting me, and so he dumped me."

She sucks in air. "Damn fool of a boy," she says. "I don't care what everyone says about him being a goddamned genius, he fucked this one up, Texas. He damn sure did."

Her words only make me cry harder.

"Aw, hell, girl, get inside."

"Is Blaine here?"

"He's in the studio," she says, referring to a separate building on the property. "It's okay. Cry all you want."

"I don't want to cry," I say. "I want him back. But he's so damned convinced he's doing the right thing."

"What the hell does he think he's protecting you from?" she asks as she leads me to the kitchen and sits me down at the table.

"The paparazzi."

"Phhht," she says. "Fuck 'em."

"I wish they were that easy to blow off." I eye her critically. "Blaine didn't tell you?"

"Tell me what?"

I don't want to go into this, but I need help. And she needs to understand why Damien left. Why he thinks that he has to leave.

"I have scars," I finally say.

She nods slowly. "There's one on the painting. On your hip. Looks to be some on your thighs, too, but the shadows make it hard to tell. So what happened to you, Texas?"

I swallow. "*I* happened to me."

The words hang there, and I wait for my tears, but they do not come. I don't know if it's me or if it's Evelyn, but it's easier to talk about now. No, that's not true. I do know. *It's me*. Damien has helped me change the way I look at my flaws.

I grimace. *Goddamn him for leaving me*.

"You're saying that Damien thinks you're going to start up with the cutting again?"

I could kiss her for being so focused, so direct. "Yes," I say. "I haven't—not since I've been in LA. But I've come close."

"The paparazzi?" She puts a glass of water in front of me, and I sip from it gratefully.

"And all this craziness about the painting. It—well, it got to me."

"Hell, that kind of crap would get to anyone."

"Now the press is saying all sorts of shit about me sleeping with a murderer, and Damien thinks—"

"That he's got to be the hero and walk away. Goddamn the boy, you two aren't supposed to be a tragedy."

"Trust me," I say wryly. "I'm not crazy about the last-minute script change, either. So what can I do?"

"You can haul your ass to Germany and get the boy back."

"But he'll just send me home again. He thinks he's being chivalrous, remember? I have to prove to him I can handle it, but how? It's not like I can go a year without cutting, and then say 'I told you so.' So what can I do to prove to him right now that I'll be okay?"

"Ah, now here's why you came to the right place. Because this is exactly the kind of sneaky shit you pick up after a lifetime in Hollywood. You just need to give the press nowhere else to go."

"I'm not following."

"They're interested in you as a story. So make the story go away."

I blink, trying to process what she's saying. And then it all clicks into place. I leap out of my chair and throw my arms around Evelyn. "You're brilliant."

"Damn right, I am. Why do you think I'm a legend in this town?"

"Do you know someone who can handle the press side of things?"

Evelyn's smile is as wide as I've ever seen it. "Just leave it to me."

I do, and I watch in wonder as the pieces come together. Not two hours later, everything is on track for the first press conference of my life.

"And what makes it really unique," Evelyn says with a guffaw, "is that everything you're going to say is one hundred percent true."

I spend the next hour organizing my thoughts. I'm not shy about speaking in front of a camera—I have my mother's pageant obsession to thank for that—but I am nervous about making sure I'm clear and quotable. With lots of juicy sound bites.

When the knock at the door finally comes, and Evelyn opens it to the camera crew, I am ready. "You sure about this, Texas?"

"It's the only thing I can think of to get him back," I say. "And more important, I need to do it for me."

She nods. "Okay, then. Let's make you even more famous."

I laugh, but have to acknowledge that she's probably right. I also have to admit that this may not work, but that doesn't matter. What matters is that the princess is going out to kill the dragon instead of hiding in the tower.

The crew consists of a cameraman, a reporter, and a producer. I'm not interested in being interviewed, so the reporter says she'll tape the intro later at the studio. This is just me, and I should take my time. I stand in the spot they've lit, wait for the cameraman to signal me, and start talking.

"My name is Nikki Fairchild, and I recently accepted one million dollars as a modeling fee for a nude Blaine original. The completed portrait now hangs in Mr. Damien Stark's Malibu home, and it is an exceptional piece of art. It is both tasteful and erotic. And it does not show my face."

I pause to collect my thoughts. The reporter nods encouragement, and I smile. We've only spoken a few words, but I like her.

"I agreed to the painting, and to the million, because I needed the money. It has not been spent, nor will it be until I am ready. But I also insisted that the arrangement be confidential and that no one except Mr. Stark and the artist know that it was me in the portrait. Somehow, though, my identity has been revealed, and Mr. Stark and I have been harassed nonstop by reporters and photographers who apparently have nothing better to do with their time. And the truth is, now I have regrets."

I wonder, as I say that, if Damien will see this tape.

I soldier on. "Not about the painting. Not about the money. No, my regret is that I asked Blaine and Mr. Stark to keep my identity confidential in the first place. I will admit that there was a time when I was ashamed of my body, but that time has passed. I think the portrait is outstanding. And I think the modeling fee was fair. Then again, what is a fair price to paint a woman's body? If Mr. Stark had paid me ten dollars, would the press now be calling me a cheap harlot?"

I glance at Evelyn, who is grinning. "To be honest, I think Mr. Stark got off easy. If he wants a second nude portrait, he'll have to pay me two million dollars. At least."

Near me, the reporter nods encouragingly. "As of this morning, the gossip about me has shifted. Apparently now I'm a woman who would sleep with a murderer to get ahead. Let's think about that. Do I sleep with Damien Stark? I do, and gladly, but not to get ahead. Instead, I am honored and humbled that he wants me in his life and in his bed."

I realize suddenly that I am not nervous at all. I feel strong. This—these words—feel right. "As for the allegation that Damien Stark is a murderer, I can only say that I do not believe it. The evidence will acquit him. But if by some horrific fault in the universe he is convicted, then that will change nothing. I will not and would not leave his side."

I draw a breath and move on to my wrap-up. "I do not intend to make any more statements to the press, so I will add one final thing for the record. I am in love with Damien Stark, and I am leaving for Germany in an hour to support him through his trial. He is an innocent man, and he has been wrongly accused. Thank you."

I stand in front of the presidential suite at the scarily luxurious Kempinski hotel in Munich and draw in a breath. I owe a huge debt to Sylvia, who could lose her job if Damien decides to be angry that his assistant told me where he was staying.

I'm not sure how he's going to react to seeing me here, and I have no way of knowing if he saw my interview. And even if he did, I have no way of knowing if it moved him.

As for that interview, when I was in the taxi from the airport to my hotel, I read through Jamie's half-dozen emails describing how the press was going wild. Apparently I am no longer a harlot and Damien is no longer a murderer. Now we are star-crossed lovers.

The press is nothing if not fickle. This time, at least, we're on the warm, fuzzy side of the press.

More important, phase one of my plan worked. And knowing that gives me courage. Surely the next part will work, too. Because I really don't want to have to call Sylvia and ask her to book me into the Munich equivalent of a Motel 6.

Enough stalling.

I draw a deep breath, knock firmly on the door, and wait.

A moment later, I hear Damien's voice. "One minute!" And then I hear the lock turning and I'm holding my breath as the door is pulled inward.

And there he is. He's wearing black trousers and his shirt hangs open. He looks both dashing and distracted. He's got his arm up as he attempts to fasten the cuff, and when he sees me, he freezes.

"Nikki."

"Do you want me to get that for you?" I ask.

Wordlessly, he holds out his arm. I button the cuff from my

position in the hallway, then step inside and do the other one. Then, without speaking, I start to work on the line of buttons on the shirt.

His body is tense and wary, and I can't tell if he's happy to see me, angry, or uncertain that I am real.

"I saw your press conference," he finally says.

"Oh?" I try to sound light and encouraging, but inside my heart is breaking. If he saw it and wanted me here, wouldn't he have pulled me into his arms?

"I didn't expect you here so quickly."

"When you know you want to be with someone you love, you want to get there as fast as you can." My smile wavers, and I'm suddenly afraid I'm going to cry. I hadn't even let myself admit until now how much I wanted to hear those three little words from him. But I did—I do. And not only is he not saying them back, but he's probably going to send me away, too.

"Oh, Nikki." There are too many emotions packed into my name, and I cannot sort them out. "No matter what you tell the press, you deserve better than a relationship with a man behind bars."

"I deserve *you*," I say. "But if you think I can't handle all of this, then you're right. I can't. Not without you. Damien, don't you get it? I can't just sit on the sidelines and watch them try you for murder. I need to be here. I have to be here. I need you." I pause to draw a breath, and then tilt my head to look him in his eyes. "And I think you need me, too."

The weight of eternity seems to hang in the second that passes before he answers.

"I do," he says, and then, "God, Nikki, I do." It is as if a glass wall around him has shattered. The life returns to his eyes, the smile to his face. Suddenly his arms are around me and he's holding me close and I'm soaking up the rhythm of his heartbeat and breathing in the scent of this man I love so deeply.

"Then it's okay that I came?" My words are tentative, uncertain.

"Oh, baby, yes," he says, and the emotion in his voice almost brings me to tears. "You are my blood; without you, I'm nothing but a shell."

"You should never have walked away," I say.

"No," he says firmly. "I had to. I had to give you that one fair chance to get free of me. Because you *will* be drawn into hell, Nikki, and though you may think I'm strong, where you are concerned I am weak. I am selfish. I walked away once to protect you, but I won't do it again. If you want to go, do it now. Otherwise, I will keep you here beside me, because that is where I want you. By my side, Nikki. Always."

I am trembling with relief from his words, and can only nod stupidly.

"I've been in hell without you," he says. "Every minute was a fight against temptation. I wanted to send a plane for you. To say to hell with whatever was best for you and scoop you up for my own selfish needs."

I lick my lips. "I think I would have been okay with that."

"No," he says, with an awed shake of his head. "I was so proud of you. Those things you said. The risks you took. You exorcised the demons, Nikki. The press may be an irritation, but you've taken their power away. They can't destroy you. Not about that. Maybe not about anything."

"It was easy. I just remembered how strong you're always telling me I am."

He brushes his fingertips across my cheek. Then he closes his mouth over mine in a long, deep welcoming kiss that makes my knees go weak and the rest of my body tingle in anticipation of his touch.

"I want to make love to you," he says.

"Thank God," I reply, which makes him laugh.

"But we can't."

I look up at him, suddenly afraid that I've been wrong and that he's going to kick me out after all.

"I have to go meet with my attorneys."

"Oh. Well, later?"

"Most definitely later. And for a very long time. But right now, would you come with me? I want you beside me when I meet with the lawyers."

"Of course," I say. "So docs this mean I can stay?"

"You damn well better." He slowly smiles, his eyes bright.

"What?" I say.

"I'm just hoping that you're not a mirage."

My smile widens. "I'm real."

"Prove it," he says, then reaches into his pocket and pulls out the emerald ankle bracelet. I gasp. "Put it on," he says.

"But how—"

"I went back," he says, bending to fasten it around my ankle, the light brush of his finger against my skin sending shockwaves rippling through me. "I had to have you with me . . . even if only a talisman."

"Damien." My voice is choked, my heart too full.

He stands, then presses a finger to my lips. "Later. Say too much and we'll never get out of here. I want you right now—but I can't miss this meeting."

I grin and follow him to the door, anticipating later.

He pauses at the threshold. "Just one more thing. When I said you could stay? What I meant to say was I love you."

I'm looking right at him as he speaks, and his eyes are shining. My mouth curls up into a delighted smile, and I find myself laughing like a child.

So what that we're facing a murder trial? Damien and I love each other.

And right now, that's enough for me.

Nikki and Damien's sensual, powerfully emotional romance comes to a stunning conclusion in

COMPLETE ME

Coming soon in 2013

Continue reading for a look at what's to come . . .

1

Fear yanks me from a deep sleep, and I sit bolt upright in a room shrouded with gray, the muted green light from a digital alarm clock announcing that it is just after midnight. My breath comes in gasps, and my eyes are wide but unseeing. The last remnant of an already forgotten nightmare brushes against me like the tattered hem of a specter's cloak, powerful enough to fill me with terror, and yet so insubstantial that it evaporates like mist when I try to grasp it.

I do not know what frightened me. I only know that I am alone in an unfamiliar room, and that I am scared.

Alone?

I turn swiftly in bed, shifting my body as I reach out to my right. But I know even before my fingers brush the cool, expensive sheets that he is not there.

I may have fallen asleep in Damien's arms, but I have awakened alone.

At least now I know the source of the nightmare. It is the same fear I have faced every day and every night for almost two weeks. The fear I try to hide beneath a plastic smile as I sit beside

Damien day in and day out as his attorneys go over his defense in meticulous detail. As they explain the procedural ins-and-outs of a murder trial under German law. As they practically beg him to shine a light into the dark corners of his childhood because they know, as I do, that those secrets are his salvation.

But Damien remains stubbornly mute, and I am left huddled against this pervasive fear that I will lose him. That he will be taken from me.

And not just fear. I'm also fighting the damnable, overwhelming, panic-inducing knowledge that there isn't a goddamn thing in the world I can do. Nothing except wait and watch and hope.

But I do not like waiting, and I have never put my faith in hope. It is a cousin of fate, and both are too mercurial for my taste. What I crave is action, but the only one who can act is Damien, and he has steadfastly refused.

And that, I think, is the worst cut of all. Because while I understand the reason for his silence, I can't quell the selfish spark of anger. Because at the core of it all, it's not just himself that Damien is sacrificing. It's me.

I squeeze my eyes shut, forcing the tears to remain at bay. My anger is unfair, and I know it. But I'm just so damn scared.

I take slow, even breaths, and after a moment, I feel calmer. I realize that I am splayed across Damien's side of the bed, and I breathe even deeper, as if his scent alone can bolster me and erase my fears.

But it isn't enough. I need the man himself, and I peel myself away from the cool comfort of our bed and stand up. I'm naked, and I bend to retrieve the white, lush robe provided by the Hotel Kempinski. Damien brushed it back off my shoulders after our shower last night, and I left it where it fell, a soft pile of cotton beside the bed.

The sash is a different story, and I have to dig in the rumpled sheets to find it. Last night, it had bound my wrists behind my back. Now, I tie it around my waist and tug it tight, relishing the luxurious comfort after waking so violently. The room itself is equally soothing, every detail done to perfection. Every piece of wood polished, every tiny knickknack or artistic addition thoughtfully arranged. Right now, however, I am oblivious to the room's charms. I only want to find Damien.

The bedroom connects to an oversized dressing area and a stunning bathroom, but though I check briefly in both, I do not see him, and I continue through to the living area. The space is large and also well-appointed with comfortable seating and a round worktable that is now covered with sheaths of papers and folders representing both the business that Damien is continuing to run despite the world collapsing around our ears, and the various legal documents that his attorney, Charles Maynard, has left for Damien to study.

The room is exactly as we left it last night, even down to the two crystal high ball glasses on the coffee table that held the whiskey we'd sipped while we sat talking on the couch, my feet in his lap and his fingers casually stroking my leg. My skin tingles from the mere memory of his touch, and I cannot help but smile. Despite the circumstances, the night was sweet. This is our last night before the proceedings officially begin, and by some unspoken agreement we said nothing about the reason that we are here in Munich. There was only the two of us and the fire that is forever between us. A fire that started with only the soft glow of coals during dinner, and then exploded into a pyrotechnical display when he finally took me to bed.

Was that really only a few hours ago?

For that matter, can it really be true that Damien's trial will begin only a few hours from now?

The thought makes me shudder, and although it is far too obvious that I am alone in this massive suite, I glance once more around the room, as if by the force of my will alone I can make Damien appear before me.

No such luck.

Frowning, I wander to the table and then to the bar, hoping to find a note. But there is nothing. I pick up the receiver on the house phone and dial zero. Almost immediately there is an accented voice on the other end. "How may I help you, Ms. Fairchild?"

Relief crashes over me. "He's down there?" I whisper, though I know the answer must be yes. Why else would the concierge assume that I am the caller, and not Damien?

"Mr. Stark is in the Jahreszeiten Bar. Shall I have a phone brought to his table?"

"No, that's all right. I'll get dressed and come down."

"*Sehr gut.* Is there anything else I can do for you?"

"No, thank you." I'm about to hang up when I realize there is something. "Wait!" I catch him before he clicks off, then inveigle his help with my plan to distract Damien from whatever nighttime demons urged him from our bed and down to the lobby.

I dress quickly, literally grabbing the first thing I see. We've spent a few hours escaping reality over the last few days by shopping on Munich's famous Maximilianstrasse, and I have acquired so many shoes and dresses I could open my own boutique. Last night, Damien had been far too cavalier when he peeled a stunning trompe l'oeil patterned sheath off me. Considering that dress cost more than my first car, I thought it deserved more than a careless toss across the back of an armchair.

Now, though, I'm glad it's there. I let the robe drop where I stand and pull the dress on, then run my fingers through my hair. I force myself not to go into the bathroom to primp and freshen the make-up that has surely rubbed off. It's more challenging than it sounds; the mantra that a lady doesn't go out unfinished has been beaten into my head since birth. But with Damien at my side I have thumbed my nose at many of the tribulations of my youth, and right now I am more concerned with finding him than with applying fresh lipstick.

I shove my feet into a nearby pair of pumps, grab my bag, and hurry out the door toward the elevator. Despite the age of the building and the elegance of the interior, the hotel boasts a modern feel, and I have come to feel at home within these walls. I wait impatiently for the elevator, and then even more impatiently once I'm in the car. The descent seems to take forever, and when the doors finally open to reveal the opulent lobby, I aim myself straight for the old English style bar.

Despite the late hour on a Sunday, the Jahreszeiten Bar is bustling. A woman stands by the piano softly singing to the gathered crowd. I barely pay her any heed. I don't expect to find Damien among the listeners.

Instead, I wander through the wood and red leather interior, shaking off the help of a waiter who wants to seat me. I pause for a moment, standing idly beside a blonde woman about my age who is sipping champagne and laughing with a man who might be her father, but I'm betting is not. I turn slowly, taking in the room around me. Damien is not with the group at the piano, nor is he sitting at the bar. And he does not occupy any of the red leather chairs that are evenly spaced around the tables.

I'm starting to worry that perhaps he was leaving as I was coming when I remember the fireplace. The last time we came down here, we drank Glenfiddich and talked about all the things we were going to do when we returned to Los Angeles. But tonight, I see no fireplace.

I move to the left and realize that what I thought was a solid wall was actually an optical illusion created by a pillar. Now I can see the rest of the room, including the flames leaping in the fireplace set into the opposite wall. There is a small loveseat and two chairs surrounding the hearth. And, yes, there is Damien.

I immediately exhale, my relief so intense I almost use the blonde's shoulder to steady myself. He is seated in one of the chairs, his back to me and the rest of the room as he faces the flames. His shoulders are broad and straight, and more than capable of bearing the weight of the world upon them. I wish, however, that they didn't have to.

I move toward him, the sound of my approach muffled by both the thick carpet and the din of conversation. I pause a few feet behind him, already feeling the familiar pull I experience whenever I am near Damien, as if he is a magnet and I am inexorably drawn to him. Across the room, the singer is now crooning *Since I Fell For You,* her voice cutting sharp and clear across the room, as if she is serenading Damien and me alone. Her voice is so mournful that I'm afraid it is going to unleash a flood of tears along with all of the stress of the last few days.

No. I'm here to comfort Damien, not the other way around, and I continue toward him with renewed resolve. I press my hand to his shoulder, and bend down, my lips brushing his ear. "Is this a private party, or can anyone join in?"

I hear rather than see his answering smile. "That depends on who's asking." He doesn't turn to face me, but he lifts his arm so that his hand is held up in a silent invitation. I close my hand in his, and he guides me gently around the chair until I am standing in front of him. I know every line of this man's face. Every angle, every curve. I know his lips, his expressions. I can close my own eyes and picture his, dark with desire, bright with laughter. I have only to look at his midnight-colored hair to imagine the soft, thick locks between my fingers. There is nothing about him that is not intimately familiar to me, and yet every glance at him hits me like a shock, reverberating through me with enough power to knock me to my knees.

Empirically, he is gorgeous. But it is not simply his looks that overwhelm. It is the whole package. The power, the confidence, the bone-deep sensuality that he couldn't shake even if he tried.

He is exceptional. And he is mine.

"Damien," I whisper, because I can't wait any longer to feel his name against my lips.

That wide, spectacular mouth curves into a slow smile. "I didn't mean to wake you." He tugs my hand, pulling me onto his lap. His thighs are firm and athletic, and I settle there eagerly, but I don't lean against him. I want to sit back enough that I can see his face.

"How could I sleep without you?" I ask. "Especially to-night?" I stroke his cheek. He hasn't shaved since yesterday, and the stubble of his beard is rough against my palm. The shock of our connection rumbles through me, and my chest feels tight, my breath uneven. Will there ever come a time when I can be near him without yearning for him? Without craving the touch of his skin against my own?

It's not even a sexual longing—not entirely, anyway. Instead, it's a craving. As if my very survival depends on him. As if we are two halves of a whole and neither can survive without the other.

With Damien, I am happier than I have ever been. But at the same time, I'm more miserable, too. Because now I truly under-stand fear.

I force a smile, because the one thing I will not do is let Damien see how scared I am of losing him. "You couldn't sleep? Are you thinking about the trial?"

"A bit," he says, his eyes locked on my face. "Mostly, I've been thinking about you."

"Oh." I cannot help the flutter in my chest, and I feel the flicker of a smile tugging at my lips. "What were you thinking?"

"That I am a selfish man, but nothing that I have done in my life is more selfish than loving you."

"Damien, no. I want to be here. I need to be here. You know that." We've had this conversation before. When the German indictment came through, he'd tried to push me away, believing that he was protecting me. But he'd been wrong—and I'd flown all the way to Germany to tell him so.

"No," he says with a small shake of his head. "I mean I should never have pursued you in the first place."

"Don't even joke about that," I say. The thought that Damien never entered my life is worse than the thought of him leaving it.

"I pissed you off at Evelyn's," he says. "Remember? I should have let you stay pissed. I should have simply walked away."

My mouth is dry, and my chest feels tight. I do not want to hear these words. I don't want to believe that there is even some tiny part of him that would prefer to have never met me, not even if that fantasy is borne from a desire to protect me. "No," I say. It's the only word I can manage, and it sounds strangled and raw.

"Oh, Nikki." His fingertips stroke my cheek, and though his smile is bittersweet, his eyes are filled with so much passion that it takes my breath away. "You can't possibly know how much I love you."

"I do," I say.

The small shake of his head is almost playful. "It's too big, too powerful. There is no start and no end, nothing with which I can measure the length and breadth of what I feel for you. I look at you and wonder how I can possibly survive the riot of emotions within me."

"You make it sound almost painful." My words are soft, gently teasing.

"You and I know better than anyone how pain and pleasure walk hand in hand. Passion, Nikki, remember? And with you, it fills me."

I swallow, undone by both his words and by the intensity with which he is speaking them.

"I want to hold you close. To cherish and protect you. To draw you in until we are so close that I am lost within you. I want to take you to bed, to watch the way your skin tightens beneath my fingers, the way your body awakens under my touch. I want to trail kisses over you until you are lost in so much pleasure that you don't know where you end and I begin. I want to tie you up and fuck you until there is no doubt that you are mine. I want to dress you up and take you out, and show you off, this beautiful, vibrant, brilliant woman. Everything I've built? All my companies? All my billions? They have no value compared to you."

I open my mouth to speak, but he hushes me with a gentle finger to my lips. "So, no, Nikki. I couldn't have walked away. Selfish, yes. But I cannot wish it otherwise. I need you, and I can't regret that I have you."

"I need you, too," I say. "You know that I do."

"I don't regret having you," he repeats. "But I regret very much what that does to you. You're suffering for it, or you will." The sadness that fills his eyes is enough to melt me. "You are the one person in all the world I cannot bear to hurt, and yet I'm the one who put fear in your eyes."

"No," I lie. "I'm not scared. If you see fear, it's only because I was afraid you were going to try to push me away. But about the trial? I'm not afraid at all."

"Liar," he says gently.

"You forget that I've seen you in action, Damien Stark. You're a goddamn force of nature. They can't possibly hold you. Maybe they don't know it yet, but I do. You're going to walk away from this. You're going home a free man. There's no other way that this can end."

I don't expect his reaction—Damien laughs. "I love you even more for pretending, but I know you're scared. And you should be. This is the kind of case that has prosecutors salivating."

"But you didn't kill Merle Richter," I remind him.

"No, I didn't. But truth is a malleable thing, and once I walk into that courtroom, the truth is what a jury says it is."

"Then you need to damn well make sure the jury has the information to do that. Dammit, Damien, you didn't kill him. But even if you did, there were mitigating circumstances." I force myself not to flinch as I say the words. Despite Maynard and all the rest of his attorneys pushing him to raise a defense, Damien has continued to refuse. I fully expect to be shut down now. Which is why I'm all the more surprised when he nods slowly.

"Yes," he says, so softly I almost don't hear him. "That's one of the things I've been down here thinking about."

I hold my breath and silently urge him to continue.

"I've wanted you for so long, and now that I have you, I'm risking everything there is between us."

Yes, I want to scream. *Yes!* I realize that I'm digging my fingernails into my knee, and I force myself to relax as I try not to anticipate his next words. As I try not to get my hopes up.

"I'm not convinced that revealing what Richter did to me is the panacea you and Maynard and the rest of them think it is. But maybe I should try. If it means that the charges will go away, then maybe I should sacrifice the privacy that I've spent my whole life fighting to maintain."

I hear the bitterness in his voice, and I want to reach for him and hold his hand tight in mine. I don't, though. I stay absolutely, perfectly still.

"There is no shame in being a victim, right? So why should I care if the world knows the vile things he did to me? Why should it matter if the press writes about the dark nights in my dorm room. The things he made me do. Things I haven't even told you. Things that I wish I could forget."

He meets my eyes, but I see only the hard lines and angles of his face. "If it means that I can walk to you as a free man, shouldn't I want to shout that story from the rooftops? Shouldn't I want it plastered everywhere?"

Something cool brushes my cheek, and I realize that I am crying.

"No," I whisper, hating the truth even as I say it. But this is the heart of the man I fell in love with. A man who lives by his own code, and it is that core of him that I fell in love with. "Not even for me," I say. "Not even to stay out of prison."

I squeeze my eyes shut, and fresh tears spill out over my lashes.

The pad of his thumb brushes my cheek.

"You understand?"

"No," I say, but I mean yes, and I can see that he knows it.

"Oh, sweetheart." He pulls me to him, his arm swooping around my waist and shifting me on his lap so quickly that I gasp. The sound, however, is cut off by the pressure of his mouth closing firmly over mine. The kiss is deep and raw and all-consuming, and immediately warm desire blooms within me. His hand slides up my back, and I curse the necessity of clothing in public. I feel his body tighten under mine, the bulge of his erection under his jeans teasing my rear as I shift my weight and lean closer, deepening this kiss.

After a moment, I pull back, breathless.

"I love you," he says, and I want to wrap the words around me like a blanket.

I smile playfully and slide off his lap, my hand extended to him. "You have to be in court at ten, Mr. Stark. I think you'd better come with me."

He stands, his expression wary. "Are you going to tell me I have to get some sleep?"

"No."

His gaze slides over me, my body quivering in response as if he had physically touched me. "Good," he says, and that one simple word conveys a world of promises.

I allow the corner of my mouth to quirk up into a hint of a smile. "Not that, either. Not yet, anyway."

The confusion on his face makes my smile grow wider, but he doesn't have the chance to ask, as the concierge has approached. "Everything is ready, Ms. Fairchild."

I smile broadly. "Thank you. Your timing is perfect."

I take the hand of the very confused man that I love and lead him through the lobby, following the concierge to the front of the hotel. There, parked on the street beside a very giddy valet, is a cherry red Lamborghini.

Damien turns to look at me, amusement dancing in his eyes. "What's this?"

"I thought you could use a little fun tonight, and the A9's just a few miles away. Fast car. German autobahn. It seemed like a no-brainer to me."

"Boys and their toys?"

I lower my voice so that the concierge can't overhear. "Since we already have some interesting toys in the room, I thought you might enjoy a change of pace." I lead him closer to where the valet stands by the open passenger door. "I understand she's very responsive, and I know you'll enjoy having all that power at your command."

"Is she?" He looks me up and down, and this time the inspection is tinged with fire. "As a matter of fact, that's exactly what I like. Responsiveness. Power. Control."

"I know," I say, and then slide into the passenger seat, letting more than a little thigh show as I do.

And instant later, Damien is behind the wheel and he's fired the powerful engine.

"Drive fast enough, and it's almost like sex," I tease. And then, because I can't resist, I add, "At the very least, it makes for exceptional foreplay."

"In that case, Ms. Fairchild," he says, with a boyish grin that makes this all worthwhile, "I suggest you hold on tight."

Nikki and Damien's irresistible, emotionally charged
romance began in the bestselling

RELEASE ME

Available now in ebook and paperback

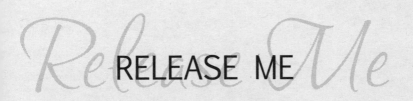

RELEASE ME

He was the one man I couldn't avoid.
And the one man I couldn't resist.

Damien Stark could have his way with any woman.
He was sexy, confident, and commanding: anything
he wanted, he got. And what he wanted was me.

Our attraction was unmistakable, almost beyond control,
but as much as I ached to be his, I feared the pressures
of his demands. Submitting to Damien meant I had to
bare the darkest truth about my past – and risk
breaking us apart.

But Damien was haunted, too. And as our passion
came to obsess us both, his secrets threatened to
destroy him – and us – for ever.

ETERNAL
ROMANCE

FIND YOUR HEART'S DESIRE...

VISIT OUR WEBSITE: www.eternalromancebooks.co.uk
FIND US ON FACEBOOK: facebook.com/eternalromance
FOLLOW US ON TWITTER: @eternal_books